A mere touch, and yet it sent a jolt of fire through him.
Anna shifted, and Devlin shook off the sensation. It must
be the brandy, he decided. He had just come from his club,
where he had been sampling a potent vintage brought up
from the wine cellar. Women had no such effect on him.

A kiss was a distraction, nothing more. A way to keep
boredom at bay.

"Go to Hell." Anna's whisper teased against his mouth
as she jerked back.

"Eventually," growled Devlin. "But first..." He kissed
her again. A harder, deeper, possessive embrace.

Her lips tremored uncertainly.

Seizing the moment, he slipped his tongue through the
tiny gap and tasted a beguiling mix of warmth and spice.
Impossible to describe.

He needed to taste more.

More.

Acclaim for the
Hellions of High Street Series

Sinfully Yours

"Sinfully fantastic!...I enjoyed this story immensely, would recommend and re-read!"

—RamblingsfromthisChick.blogspot.com

"Fun and well-written."

—RedHotBooks.com

"A pleasant and enjoyable read."

—HarlequinJunkie.com

Passionately Yours

"A classic example of romance, adventure, and fun! Only Cara Elliott could balance all these elements and keep them equally as interesting...Carolina Sloane is such a fantastic character!"

—RamblingsfromthisChick.blogspot.com

"Entertaining...She writes with a very engaging and funny style."

—SweptAwaybyRomance.com

"Engaging characters and an intriguing storyline will keep you up all night turning pages...a very enjoyable read!"

—MyBookAddictionReviews.com

Scandalously Yours

"Excellent!...witty and fun...an entertaining Regency romance."
—DreysLibrary.com

"A promising start to a new series. It's an easy, undemanding read, the characters are likeable, and the writing is intelligent and often humorous."
—All About Romance (LikesBooks.com)

"Delightful...What a beginning!...a must-read...Ms. Elliott has done a wonderful job of mixing romance with politics and passion. Well done indeed!"
—MyBookAddictionReviews.com

Acclaim for the Lords of Midnight Series

Too Dangerous to Desire

"What a wonderful storyteller and a wonderful way to end a trilogy. A must-read."
—MyBookAddictionReviews.com

"The well-paced storyline, brimming with several nail-biting escapades, keeps readers glued to the pages as much as the love story. Quite simply, this fast, sexy read is a pleasure."
—*RT Book Reviews*

"What a fun, little guilty pleasure read this turned out to be. I ate this book up like a fine dessert... A romance that should be on everyone's keeper shelf."

—GraceBooksofLove.com

Too Tempting to Resist

"Elliott provides readers with a treat to savor in this fun, sexy, delicious tale. With smart, sassy characters, a charming plot, and an erotic bad boy/good girl duo, this fast-paced story will keep readers' attention."

—*RT Book Reviews*

"Nothing is more sensuous than a delicious meal, and Cara Elliott's food-inspired sex scenes are, quite literally, *Too Tempting to Resist*... likeable characters, a fast-moving plot, and unique, engaging sex scenes that are deliciously tempting."

—HeroesandHeartbreakers.com

"Haddan and Eliza's charming wit and banter will absolutely capture the reader from their first meeting... [It] can easily be read as a stand-alone, though most readers will want to rush out and find a copy of the first book to get more of Cara Elliott's Hellhounds. A real page-turner, readers will not be able to put this book down."

—RomRevToday.com

Too Wicked to Wed

"Elliott packs the first Lords of Midnight Regency romance with plenty of steamy sex and sly innuendo... As

Alexa and Connor flee London to escape vengeful criminals, their mutual attraction sizzles beneath delightful banter. Regency fans will especially appreciate the authentic feel of the historical setting."
—*Publishers Weekly*

"A surprisingly resourceful heroine and a sinfully sexy hero, a compelling and danger-spiced plot, lushly sensual love scenes, and lively writing work together perfectly to get Elliott's new Regency-set Lords of Midnight series off to a delightfully entertaining start."
—*Booklist*

"The romance, adventure, and sensuality readers expect from Elliott are here, along with an unforgettable hoyden heroine and an enigmatic hero. She takes them on a marvelous ride from gambling hells to ballrooms, country estates, and London's underworld."
—*RT Book Reviews*

Praise for the Circle of Sin Trilogy

To Tempt a Rake

"From the first page of this sequel…Elliott sweeps her readers up in a scintillating and sexy romance."
—*Publishers Weekly*

"An engaging cast of characters...Readers who thrive on empowered women, sexy and dangerous men, and their wild adventures will savor Elliott's latest."

—*RT Book Reviews*

"Elliott expertly sifts a generous measure of dangerous intrigue into the plot of her latest impeccably crafted Regency historical, which should prove all too tempting to readers with a craving for deliciously clever, wickedly sexy romances."

—*Booklist*

To Surrender to a Rogue

"4 stars! Elliott's ability to merge adventure, romance, and an intriguing historical backdrop will captivate her readers and earn their accolades."

—*RT Book Reviews*

"With mystery, intrigue, laughter, and hot, steamy passion...what more could any reader want?"

—TheRomanceReadersConnection.com

"Another fantastic read from Cara Elliott. Can't wait until the next book."

—SingleTitles.com

To Sin with a Scoundrel

"HOT...Charming characters demonstrate her strong storytelling gift."

—*RT Book Reviews*

"Has everything a reader could desire: adventure, humor, mystery, romance, and a very naughty rake. I was absorbed from the first page and entertained throughout the story. A warning to readers: If you have anything on your schedule for the day, clear it. You won't be able to put *To Sin with a Scoundrel* down once you start reading."
—SingleTitles.com

"Steamy ... intriguing."
—*Publishers Weekly*

ALSO BY CARA ELLIOTT

Circle of Sin Series

To Sin with a Scoundrel
To Surrender to a Rogue
To Tempt a Rake

Lords of Midnight Series

Too Wicked to Wed
Too Tempting to Resist
Too Dangerous to Desire

Hellions of High Street Series

Sinfully Yours
Passionately Yours
Scandalously Yours

Sinfully Yours

CARA ELLIOTT

FOREVER

NEW YORK   BOSTON

Copyright © 2014 by Andrea DaRif
Excerpt from *Passionately Yours* copyright © 2014 by Andrea DaRif

Forever
Hachette Book Group
1290 Avenue of the Americas
New York, NY 10104
forever-romance.com

Printed in the United States of America

Originally published as an ebook by Forever in February 2014
First mass market edition: April 2015
10 9 8 7 6 5 4 3 2 1

OPM

Forever is an imprint of Grand Central Publishing.
The Forever name and logo are trademarks of Hachette Book Group, Inc.

The Hachette Speakers Bureau provides a wide range of authors for speaking events. To find out more, go to www.hachettespeakersbureau.com or call (866) 376-6591.

The publisher is not responsible for websites (or their content) that are not owned by the publisher.

For my fellow Word Wenches,
Jo Beverley, Joanna Bourne, Nicola
Cornick, Anne Gracie, Susan Fraser
King, Mary Jo Putney, and Patricia Rice,
who are my Sisters-in-Writing.
You are always there to make me laugh
and feed me cyber chocolate when the
Muse is in a cranky mood.
No author could have better friends.

Sinfully Yours

Chapter One

Alessandro twisted free and fell back against the rough stones just as a dagger thrust straight at his heart. Steel sliced through linen with a lethal whisper, but the blade cut naught but a dark curl of hair from his muscled chest.

"Tsk, tsk—you're losing your edge, Malatesta," he called, flashing a mocking smile. "In the past, your strike was quick as a cobra. But now…" He waggled an airy wave. "You're sluggish as a garden snake."

"You're a spawn of Satan, Crispini!" Another slash. "And I intend to cut off your cods and send you back to Hell where you belong."

"Oh, no doubt I shall eventually find my *testicolos* roasting over the Devil's own coals. But it won't be a slow-witted, slow-footed oaf who sticks them on a spit."

With a roar of rage, Alessandro's adversary spun into a new attack.

Whoosh, whoosh—*moonlight winked wildly off the flailing weapon, setting off a ghostly flutter of silvery sparks.*

As he danced away from the danger, Alessandro darted a quick glance over the tower's parapet. The water below was dark as midnight and looked colder than a witch's—

"Crispini—watch out!" The warning shout had an all too familiar ring. "Le Chaze is behind you!"

"Damn!" muttered Alessandro. He had told—no, no, he had ordered—*the young lady to flee while she had the chance. But no, the headstrong hellion was as stubborn as an—*

"Damn!" muttered Miss Anna Sloane, echoing the oath of Count Crispini, the dashingly handsome Italian Lothario whose sexual exploits put those of the legendary Casanova to the blush. Throwing down her pen, she took her head between her hands. Several hairpins fell to the ink-spattered paper, punctuating the heavy sigh. "That's not only drivel—it's *boring* drivel."

Her younger sister Caro looked up from the book of Byron's poetry she was reading. "What did you say?"

"Drivel," repeated Anna darkly.

Caro rose and came over to peer over Anna's shoulder. "Hmmm." After a quick skim of the page she added, "Actually, I think it's not half bad."

"I used a knife fight to liven things up in the last chapter," said Anna.

"What about those clever little turn-off pocket pistols we saw in Mr. Manton's shop last week?" suggested Caro.

"Chapter three," came the morose reply.

"Explosives?"

Anna shook her head. "I need to save that for when they hijack the pirate ship." She made a face. *Hijacking*—even that sounded awfully trite to her ears. "I don't know what's wrong with me. I seem to be running short of inspiration these days."

Caro clucked in sympathy. Like their older sister Olivia, the two younger Sloane sisters shared a secret passion for writing. "You've been working awfully hard these past six months. Maybe the Muse needs a holiday."

"Yes, well, the Muse may want to luxuriate in the spa waters of Baden-Baden, but Mr. Brooke expects me to deliver this manuscript in six weeks and I'm way behind schedule." Anna was much admired by London's *beau monde* for her faultless manners, amiable charm, and ethereal beauty. Little did they know that beneath the demure silks she wore a second skin—that of Sir Sharpe Quill, author of the wildly popular racy romance novels featuring the adventures of the intrepid English orphan Emmalina Smythe and the cavalier Count Alessandro Crispini.

"Perhaps you can bribe Her with champagne and lobster patties," quipped Caro, whose writing passion was poetry. "We are attending Lord and Lady Dearborne's soiree tonight, and they are known for the excellence of their refreshments."

Anna uttered a very unladylike word. In Italian.

"You would rather wrestle with an ill-tempered Word Goddess than waltz across the polished parquet in the arms of Lord Andover?"

"Andover is a bore," grumbled Anna. "As are all the other fancy fops who will likely be dancing attendance on us."

Caro lifted a brow. "Lud, you *are* in a foul mood. I thought you liked Andover." When no response came, she went on, "I know you'll think me silly, but I confess that I'm still a little dazzled by the evening entertainments here in London. Colorful silks, diamond-bright lights, handsome men—you may feel that the splendors of Mayfair's ballrooms have lost their glitter, but for me they are still very exciting."

A twinge of guilt pinched off the caustic quip about to slip from Anna's lips. Her sister had only recently turned the magical age of eighteen, which freed her from the schoolroom and allowed her entrée into the adult world. And for a budding poet who craved Worldly Experience, the effervescence of the social swirl was still as intoxicating as champagne.

"Sorry," apologized Anna. "I don't mean to cloud your pleasure with my own dark humor." She shuffled the stack of manuscript pages into a neat pile and shoved it to the side of her desk. "I supposed we had better go dress for the occasion." Knowing Caro's fondness for fashion, she forced a smile. "Which of your new gowns do you plan to wear? The pale green sarcenet or the peach-colored watered silk?" Her own choice she planned to leave in the hands of her new lady's maid. The girl was French and had already displayed a flair for choosing flattering cuts and colors.

"I haven't decided," replied Caro with a dreamy smile. "What do you think would look best?"

"You are asking *me*?"

"Only because I am hoping you'll ask Josette to come with you and give her opinion."

Anna laughed.

"Not that you don't have a good eye for fashion," said her sister. "You just refuse to be bothered with it."

"True," she conceded. "I find other things more compelling."

Caro cocked her head. "Such as?"

"Such as..." *A restless longing for something too vague to put a name to.*

Anna had carefully cultivated the outward appearance of a quiet, even-tempered young lady who wouldn't dream of breaking any of the myriad rules governing female behavior. Up until recently it had been an amusing game, like creating the complex character of Emmalina. But oddly enough, a very different person had begun to whisper inside her head.

The saint dueling with the sinner? As of yet, it was unclear who was winning the clash of wills.

"Such as finishing my manuscript by the due date," she replied slowly.

"Well, seeing as you are so concerned about being tardy," said Caro dryly, "perhaps we ought to start off this new resolve of good intentions by heading upstairs now to begin dressing for the evening."

Much as she wished to beg off and spend a quiet evening in the library, hunting through her late father's history books for some adventurous exploit that might spark an idea for her current chapter, Anna hadn't the heart to dampen her sister's enthusiasm. She dutifully rose.

"Oh, come now, don't look so glum," said Caro. "After all, inspiration often strikes when you least expect it."

Slipping behind a screen of potted palms, Anna exhaled sharply and made herself count to ten. The air hung heavy

with the cloying scents of lush flowers and expensive per-
fumes, its sticky sweetness clogging her nostrils and making it difficult to breathe. Through the dark fronds, she
watched the couples spin across the dance floor in a kalei-
doscope of jeweltone colors and glittering gems. Laughter
and loud music twined through the glittering fire of the
chandeliers, the crystalline shards of light punctuated by
the clink of wine glasses.

Steady, steady—I mustn't let myself crack.

"Ah, there you are, Miss Sloane." Mr. Naughton, second
son of the Earl of Greenfield and a very pleasant young
man, approached and immediately began to spout a pro-
fuse apology. "Forgive me for being late in seeking your
hand for this set. I've been looking for you everywhere."

Forcing a smile, Anna made no effort to accept his outstretched hand. "No apologies necessary, sir. The blame is
mine. I—I was feeling a trifle overwarm and thought a moment in the shadows might serve as a restorative."

His face pinched in concern. "Allow me to fetch you a
glass of ratafia punch."

"No, no." She waved off the suggestion. "Please don't
trouble yourself. I think I shall just pay a visit to the
ladies' withdrawing room"—a place to which no gentleman would dare ask to escort her—"and ask the maid for a
cold compress for my brow."

Naughton shuffled his feet. "You are sure?"

"Quite." Suddenly she couldn't bear his solicitous smile
or the oppressive gaiety a moment longer. Lifting her
skirts, she turned before he could say another word and
hurried down one of the side corridors.

Her steps quickened as she passed by the room reserved
for the ladies and ducked around a darkened corner. From

a previous visit to the townhouse, Anna knew that a set of French doors in the library led out to a raised terrace overlooking the back gardens. It was, of course, against the rules for an unchaperoned young lady to venture outdoors on her own. But she had chosen the secluded spot with great care—the chances of being spotted were virtually nil.

The night air felt blessedly cool on her overheated cheeks. "Thank God," she murmured, tilting her face to the black velvet sky.

"Thank God," echoed a far deeper voice.

A pale plume of smoke floated overhead, its curl momentarily obscuring the sparkle of the stars.

"It was getting devilishly dull out here with only my own thoughts for company."

Speak of the Devil!

Anna whirled around. "That's not surprising, sir, when one's mind is filled with nothing but thoughts of drinking, wenching, and gaming. Titillating as those pursuits might be, I would assume they grow tiresome with constant repetition."

"A dangerous assumption, Miss Sloane." Devlin Greville, the Marquess of Davenport—better known as the Devil Davenport—tossed down his cheroot and ground out the glowing tip beneath his heel. Sparks flared for an instant, red-gold against the slate tiles, before fading away to darkness. "I thought you a more sensible creature than to venture an opinion on things about which you know nothing."

Anna watched warily as he took one...two...three sauntering steps closer. Quelling the urge to retreat, she stood her ground. The Devil might be a dissolute rake, a rapacious rogue, but she would not give him the satisfaction of seeing her flinch.

"Sense has nothing to do with it," she countered coolly. "Given the rather detailed—and lurid—gossip that fills the drawing rooms of Mayfair each morning, I know a great deal about your exploits."

"Another dangerous assumption." His voice was low and a little rough, like the purr of a stalking panther.

Anna felt the tiny hairs on the nape of her neck stand on end.

He laughed, and the sound turned even softer. "I also thought you a more sensible creature than to listen to wild speculation."

"Indeed?" Feigning nonchalance, she slid sideways and leaned back against the stone railing. Which was, she realized, a tactical mistake. The marquess mirrored her movements, leaving her no way to escape.

"I—I don't know why you would think that," she went on. "You know absolutely nothing about me."

"On the contrary. I, too, listen to the whispers that circulate through the *ton*."

"Don't be absurd." She steadied her voice. "I am quite positive that there's not an ill word spoken about me. I am exceedingly careful that not a whiff of impropriety sullies my reputation."

"Which in itself says a great deal," he drawled.

"You're an idiot."

"Am I?" He came closer, close enough that her nostrils were suddenly filled with a swirl of masculine scents. *Bay rum cologne. Spiced smoke. French brandy. A hint of male musk.*

Her pulse began to pound, her breath began to quicken.

Good Lord, it's me *who is an idiot. I'm acting like Emmalina!*

Shaking off the horrid novel histrionics, Anna scowled. "You're not only an idiot, Lord Davenport, you are an *annoying* idiot. I'm well aware that you take perverse pleasure in trying to…"

Cocking his head, he waited.

"To annoy me," she finished lamely.

Another laugh. "Clearly I am having some success, so I can't be all that bumbling."

To give the Devil his due, he had a quick wit. Biting back an involuntary smile, Anna turned her head to look out over the shadowed gardens. Flames from the torchieres on the main terrace danced in the breeze, their glow gilding the silvery moonlight as it dappled over the thick ivy vines that covered the perimeter walls.

She shouldn't find him amusing. And yet like a moth drawn to an open fire…

"What? No clever retort?" said Devlin.

Anna willed herself not to respond.

"I see." Somehow he found a way to inch even closer. His trousers were now touching her skirts. "You mean to ignore me."

"If you were a gentleman, you would go away and spare me the effort."

"Allow me to point out two things, Miss Sloane. Number one—I was here first."

The marquess had a point.

"And number two…" His hand touched her cheek. He wasn't wearing gloves and the heat of his bare fingers seemed to scorch her skin. "We both know I'm no gentleman."

* * *

Devlin saw her eyes widen as the light pressure on her jaw turned her face to his. It wasn't shock, he decided, but something infinitely more interesting. Miss Anna Sloane was no spun-sugar miss, a cloying confection of sweetness and air that would make a man's molars stick together at first bite. He sensed an intriguing hint of steel beneath the demure gowns and dutiful smiles.

If I had to guess, I would say that she's not averse to the little game we have been playing.

She inhaled with a sharp hiss.

Or maybe I am simply in a state of drunken delusion.

It was entirely possible. Of late he had been imbibing far more brandy than was good for him. Only one way to find out.

He would give her a heartbeat to protest, to pull away. Yes, he was dissolute, but not depraved. A man had to draw the line somewhere.

She made a small sound in her throat.

Too late.

The tiny throb of her pulse beneath his fingertips had signaled her time was up. Devlin leaned in and felt their bodies graze, their lips touch.

A mere touch, and yet it sent a jolt of fire through him.

He froze. The distant laughter, the faint trilling of the violins, the rustling leaves all gave way to a strange thrumming sound in his ears.

Anna shifted, and Devlin shook off the sensation. It *must* be the brandy, he decided. He had just come from his club, where he had been sampling a potent vintage brought up from the wine cellar. Women had no such effect on him.

A kiss was a distraction, nothing more. A way to keep boredom at bay.

"Go to Hell." Anna's whisper teased against his mouth as she jerked back.

"Eventually," growled Devlin. "But first..." He kissed her again. A harder, deeper, possessive embrace.

Her lips tremored uncertainly.

Seizing the moment, he slipped his tongue through the tiny gap and tasted a beguiling mix of warmth and spice. Impossible to describe.

He needed to taste more.

More.

Clasping his arms around her waist, Devlin pushed her back a little roughly, pinning her body to the unyielding stone. She tensed and twisted...

I am Satan's spawn.

...and then went still.

Time seemed to stop, to hang suspended within the shifting shadows of the fluttering leaves. A myriad of sensations seemed to skate over his skin. *Fire. Ice. The slow softening of her resistance.*

Anna made another sound. No words, just a soft feline purr that drifted off into the darkness. She moved, tilting forward in a tentative tasting of her own. Entwined, they swayed, weightless in the cool caress of the night.

Somewhere close by, a door opened and shut.

The echo broke the strange spell. With a shudder, Anna wrenched free of his hold, a gasp fluttering through her gloved fingertips as she touched her lips.

Disgust? Disbelief?

Devlin blinked, not quite certain of his own feelings.

For a fleeting moment it looked as though she were going to speak, but instead, she shoved him aside and walked off without a word.

Walked with her head held high, her spine ramrod straight, he noted, rather than pelter off in a torrent of tears and sobs.

Hard and soft—no question Anna Sloane was a contradiction.

Which made her a conundrum.

But Devlin liked puzzles. They kept his own inner demons at bay.

Chapter Two

"Are you feeling ill, my dear?" Anna's mother squinted through the dim light of the carriage lamp. "You look a trifle peaked."

Piqued was perhaps a more accurate word, thought Anna, but she kept such thoughts to herself. Unlike her daughters, Lady Trumbull was not overly interested in the nuances of language.

"I confess, I am not feeling overly well either." Caro shifted on the seat next to her and exhaled loudly. "My head hurts. I think I drank one too many glasses of that lovely champagne."

"You must learn to control your impulsive urges," scolded their mother. "Really, Carolina, do try to emulate your older sister's example."

Anna closed her eyes, unwilling to meet the fond smile.

"Discretion, discipline," continued Lady Trumbull. "Follow her lead and you won't go wrong."

"Yes, Mama," replied Caro. But, being Caro, she

couldn't resist adding, "However, not all of us are graced with the good fortune to be a saint."

"Don't be impertinent, Carolina."

"No, Mama."

To Anna's relief, Caro left it at that. Not that the ensuing silence was any more comfortable. Left to brood on her own inexplicable impulses, she, too, felt a beastly headache coming on.

Davenport is a disgrace, but so am I.

Of all the buffle-headed, bird-witted things to do, kissing a rapscallion rogue ranked awfully high on the list of Supreme Follies. And to think she had called him an idiot. The epithet was better directed at herself.

Idiot. For good measure, Anna repeated it in Italian. *Cretina.* She wished she knew German, for no doubt it would sound suitably harsher. Or Russian...

Thankfully, the carriage rolled to a halt, putting an end to her multilingual self-loathing.

"If you will excuse me, I think I shall go straight up to my room," she mumbled, after handing her cloak to their manservant.

"Shall I have Cook fix you a posset?" asked Lady Trumbull.

"No, no, I'm just fatigued is all. A good night's sleep is the only restorative I need." Assuming sleep would come. Anna rather doubted it.

Their mother looked unconvinced but yielded with a reluctant nod. "Very well. However, if you are still feeling unwell in the morning, I shall send for a physician." A tiny pause. "Lord Andover mentioned that he wishes to take you to Lady Riche's Venetian Breakfast on Thursday and it would be a pity if you had to refuse him." Another pause, punctuated by a sigh. "He is such a pleasant young man. Handsome and considerate—"

"Rich and titled," added Caro under her breath.

"Not to speak of possessing a handsome fortune and being heir to an earldom."

Anna stripped off her gloves, feeling further unsettled by her mother's ham-handed hints on marriage. Up until recently, she had dutifully accepted the notion that it was up to her to marry well in order to provide security for her family—money, not love, was all that mattered. But now...

"Now that Olivia has married Lord Wrexham, we need not be so desperate to catch a rich peer," she pointed out.

A frown furrowed between Lady Trumbull's brows. "I wish to see *all* my daughters well settled, my dear. Money and position are very important in Polite Society."

Even if they don't make you happy?

Anna turned away, leaving the retort unvoiced. What right had she to talk of happiness when she hadn't the foggiest notion of what it was or how to achieve it?

After lighting a taper from the candelabra on the side table, Anna started up the stairs. Perhaps she, too, had imbibed too much bubbly. Her thoughts usually did not sink to such depths of cynicism.

The patter of steps right behind her warned that Caro was not as easily put off as their mother.

"What's wrong?" demanded her sister as soon as they reached the top of the landing.

"I'm tired," she snapped.

"Oh? And since when has fatigue grown clever enough to give a girl kiss-ravaged lips?"

Anna clapped a hand over her mouth. "What do you know about kissing?" she said through her fingers.

"You describe it in excruciating detail in your novels," replied Caro smugly.

"I'm sorry that Olivia and I taught you how to read." Anna wrenched open her bedroom door and kicked it shut behind her. No wonder men liked hitting each other. There was something very satisfying about lashing out a solid *thwock*.

"Ha, ha, ha." Caro slipped in just before the paneled oak fell into place. "Who was it?"

"Never mind."

Ignoring the order, her sister took a seat on the edge of the bed and began fingering her chin. "Not Andover. He's much too polite. And Chittenden wouldn't dare—he's far too in awe of you."

"Kindly stubble the speculation. I'm really not in the mood for it."

"Major Grove is a possibility. Or perhaps that American merchant, Mr. Hale. He's a little rough around the edges."

"Caroooo."

"But it's amusing to try to guess," responded her sister with a grin. "Who in the name of the Devil would be bold enough—" Her words suddenly came to a halt in midsentence.

Drat.

"Ye gods. Not Lord Davenport."

Anna dropped her reticule on the dressing table and sat down. A hard yank freed a handful of hairpins. The stinging in her scalp actually felt rather good.

"That is to say, he, of all people, would be bold enough," went on Caro. "But you would never allow it. You dislike him."

She picked up her brush and set to combing out the top-knot of curls.

"*Intensely*," added her sister.

Anna continued to work in steadfast silence.

"Though I confess, I've never quite understood why. You once tried to explain it, but it didn't make a great deal of sense." Caro's voice turned more tentative. "Something about how the two of you were more alike than you wished to acknowledge because you were both forced to be on the hunt for a plump-in-the-pocket pigeon to marry."

Caro had a habit of making rambling speeches, mused Anna. Perhaps she would simply tire herself out and go off to bed.

"But that's a moot point now. Wrexham is rich as Croesus, and Olivia has assured me that neither of us has to worry about marrying for money anymore."

Their eldest sister had recently wed the Earl of Wrexham—much to the surprise of Society, for Olivia was regarded as an outspoken, opinionated hellion while John was admired as the oh-so-proper Perfect Hero. However, both portrayals were only skin deep. Beneath the surface were hidden complexities. Hidden secrets.

Anna repressed a sigh. Secrets seemed to run in the family.

"So if you ask me..." Caro's voice drew her out of her brooding. "I think the Devil's aura of danger is exciting."

That a part of her—a very small part—obviously agreed with Caro turned Anna's mood even more prickly. Abandoning the I-Will-Not-Say-A-Word strategy, she huffed out a sharp "hmmph" and turned in her chair.

"My head is aching enough right now without having to listen to you prattling on like a silly schoolgirl about something of which you know virtually nil. So could we kindly continue this conversation in the morning?"

As soon as the words were out of her mouth, Anna wished she could summon them back. Caro, who usually accepted the set-downs from her older sisters with cheerful good grace, flinched and went white as the down-turned linen sheets.

"Oh, sweetheart, I'm so sorry." Rising, she hurried to the bed and enveloped Caro in a fierce hug. "I don't know what's wrong with me of late—I've not been myself." And the trouble was, she wasn't quite sure who "myself" was anymore. "It wasn't you I was sniping at—it was my own tangled thoughts. Please forgive me."

"The fault is mine," mumbled Caro through a teary sigh. "I should have known better than to tease you when clearly you are feeling blue-deviled. Mama is right, I must learn to control my impulsive urges. It's childish. And selfish."

"Don't *ever* let anyone tell you to bridle your exuberance." Anna stroked a hand over her sister's dark curls. "It's part of your essence, and without it you wouldn't be you." Lifting Caro's head, she pressed a light kiss to her brow. "Or a poet."

"I—I'm not a very good poet, but perhaps if I work as hard as you and Olivia do at writing, I shall have a hope of improving."

"You are exceedingly good, Caro. And you're going to get even better. You have a rare talent for expressing emotions."

Sniff. "Even though they sometimes get out of control?"

"Emotions are perverse little devils." *Devil*—the word brought a fresh rush of heat to her cheeks. "They seem to have a will of their own and defy any attempts by us mere mortals to control them."

Caro quirked a watery smile. "Perhaps I'll write an Ode to Hellfire Emotion."

"An excellent idea. But it's probably best left until morning, when the flames of Passionate Feelings have burned down a bit."

"Yes, yes, quite right." Her sister smoothed her skirts and rose. "I'll leave you to sleep…" She opened the door and then looked back over her shoulder with an impish grin. "And to dream of the Devil."

"Minx." Letting out a rueful laugh, Anna tossed a pillow at the paneled oak as it clicked shut.

Which left her alone with her own thoughts.

Touching her tongue to her kiss-ravaged lips, she fell back upon the counterpane and stared up at the ceiling, where the play of shadows cast by the candleflame were dancing like underworld imps of Satan flitting across the plaster.

Shadows, not imps of Satan, Anna reminded herself, trying not to let Caro's penchant for exaggerated exuberance color her own already overheated imagination. The night promised to be uncomfortable enough without added demons.

"You look like Hell warmed over."

Devlin slouched into the leather armchair and poured himself a glass of brandy. "Have you any idea how often I hear such thoroughly unoriginal witticisms? From you, I expect a tad more cleverness."

"I'm not feeling terribly clever at the moment," replied Anthony Thorncroft, pinching at the bridge of his prominent nose. Dark smudges of fatigue underlined his gunmetal-gray eyes and his usual predatory smile was looking a little taut around the edges.

"Nor am I. It requires far too much effort, especially at this hour of night." He lit a cheroot and took several long puffs before leaning back and exhaling a perfect ring of silvery smoke. As it hovered for an instant overhead, he let out a rumbled laugh. "Oh, look. I've got a halo."

"You," growled Thorncroft, "are an ass."

"So I've been told." Devlin tapped a bit of ash on the expensive Turkey carpet. "And I don't disagree."

Thorncroft slid his boot out and stamped out an errant spark.

"Which raises the question of why you asked me here."

"I have a job that might suit you."

Devlin took a long moment to consider the statement. The ancestral title and estate passed down by his profligate father had come with crushing debts piled upon the fancy family crest, whose fancy Latin motto translated as *Restraint and Resolve.*

Ah, yes, the Gods of Greed had a wickedly cynical sense of humor.

Not that I have any right to be holier than thou. The task of repairing decades of damages had been daunting to a callow youth of seventeen. Instead, he had chosen to emulate the example of his predecessors. Devilry, like brandy, ran hot and potent in the Davenport blood. Why fight Fate when it was far easier to give in to temptation than try to be...

A better man?

Ha! And pigs might fly.

"How much does it pay?" asked Devlin after blowing out another series of tiny rings.

A grimace spasmed across Thorncroft's face. "You're not in any position to negotiate, Davenport. According to my sources, you're badly dipped at the present moment."

"I'm always badly dipped," retorted Devlin. "The degree really doesn't matter."

"Considering what we paid you for the last job, I would have thought you would have settled some of the accounts at your gaming hells."

"Good God, why?" he drawled.

The comment drew a ghost of a smile from the other man. "I confess, your utter lack of morality has a certain charm."

"Of course it does. It suits your purpose." Devlin tossed back a long swallow of his spirits. In truth, Thorncroft might faint if he knew what the money was really spent on. "Now that we've exchanged pleasantries, shall we get down to business?"

Settling back in his chair, Thorncroft tapped his well-tended fingertips together. "It's actually a very simple and straightforward task, though it does require you to be absent from the pleasures of London for several weeks."

Which might, mused Devlin, be an excellent idea. Given his inexplicable reactions to a casual kiss, a respite from the usual revelries was needed to reorder his wits.

"I will warn you though, the spot is remote."

Even better.

"I'm willing to listen," he said softly.

Tap, tap. "And I," replied Thorncroft, "am willing to negotiate the price."

The first slender fingers of dawn's light poked through the draperies, pulling Anna fully awake. Strange dreams had plagued her sleep. Teasing, taunting dreams, filled with a whirling dervish tangle of menacing creatures and threatening whispers. *A black cat—there had been a black cat, a tiny tabby who had, in an instant, transformed in a burst of flame and brimstone smoke into a terrifying beast. Ha, ha, ha! Its topaz eyes had turned scarlet, with flames spitting out to scorch her face—*

"Drat." She covered her face with her hands, trying to cool her burning cheeks. "Would that I could dream of something useful." A wry sigh. "Like the plot for my next chapter."

It was, Anna decided, the unaccountable absence of her creative muse that had her emotions in a muddle. Perhaps the perverse goddess had heeded Caro's suggestion and headed off to the spa at Baden-Baden on her own for a prolonged stay, taking all her clever words with her.

Leaving me to face a looming deadline without so much as a dribble of inspiration.

Slumping back against the pillows, Anna tacked on a few well-chosen oaths to her grumbling. *Think!* Surely it shouldn't be so hard to strike a few fresh sparks of imagination. All that was needed was to find the right flint and steel…

Determined to banish her brooding mood, she quickly dressed on her own and headed downstairs. Her late father's library, a cozy, comfortable refuge that always seemed to help focus and clarify her thoughts, offered far more prospects for helpful ideas than a jumble of twisted bedsheets.

She had been reading for an hour or two when the door pushed open and Caro entered, patting back a yawn.

"You're up awfully early," murmured Anna as she jotted down a few notes before turning the page of the book.

"I was having trouble sleeping." Her sister grimaced.

"Ugh, my head feels even worse than last night and my stomach is a little queasy."

"Champagne's sparkle turns a little flat when one overindulges," replied Anna, with a tiny smile.

"But it tasted so good."

"So said Eve about the Serpent's apple," she pointed out. "Temptation usually does."

"Thank you, but wisdom isn't easy to swallow at this hour in the morning." Tightening the sash of her wrapper, Caro pushed one of the armchairs closer to the hearth and curled up on the well-worn cushion. "What are you reading?"

"Lady Mary Wortley Montagu's *Letters from Turkey.*" Another turn of the page. "They contain some really fascinating details about the Ottoman Sultan's court in Constantinople."

"You've already had Emmalina imprisoned in a pasha's harem in Tripoli."

"Yes, yes, but Lady Mary also explored the country along the coast, including a fabulous city of classical ruins at Ephesus. Her descriptions of the towering marble columns silhouetted in the moonlight are quite wonderful." Anna read aloud a short passage. "She says the Temple of Artemis was one of the Seven Wonders of the Ancient World."

"A midnight chase scene through the stones offers some interesting possibilities," mused Caro.

"Precisely. I have a few rough ideas taking shape, but they need to be refined." Plotting her novels was usually a very personal and private process, but on occasion she did find it helpful to talk out ideas with her sisters. This morning, however, aside from the purely practical advantage of stimulating ideas, Anna decided that involving Caro would help assuage the hurt of her thoughtlessly cruel comment from the previous evening.

"Would you care to hear them?" she asked. "I would welcome your suggestions, seeing as my own brain seems to be acting a trifle sluggish."

Caro's face lit up.

Anna bit her lip, feeling even more guilty. Caught up in her own moods, her own worries, she had forgotten that this transition from schoolroom to ballroom was still new and perhaps a little daunting for her younger sister. And with all the recent changes to life at High Street—Olivia's marriage to Lord Wrexham, the myriad alterations in their household routine now that finances were no longer so pinched—Caro and her concerns had been shunted into the shadows.

It was, mused Anna, not easy being the youngest of three very strong-willed siblings. Caro's penchant for melodrama was...

"Balloons!" exclaimed her sister. "What about a chase that leads up and up through the Temple columns, and then suddenly Count Alessandro swoops down in a hot air balloon to rescue Emmalina from La Chaze."

"Hmmm. Intriguing." Anna considered the idea for a moment. "But where has the balloon come from? It's not exactly something he can conjure up out of thin air."

"Oh. Right." Caro scrunched her mouth in thought.

Coals crackled as the burning logs suffused the companionable silence with a mellow warmth. Watching the dancing flames slowly melt the early morning shadows, Anna felt her own mood begin to brighten. It was silly to let thoughts of a hellfire rogue upset her.

"Ah! How about this?" Caro slapped her palms together. "It's a gift to the Sultan from Napoleon, who is trying to win allies in the Mediterranean. The Sultan's Janissary Guards have been making a test flight along the coast, to make sure it is safe for His Imperial Highness. And they stopped for the night at the ruins."

"Perhaps you should give up poetry for prose," said Anna dryly. "You are showing a frightfully good knack for imagining exuberant adventures."

"Really?"

"Perhaps I will hand over Sir Sharpe Quill's pen and travel to Baden-Baden after all."

Caro laughed, the sound signaling that any hurt feelings were now forgotten. "You would soon become terribly bored. And besides, it's much more fun to read Emmalina's exotic adventures than to actually have to sit down and write them."

"Thank you for reminding me of that fact." Anna blew out a long sigh. "Let's pursue this balloon idea…"

The lively discussion was still in full flight when their mother entered the library well after the breakfast hour. "La, I've been looking all over for you, girls." Her eyes narrowed in disapproval as she slanted a look at the massive oak bookcases crammed full of scholarly volumes and arcane manuscripts. "What are you doing in here?"

"Discussing Sir Sharpe Quill's latest novel," answered Anna as she quickly hid her notebook in her lap.

Lady Trumbull thought that learning anything other than needlework, sketching, dancing, and perhaps playing the pianoforte was unnatural for a young lady. That the late baron had taught his daughters all about literature, history, science, and philosophy still provoked a litany of bitter recriminations about Things That Discouraged A Gentleman From Making A Marriage Proposal.

Popular novels, were, however, exempt from censure. The *ton* had deemed them acceptable entertainment for the fairer sex.

Their mother's expression relaxed ever so slightly. "I grant you, such silly adventures are mildly amusing, but I've got some exciting news that will quickly put all thoughts of novels out of your head."

Anna felt a prickling of unease run down her spine.

"I just received a letter in the morning post from my dearest school friend, the Countess of Dunbar..."

A "dearest" school friend who had pointedly ignored the baroness when the Sloane family had been dancing on the razor's edge of poverty, thought Anna with an inward sigh.

"Just look!" went on Lady Trumbull, a triumphant flourish producing the missive in question. The paper was indeed festooned with the remains of an ornate red wax seal. "Of course, it is only a Scottish title, and not nearly as impressive as Wrexham's earldom, but still..."

A title is a title, mouthed Caro, careful to mask the impertinence by brushing a lock of hair from her cheek.

The paper fluttered again, emitting the discreet crackle that only expensive stationery could achieve. "I am sure you girls are all agog to learn what exciting news it contains."

"I am holding my breath," murmured Anna. Whatever it was, she was certain that she wasn't going to like it.

Lady Trumbull inhaled deeply and held her breath for a moment, savoring the coming words like a fine wine. "We are invited to a shooting party for the month of August at dear Miriam's castle in Scotland."

Scotland. Anna cocked an ear. A country house party in the remote wilds of the north was not something that would normally send her mother into a fit of raptures. Not unless...

"And she informs me that the other guests will include several Prussian nobles—and a prince!"

Of course. The party included eligible men. Now that Olivia had captured an earl, their mother had apparently raised her sights to royalty.

"Which prince?" asked Caro curiously.

Lady Trumbull waved off the question. "Oh, Schlezzie-Whatsie or some such thing. All those little German fiefdoms are so dreadfully confusing." Turning a beatific smile on Anna, she continued, "What matters is that Miriam says he is rich, handsome, charming—and unmarried."

Anna looked down at her lap. In the past, she had accepted the fact that her beauty must be bartered in order to provide for her family's security. However, things had changed.

"And since Lord Andover has not come up to scratch, Anna..."

The truth was, after fueling his courage with one too many glasses of claret, Andover *had* broached the subject of marriage to her several weeks ago, though he had been wise enough to do it in private. Wisdom, along with a kind nature and self-deprecating sense of humor—that was more than most ladies were offered. And yet it wasn't enough. She had gently but firmly informed him that while she valued his friendship, she did not think they would suit as husband and wife.

He had actually seemed rather relieved, mumbling something about perfection and pedestals.

"You have every right to look elsewhere," finished their mother.

Elsewhere being Dunbar, Scotland.

As if she didn't have enough worries here in London. Now that Andover had gracefully withdrawn his attentions, two other gentlemen had become more ardent in their attempts to win her regard. Both were very pleasant, and yet...

A quip from Caro interrupted her musings. "So, grouse and pheasants will not be the only hunted creatures on the windswept moors. The royal party of foreign blue bloods is going to find itself fair game."

"Bite your tongue, Caro!" admonished their mother. "A lady must never, ever give voice to such vulgar speculations."

"Especially when they are true," retorted the youngest Sloane in a low whisper.

Anna shook her head ever so slightly in warning.

"Don't be impertinent. Men dislike ladies who express opinions as if they possessed..."

A brain? thought Anna.

"...any understanding of the world," said Lady Trumbull with a huff of exasperation. "As I've told you repeatedly, you must try to follow your sister's example. She understands exactly what is expected of a paragon of propriety, and does not disappoint."

"Yes, Mama," said Caro after a tiny hesitation. For the moment, she seemed to have taken the talk on controlling impulsive urges to heart.

Turning her attention to Anna, Lady Trumbull softened

her tone. "Now, my dear, when you think of it, a retreat to the quiet of the country for a month will be a welcome interlude for rest and relaxation after the whirlwind weeks of the Season." The predatory smile did not bode well for the unpronounceable prince and his peace of mind. "Don't you agree?"

Anna was about to respond with a careful calculated list of reasons why the invitation ought to be rejected. But the words "retreat," "quiet," and "country" suddenly stirred second thoughts.

A remote Scottish castle. A month of precious few distractions, save for the prince and his party of noblemen— and they would be easy enough to deal with.

Perhaps meeting her deadline was not yet beyond hope. Her writing had always been a source of solace and satisfaction, providing an escape from the pressures of the real world. That she was suddenly struggling with her story was a little frightening, especially with all the other uncertainties tugging at her emotions. So the date had become a talisman of sorts. If she could reach it, all of her usual well-ordered discipline and detachment would return...

"I think," said Anna slowly, "that Lady Dunbar's hunting party would make a lovely getaway from London."

Caro stared at her in confusion.

"Excellent, excellent! I knew you would adore the idea." Clapping her hands together, Lady Trumbull lost no time in turning for the door. "I shall go write to Miriam right away."

"Are you mad?" hissed Caro as soon as their mother had left the room.

Anna smiled.

"What about your deadline—" A look of dawning comprehension suddenly lit her sister's face. "Oh, brilliant!"

Peace and quiet. A respite from the swarm of suitors in London.

"Yes, I rather thought so myself."

Chapter Three

*I*gnoring the censorious stares from a trio of dowagers, Devlin continued whistling an aria from Mozart's *Don Giovanni* as he sidestepped around their elegant barouche and turned down the side street. The morning hours were not often cause for songful celebration. For the most part he passed them sprawled in bed, sleeping off the long evenings spent drinking, gaming, or...indulging in other more engaging activities. Today, however, the grumbling protest from his weary bones took second fiddle to a more cheerful melody—the whisper of money.

Even though the blade of bright sunshine that cut across his path did make him wince.

It was, he decided wryly, an interesting question to ponder whether he, like the Vampyre in John Poldari's novel, grew weaker in daylight...

But not at the present moment.

The early start had been impelled by the thick wad of bank notes that were at present making such a pleasant sound within in his waistcoat pocket. Thorncroft had, with surprisingly little argument, agreed to fund his request for a pair of special turn-off pocket pistols from Joseph Manton's shop. Delighted with the stroke of luck, Devlin was itching to get his hands on them without delay and examine the workmanship, for the weapons were exquisitely crafted—not to speak of sinfully expensive.

But however superb, he had already come to the decision that he was only going to buy one. The other half of the funds would be spent at a nearby shop, procuring a special assortment of...

A high note of the aria died on his lips as a frown strangled all further sound.

He stared for a long moment at the front of Manton's shop, trying to quell the erratic quickening of his pulse as he suddenly recognized the figure standing there. Shaking off the physical response to the person in question, Devlin made himself concentrate on the practical question her presence raised. *What was she doing there? Ladies did not usually linger in front of a gunsmith's display window.*

Lightening his footsteps, Devlin approached in silence. "Planning on murdering someone, Miss Sloane?"

Anna started, nearly dropping the small notebook in her hands, and then whirled around. "Some men," she snapped, "deserve to be shot."

"More than a few," he agreed, angling his head to try to catch a glimpse of what she had been writing.

The covers quickly snapped shut.

"If you like," he went on, "I could draw up a list of the most offensive characters."

Chuffing a rude sound, Anna darted one more look at the pistols on display before shoving her pencil and notebook into her reticule. "Come along, Nettie," she called to the young maid hovering near the corner of the storefront. "Let us be on our way."

Devlin shifted his stance just enough to block her path. "It's unusual for a lady to have an interest in firearms. I confess, I am curious as to why."

"There is an old adage about curiosity killing the cat," she shot back.

He smiled, which appeared to annoy her even more. "Then it is lucky that I am an imp of Satan."

"Why is it that I have a feeling Luck has nothing to do with your choice of habits?"

Because your wit and your tongue are lethally sharp.

Keeping such thoughts to himself, he merely said, "An interesting question. But you haven't yet answered mine, and I asked first."

A glare, which he countered by stretching his smile into a grin.

Her nostrils flared as she drew in a sharp breath. "Not that it is any of your business, but I—I am looking to find a special gift for Wrexham."

A reasonable reply. So why did he have the feeling that she was lying?

"Manton's pistols are frightfully expensive," responded Devlin, carefully watching her face. "Dare I assume that the poor-as-churchmice Sloane family is now no longer under the hatches, thanks to the generosity of your older sister's new husband?"

A light breeze ruffled the ribbons of her bonnet, and for the space of a heartbeat a flutter of a shadow seemed to hang on her gold-tipped lashes.

"Indeed, knowing the earl's noble nature, I would imagine that you and Miss Caro are now in possession of a very generous dowry."

Her cheeks darkened to an angry shade of red. "You are not only impertinent, you are offensive, Lord Davenport. Kindly step aside."

"But of course." He slowly shifted, deliberately dragging his boots over the paving stones to make a loud rasping sound. It was ungentlemanly to goad her into a temper, but the fire in her eyes was mesmerizing to watch. Heat blazed in a burnt-gold swirl of sparks, turning their deep green hue into a pool of molten jade.

"Allow me to make amends for my churlish manners by offering a recommendation on which of Manton's models the earl might like."

"On second thought, I have decided to look elsewhere for a gift," replied Anna tightly.

"A simple but elegant watch fob, perhaps? A bejeweled cravat stickpin would not be at all in keeping with the earl's sense of style."

"I can't help but wonder something, sir," she said in reply.

"Which is?"

"Why you take such fiendish delight in tormenting me."

"Perhaps because you react with such delightfully explosive ire." Devlin waggled a brow. "Most young ladies are afraid to stand up for themselves. But not you."

She brushed past him without comment.

Devlin watched her stalk away. Miss Anna Sloane was known for her effortless grace, and yet there was no other word than "stalk" for her stiff-legged gait. Which in itself spoke volumes about her state of inner agitation.

Again, he wondered why.

Turning, he moved to where she had been standing and made a careful study of the display window.

Interesting.

Devlin stood for some moments deep in thought, alternating his gaze between the weapons laid out on the dark green felt cloth and the fast-fading reflection of a feminine figure glimmering in the paned glass. Anna had been quick, but not quick enough. He had caught just a fleeting glimpse of the page, a flutter of white and graphite, but he had the distinct impression that it had not been writing, but rather a drawing that she had been scribbling in the notebook.

A drawing of a turn-off pocket pistol?

He frowned. It was conceivably the sort of firearm a lady might tuck in her reticule...

Assuming she had reason to fear for her safety.

Anna Sloane in danger? For an instant, his hands fisted, but he quickly dismissed the idea as absurd.

Absurd.

She was the very soul of tactful charm and grace. Even the Mamas with daughters on the Marriage Mart found it impossible to dislike her. That was because, mused Devlin, they couldn't help but notice how kind Anna was to the plain or painfully shy girls who decorated the ballroom back walls like so many fragile pastel blooms. He, too, had seen how she had discreetly asked her own swains to favor them with a dance or take them in to supper.

In truth, she was so kind and considerate to everyone— granted, with one notable exception, but he readily admitted the fault was his—it was almost as if she were too good to be true...

"I have been reading too many adventure novels."

Devlin blew out his breath along with the harried growl. "Clanging chains, subterranean dungeons, evil villains, damsels in distress...ye gods, perhaps I should send Sir Sharpe Quill a few ideas for his next book." Some of the things he had been thinking were outrageous enough for the pages of London's favorite author.

The glass caught the mocking curl of his lips. Speaking of advice, the fellow definitely needed some help with his sex scenarios. Given the exotic settings, the virile hero, and the bold-as-brass heroine, they were surprisingly...tame.

The workshop door opened with a muted tinkling of bells, drawing Devlin from his musings.

"I'm surprised to see you here, Davenport," said the Duke of Leverett, as he and his gunkeeper exited the premises. "Thought you were too dipped to be able to afford any of Manton's creations."

"I've come into an unexpected windfall," he replied.

"Then use it to pay off your debts, man," snapped the duke.

Devlin suspected he owed the fellow money but couldn't quite remember for what. "Actually, there is an alternate way to settle my accounts," he replied. "I could use the funds to purchase a double-barreled coaching gun." A pause. "And then use it to eliminate all my creditors. Poof! My troubles are gone, and I end up with a very fine precision instrument."

The duke took a step back and looked as though he might faint.

"A jest, Your Grace," murmured Devlin. The man was notorious for having no sense of humor. "Merely a jest."

"A damnably bad one," groused the duke, as he crabbed

his way to the street and waved for his carriage. "You're a disgrace to the peerage."

Lifting his shoulders in a shrug, Devlin cocked a sardonic salute. "Shocking, isn't it, how low the standards have fallen."

"Go to—"

"Yes, I know—go to the Devil," murmured Devlin. "I do wish someone would come up with a more original insult."

"You look very lovely, Mademoiselle Anna." Josette stepped back to survey her handiwork. "That is, if I may say so myself."

"You may indeed—you deserve all the credit," said Anna. She slowly turned in front of the cheval glass, setting off a soft swish of silk and satin. This was the first ballgown that her French maid had taken charge of designing, and the result was quite striking.

"I look...different." Somehow more worldly, more mysterious, though she couldn't quite describe why.

Josette nodded sagely. "It is a matter of subtle details. Fabric, cut, color, texture. Your Mama had you swathed in unflattering styles that made you look like a morsel of spun sugar. Too sweet! Too fluffy! And as for all the girlish ribbons and bows..." The maid's hand gestures eloquently expressed what she thought of such decorative frills. "I have put most of them in the rag bin," she confided.

"I am happy to defer to your judgment on fashion," said Anna, still taking in the fact that a few yards of fabric could make such a difference.

"*Bon*," went on Josette, after circling around Anna for a final look. "Simplicity lets your delicate beauty shine.

As do the richer hues." She pinched the slate blue watered silk between her capable fingers. "Pastel shades are too in…in…"

"Insipid?" suggested Anna.

"*Oui*, that is the word! Too many of the young ladies here in London look as though they have had all the color scrubbed out of them."

A very perceptive comment, thought Anna. But then, her maid was an émigré from Paris who had lost her parents during the last tumultuous days of the Terror. Despite her young age, she had few illusions about human nature.

Josette made a face. "*Pffaugh*. What man wants to flirt with a piece of pasteboard? He wants to be intrigued, entranced."

"I'm afraid that here in London, a lady is meant to be seen and not heard," pointed out Anna. "She is not supposed to intrigue or entrance a man. She's supposed to smile and simper—and get him to the altar as soon as possible."

"*Pffaugh*. What fun is that?"

"It's not meant to be fun," replied Anna. "It's serious business."

Josette blew out a low snort. "*Oui, oui*, I know. For you English, marriage is all about money, power, and prestige, eh? It is not so different in France." The maid paused to take a needle and thread from a pincushion on the dressing table, and quickly stitched a small tuck into the sarcenet overskirt. "But we also understand that life is far more fun when there is a spark of romance to it."

Finished with the sewing, she raised a hand to her lips and kissed the tips of her fingers. "Put a man and woman together, it is inevitable that passions will flame."

"And likely one of them will get burned," remarked Anna dryly.

"Don't be a pess...a pessimist, mademoiselle."

"I'm not. I'm simply being a pragmatist."

Josette shook her head. "Fire can burn, but it can also be a source of warmth and light."

"Oh, my goodness!" Caro pushed open the bedchamber door, interrupting the exchange. "You look...like a completely different person in that gown."

Josette set a hand on her hip. "Is that good or bad?"

"Most definitely good," said Caro. "Marvelous, in fact. That shade of smoky blue suits you perfectly, though I can't explain why."

Anna felt a shiver skate across her skin. Strangely enough, it felt as if a layer of herself had been peeled off, leaving her naked.

Ye gods, my thoughts are in such a tangle that nothing is making any sense.

"You look," mused Caro, tilting her head to one side and then to the other, "not only beautiful but a little...I dunno..."

"Dangerous?" suggested Josette. "Even better than good. A lady should be little dangerous."

Anna cast a last sidelong look at her reflection before turning for the dressing table. Come-hither shadows seemed to ripple within the folds of silk as she moved, whispering softly, softly.

Siren songs, luring unsuspecting men...

Jerking her eyes away from the glass, Anna gave herself a mental scold. Far more dangerous than a lady in the flesh were the wild fancies that could spring to life inside her head.

"We had better go downstairs," she murmured, taking up her shawl and reticule. "You know how cross Mama gets if we keep her waiting."

Slouching a shoulder to the faux marble column, Devlin quaffed a swallow of his champagne and watched the dancing couples caper through the figures of a country gavotte.

"What brings you out into the gilded glitter of Mayfair, Davenport?" Lord Osborne, a rake with nearly as dreadful a reputation as his own, strolled into the recessed alcove. "I thought that you, like a toadstool, much prefer dank, dark spots that never see a sliver of light."

"I am surprised that you are so conversant with the habits of primitive plant life like *Lepista nuda*. I thought your specialty was the female species of *Homo sapiens*," replied Devlin.

"Ha, ha, ha." Osborne smiled. "I did attend Oxford, you know."

"For less than a term. As I recall, you were sent down for seducing the Provost's wife."

"Actually, it was the other way around," corrected Osborne. "But nonetheless, I had already decided that a scholar's life was not for me."

"Neither is that of a monk," quipped Devlin.

"I don't pretend to be a saint." Osborne regarded a group of young ladies fresh from the schoolroom who were waiting their turn at dancing. "Nor do you." He flicked a mote of dust from his sleeve. "Though I daresay there isn't much here to tempt a man to sin. Innocence is so terribly boring, don't you think?"

Devlin didn't answer right away. His gaze was on the

arched entryway at the far end of the ballroom, where a quicksilver flutter of blonde and blue had just disappeared into one of the side salons.

"What a pity that a plump purse is so rarely attached to aught but a dewy-eyed virgin."

"I wasn't aware that you had to marry for money," said Devlin absently. He shifted his stance, trying to find a better vantage point. Quite likely it was just a quirk of the swaying candlelight that had him imagining things.

"I don't. Which is why I have no intention of riveting on a legshackle anytime soon. Word is that you, however, are sinking fast in the River Tick and need a rich heiress to bail you out of your debts."

"Perhaps," said Devlin softly, "you have been listening in the wrong places."

"I keep my ears open wherever I go," replied Osborne. "And I find it curious..." He paused to watch a new set of dancers take their places for a cotillion. "Speaking of dewy-eyed virgins, the only one who has a glimmer of interest to her is Miss Anna Sloane."

Damnation, swore Devlin to himself, as the lady in question turned to face her partner, setting off a soft swirl of smoke-dark silk around her ankles—and sin-dark thoughts inside his head.

"And now that Wrexham has married her older sister, I imagine he will do the pretty and provide a handsome dowry." Osborne's mouth curled to a scimitar smile. "If so, I might reconsider my objections to matrimony to get her into my bed. My hunch is that beneath all the delicious beauty and demure smiles, there's a tantalizing streak of wildness just waiting to be unleashed."

A sudden surge of fury, all the more powerful for being

so unexpected, welled up in Devlin's chest. For an instant, the music and the rhythmic scuff of shoes on the polished parquet was overwhelmed by the thrumming rush of boiling blood reverberating in his ears.

If his newly purchased pocket pistol had been in his pocket, another hellfire scandal would likely have been branded on his name.

Gritting his teeth, he waited for the pounding of his pulse to subside before he looked around. "I wouldn't, if I were you."

"Oh? Have designs on the chit yourself?" A laugh. "I doubt the Perfect Hero would let either of us near her. Pistols at dawn, without a doubt. And no woman, however well dowered, is worth the trouble."

Devlin repressed the urge to shove the supercilious sneer—and several pearly teeth—down the other man's throat. "A wise philosophy. Especially when one is a notoriously lousy shot."

Osborne arched a brow. "You seem to have swallowed your usual sense of humor tonight, along with the last of your wine."

"Bilious stomach," muttered Devlin. A strangely sour taste had left his throat feeling dry as dust.

"Drinking to excess tends to do that."

"For a fellow who makes no claim to sainthood, you are doing a bloody awful lot of moralizing this evening."

"Ye gods, you *are* in a touchy mood. My comments on excess have to do with curiosity, not morality."

Devlin scowled a warning.

"I can't help but wonder something," went on Osborne. "As I said, I listen carefully when people talk, and from what I have gathered, your losses and winnings at the gaming hells are deceptively even. In fact, the winnings may hold a slight edge. Yet your debts are quite large. So it raises the question—on what are you spending your money?"

"If you'll excuse me, my glass is empty." Turning on his heel, Devlin walked off, ignoring the last murmured question that trailed in his wake.

"What secrets are you hiding, Davenport?"

Chapter Four

*H*ands lightly touching, Anna followed Lord Andover's lead through the figures of the country dance. *Step-turn, step-turn.* She knew the movements by heart so there was little danger in letting her mind wander to more personal concerns.

Had it been a wise decision to agree to the journey north? She was having second thoughts...

"So sorry—how clumsy of me," murmured Andover as he steadied her stumble.

Anna jerked her gaze away from the figure moving in and out of the shadows cast by the decorative colonnade. "I appreciate your gallantry, sir, but the fault is all mine—as you well know," she replied.

"You seem...distracted this evening," he said. "Is something wrong?"

"No, no," assured Anna, essaying a smile as the music came to an end. "I think I am just a trifle fatigued, is all."

"The social swirl can be tiring," agreed Andover, as he escorted her off the dance floor. "Miss Caro mentioned that you will soon be journeying to Scotland, and I have to confess that I'm rather jealous. An interlude of peace and quiet in the country sounds very inviting after the rigors of the Season."

"The castle is surrounded by wild moors and rugged cliffs overlooking the North Sea, so unless you enjoy shooting birds or watching rain squalls darken the horizon, I daresay you might be bored to flinders."

"And you? How will you keep yourself occupied in such a remote spot?" asked Andover.

"Books," said Anna. "One can never be bored with books as company."

The comment drew a chuckle in response. "I've never known a lady so passionate about reading."

"Yes, well, there are those who love music or watercolors. I happen to find the printed word endlessly inspiring." Anna fanned her face, using the cover of her kidskin-clad fingers to take another peek at the far end of the room.

The shadows showed no sign of life. Perhaps the Underworld specter was only a figment of her own overwrought imagination.

"I shall have to try to find you a novel that you haven't read for the trip north," said Andover lightly. "A daunting task."

"You need not trouble yourself. I've plenty of reading material to keep me occupied," Anna assured him.

"Miss Caro also tells me that a bevy of German nobles, including a prince, will be among the guests. So perhaps you will find romance outside the pages of a book," he replied.

"Real-life romance is the last thing I am looking to find in Scotland," said Anna. "Prince Charming will have to look elsewhere for a bride." Spotting her sister conversing with a childhood friend behind a large decorative urn filled with tuber roses, she quickly added, "If you don't mind, sir, I think I shall beg off from this next set and join my sister."

Ever the gentleman, Andover was far too well mannered to protest. Taking his leave with a polite bow, he strolled off in the direction of the card room. A moment later, Caro's friend was quickly claimed by her next partner, leaving the two sisters alone.

"Christabel thinks your new gown is shockingly lovely," said Caro. "All the girls do. They are yearning to cast off their pale hues and wear more daring colors."

"Perhaps, like Beau Brummel, you will become the arbiter of fashion," added a masculine voice from somewhere close by. "The Sovereign of sarcenet and satin."

Anna didn't need to turn around to know who was standing just behind her left shoulder. She could swear a faint whiff of brimstone suddenly sharpened the sweet fragrance of the flowers.

"It's rude to eavesdrop, Lord Davenport," she said.

"So it is," he murmured, moving in a half circle to face her. "Which is why I shall step in and join the conversation." His eyes locked with hers for just a moment, before sliding down to make a long, leisurely inspection of her gown. "Unless, of course, you have any objection."

Damnation. She felt herself growing uncomfortably warm. *Damn, damn, damn.* Her rebellious body seemed intent on responding to the man, despite all orders to the contrary.

"Not at all," answered Caro quickly. To Anna's consternation, her sister had decided on their first encounter several months ago that the dark, disreputable marquess was "Exceedingly Interesting," an accolade she bestowed on precious few gentlemen of the *ton*.

Poets, thought Anna wryly, were Exceeding Hard To Please.

"What do you think of Anna's new gown, Lord Davenport?" added her sister.

"It is indeed daring," he replied, after a prolonged pause. "That particular shade of blue makes an intriguing contrast to her fair coloring. One can't help but notice the striking contrast between dark and light."

A shiver of ice now joined the heat prickling over her flesh.

"I think it makes her look slightly dangerous, and so does our new French maid," confided Caro. "Josette says a lady *should* be dangerous. Do you agree, sir?"

"That depends," said Devlin.

"Caro..." began Anna, anxious to turn the talk to a safer subject.

"On what?" challenged her sister.

"On the lady." His eyes were on her again, and Anna felt her body clench in response to the low laugh that rumbled in his throat. "That smoke-dark hue conjures up thoughts of midnight and all the many sins that are hidden by darkness..."

Anna did not want to think of sin, not when the word stirred vivid memories of how good his body had felt pressed up against hers.

"...So yes, I would agree with you that your sister looks slightly dangerous."

"Looks can be deceiving," she quickly pointed out.

"So can words be deceiving," responded Devlin.

She felt her pulse start to skitter, and suddenly it was hard to breathe. Surely he couldn't suspect the truth. *Could he?* Lucifer and his legions were said to possess dark powers.

"So can gestures be deceiving," he added. "So can kisses be deceiving."

"Are you always so cynical about life, Lord Davenport?" asked Caro, sounding far more intrigued than a young lady should be by a thoroughly disreputable rogue.

"The answer is yes," replied Anna. "Always."

His lips quirked, and the memory of his wicked, wanton mouth on hers made her skin begin to tingle all over.

"Your sister knows me too well, Miss Caro."

"On the contrary," protested Anna. "I know you not at all, sir."

"A more accurate statement would be that you know me better than you think."

A frightening thought.

"However, in the spirit of furthering the acquaintance, might I request the next dance?" asked Devlin abruptly.

Taken by surprise, Anna stammered, "I—I am fatigued, sir."

A glint of unholy amusement seemed to light in his eyes. "I promise to move very slowly. As you know, I am loath to exert myself any more than necessary."

Caro stifled an unladylike chortle. "That's not what is whispered in all the drawing rooms, sir."

"It's dangerous to listen to idle speculation, Miss Caro." Devlin held out his hand to Anna. "Well?"

"But you *never* dance at these parties," she said.

"Aren't you just a little curious as to why I wish to do so now?"

"No," lied Anna. Against all reason, the desire to feel his touch again impelled her to add, "But to avoid drawing unwanted attention, I shall accede to your request. People are already staring."

"Let them," drawled Devlin, as he led her to the far corner of the ballroom floor. "Do you really give a fig for what bumbleheaded idiots think of your actions?"

"Ladies are not as free as you gentlemen are to thumb their noses at Society," she answered obliquely. "The rules are far stricter."

"Don't the rules ever chafe, like the whalebone stays of a corset that's been laced too tightly?"

Anna avoided the uncomfortable question by snapping back with a tart retort. "Somehow I doubt you have much experience with too-tight corsets, Lord Davenport. Unlike the Prince Regent, you have no need yet to wear such an intimate garment to enhance your manly figure."

A silent laugh, warm and wicked, teased against her cheek. "True. But I have unlaced enough wasp-waisted women to know that they must be deucedly uncomfortable."

Drat the rapscallion rogue—he was impossibly awful. Anna looked away to a distant spot over his left shoulder, hoping a telltale flush of color was not betraying the terrible tickle of heat that suddenly flared inside her. *And impossibly intriguing.* The thought of his long tapered fingers unknotting her undergarment stirred a strange shiver. What a pity she could not ask him for a detailed description of the process. It would be quite useful in writing Count Alessandro's next seduction scene.

"Forgive me, am I boring you?" inquired Devlin, as the musicians struck up the first lilting notes of the new dance.

It was a waltz, Anna realized belatedly.

"Your thoughts seem to be wandering," he added.

"I…" His palm pressed lightly on the small of her back, drawing her close, and all of a sudden, the rest of her words seemed to trip away.

Strangely enough, the floor was behaving oddly as well. The parquet took on a tiny tilt, pitching her off-balance.

"Too much champagne, Miss Sloane?" Devlin's voice held a hint of amusement.

"As I said, I'm tired, sir, and not much in the mood for dancing." The first twirling steps left her feeling even more lightheaded. "So perhaps you could stop spinning in circles and simply get to the point of why you have dragged me out here."

"Ah, and here I thought my technique was not quite so clumsy."

In truth, he was an excellent dancer, lithe and light on his feet. For someone who claimed to be an indolent idler, he had a panther-like grace, an impression sharpened by the rippling of muscle beneath the tailored black wool of his evening attire.

"If you are fishing for flattery, cast your lures elsewhere, sir." Anna tried to sound stern, but there was, she admitted to herself, something exhilarating about crossing verbal swords with the marquess. Yes, his clever, caustic tongue could cut like a rapier, but the fact that he expected her to be able to defend herself with equal skill was in itself a great compliment. It added an unexpected edge to their thrusts and parries.

And interestingly enough, their recent clashes had given a hint of hidden steel beneath his devil-may-care…

"You wound me, Miss Sloane," murmured Devlin, once they had spun by a pair of other couples.

"I doubt that I've drawn blood. And if I have, it could only be a pinprick to your vanity."

He laughed in a low, intimate way that stirred thoughts of rumpled sheets and musky perfume. "If I were a puffed-up popinjay, the injury might be mortal. However, as I can readily laugh at my own foibles, as well as those of others, I don't think I can be accused of taking myself too seriously."

"I grant you that, Lord Davenport. Your faults may be legion, but overweening conceit is not one of them."

"Ye gods, praise from you? I think I may need smelling salts to keep me from falling into a swoon."

"I have a feeling that very little in this world could render such a shock to your sensibilities, sir."

Another laugh—which sent another frisson of heat tingling through her body.

"By the by, it wasn't praise," Anna added softly, telling herself that it was too dangerous to play with fire. No matter how pleasantly seductive the sensation was now, she would only end up getting burned. "It was merely an observation."

They danced through a slow turn in silence before Devlin replied, "I, too, have made an observation, which brings us in a roundabout way to what I wished to discuss with you."

"At last," she responded, "we stop spinning in circles."

"Indeed, the dance is almost at an end." His hand tightened on hers as the tempo of the music quickened into its crescendo. "My apologies again if I have subjected you to a tedious interlude."

It hadn't been tedious, it had been...tempting.

Too tempting.

"You had better get to the point, sir, before it's time for us to part company."

"Very well." And yet, he hesitated as their bodies whirled in perfect harmony with the lilting rhythm of the waltz.

For a moment Anna felt as if she was dancing on air.

"Is there a reason you were making a sketch of the pocket pistol in Manton's display window?"

The question brought her girlish reverie thudding back down to earth. *Thud, thud, thud.* Her heart began to hammer against her ribs.

"Your eyes must have been deceiving you, sir."

"On the contrary, I have excellent vision." His steps skimmed smoothly over the parquet. "So I would say that the deception must lie elsewhere."

Anna swallowed hard, unsure of how to reply.

Damn the man—he must have a basilisk gaze to go along with his Lucifer smile.

"You're a bad liar, Miss Sloane," he whispered. "The question is why."

"W-why..." she repeated, trying to gather her wits. "W-why... why is it any business of yours what I put in my private notebook?"

"It isn't," replied Devlin calmly. "However, given the oddity of a young lady being so intrigued with a firearm, it occurred to me that you might feel yourself in some imminent danger."

Ha! The only imminent danger was to her peace of mind. And for that, bullets and gunpowder would provide precious little protection.

"Are you?" he pressed.

Anna hitched in a breath as the violins finished their last

notes with a flourish and the music came to an end. Laughter rose from the crowd milling near the punch table, the gaiety punctuated by the sharp-edged clink of crystal.

The urge to echo their amusement rose up in her throat. Lud, the evening was fast descending from drama to farce. The only thing more absurd than the notion that she might be threatened by some unknown enemy was the idea that Lord Davenport might feel honorbound to offer aid to a damsel in distress.

"No," she answered.

The surrounding couples were beginning to drift away from the dance floor in a muted rustle of silk and well-tailored wool. Looking up through her lashes, she saw that Devlin had fixed her with an inscrutable stare.

"No," she repeated a little more forcefully. "Ye gods, the idea is absurd."

"True. But stranger things have happened," he murmured.

"Perhaps in novels," she shot back. "Not in real life."

"And how much experience have you had in real life, Miss Sloane?"

She lifted her chin a notch. "Enough to know that we had better not remain standing here together in the center of the room, else risk becoming fodder for the morning gossip mills."

Devlin didn't move.

"I see my sister near the entrance to the card salon," went on Anna. "If you will kindly escort me there, you can shed your suit of shining armor and walk away without the weight of *noblesse oblige* making any further dents on your shoulders."

His lips twitched. "I imagine armor can be cursedly uncomfortable. As can a conscience. That's why I make no pretensions to possessing either." Devlin finally offered her his arm. "I was not about to suggest you look to *me* for help. If you are in trouble, you had best turn to your older sister's new husband. It is Wrexham who is the perfect hero, not I."

"I shall bear that in mind, should I ever be in peril."

To her dismay, Devlin seemed in no hurry to end their tête-à-tête. Rather than taking a direct line toward Caro, he chose a roundabout route through the leafy shade of the decorative potted palms. The fronds cast a fluttering of knife-edged shadows, making it impossible to read his expression.

Muddled grays, charcoal blacks—the play of hues seemed to mirror the marquess's own inner thoughts, which he kept shrouded in darkness.

Let them remain wrapped in whatever sins he chose to live with, Anna told herself. It was of no interest to her.

Liar. The leaves caught in a current of air, the low whisper echoing Devlin's earlier word. *Liar, liar, liar.*

"About the pistol, Miss Sloane..." Like a mastiff with a bone between his teeth, Devlin seemed stubbornly unwilling to let the subject drop.

She thought quickly—surely she could improvise.

"Really, sir, I hardly think I owe you any explanation. However, to put an end to your tedious interrogations, I shall explain."

He waited.

"If you must know, my sister and I are writing a play, to be performed at an upcoming house party to which we've been invited. Amateur theatrics are always a source of entertainment at such gatherings, and Caro thought it would be amusing to come up with a fanciful plot involving pirates and a kidnapped heiress in need of rescuing."

A cough—or was it a laugh?—caused her to pause. "Forgive me," Devlin murmured, clearing his throat. "Do go on."

Odious man. Why he took such fiendish delight in tormenting her was a mystery. But at the moment, all she cared about was escaping from his devil-dark gaze. "My maid, who is a very talented seamstress, is willing to help with creating costumes, and so, well, we thought that having colorful props, such as pasteboard pistols, would add to the spectacle. I happened to be passing Mr. Manton's shop, and decided that accuracy would be a nice touch."

"Accuracy. Yes, that's rather important when it comes to pistols," said Devlin dryly.

Ignoring the comment, Anna hurried to add, "But it is all meant to be a surprise. So I would ask that you not make mention of it to anyone, sir."

"I'm good at keeping secrets." Devlin smiled, but it didn't quite reach his eyes. Lurking beneath the thick fringe of his lashes was something deeper and darker than humor. It was…

Puzzling. The marquess had a surprising number of hidden facets, which was at odds with his image as a frivolous, indolent rake.

"I'm glad to hear it," she answered. "Then may I count on your silence?"

Devlin led her through a sliver of space between two of the potted trees, and all at once they were back in the gilded light of blazing candles. "Very well. But be advised that when you ask a favor, you must be prepared to grant one in return."

On that note, he turned and walked away.

* * *

Pasteboard pistols. Devlin chuckled under his breath. The explanation was diverting, but just as much a lie as her earlier denial.

Which raised the question of what she was really hiding.

But intriguing as that conundrum was, he had another more pressing matter to deal with at the moment.

Taking the steps of the carved staircase two at a time—a lapse in manners that earned a reproving stare from the head footman stationed in the entrance hall—he made a quick check of his pocketwatch. He was going to be late, though not unconscionably so. Thorncroft would expect no less. They were both becoming familiar with each other's habits.

His were likely more irritating, he thought with an inward smile. However, the other man had no choice but to tolerate them.

Once on the street, he flagged down a hackney and arrived at St. James's Street just a few minutes past midnight.

"How kind of you to show up," said Thorncroft, looking up from perusing a sheaf of papers.

Devlin closed the door to the private meeting room and poured himself a drink from the decanter set on the sideboard. "A passable port," he said after a meditative swallow. "But given the distance I'm being asked to travel, you might have chosen a better vintage."

"Beggars can't be choosy," retorted the other man.

Taking a seat in the facing armchair, Devlin stretched out his legs and crossed them at the ankles. "I wouldn't have to dance for my supper if you weren't such a nipcheese about paying me for my services."

"You are well compensated for your efforts, Lord Davenport. Perhaps if you curtailed your other habits, you would have more blunt in your pocket."

"My other habits, as you so charmingly refer to them, have proved exceedingly useful to you in the past."

"Some of them," stressed Thorncroft. "However, let us not waste time in trading barbs. I've several papers here that you must read. For obvious reasons, I can't allow them to leave the room."

Devlin heaved a pained sigh.

"You *do* know how to read, don't you?"

"It will cost you extra."

Thorncroft stifled a snort of laughter. "I shudder to think what you would charge if I asked you to look at the original German versions."

"Best not to ask," agreed Devlin as he accepted a handful of documents. "All these? Ye gods, pour me another drink."

Silence settled over the room, broken only by the intermittent crackle of paper. A half hour passed before he looked up. "The prince appears to be a thoroughly amiable, if thoroughly feather-headed fellow. Who would want him dead?"

"That is what we are hiring you to find out," answered Thorncroft a little testily. "We aren't sure that anyone does. The report the Foreign Office received is awfully vague, but given that the fellow is a relative of our Royal family, we have to take the threat seriously. To begin with, there are any number of Scottish radicals who would like nothing better than to foment a crisis by striking a blow at the British Crown."

"With the King mired in madness and the Prince Regent

even more of a wastrel than I am, the Scots should simply sit back and let House of Hanover destroy itself."

Thorncroft waggled a warning finger. "Watch your tongue, lest I have you arrested for sedition."

Devlin shrugged.

"The Scots are not the only potential threat," went on Thorncroft. "As you should know, Russia and the Kingdom of Saxony are our key Eastern allies in the fight against France. However, their rulers are currently at each other's throats over some sliver of land, and the prince may be used as a pawn in the squabble. We can't afford to have any ill befall him on British soil, lest the entire region blow up like a powder keg in our face."

Devlin reread one of the documents. "According to your envoy's report, there may be a paid instigator within the prince's hunting entourage."

"Perhaps. Several French émigrés will also be attending the party, so we can't overlook the fact that one of them may be an agent of Bonaparte."

"Or he may have a spurned mistress who is out for blood." He tapped his fingertips together. "In other words, you haven't uncovered any real clue, so I must consider everyone a suspect."

"Yes. But in truth, it is more than likely you will have nothing to do but drink and flirt for the coming month."

"And freeze my bones in the damp, desolate moors," muttered Devlin.

"Whisky will chase the chill from your blood," quipped Thorncroft. "And the Countess of Dunbar is inviting a number of ladies from London to visit, so I'm sure you'll find someone willing to warm your bed." He paused. "Apparently two rich heiresses will be among the guests. If for once you play your cards with some skill, you may end up with a long-term solution for your money problems."

"The question is whether the price I would have to pay is worth the blunt. What makes you think I wish to be encumbered with a wife?"

"Because your clever little hobby is rather expensive, that's why."

Devlin straightened from his slouch. "How—" he began, and then snapped his teeth shut. *Bloody Hell.* He should have guessed that the Foreign Office would make a thorough investigation of his habits before asking him to undertake this mission.

Thorncroft looked pleased with himself. "Yes, yes, I know all about those exquisitely detailed mechanical objects that you design and build. I became curious after you sold us that ingenious telescope and folding slingshot. Where did you acquire such skills?"

"Never mind," growled Devlin. He wasn't about to reveal any more private secrets. "Now, might we return to the business at hand?"

"But of course." Thorncroft first took a sip of his brandy. "By the by, did you know Dunbar Castle houses a very fine collection of seventeenth- and eighteenth-century *automata*?"

Devlin spun his glass between his palms, and watched the ruby-red liquid swirl around and around. "Is that a bribe?"

"Consider it a bonus."

"You are too kind," replied Devlin sourly. He didn't like feeling manipulated, but he couldn't really blame Thorncroft for being good at his job.

Thorncroft raised his drink in mock salute. "I am. I've

just paid you a King's ransom to do little but dance, drink, and tinker with your mechanical creations."

"And what if I do discover something havey-cavey is afoot?"

"We don't expect you to rouse yourself to perform any heroics. One of our operatives will be stationed in the town. You have only to alert him of the details and he will take care of ensuring the prince's safety."

"Sounds easy enough."

"Yes, as I said, you will likely have nothing to do but enjoy a month of pampering and pleasures at Dunbar Castle." Thorncroft set a small packet on the side table. "Here are funds for the journey. I've arranged for a traveling coach to call for you in the morning."

Chapter Five

*B*edbugs," said Lady Trumbull darkly, as the ostler closed the door to their coach. "The inn came highly recommended by Lady Herrington, but I am sure the bedsheets had bedbugs."

"I'm sure you are mistaken, Mama," soothed Anna. Their mother was a fretful traveler who tended to find fault with everything. And the journey north to Scotland had been a long and tiring one. "The scent of fresh lavender perfumed the linens."

"Yes, yes," agreed Caro. "It was quite sweet."

"Well, if you girls are sure." Their mother retrieved her embroidery from one of the bandboxes on the floor. "How much longer until we arrive?"

Caro consulted the map. "No more than a few hours, I think."

"It can't be soon enough," sniffed the baroness. "It feels as if we have been bouncing over these rutted roads forever."

Thank heaven the Earl of Wrexham had put his well-appointed barouche at the family's disposal while he and Olivia were visiting Rome for their wedding trip. The interior was spacious, the seats were soft, the lap robes were warm—Anna dreaded to think what expressions of horror a hired vehicle would have drawn from their mother.

Heaving an inward sigh, she opened her book to resume reading where she had left off the previous day. But after a few minutes, she found her attention wandering to the square-paned windows and the rain-drizzled landscape outside the glass.

Scotland was, to her eyes, a starkly beautiful country, its austere angles and muted earthtone colors possessing a rough-cut appeal. The wind-carved granite had a chiseled strength, and the hardscrabble heather covering the mist-shrouded moors showed a rugged toughness in withstanding the force of the salt-tinged squalls blowing in from the North Sea.

"What a dreary place," announced Lady Trumbull. "I do hope that Miriam has plenty of entertainments planned." Her face suddenly brightened. "Ah, but if the weather is too beastly for hunting, the prince and his party will be forced to remain indoors."

"It would have to be a full-force gale in order to convince the men to give up their shooting," observed Caro.

"Hmmph." Lady Trumbull smoothed at her skirts. "I have never understood why they would want to be tramping around in the cold and mud, when they could be indoors enjoying the company of the ladies."

"Perhaps because there is some primal force that still resonates inside them—at heart they are hunters and gatherers," murmured Anna.

Her mother made a pained face. "Nonsense, my dear.

The gentlemen invited to Dunbar Castle are civilized aristocrats, not heathen savages."

Were they? Anna did not bother to argue, but went back to reading her book on the history of Scotland. Accepting the countess's invitation had been a stroke of inspiration, she decided. Given the country's tumultuous past and its wildly atmospheric landscape, she was already envisioning a number of intriguing scenes for the last part of her novel.

"Oh, look!" As if reading Anna's thoughts, Caro pressed her nose to the rain-spattered windowpane and peered up at an ancient stone fortress. Perched atop a craggy cliff, it overlooked the gray-as-gunmetal waters of a broad loch, looking like a silent, solitary Highland warrior keeping a watchful eye on the surroundings. "Isn't that romantic!" she exclaimed.

Anna leaned over for a look.

"Surely there are deep, dark dungeons cut into the ancient rock," went on Caro. "And no doubt there are subterranean passageways that wind down and down to the water's edge."

Anna repressed a smile as her sister added, "One can't help but imagine all sorts of interesting stories taking place within a Scottish castle."

"Indeed," she replied.

Lady Trumbull gave a mock shiver. "Really, Caro, how you can wax poetic over a pile of moldering stones is puzzling. And Anna, please don't encourage such girlish fantasies. I sometimes think that reading all those horrid novels is too overstimulating for a young lady's sensibilities."

"On the contrary, Mama," assured Anna. "Even so high

a stickler as the dowager Duchess of Kirtland agrees that such stories are a harmless source of amusement."

Just as she suspected, mention of Society's most influential arbiter of style quickly caused their mother to revise her opinion.

"Oh, well, of course I agree with Her Grace that there is nothing wrong with enjoying a diverting tale. I simply meant that they ought to be enjoyed in moderation, especially by someone just out of the schoolroom."

Caro scowled, though she took pains to hide it.

"It is, after all, an impressionable age, and your sister has not yet gained experience in the ways of Society."

"I have learned a great deal just by listening to Olivia and Anna," protested Caro.

"You would do well to emulate your sisters." Sensing she was on the defensive, Lady Trumbull cut short the conversation by patting back a yawn. "I think I shall take a nap. Let us hope we arrive before suppertime."

Devlin hunched low and angled the brim of his hat in a vain attempt to keep the chill rain from dripping beneath his coat collar. Swearing under his breath, he turned in the saddle and surveyed the soggy moors. The low, leaden clouds were thick as porridge and with the mists pooled in the low-lying heather, it was impossible to make out anything but a gray-green wash of blurry color.

"Are you enjoying Scotland, Lord Davenport?" The burred voice held a slightly sarcastic note. Alec McClellan, a Scottish baron who had reluctantly agreed to serve as a guide for an afternoon ride, had chosen to halt on a high knoll where the gusting wind hit them with its full force. He was, noted Devlin, wearing an oilskin riding cloak and wide brimmed hat designed to withstand the elements. As for himself, he was soaked to the bone.

"I can't say that I will echo Robert Burns's rapturous odes to your country anytime soon," he replied.

"Like our national dish, haggis, our weather is an acquired taste."

"Sorry, but I find both equally foul," muttered Devlin.

"That's not surprising. Few Sassenachs appreciate the unique charms of Scotland or its people."

Sassenach was the Gaelic term for people from England. And Devlin knew it was not meant to be flattering.

"Shall we ride on to the coast?" asked McClellan. "The nearby cliffs offer a superb vista of the North Sea."

The mocking tone had become more pronounced. The fog rolling in from the ocean was now so thick that Devlin couldn't see the ears of his stallion.

"Or have you had enough of the local scenery?" went on his guide.

The baron had arrived at the castle the previous evening, and from his sullen demeanor and abrasive comments to the guests from south of the border, it was clear he had no love for the English. The Germans he had simply ignored.

The countess had murmured a discreet apology for his behavior, explaining that he held strong views on the subject of Scottish independence. Or to put it less politely, her cousin was a flaming radical nationalist, mused Devlin. Which raised the question...

Is he merely a boor who lacks social graces? Or something more dangerous?

"The scenery is splendid," replied Devlin. "By all

means, let us continue on to the cliffs. I look forward to you pointing out all the local landmarks."

That drew a bark of laughter from McClellan. "You're not as soft as you look, milord."

"That depends."

"On what?" asked the baron.

"On how much whisky I've imbibed," drawled Devlin. "Usually I loathe exposing myself to any physical hardship. But having enjoyed a few wee drams at breakfast, I'm currently feeling no discomfort."

"In that case, let us return to the castle," came the barbed reply.

"Because there's no sport in tormenting a Sassenach if he can't feel the pain?"

McClellan didn't respond to the quip. "Stay close, Lord Davenport," he said brusquely. "There are dangerous peat bogs close to the trail and it would be a great pity to see you swallowed by the Celtic mud."

Thankfully, his frigid flesh was soon submerged in steaming, pine-scented bathwater rather than slimy muck. Flexing his stiff shoulders, Devlin leaned back in the tub and stared up at the massive age-dark oak beams set in the plastered ceiling of his bedchamber.

Only half of the invited guests had arrived as of yet—the rest were expected over the next few days—and aside from the ill-tempered baron, the other gentlemen seemed pleasant enough. A trifle dull, but inoffensive. Save, of course, for the fact that one of them might be a cold-blooded assassin. As for the German prince, he and his entourage were cheerful fellows who talked enthusiastically about the upcoming hunting opportunities and flirted politely with all the ladies.

So far, the feminine presence numbered ten—six had arrived together from London, while two French noble ladies-in-exile had come from Bath, and the final pair were the wives of the prince's military attachés. Five more were expected, making a total of fifteen to balance the same number of men.

Thirty guests in all.

Devlin pursed his lips and blew out a sigh. Thorncroft hadn't bothered to mention the exact number, no doubt secretly enjoying the fact that it would require a great deal of effort to become acquainted with everyone and assess what possible threat they might present to the prince.

Damnation. He would have charged double for the mission had he known the facts.

He consoled himself with the thought that an attempt at murder seemed even more implausible now that he was here than it did in London. Aside from McClellan, whose surliness and overt Scottish nationalism made him too obvious a suspect, none of the other guests seemed out of the ordinary.

The most likely danger was that he might expire from ennui.

Lathering a sponge, Devlin circled it slowly over his chest and the soft caress stirred a more pleasant thought. There were several strikingly pretty ladies here already, including the young London heiress and a sultry Parisian widow who was part of the French party from Bath.

The heiress was under the watchful eye of her Mama, so the chances of gaining any intimate acquaintance with her fortune seemed slim. As for the other plump-in-the-pocket English pigeon that Thorncroft had mentioned, she had not yet arrived.

No doubt she would be just as closely guarded...not that he had any interest in seducing an innocent. Despite Thorncroft's low opinion of his morality, he did have some scruples.

For an instant, his thoughts strayed to Anna, but he quickly reeled them back. *Thank God she was in London—that should be far enough away to keep her from being a constant distraction.*

Forcing his mind back to the mission, he decided the best prospect for an enjoyable interlude lay in *la magnifique* Marie-Hélène de Blois. After all, everyone—even the ladies—had to be considered a possible suspect, so a closer acquaintance with the comtesse was part of his mission. If a casual dalliance developed, well, both of them were experienced enough to know the rules of the game. There would be no expectations, no recriminations, no tears when it was over.

The prospect served to warm the last lingering chill from his limbs. Devlin dressed quickly and, after combing a careless hand through his hair, he made his way down to the drawing room.

"I hope you did not venture out for a ride today, Lord Davenport," said Lady Dunbar in greeting, as she placed a hand on his sleeve and steered him to the drinks table. "The moors can be dangerous if one loses the way and strays off the trail in one of our North Sea gales."

"Actually, I did," replied Devlin. "Lord McClellan was kind enough to accede to my request when I asked at the stables whether I might accompany him."

"Oh, dear," murmured the countess.

Devlin arched a brow. "Is he in the habit of disposing of your unwanted guests in the peat bog?"

"Horrid man—Alec, that is, not you," responded Lady Dunbar. "Did he try to frighten you with that farrididdle?" She chuffed an exasperated sigh. "They aren't nearly as dangerous as he claims. But it's easy to take a nasty fall if your horse gets entangled in the heather or gorse."

"It wasn't fear that had me quaking in my Hessians, Lady Dunbar, it was the toe-curling cold of your Scottish squalls. Do you not have summer here?"

"The seasons are different from what you are used to in London." She lowered the lens. "As are a great many things."

Devlin sipped his champagne. "Thank heaven that sparkling wine is not one of them. This is an excellent vintage."

The countess accepted a glass from one of her footmen and then drew Devlin aside to a quieter spot by the diamond-paned windows. "I apologize again for my cousin. He is rather passionate about his political beliefs and doesn't much like the English."

"So I gathered," he said dryly.

"But he is an excellent shot and knows the moors like the back of his hand," explained Lady Dunbar, "So I pressed him to be part of the party and to serve as a hunting guide to the prince and his companions."

"I'm surprised he accepted," said Devlin, making private note of the baron's proficiency with firearms. "McClellan doesn't appear to give a fig for social niceties." The irony of his observation was not lost on him. It was, he thought wryly, rather like the pot calling the kettle black.

"No, he doesn't," agreed the countess. "But I am a very generous donor to his local charitable initiatives for the crofters, so he humors me."

To a degree, thought Devlin.

"And now, enough about Alec. Let us mingle with the others." The French trio had just entered the room, followed by several of the German nobles. "The last of the guests arrived this afternoon, so everyone is now here."

Devlin watched as Madame de Blois turned and held his gaze for a moment before joining a group of gentlemen clustered by the marble hearth.

"But of course," he murmured. Between having ample quiet time for his own private project and an attractive widowed lady with whom to play provocative games, the decision to accept Thorncroft's assignment was beginning to seem like a stroke of genius. *No tedious creditors to disturb his work, no beguiling blonde beauty to torment…*

"By the by, Lord Davenport," said the countess, "I hadn't realized you were such an avid sportsman. Had I known you were so fond of grouse shooting, I would have invited you to our annual hunt parties before now."

"Ah, we all have our little secrets," he replied lightly.

"Well, I am glad that Sir Thorncroft made mention of the fact to my husband. I do hope you will find your stay a rewarding one." With that, she drifted off to greet a contingent of local gentry who had just entered through the side salon.

A small smile played on his lips. Rewards came in many guises, and although a rich heiress was not likely to fall into his arms, the sojourn was still going to prove highly lucrative, assuming all went according to plan.

But no sooner had the thought popped into his head when a sudden flutter of moss-green silk at the drawing room's main door knocked all such assumptions to flinders.

* * *

Anna smoothed at her skirts, feeling unaccountably reluctant to join a crowd of strangers. Her mother's constant carping had provoked a dull ache in the base of her skull, and for a moment she was tempted to cry off from the gala welcoming supper and retreat to her room.

But good manners triumphed over the longing to curl up in bed with a cup of tea and her book on Scottish history. Heaving an inward sigh, she pasted on a smile and made herself step over the threshold.

"Oh, look," said her mother a bit smugly, "here is the Lady Dunbar coming to greet us. No doubt she wishes to introduce you to the prince. I wonder which one…" Her words trailed off in an aggrieved huff as she caught sight of the figure by the arched windows. "Good heavens, what possessed Miriam to invite *him* to Scotland?"

Anna followed her mother's gaze and suddenly felt the ache in her head turn into a stab of fire. *An imp of Satan, perhaps?* A strange crackling heat seemed to spread through her limbs.

"Who?" asked Caro, trying to see over her mother's shoulder.

"The Devil," grumbled Lady Trumbull. However, the approach of their hostess forestalled any further complaint.

Anna performed the rituals of introduction by rote, for her thoughts were knotted in a tangle. *Davenport is here?* Not in her wildest dreams had she imagined that the marquess might be part of Lady Dunbar's house party.

The idea ought to appall her, and yet…

She slanted a sidelong look at Devlin and felt her pulse skitter. With his dark, disheveled hair and his dark, disheveled evening clothes, he looked like some wild Celtic wraith from the black-misted moors. In contrast, all the other gentlemen looked tame as well-fed tabby cats.

Yes, that was it, she realized with a jolt. The marquess always looked hungry for something, though God only knew what it was. His predatory gaze was always hunting, hunting—

Their eyes locked for just an instant, and then she quickly looked away.

"...What lovely daughters, Hermione." Anna caught the last of Lady Dunbar's compliments to their mother. "Come along, girls, I must introduce you to the other guests, starting with visitors from the German principality of Schwarzburg-Rudolstadt. Prince Gunther has not yet come down, but his friends are a very amiable group of gentlemen."

Anna listened with only half an ear as the countess rattled off several names and titles.

"Did you hear that, girls?" said their mother in a hushed whisper. "Not only a prince, but a *margrave* and a *graf*. That is the equivalent of an English marquess and an earl."

"I think Mama is already hearing the ringing of church bells," murmured Caro, as Lady Trumbull turned back to converse with her old friend. "Which title would you prefer to wed? As the elder sister, you ought to have the first choice."

"Hmmm?" answered Anna absently as she checked the reflection in a large glass-front curio case, trying to spot Devlin among the blurred shapes and flickering light.

A playful smile tugged at her sister's lips. "Or have you decided that you will settle for nothing less than the prince?"

"Hmmm?" He seemed to have melted into the shadows.

"You aren't paying the least attention, are you?" Caro raised a quizzical brow. "What are you looking for?"

"Nothing," she replied, forcing herself to push aside the distraction. "I was simply making mental note of the details. It's an unusual room."

It was far larger than a traditional London drawing room, with soaring stone columns rising up to a vaulted ceiling. Beneath its arch, massive oak beams ran the length of the space, and from the center beam hung an ornate chandelier wrought of stag horn and silver. Tapestries of hunting scenes hung on the honey-colored pine paneling—rather fiercely graphic scenes that were not for the faint of heart.

The Scots appeared to be a bellicose, bloodthirsty people, noted Anna, as her gaze came to rest on a display of ancient claymores and crossbows.

"The fireplaces look large enough to roast an ox," observed Caro. There were two set at opposite ends of the room, with high granite mantels and fanciful fire-breathing dragons carved into the decorative stone work above them.

"Or two English nobles," said a deep, hard-edged voice.

"That is *not* amusing, Alec." Lady Dunbar whirled around and fixed the sandy-haired gentleman who had just stepped out from the recessed book alcove with a reproving glare. "Miss Sloane, Miss Caro, please forgive my cousin. His sense of humor can be a little rough around the edges."

"You don't like the English, Lord McClellan?" asked Caro, once Lady Dunbar had performed the introductions.

"No," came the blunt reply, which earned another pained look from the countess.

"Why?" demanded Caro, ignoring their mother's surreptitious warning pinch to maintain a ladylike silence.

"Don't you south-of-the-borderlands schoolgirls study history?" he shot back. "If you did so, you would know that the history between our two countries is a violent and bloody one."

If sufficiently provoked, Caro could display a fiery temper to go along with her flair for drama. Sure enough, her sister was quick to fling back a retort. "Don't you north-of-the-borderlands nobles study social etiquette?" she asked. "If you did so, you would know that I would not be a guest at your cousin's house party if I were still in the schoolroom."

Hoping to forestall further pyrotechnics, Anna took her sister by the arm. "Perhaps we ought to move on, before Lord McClellan decides to roast *us* as a sacrifice to the Celtic God of War."

His mouth twitched, softening for just a fleeting instant his stony visage. "It would be too great a waste of beauty, so I shall confine my murderous impulses to the males of your country."

Caro's eyes narrowed. *If looks could kill…*

As her sister hitched in an angry breath, Anna nudged her forward before any retort could be uttered. "Let us try not to spark an international incident on our first night here," she counseled.

"Ill-mannered oaf," muttered Caro.

"True, the man does display a decided lack of charm and good manners." Her gaze unconsciously darted around the room again. "If he annoys you, the best thing is to simply avoid any further contact with him."

"With pleasure," replied her sister darkly.

The chance for any further exchange was ended by Lady Dunbar's cheerful summons to the German gentlemen to come greet them.

Lord Saxe-Colza and Count Rupert, two of the unmarried gentlemen among the prince's party, proved far more polished and polite than the countess's cousin. Their English was excellent, and they made amiable conversation about their fondness for London and how much they were looking forward to hunting in Scotland.

The count was especially delighted with Anna's ability to converse in his native tongue. "I am impressed, Miss Sloane. Most English ladies know only French."

"My father was a serious scholar and spoke many languages. I had a good ear for them and he encouraged my interest."

"What others do you speak?" inquired Saxe-Colza.

"French, along with a little Russian and Italian," replied Anna. "And I can read classical Greek and Latin."

"You speak Russian?" remarked Lady Dunbar. "How nice. One of the other guests is Colonel Polianov, an attaché from the Russian embassy in London."

"La, but you mustn't think my daughter is a bluestocking, Count Rupert," interjected Lady Trumbull. To Anna she added, "Pray, my dear, don't give the gentlemen the wrong impression. They might think you are bookish."

Rupert looked bewildered. "Blue stocking? Is this some new English fashion?"

Anna smiled. "No, my lord. It is a rather unflattering term for a lady who has an interest in intellectual pursuits. You see, in our country, a lady is not supposed to be *too* clever."

"Indeed, beauty, not brains, is all that matters to a

proper Englishman." Devlin joined their little circle and tossed back a swallow of his champagne. "Is it the same in Schwarzburg-Rudolstadt?"

The count looked uncertain of how to reply. Clearing his throat with an embarrassed cough, he shot an appealing look at their hostess.

"Ah, I see that the crown prince has come down from his quarters," announced Lady Dunbar loudly. Offering her arm to the beleaguered count, she signaled her footmen to throw open the double doors leading to the dining salon.

"Come, let us all go in to supper."

Chapter Six

The meal over, the ladies returned to the drawing room for tea and cakes while the gentlemen remained in the dining salon to enjoy their postprandial cigars and port. The French duo immediately chose to sit together and seemed little inclined to socialize, despite the efforts of their hostess. The two German countesses were a little more gregarious, observed Anna, although their loud voices and brusque comments did not bode well for prolonged conversation. As for the two local Scottish gentry, they quietly helped to pass the cups, and when they did speak, it was hard to understand their burred speech.

No doubt the initial reserve would soon melt, but for the moment, an air of stiff formality seemed to pervade the room.

After exchanging pleasantries with the other group of ladies from London, Anna sought refuge in one of the side display alcoves, where a collection of hand-colored botanical engravings offered the perfect opportunity to enjoy an interlude of quiet contemplation.

Perfect, that is, until the murmur of male voices announced that the gentlemen guests hadn't lingered long over their masculine rites of pleasure.

Anna slipped deeper into the alcove, hoping her presence would go unnoticed. The candles in the wall sconces had burned low, and the encroaching shadows were deepening the fluttery light to a soft, bronze-hued glow. With any luck, no one would think to enter the secluded space.

Just then, the light tread of steps sounded just outside the narrow archway...

Anna held herself very still. But Luck appeared to be in a perversely mischievous mood this evening.

"I wasn't aware that you are fluent in German," said Devlin as he slid through the opening and slouched a shoulder against the wall. "Or Russian."

"There are a lot of things you don't know about me, Lord Davenport," answered Anna. "Do be careful of the engravings," she added. "I imagine that they are quite valuable."

"No doubt. I've heard that the castle is full of priceless art." The wavering flame caught the spark of amusement in his eyes. "Perhaps you would care to explore some of the other dark nooks and crannies together. I'm sure we would discover some very interesting things."

Anna turned away to hide the smile tugging at her lips. She shouldn't find his humor appealing. He was too dissolute.

Too dangerous.

"Please go away, Lord Davenport."

He shifted his stance and somehow his lean body was now too close for comfort. "But we've barely begun to talk."

"I'm in no mood for conversation, if you don't mind." Suddenly feeling a bit breathless, she inhaled, only to find her nostrils filled with the faint sweetness of the wine on his breath and the earthier spice of his sandalwood cologne.

"Oh?" He leaned in closer, the movement causing a lock of his hair to brush against his jaw. Anna was intimately aware of the subtle fragrance of pine soap clinging to the dark strands.

Was it possible to become intoxicated from mere scent? All at once her head was feeling woozy. Leaning back, she steadied herself against the wainscoting.

"No matter—I can think of other activities that don't require speech."

"Oh, you wouldn't dare." As soon as she said it, Anna realized her mistake.

"That," replied Devlin slowly, "is exactly the wrong thing to say to a Devil like me."

"I—I meant…" She wasn't sure what she meant. But it was *not* to be staring at the sinuous shape of his mouth and wondering what the trace of port would taste like on his lips.

"Perhaps you meant that *you* wouldn't dare," whispered Devlin, after the silence had stretched out for several heartbeats.

Anna wanted to respond with a clever answer, and yet some force seemed to have squeezed the air from her lungs.

"But I think you are wrong," he went on. "I have a feeling that deep down inside that delectable body, the well-behaved Miss Sloane is not quite as angelic as she wishes to appear."

A light touch of his finger tipped her chin up, forcing her eyes to meet his. A strange sound—something akin to the crackling of burning coals—began to echo in her ears.

"Unless I am much mistaken," he said in a whisper, "there are devilish desires swirling in intimate places you don't wish to admit exist."

Anna shook her head and the movement seemed to dispel her momentary dizziness. "You are quite wrong, sir."

A breath of air teased against her cheek. *A silent laugh?* Or was it merely a draft sneaking in through some unseen gap in the woodwork?

"Then prove it," said Devlin.

"How? You seem unwilling to take my word for it."

"It's simple. All you have to do is not react to my kiss."

"That's an unfair challenge, sir. I'm damned as a coward if I say no, and damned as a fool if I say yes."

This time there was no mistaking his mirth. "See what I mean? No angel would dream of uttering an oath."

"On the contrary. I could have blistered your ears in German or Russian as well. But I showed an angelic restraint."

"That's what is so intriguing about you, Miss Sloane. Like all truly interesting individuals, you have a dark and a light side."

His words sent a serpentine shiver slithering down her spine. "That's completely untrue, sir."

"Is it?"

Flustered, Anna quickly returned to the heart of his challenge. "It seems to me that the risk is all mine."

"On the contrary," replied Devlin ever so softly. "According to you there is no risk at all."

"Honestly, you and your silver tongue could probably

convince St. Peter to throw open the Pearly Gates and invite you to tea."

"A kiss," he murmured. "A mere touch of the lips."

Loath to appear uncertain of her resolve, Anna decided to settle the matter once and for all. In London, he had caught her at a vulnerable moment. She had been off balance, taken by surprise.

He had no such advantage this time.

"Very well, sir. You may test your theory. But be prepared to have your pride piqued."

"Pride goeth before a fall," he quipped. "We shall see which one of us takes a tumble."

Anna backed up a step. "Just to clarify the rules, sir. Just a touch of the lips, nothing more."

He hesitated, and then nodded. "As you wish."

A shift of his shoulders threw her face into shadow. Her skin felt suddenly cooler—a mere illusion, she knew, for the candleflames gave off only a weak stutter of light. Closing her eyes, she waited.

And waited.

Her pulse began to skitter, and she was just about to cry off from the challenge when a gossamer feathering of flesh against flesh stilled the protest.

Just as suddenly, the coolness gave way to warmth. The sensation was so slight that it may only have been a figment of her imagination. And yet her mouth began to tingle.

A rake would be more ruthless, Anna thought. More demanding. She had prepared herself to withstand a hard, possessive attempt to win her surrender. But this soft-as-silk caress had her insides slowly melting into a slow spin of topsy-turvy somersaults.

This dreadful dizziness will pass in a moment—it's just fatigue that is addling my wits.

Anna steeled her spine, willing her resolve to reassert itself. Instead, the gentle warmth of Devlin's mouth flared to a fierce burn. The beguiling whisper of port—a potent mix of sun-ripe sweetness and fire—was tantalizing.

Just a tiny taste more and then I will stop, she decided, tentatively tracing the sensuous shape of his lips.

It felt good—no, beyond good. Rising on tiptoes, she steadied herself with a hand on his shoulder...

"Anna?" Her sister's voice cut through the haze. "Are you there? Mama is looking for you."

Thank God for the gloom and the Devil's coal-black evening clothes.

Coming back to her senses, Anna broke off the challenge with a ragged gasp. "Yes, yes, I'll be out in a moment."

Devlin's expression was impossible to read. All she could tell was that he seemed to be watching her intently with a heavy-lidded gaze.

Fisting her skirts, she edged past him, praying that he would be gentlemanly enough not to follow.

Caro cast a second look into the alcove as Anna emerged from the shadows and paused to allow her eyes to adjust to the brightly blazing light.

"Since when have you become so engrossed in art that you'll stay to study it even when the candles are in danger of burning out?"

"My garters had come loose," she fibbed. "I could hardly retie them in full view of the other guests."

"Well, that might have roused the elderly Baron McIntire from his after-supper slumber," replied her sister.

"Instead, two footmen had to carry him up to his room when the snoring grew too loud." However, the bantering tone did not quite dispel the question lingering in her eyes.

Anna avoided meeting her gaze. "Where is Mama?"

"In the side salon, having a nip of sherry with the countess and her husband." Lord Dunbar had finally arrived halfway through supper, having been delayed in his journey home from Edinburgh by a broken carriage axle. "You know how garrulous she gets when she's had several glasses of spirits. We had better go trundle her off to bed before the poor earl faints from exhaustion."

"No doubt we could all use a good night's rest." Perhaps in the morning she would wake and find the last little interlude had been nothing but a strange dream. Even now, it seemed a strange, smoke-swirled fantasy brought on by too much rich food, too much fine wine, and too many new faces.

"You look odd," said Caro. "Are you feeling ill?"

"Just overtired." Just overwhelmed with sensations that no proper young lady ought to be feeling. "I'll be fine by tomorrow."

Devlin held himself very still, waiting for the sound of her retreating steps to trail off. He knew he was playing with fire—and Anna would suffer the worst of the burns if anyone spied their private encounters.

Damnation. He had meant to escape all thoughts of Anna Sloane's kiss and the terrible, sinful urges it sent spiraling through his body. A jaded rake ought to be impervious to innocence. Instead, he found himself feeling...protective. For some reason, he couldn't shake the suspicion that she was hiding a secret that could draw her into trouble.

Expelling a pent-up breath, Devlin ran a hand through his hair. "Ha! As if I am some pure and noble knight, ready to slay dragons for a damsel in distress." He was the first to admit that nothing could be further from the truth. Nobility took too much effort—it was far easier to be a hellbent rascal. No one expected anything from the Devil Davenport.

Including himself.

Cocking an ear, he heard nothing but the muted murmurs of the few guests left lingering in conversation by the hearth. The others seemed to have wandered off to the card room, and so, after waiting a few moments longer, he slipped out of the alcove and made his way out through the double doors to the castle's central corridor.

Straight ahead would take him to the main staircase and the wing housing the gentlemen guests. But feeling too agitated to sleep, Devlin chose instead to turn left and wander down to the row of leisure rooms, where the guests had been invited to explore the various activities available for their amusement.

After pouring himself a glass of whisky from the decanters in the music room, he cut between a pianoforte and an ancient harpsichord and went to stand by the glass-paned doors overlooking the terrace. The rain had ceased and the lawns sloping down to the rock-ringed lake were bathed in a dappling of pale moonlight. In the silvery glow, the wet grass took on a fanciful glitter, as if some Scottish silkie had risen from the dark water and flung handfuls of diamond-bright crystals into the night. Wraith-like fingers of mist swirled in and out of the pine trees bordering the far garden wall, adding to the aura of primitive enchantment.

Angling his gaze upward, Devlin watched the scudding clouds, wondering why he was in such a strange mood.

He ought to be celebrating a clever triumph over Miss Anna Sloane. He had won—he was sure of it.

Well, almost sure.

She *had* reacted. Her mouth had quivered at his touch, and she had softly, ever so softly, let herself explore his shape, his taste.

Raising his glass to his lips, Devlin drew in a mouthful of the amber spirits and let it trickle down his throat.

Or perhaps it was just another figment of his imagination.

Draining the rest of his whisky in one gulp, he turned abruptly, determined to shake off his brooding. Anna Sloane's presence must not distract him from the reason he was here. Between finishing the intricate mechanical model he was making for a wealthy collector and doing a bit of sleuthing to determine whether Thorncroft's fears were justified, he had more than enough to keep his mind occupied.

Stepping lightly, Devlin exited the room and began prowling the length of the corridor. The library was dark, and the only sounds emanating from within were the faint creaking of the wooden shelves and the rattle of the brass-framed windows in the gusty wind.

The study was also deserted. Moving on to the billiard room, he paused by the half-open door, listening to the rumble of laughter punctuated by the click of the ivory balls. The prince and his unmarried friends appeared to be deep into a competitive match. Angling a look through the opening, Devlin saw through the haze of cigar smoke that they had stripped off their evening coats and rolled up their shirtsleeves. And though they were speaking in German, the language of masculine needling was universal. There must be a hefty sum riding on the outcome of the games, for a scowling Count Rupert took his time in lining up his next shot.

They would likely be at it for some time, thought Devlin, and judging by the array of wine and brandy bottles on the sideboard, play was only going to get more erratic. There was no reason not to take advantage of the opportunity to have a quick look around in the rooms of the prince's three friends.

The German contingent was quartered on their own floor in the tower, and to avoid being spotted by any of the other guests, he decided to retrace his steps to the music room and circle around the gardens to gain access through the entrance on the north side of the castle.

It was probably a wild goose chase. But his mind was unsettled, and to work on his mechanical model required meticulous concentration. As for thinking of any amorous diversions, he had not yet had a chance to begin a flirtation with the sultry Madame de Blois.

And Anna? Ye gods, he didn't even want to begin thinking of that complication. "Bloody Hell," Devlin muttered under his breath, forcing himself to concentrate on the German guests. "I suppose I've nothing better to do."

Leaving their mother finally settled for the night and snoring softly in her canopied bed, the two sisters quietly made their way down the corridor to their own rooms. It was late, but any hope Anna had of gaining some much-needed solitude was quickly put to rest by Caro's assertion that she was far too wide awake to sleep.

"You may have the stamina of youth..." She feigned a yawn. "However, I'm exhausted. It's been a very long day."

"We can have a comfortable coze while you ready your ancient bones for bed," replied her sister.

Recalling the hurt her earlier rebuff in London had caused, Anna didn't have the heart to say no. This was Caro's first country house party and it was no wonder that she was abuzz with excitement. Count Rupert had been particularly attentive over supper—so with any luck, that first heady taste of flirtation would keep her sister distracted from discussing any of the other gentlemen guests.

But no sooner had the door closed when the first words out of Caro's mouth quickly dispelled that hope. "It seems to me that you have changed your tune and are now willing to dance with the Devil."

"You are mistaken," scoffed Anna, as she untied the tabs of her gown and stepped out of the layered skirts.

"Oh, pish. Don't deny it." Planting herself in the armchair by the hearth, Caro crossed her arms in a silent signal that the conversation wasn't going to be a short one. "It was dark in the far corner of the alcove, but no amount of shadows could disguise a certain set of broad shoulders and long legs."

"Oh, very well." She expelled a sigh. "I admit that the mistake is not yours but mine. I don't know how to explain it, but when I am around the dratted man I can't seem to think clearly."

"Actually, there is a very simple word for what's clouding your head," said her sister. "It's—"

"Don't you dare say what I think you are going to say," warned Anna. "Life isn't as simple as a sonnet."

"Sonnets are deucedly hard," protested Caro. "Odes are even harder."

Anna allowed a reluctant smile as she unpinned her hair and began to brush it out. "I was speaking metaphorically. What I meant was, things aren't always black and white. Sometimes they are more..."

A muddle of grays.

Her sister looked thoughtful. "Sometimes they are more confusing?" she suggested.

"Yes." The shadowy reflection of her face in the looking glass seemed to reveal all her myriad inner doubts. "I suppose so."

Silence greeted the admission, rather than one of her sister's exuberant opinions. Anna unwound the braided ribbon in her topknot and slowly worked the brush through a small snarl of curls. Outside, the raw, wind-roughened sounds of the Scottish night rose and fell with the gusting breeze, its cadence so elementally different from the familiar street music of London. Which only accentuated the feeling of having lost her way in a dark woods.

"And yet, you always seem so sure of yourself." Caro's tentative voice pierced the gloom. "I thought I was the only one who struggles with how to untangle my uncertainties."

Anna hesitated. Their older sister, Olivia, had considered Caro too young and too impetuous to share in any serious heart-to-heart confidences. But of late, Caro had begun to show a newfound maturity, so perhaps it was time to stop treating her like a schoolgirl.

"If I seemed sure of myself in the past, that's because I knew exactly what was expected of me," she said slowly. "Mama had pinned her hopes for our family's future on my ability to attract a wealthy husband, and I was determined to live up to that responsibility in order to make sure none of us would ever have to worry about having a roof over our heads."

Caro sucked in a ragged breath. "I never quite realized what a terrible burden you bore. I saw that you had swarms of suitors, and it all seemed like such marvelous fun." A grimace tugged at her mouth. "I suppose that I thought it was all an enchanted fairy tale, and that you were sure to find a handsome storybook prince who would sweep you off your feet."

"Mama no doubt still shares your fantasy about the prince," said Anna dryly. "But Olivia and Wrexham's generosity has freed me from such responsibilities."

"Yes, now you may choose a man who enriches your soul, not your purse."

The burst of poetic passion stirred a snort of amusement, and Anna found herself hoping that at age eighty Caro would still display the same exuberant excess.

"Did you say something?" asked her sister.

"No, no, just something lodged in my throat."

"Not an unsuitable husband, thank goodness," quipped Caro. "You don't have to swallow your dreams and compromise on someone who doesn't make you completely happy."

Happy? Ah, that was the very heart of the problem.

"If only I knew what my soul needs to make it overflow with happiness," she responded. Not wanting to sound too wistful, she quickly added, "It hasn't yet penned me a note with all the requirements spelled out."

Caro didn't laugh.

Shedding the last of her evening clothes, Anna slipped on her nightrail and a thick banyan-style wrapper to shield her from the chill. "Now that you've quizzed me on my evening's interactions with the male guests, tell me about your time with Count Rupert. He seemed extremely attentive to you during supper."

"Oh he's pleasant enough." She shrugged. "And undeniably handsome. But he doesn't set off any sparks."

"Sparks aren't necessarily a good thing," pointed out Anna. "They can be unpredictable."

"But shouldn't love be full of unexpected explosions of beautiful, brilliant little flames?" countered her sister.

"Sparks may look lovely flying up in a bright burst of light, but you never know when they will fall in the wrong spot and start an unwanted fire."

"Better to have some degree of risk in flashes of fire than safety within the confines of a dull, colorless box of boredom."

Caro's eloquence was beginning to reflect some interesting insights. "I hope you are not speaking from experience. Of the three of us, you have the sort of passions that can ignite into trouble."

"I am not the one dallying with a hellfire rake."

"I am *not* dallying, I am simply..."

"Doing research for your novel?" asked Caro with an impish grin.

Anna tossed a pillow at her. "Go to bed, before your imagination becomes too overheated."

"It's not *my* mind that's afire with forbidden fantasies," said her sister as she batted the feathery missile aside. Rising, she sauntered toward the door. "Sweet dreams." A teasing wink hung for an instant in the light of the lone candle. "Though I daresay they will be flavored with far more spice than sugar."

Another pillow winged through the air, but this one bounced off only polished oak.

"Minx," muttered Anna with a rueful smile, uncomfortably aware that Caro's new sharp-eyed insights might prove to be a double-edged sword. Still, she had missed sharing sisterly confidences. Olivia's sage advice had been a steadying force.

And if ever I needed to keep my balance...

A faint rumble of thunder in the distant moors warned that another storm was blowing in. Moving to the tall bank of leaded windows, Anna pressed her forehead to one of the panes, hoping to cool the feverish thoughts inside her head.

Pitchforks—it felt as if tiny pitchforks were jabbing at the backside of her brow. That, she decided, was because she was letting the Devil Davenport get under her skin. Rather than allow his little games to tease and torment her peace of mind, she ought to channel her emotions into something more positive than brooding.

Ha! All at once, the chill glass suddenly felt remarkably soothing against her skin as Caro's offhand comment about research suddenly stirred an idea—no, more than an idea—to life.

She was about to turn to the escritoire for her pen and notebook when a flicker of movement in the gardens below caught her eye.

A man was stealing through the slanting shadows cast by the tall yew hedge. Keeping to the verge of grass rather than the graveled walkway, he crossed through a pool of moonlight before disappearing through the arched opening in the garden wall.

Anna stared at the slivered darkness, watching the thick

twines of ivy ruffle for just an instant against the stonework before going still. From somewhere in the nearby trees rose the hoot of an unseen owl.

A creature of darkness who did its hunting at night.

"Predators are on the prowl," she whispered, and then reached up to draw the draperies shut.

Chapter Seven

The door was unlocked. Easing the latch open, Devlin stepped inside Count Rupert's set of rooms, and after listening for any sounds of a servant stirring, he stepped to the center of the carpet and slowly turned in a circle to survey his surroundings. There was nothing out of the ordinary. The furnishings were a trifle worn with age, but displayed a tasteful rustic elegance.

A settee and several armchairs upholstered in muted earthtone stripes, a massive pine sideboard stocked with various libations, a pair of mahogany tea tables…a pine desk, already cluttered with various personal items.

Devlin really didn't expect to find anything momentous. However, he had found that having a sense of an individual's personality was often an advantage in gambling. And as discerning whether the prince faced any real danger was a game of chance, he went over for a quick look.

The desktop showed none of the usual Germanic penchant for order. A set of meerschaum pipes lay carelessly atop several sporting journals. Next to them sat a book—

poetry by Goethe, discovered Devlin, as he thumbed through the pages. Moving on, he found gloves, an oilskin hunting hat still in its wrappings, a pen case, and a portfolio of letters.

Count Rupert appeared to have a number of ardent female admirers scattered throughout Europe.

Finding nothing else of interest, he headed for the half-open bedchamber door. If discovered there, he could always feign drunken disorientation. House parties were notorious for guests stumbling into the wrong rooms, and he had taken care to splash a good amount of whisky on his coat. However, there was no need to linger, for a search turned up nothing, save for the fact that the count had expensive taste in clothing and boots.

Devlin checked the clock on the mantel and decided it was safe to move on to the margrave's quarters. And depending on how long it took to take a look around, he might also have time to explore Prince Gunther's quarters. However slight the chances, it was possible that some hint as to why anyone would wish him ill might be there among his belongings.

Too unsettled for sleep or for writing, Anna wandered first to her dressing table, and then to the armoire. But neither the rhythmic strokes of her hairbrush nor the rearranging of her evening slippers and reticules helped to quiet the nagging question echoing in her head.

Why was Lord Davenport sneaking through the garden at this late hour?

"An assignation, that's why." Muttering the answer aloud seemed to give it more force. "Good heavens, the man is a notorious rake, and that is what rakes do at a country house party—they steal into a willing lady's bed-chamber for a night of passionate *amour*."

And yet, on her arrival, the layout of the castle had been carefully explained by the butler to help avoid becoming lost in the various wings. Devlin had been heading to the section that housed only the prince and his friends.

Which raised yet another question.

Why?

After pacing the perimeter of her room several times, Anna gave up any pretense of silencing her speculations. Tightening the sash of her wrapper, she decided there was no harm in doing a little reconnoitering. If spotted, she could claim that she had become disoriented in trying to find her way to the library for a book.

Easing her door open, she tiptoed past Caro's room, praying her sister was not still awake. At the end of the corridor, the low-burning wall sconce by the carved staircase illuminated several choices. Recalling the neatly inked floor plan posted in her room, she chose the right-hand turn.

The shadows deepened, and the gloom seemed amplified by the flitting black shapes that dipped and darted over the ancient tapestries and *objets d'art* decorating the passageway. The little creaks and groans of the floorboards grew louder, the sounds stirring a prickle of uneasiness at the back of her neck.

Anna paused for a moment, suddenly feeling foolish. There were any number of perfectly plausible reasons why Davenport would be visiting the German gentlemen in the privacy of their rooms. *A high-stakes card game...a comparison of Continental and English women over brandy and cigars...a look at the latest sporting rifles from the famed gunsmiths of Prussia...*

She sucked in a breath on hearing the light tread of steps in the adjoining corridor, trying to gauge whether there was time to make a hasty retreat. Or was it better to seek shelter in one of the many display rooms?

There wasn't a moment to lose—the steps were coming on faster than she anticipated.

Curiosity getting the better of her, Anna decided to hide behind the suit of armor standing guard by the entrance to the display room of ancient weaponry. Having come this far, she might as well see if her suspicions were correct.

A wiggle, a squeeze . . . a whispered oath.

"Hell's Bells."

She hadn't realized how short the men of the Middle Ages were, or how many moving metal parts their fighting regalia contained. Already she had caused a slight jangle by bumping against a hinged kneepiece. And there was a most peculiar odor emanating from inside the helmet.

Perhaps mice had made a home in the pointed visor. She could swear she heard a scrabbling of tiny claws.

I really must find a way to include this scene in one of my next chapters, she thought wryly as she flattened her back to the wall and sank down into an awkward crouch. At least her own outrageous escapades were proving useful in inspiring ideas for Emmalina's adventures.

A flicker of movement, dark on dark, made her go very still. No glimmer of a candle—like her, the person preferred to move about unnoticed. However, the moonglow coming in through a pair of narrow windows was just bright enough that the shape slowly materialized into a distinct figure as it came closer.

There was no mistaking the broad shoulders and long, muscular legs.

The marquess was moving with a stealthy grace, his steps quick but careful as he kept close to the paneling.

Closer, closer.

Was there an odd bulge in his coat pocket? Anna shifted just a fraction for a better angle of view.

He was just about to pass her hiding place when all of a sudden he came to a halt and shot a hard look at the door of the Weapon Room.

Anna didn't dare breathe.

His boots shifted.

Squeezing her eyes shut, she prayed that Lord Dunbar's ancient ancestor was stout enough to protect her from the marquess's prying eyes.

Silence.

Surely he must hear the hammering of her heart. It was loud enough to wake the dead knight, wherever his bones might be resting.

Leather scuffed against wood as Devlin started to move away. He paused at the corner, and then to her surprise, turned down the corridor that led to the most ancient part of the castle, which held nothing of interest to any house-guest.

Anna made herself wait several moments before crawling out from behind the armor. Repressing a wince, she picked a cobweb out of her hair. Crouching in a cramped space was deucedly uncomfortable.

"Thank goodness Emmalina is a hardier soul than I am," she murmured, shaking the dust from the hem of her wrapper. Otherwise her intrepid heroine would long since have succumbed to the evil machinations of the villainous Lord Malatesta.

Villain. What in the world was Lord Davenport doing

creeping into a part of the castle that held only the earl's most ancient art collections? Anna drew a deep breath, knowing she should ignore the question and head back to bed. And yet...

Tiptoeing to the corner, she darted a look around and then followed after him.

The passageway narrowed and wound up and down several sets of roughhewn stairs. There were few windows, so Anna could barely see more than several yards ahead. More than once, she hesitated, knowing she was asking for trouble by acting on impulse. But the sound of the marquess's footsteps echoing further off assured her there was little danger of being caught.

So some inner demon impelled her to go on.

Suddenly the steps ahead stopped. A raspy clang of metal against metal rang out.

Inching forward to the next turn, Anna ventured a peek around the corner.

Davenport's back was to her. He had just finished unlatching the last of three massive bolts and was pushing up an iron-banded oak door. After striking a flint to the lantern he had unhooked from the wall, he disappeared through the opening.

What...

Anna was about to creep forward, when all at once reason reasserted itself. The realization that he might return at any moment spurred her to gather her wits and make a quick retreat. Picking up her pace, she hurried back through the twists and turns, giving thanks as she made it to her own rooms that no one had spotted her.

Closing the door, Anna slumped against the paneled oak and felt her limbs go a little limp.

So much for the peace and quiet of the country. Perhaps she should have gone to Baden-Baden after all.

Rat-a-tat-tat. Anna awoke to a downpour pelting against the windows. The skies were a sullen gray, and the dark clouds hanging low over the moors looked heavy as Scottish granite.

"Nay, miss, the storm looks te be a stubborn one," said the young chambermaid who scuttled in to light a fire in her hearth. "I dunna think it will blow over today."

"What filthy weather," groused Josette, as she entered with a freshly pressed gown for the evening's supper. "No wonder the Scots all drink whisky instead of wine. You need a potent fire to warm the chill from your bones."

Anna shivered as a damp gust rattled the windowpanes. "Lady Dunbar assures me that it's quite warm when the sun shines."

"Hmmph." Throwing open the armoire, her maid began to rearrange the various items of clothing. "*Mon Dieu!* Speaking of filthy, what has happened to your wrapper, mademoiselle? I am quite sure I would never have hung it in here looking as if the cat had dragged it in from a mousehole."

"The fault is mine," apologized Anna. "I couldn't sleep and went down to fetch a book from the library."

"A book?" The maid eyed the two stacks of novels and travel guides piled on the desk.

"Yes, well, I was hoping to find something boring, like an essay on agriculture, to help put me to sleep."

"Ah, *oui.*" Josette nodded. "It's true—a novel can be so entertaining that it keeps you up all night." She made a clucking sound as she surveyed Anna's face. "And you, mademoiselle, ought to be sure to have an early evening. You are looking—how do you say it in English—a bit mountained."

"Peaked," corrected Anna.

The maid repeated the word, then added, "When I suggested dark hues to highlight your fair coloring, I did not mean for you to put purple smudges under your eyes."

"Forgive me for reflecting badly on your artistic genius."

Josette grinned. "I am passionate about the things that matter to me." She carefully shook out the wrapper and set it aside for cleaning. "If that offends you," she added in a softer voice, "I am sorry."

"Passion is important," mused Anna. "It makes you feel alive."

"*Oui.*" After pulling out a sprigged muslin morning dress, Josette bent down to choose a pair of matching slippers. "However, if I don't have you ready to go down to the breakfast room while the prince is still there, your Mama will have my head on a platter."

Other than the prince, who was cheerfully wolfing down a plateful of shirred eggs and sausage, none of the gentlemen of the party had yet made an appearance at the morning meal. Most of the ladies had also chosen to sleep late, for the pouring rain promised to keep everyone indoors for the day.

It was, decided Anna, a good thing that their mother was among them, for she would have been aghast to see Prince Gunther push back his empty plate and politely take his leave without engaging in any flirtations.

"Forgive me, ladies, but I must see to oiling my fowling guns," he explained. "Just in case the weather clears."

After finishing their tea and toast, Anna and Caro decided to wander to the library, which was said to house one of the best private book collections in all of Scotland. The vast main room was empty, noted Anna, save for the elderly baron, who was napping in one of the armchairs, the London heiress's father, who was searching for a sporting book on races at Newcastle, and—

Lord Davenport?

"Are you an avid reader, sir?" inquired Caro, spotting the marquess as he emerged from one of the many alcoves. "There looks to be a wealth of wonderful old volumes here."

"Not really. I was only hoping I might find a new novel by Sir Sharpe Quill somewhere here," he replied with a theatrical flourish at the shelves.

The mention of her *nom de plume* set off a prickling of alarm at the back of her neck. Still, Anna did not miss the subtle shift of his other hand as he quickly shoved a small book into his coat pocket.

Why the secrecy? she wondered. Unless he meant to take it with him when the house party was over.

"Actually, there won't be a new Sir Sharpe novel available until after Christmas," said Caro.

"Indeed?" drawled Devlin. "You appear extremely well informed on the author's publishing schedule."

"Um, yes, well, I am a very devoted fan," stammered Caro.

"And you, Miss Sloane?" he asked, turning to her.

Anna forced herself to release the pent-up breath in her lungs.

"Are you a devoted fan as well?"

The mischievous glint in his eyes might only have been

a quirk of the candlelight. Still, his gaze stirred an uncomfortable tickle as it flitted over her face. "Like most young ladies," she answered, hoping he wouldn't notice the tightness of her voice, "I find horrid novels amusing."

"Ah, but I would venture to guess that you rarely behave like most young ladies."

She felt a flush rise to her cheeks. "No guessing is required to know that *you*, sir, rarely behave like most gentlemen."

"Touché," he murmured.

"Now, if you will excuse us, sir, my sister and I are anxious to explore Lord Dunbar's collection." Having no desire to continue the verbal duel, Anna looked at Caro. "I'm sure we shall find a complete set of Robert Burns's poetry somewhere on the shelves."

"There is also a fascinating selection of picture books on ancient armor located near the back wall," said Devlin.

Anna's feet tangled in the fringe of the carpet, causing her to bark a shin against the leg of a worktable. "W-w-what makes you think I have any interest in armor?"

"Given your fascination for weaponry, I thought you might enjoy them," said Devlin. "The engravings are quite detailed, and who knows, they might serve as inspiration for the play you two are writing."

"Play?" repeated Caro blankly.

"Oh, yes, the play," exclaimed Anna quickly. "There is no medieval scene in it, so a suit of armor would be out of place."

"Oh, come—use your imagination, Miss Sloane."

"Mine is clearly not nearly as vivid as yours, Lord Davenport." Taking pains not to limp, she set off for the sanctuary of the shelves, hoping her sister would have the good sense to follow along instead of lingering in conversation with the marquess.

Caro did—but only because her curiosity was piqued. "What play?" she whispered.

"He spotted me sketching a pistol in Mr. Manton's display window. I had to make up as story as to why," replied Anna in equally low tones.

"Come to think of it, writing a play for the guests to perform could be quite a lark," mused Caro.

"Not for me. In case it has slipped your mind, I've got a deadline, and precious little time in which to finish my manuscript." She made a face. "Speaking of which, after I find a book describing the historical ruins in this area, I had better spend the rest of the morning in my room, working on the next chapter."

"And I think I shall search out a copy of Shakespeare's *Midsummer Night's Dream* and have a look at the play within a play."

Lord Dunbar's assistant secretary helped them in locating the desired books, and after a longing look at the rest of the magnificent collection, Anna reluctantly returned to her quarters.

Work, she reminded herself. She had come here to work, not to moon over a rakish rascal's kisses and the terrible temptations they stirred inside her.

Sharpening her pen, Anna slapped a fresh sheet of foolscap onto the blotter and uncapped her inkwell. The best way to exorcise the Devil was through writing, and she had come up with some interesting ideas for a new plot twist.

And yet, as the nib touched the paper, she hesitated for a moment, thinking about fact before starting in on fiction.

The fact was, Davenport was acting very havey-cavey. *Prowling around the castle in places he had no right to be, stealing a book from the earl's library...* which yet again raised the unsettling question—what was he up to?

It was no secret that the marquess was always desperately in need of money. It was assumed by the *ton* that he meant to marry a rich heiress. But perhaps he had other ideas on how to refill his coffers.

Hmmm.

Some time later, she was still musing over the conundrum when Caro's light knock pulled her out of her reveries.

"Any progress?" Her sister's brows shot up as she spotted the blank page. "Um, is there a problem?"

"Men," muttered Anna through her teeth. "Or, rather, one gentleman in particular."

"Let me guess." Caro's mouth curled up at the corners. "Did he steal another kiss?"

"No!" She slapped down her pen. "I have a feeling that he may be planning to purloin something far more valuable than that."

"Ooooo, the plot thickens!"

"Stop that," groused Anna. "It's not a jesting matter."

Her sister's grin disappeared. "You're serious?"

She nodded. "Quite."

"What makes you think that?"

After hearing the terse account of the previous evening's hide and seek, Caro pursed her lips. "It's intriguing, but hardly incriminating. Maybe he was just restless after visiting the prince's quarters and decided to explore the ancient part of the castle."

"I know, I know." Her fingers began to drum on the blotter. "At this point it's pure speculation, and yet I feel certain there is some mischief afoot here. I just have to find the proof."

Caro's reply was uncharacteristically restrained. "That has an ominous ring to it. You are beginning to sound like Emmalina."

"I *am* Emmalina."

The comment drew a laugh, but it quickly gave way to a quizzical huff. "Yes, yes, but she is the devilish side of you that exists only on paper. The real you is too carefully composed to do anything rash."

Am I?

"You wouldn't want to do anything risky that might expose your secret," went on her sister. "Playing sleuth with Lord Davenport could be dangerous. Whatever he is up to is no concern of yours."

"But I can't help being curious," murmured Anna.

"You know what they say—curiosity killed the cat," pointed out Caro.

"Cats have nine lives," she countered, feeling rather pleased with her cleverness. "Ha, ha, ha."

"That may be so, but racy romance novelists have only one," shot back her sister. "And trust me, just a small slip could prove mortal to your reputation."

"Perhaps I don't care about my reputation," muttered Anna.

"You wouldn't be able to write any more books."

The quill seemed to stir against the blotter, adding its own flutter of warning.

Anna didn't wish to confess her fears that her inspiration may have gone missing for good, so instead she merely muttered, "Hell's bells, since when have you become the Voice of Reason?"

"Now that I've turned the age to be admitted into the adult world, perhaps I've decided that certain excesses of emotion ought to be left in the schoolroom."

She sighed. "You are right, of course, to counsel caution. I won't do anything rash. However, don't become *too* much of a stick-in-the-mud."

"I doubt there is any danger of that happening. Exercising restraint is deucedly difficult." Caro cracked her knuckles and began pacing in front of the hearth. "I swear, I was sorely tempted to punch Lord McClellan in the nose this morning."

"Talk about slaying one's reputation in one fell swoop," said Anna dryly. "What did he do to provoke your ire?"

"He saw me leaving the library with the volume of Robert Burns's poetry as well as the Shakespeare play and a book of the Bard's sonnets—and made a *very* mocking comment about simpering schoolgirls and their silly infatuation with poetry and true love."

"I'm surprised you didn't cram the books down his throat, along with making him eat his words."

"I was sorely tempted," grumbled Caro.

"I'm very glad to hear that you haven't become *too* staid in your old age," said Anna.

"I fear there's little chance of that." Her sister grinned. "As Josette says, a lady should be a little dangerous."

The word stirred an uncomfortable prickling in her fingertips. "Which reminds me that I had better get back to work on Emmalina's adventures, else I really will be in peril of missing my deadline."

"I, too, plan to spend the rest of the day writing," said Caro defiantly. "A satirical ode about gentlemen who have no more sense of romance in their soul than a garden slug."

Chapter Eight

The unrelenting rain continued, keeping the guests cooped up indoors for the rest of the day. Cards, billiards, and backgammon provided diversion for the gentlemen, while reading, letter writing, and playing the pianoforte kept the ladies occupied. By suppertime, however, everyone seemed a little restless.

"Is it my imagination," murmured Caro, as she and Anna entered the drawing room with their mother, "or is the champagne flowing a little faster tonight?"

"Given the dreary wetness outside, Lord Dunbar does appear anxious to add a bit of sparkle to the evening's proceedings," answered Anna.

Caro repressed a laugh as the elderly Scottish baron became a trifle too animated and nearly spilled his wine down the ample cleavage of Lady Hohenzugger, the older and stouter of the two German nobles. "Things are already getting more than a little effervescent."

"Don't giggle, girls," commanded their mother in a low voice. "It's most unbecoming."

"Yes, Mama," answered Anna.

Lady Trumbull was distracted from further chiding by the approach of Prince Gunther and Colonel Polianov, the Russian attaché. In contrast to the prince's fair-haired Nordic good looks, Polianov was dark—dark hair, dark eyes, dark scowl twisting his handsome mouth.

Anna had met him only in passing, but her impression was that the man did not possess a sense of humor.

"Ah, good evening ladies," said the prince cheerfully. "I am so glad to see you in particular, Miss Sloane."

Lady Trumbull's lips curled up in a cat-in-the-creampot smile.

"You see, the colonel and I are hoping you can help us resolve a little disagreement."

"*Da*," added the colonel brusquely. "His Highness thinks the Russian word '*олень-самец*' means 'stag' in English. While I am quite certain it means 'doe.' I have been informed that you are familiar with my native language, so perhaps you could confirm that he is wrong."

"Damned if you do, damned if you don't." Devlin had come up right behind her, and his whisper was only loud enough for her to hear.

The marquess was certainly not lacking in a sly sense of humor, thought Anna, however caustic and cutting it might be.

"Actually, the prince is right, sir," she answered, trying to ignore the pulsing heat of Devlin's presence. It felt as if the silk of her gown would burst into flames if he came any closer.

"You must be mistaken," replied the colonel.

"I don't claim to be fluent in your language, sir, so that may well be true," answered Anna diplomatically.

"Perhaps there is a Russian-English dictionary in Lord Dunbar's magnificent library that you might consult for a definitive answer."

"I shall inquire." Clicking his heels together, Polianov inclined a curt bow and walked off, not before giving the prince a daggered look.

"Dear me, what a dreadfully serious fellow," commented Prince Gunther, with a wry grimace. "Please accept my apologies, Miss Sloane. I did not mean to put you in an awkward position."

"Thank goodness she sent him scampering off to vent his ire on the bookworms and dust motes," said Devlin loudly. "That grim face and grating voice were ruining my appetite."

"But not your thirst," murmured Anna softly.

He grinned and took another swallow of his wine.

"The Russians do have a penchant for melancholy," said the prince. "Their brooding makes Shakespeare's Hamlet look like a jolly fellow."

"By the by, Your Highness," asked Devlin abruptly. "Is there bad blood between you and the colonel?"

Prince Gunther looked perplexed. "I've never met the fellow before. Why do you ask?"

"Idle curiosity," he answered with a shrug. "His manner seemed decidedly unfriendly. But then, Russians appear to dislike everyone."

The comment drew a laugh from the prince. "True," he agreed. Turning to Anna, he offered his arm. "I, on the other hand, do not wish to appear as churlish, so to make amends for subjecting you to such unpleasantness, please allow me to escort you the refreshment table."

Leaving her mother beaming in delight, Anna walked

with him across the room and accepted a flute of champagne. "No doubt you are disappointed that the shooting has been delayed," she said, to make polite conversation.

"I do look forward to seeing Scottish moors, for in hunting circles they are renowned for both their beauty and their sporting challenges," he replied. "However, I am happy to have a chance to explore Lord Dunbar's library. It, too, is famous among those of us who appreciate the art of medieval illuminated manuscripts."

His answer was unexpected. She hadn't been led to believe that he had the slightest interest in books or art.

Her face must have betrayed a spasm of surprise for he smiled over the rim of his glass. "Most people assume I'm a frivolous fellow because I am an avid sportsman. But I also believe in exercising the mind as well as the body."

Intriguing. The tiny bubbles of the wine tickled against her tongue. So, she was not the only one who had hidden facets.

"I gather that you, too, have an interest in intellectual pursuits, Miss Sloane?" he went on.

"Yes," she responded. "I am fascinated by history—"

"And firearms," interrupted Devlin. He held out his empty glass for a servant to refill. "Perhaps we should invite you to accompany us on the hunt. Are you fond of shooting?"

Only rascally rogues who make a habit of teasing me to distraction.

"Or do you just prefer to make drawings of weaponry?"

"You are an artist of weaponry?" exclaimed Prince Gunther. "Lord Dunbar's collection of antique armaments is said to contain many unique examples of Scottish claymores and crossbows. For someone interested in the subject, they must afford some superb opportunities for sketching."

"Lord Davenport is jesting," she replied tightly. "Please pay no attention to him. I assure you, my drawing skills are no more than ordinary."

"You are far too modest," said Devlin. "From what I saw, your rendering of a pistol was extremely accurate."

"Oh, but pistols and poniards are such dreadfully boring subjects." Lady de Blois, the widowed French comtesse who had accompanied her sister and brother-in-law to Scotland, sidled up to the table. A buxom blonde, she was wearing an emerald-colored velvet gown with a plunging neckline and a glittering array of matching gems.

"I much prefer to sketch handsome men." Tracing a finger over the teardrop-shaped pendant nestled between her breasts, the comtesse added, "And beautiful baubles."

"Lord Dunbar has a lovely collection of Renaissance jewelry on display in the Sculpture Room," said the prince.

The comtesse batted her kohl-darkened lashes. "Oh, really? Perhaps you would help me locate it sometime tomorrow. I find it impossible to navigate my way around the castle."

"The prince likely has many official documents to review and decisions to make during his leisure time," interrupted Devlin smoothly. "While I, indolent idler that I am, have no responsibilities at all. So I would be delighted to serve a guide whenever you like."

"How accommodating of you, sir. I, too, have no responsibilities, so it seems we are well matched." Lady de Blois tapped his sleeve coyly with her fan. "I imagine there are many fascinating things to see here, especially for two people with no other distractions."

Anna couldn't help but notice that Devlin's gaze was glued on her décolletage.

"Indeed there are." He smiled.

A wolfish smile.

"Perhaps we should leave these two to arrange their Grand Tour while we discuss books, Your Highness." Forcing her eyes away from the sinuous stretch of Devlin's lips, Anna suddenly felt compelled to show that that she, too, knew how to flutter a flirtatious look. "Shall we find a quiet spot to sit and talk? I would love to hear more about medieval manuscripts."

"I could ask one of the servants to fetch an example so that I can point out some of the artistic nuances," said Prince Gunther. "That is, if you are sure that I will not be boring you."

"Oh, not at all," answered Devlin for her. "Miss Sloane greatly enjoys expanding her knowledge of the world…" His pause was almost imperceptible. Quite likely only she noticed it. "…Intellectual and otherwise."

Anna tried to remain annoyed, and yet his Be-Damned-to-the-Devil sense of humor couldn't help but provoke an inner laugh.

He must have sensed her reaction, for as she passed on the prince's arm he flashed a roguish wink.

She pretended not to see it.

"Enjoy perusing the painted pages," he murmured.

"Enjoy admiring the baubles," she shot back.

His laugh was light as a zephyr and lasted only an instant. And yet its sound seemed to tickle against the nape of her neck long after she had crossed to the other side of the room.

* * *

Rising early, determined to spend the day at work in her room while the others spent their hours in play, Anna made her way down to the breakfast room. Given the copious amount of wine consumed by everyone the previous evening, she was sure that she would have little company.

However, the sounds coming out through the doorway announced that she was wrong.

"...an emerald ring!"

Anna recognized Lady de Blois's voice, although this morning it was more shrill than sultry.

"The stone was *very* large, and *very* valuable."

As she entered the room, she saw Lady Dunbar, flanked by her solemn butler and housekeeper, facing the comtesse. "Perhaps it inadvertently fell from your dressing table?" suggested the countess in some concern. "Have you made a careful search of the room?"

"My maid has looked," replied Lady de Blois, clasping her hands to her chest. "It is nowhere to be found."

"I am quite sure it will turn up," soothed Lady Dunbar. "Please, come sit in my private parlor and have a calming cup of chocolate while Givens and Mrs. Gorman organize a thorough combing of your quarters."

"Very well," sniffed the comtesse. "Cook may send some pastries too. I am feeling faint."

"Yes, yes, of course."

"This way, madam." The silver-haired butler offered his arm and led her away into the corridor.

"Dear me," fretted Lady Dunbar as the housekeeper moved off with a muted jangling of the massive ring of keys fastened to her apron. "Pouring rain and missing gems—this is hardly an auspicious start to the party."

"I take it the comtesse has lost a piece of jewelry?" murmured Anna.

"So it seems. I would venture to guess that it's simply snagged in a fold of her evening gown, or has dropped from the dressing table and lodged in some crack or crevasse."

"Yes, of course," agreed Anna, forcing a far more unsettling suspicion concerning Devlin and his need for money back into a dark corner of her mind.

"Well, I had better go join Mrs. Gorman in overseeing the hunt." Taking her leave with a distracted wave, Lady Dunbar hurried away.

However discreet the search party was, the news soon spread through the upper floors, and Anna was shortly joined by a number of the other guests.

"Do you think we have a thief in our midst?" Her mother seemed to be relishing the thought even more than the deviled ham and eggs heaped on her plate. "How very exciting."

Caro paused in buttering her toast. "Actually…" She shot a quick look at Anna. "I think it's a very silly suggestion. The comtesse has likely misplaced it and is making a fuss over nothing."

"She does seem to have a flair for the dramatic," commented Devlin, as he entered the room and paused by their chairs to straighten his cravat. His hair looked a little damp and windblown, as if he had been out riding.

Damn the Devil for looking so… divinely disheveled.

Anna swallowed quickly to loosen the sudden constriction in her throat, and then couldn't resist doing a little needling of her own. "You were the one who had the closest look at her baubles. Is it your opinion that one could have come loose from its settings?"

Their eyes met, and his were dancing with mirth.

No man ought to have such a molten gold gaze. She felt herself falling, falling, into a liquid pool of sun-warmed honey...

"Alas." Devlin exaggerated a sigh. "I did not ask permission to make a thorough examination of her jewels. However, from what I could see, they looked quite well made to me."

"Mark my words," said her mother darkly. "I say there's something havey-cavey afoot here."

"Let us not look for trouble where there is none, Mama," cautioned Anna, shifting her attention away from his half-mocking smile. "I'm sure your dear friend Miriam would not wish for us to stir up any rumors."

"A very wise suggestion," agreed Devlin.

Lady Trumbull looked miffed, but contented herself with a bite of her sultana muffin.

"What are your plans for the day, sir?" asked Caro quickly. "Has the weather cleared enough for a hunt?"

"There is still a light mizzle falling, but our German guests have decided they are hardy enough to brave the elements, so we British fellows can hardly fail to do the same. All but the elderly baron and Lord Dunbar have agreed to meet in the Gun Room shortly," he answered. "And you, ladies?"

"Lady Dunbar has arranged for carriages to take us on a shopping expedition into town," replied Caro.

"I hear there are some lovely woven blankets and shearling muffs in the shops," said their mother.

"Are you looking to make some purchases as well, Miss Sloane?" he inquired politely.

"I haven't decided," she replied tartly, a little unnerved

by the effect he was having on her rebellious body. "I may simply pass the day with a book."

"That may be the wisest decision of them all, judging by the clouds hovering on the horizon." Devlin inclined a casual bow. "Now if you will excuse me, I had better fortify myself for the moors with some hot porridge and coffee. Enjoy your day of leisure."

"Leisure? Ha!" Setting down her pen, Anna flexed her hunched shoulders and slowly massaged the crick in the back of her neck. The muscles were knotted, but the pile of finished pages more than made up for the twinges of discomfort.

"Well, at least I am making some progress," she announced to the inkwell.

The silver-capped crystal did not echo her satisfaction.

"You have no idea how much mental effort is required to create a story," she added. "It is *very* hard work."

Her stomach growled in agreement. It had been several hours since the midday meal.

Deciding to reward her diligence with a break for some tea and pastries, Anna set off for the main parlor, where a collation of light refreshments were laid out for the guests throughout the day. After nuncheon, most of the ladies—including Caro, who had decided to visit the local book-shop—had gone on the shopping expedition with Lady Dunbar. And with all but a few of the men off tramping the moors, the house felt eerily empty.

It was silly, she knew, but the silence seemed to be whispering to her as she made her way through the corridor.

She was simply faint with hunger, Anna told herself.

And her mind was half-lingering in its own inner world of imagination.

The suggestion was too brash—even for one of the Hellions of High Street.

She tried to ignore it, but the rustle of her skirts kept repeating the message.

A lady ought to be a little dangerous.

Exhaling an oath, Anna hurried across the landing instead of turning for the stairs and darted into the corridor housing Devlin's rooms. At the midday meal, she had confirmed that he and the two other single gentlemen quartered here had elected to be part of the hunting party. So there was hardly any danger of being caught.

She promised herself that she wouldn't spend long.

Just a quick look around.

For what? A horde of stolen jewels hidden in a waistcoat pocket? Priceless paintings rolled up and stuffed in a boot?

Shutting her ears to the voice of reason, she carefully counted her way down the doors. A peek at the housekeeper's chart had revealed which room was his.

Holding her breath, Anna pressed the latch...

Only to find it locked.

Pulling a hairpin from her chignon, she offered up a silent prayer of thanks to her late father. His expeditions had often taken him to wild places, and he had thought it important to teach his daughters basic survival skills so that they could fend for themselves if need be. Opening locks was one of them.

A deft jiggle released the catch.

Hoping her luck would hold, Anna slipped inside.

Considering Devlin's dissolute reputation, the sitting

room was surprisingly tidy. The furniture was free of rumpled clothing, the decanters appeared untouched, the desk was neat, with papers and books arranged in orderly piles.

Though she was curious as to what he was reading, Anna forced herself to head into the bedchamber. Averting her eyes from the large canopied bed, she opened the massive armoire and hurriedly checked through the clothing and bandboxes for anything suspicious.

Finding nothing, she looked around a little guiltily. It appeared she had let her imagination run wild. There was really nothing out of the ordinary about the marquess's personal effects. Granted, a bejeweled ring—assuming it had actually been stolen—was small enough to hide anywhere. But suddenly it felt absurd to have fantasized that the man was a thief.

After taking a half-hearted look inside the chest of drawers, Anna was about to leave when she remembered the adjoining dressing room. It was unlikely that there would be anything other than an assortment of sporting boots and oilskin cloaks within the small space, but since she was here...

"How odd," she murmured, giving the door latch another jiggle.

It, too, was locked. Which made no sense at all.

Once again, the hairpin made quick work of manipulating the levers. With a soft *click*, the door swung open several inches.

Pressing her hand to the waxed wood, Anna felt her pulse kick up a notch.

The *thump, thump, thump* began to hammer in her ears as she tentatively gave it a small push.

"Oh, stop acting like a peagoose," she muttered. "There is likely a perfectly plausible reason for locking..."

As a dappling of daylight from the narrow window illuminated the alcove, she froze in place, staring in mute shock at the sight before her eyes.

A small worktable had been set up in the center of the space. An unlit argent lamp sat on a pedestal next to it, the oil-fueled glass globe angled to cast its intense light over the square of white felted wool that covered nearly the entire surface.

Swallowing her surprise, Anna ventured a step closer and leaned in for a closer look at what lay upon the fabric.

The pocket pistol from Manton's shop had been disassembled, and all the parts laid out in an orderly grouping on one side of the table. But it was the weapon on the other side that wrenched a tiny gasp from her throat.

It was a copy of Mr. Manton's design—and yet, it wasn't. Some of the small metal workings had been made out of steel. But the majority were crafted out of beautiful burnished gold.

Hardly daring to breathe, she carefully picked up a magnifying glass from among the set of precision tools wrapped in chamois and peered through the lens at the exquisite detailing of the half-finished model. Along with the intricate decorative patterns etched on the surfaces, some of the pieces were also covered by delicate indigo blue enamelwork highlighted by seed pearls. Looking up, Anna saw a number of glass vials containing powdered pigments grouped together with an assortment of small tweezers and paintbrushes.

"Good Lord," she whispered.

Even more astounding than the partly finished golden

pistol was the sight of a colorful miniature bird lying half assembled in the middle of the felt. Its eyes were two emeralds, and the tiny wings had been fashioned with a deft artistry that created the illusion of myriad feathers. Next to the golden claws was a bewildering array of impossibly small gears and levers.

The marquess wasn't a thief, he was...

An artist? An alchemist with otherworldly powers to transmute ordinary elements into magic?

Feeling a little dizzy, Anna put the magnifying glass back in its place and slowly circled the table, checking to see if there was anything else that could shed light on what Devlin was doing.

It was then that she spotted several books stacked by the lamp. She opened the top one and saw that it bore Lord Dunbar's bookplate, indicating that it had come from the library downstairs. Thumbing to the next page, she read its title—

A History of Automata
Being a Detailed Account of
Ingenious Mechanical Devices
Throughout the Ages

The term "automata" was vaguely familiar. Her father had several books in his library on the subject. It referred to complex mechanical devices that performed some sort of movement, mostly for sheer entertainment—a majestic eagle that flapped its wings, a lute player who could strum his instrument, a ferocious tiger that could paw its prey. Popular since ancient times, there were, she knew, some very clever and complex constructions.

Intrigued, Anna paged through the chapters of the book in her hand, stopping occasionally to study the detailed engravings of various examples, including an elaborate thirteenth-century Arabic model of a jewel-encrusted peacock fountain and an eighteenth-century French flute player. But much as she wished to read the text, she needed time to think over what she had discovered before confronting the marquess.

As she closed the book a folded piece of paper fell out of it. Smoothing it open, she read over the list of names carefully before putting it back between the pages.

Ye gods—what is the marquess up to?

Reluctantly placing the book back atop the others, she quitted the dressing room and relocked the door. After checking that the corridor was clear, she reset the main lock and hurried back to her own chamber.

Shrugging out of his hunting coat, Devlin draped it over one of the armchairs of his sitting room and went to pour himself a drink. The first swallow of whisky burned a trail of welcome fire down his throat, but as he turned away from the sideboard, a tiny chill teased against the nape of his neck.

Something wasn't quite right.

The desk blotter was slightly askew, and a pillow on the settee had been shifted several inches.

Setting down his glass, Devlin moved into his bedchamber, and the sensation grew even more pronounced.

His eyes were attuned to notice minute details, but even an unschooled gaze could see that someone had been in here going through his belongings. And whoever it was hadn't been particularly skilled at it. The clothing in the armoire hung at odd angles and several lids of the bandboxes were not quite closed.

Ignoring the chest of drawers, he quickly crossed the rug to check the dressing room door. That the bolt was in place brought some measure of assurance that his secret was still safe.

Until he fitted his key into the lock and clicked it open.

Damn. Damn. Damn.

The intruder had been more careful in here, but not quite careful enough. His work-in-progress was undisturbed, but the tools and books showed small signs of tampering.

Frowning, he crossed his arms and considered the conflicting evidence. On one hand, the clumsiness of the search betrayed an inexperience in spying. On the other, the lock-picking skills said otherwise.

"Damn." Uttering the oath aloud, Devlin lit the lamp and angled the beam of light into every nook and cranny of the far wall. He worked his way back methodically around the rest of the room's perimeter, then concentrated his efforts on the area beneath his work table.

There, between a narrow joint of the floor planks, was a colored thread caught on a splinter. He picked it out and carefully folded it in his handkerchief, though the chances were slim that it meant anything. Tucking it into his pocket, he redoubled his efforts. But after a thorough search turned up no other clue that might help him identify the intruder, he finally gave up and returned to his sitting room.

Picking up his whisky, Devlin set the amber liquid to swirling in a slow, spinning, vortex. He disliked being at a disadvantage. However, for the moment there was nothing to do but wait for his unknown adversary to make the next move.

Or was there?

After a meditative sip, he returned to his temporary workroom and took out his most powerful magnifying glass from a wooden case beneath his paintbox. Fishing his handkerchief from his coat, he smoothed out the snowy white square of cambric and arranged the thread in its center.

Light winked off the highly polished lens.

"Well, well, well."

It was, perhaps, a flimsy scrap of evidence to go on. However, he had a keen eye for color and could only recall having seen this exact hue once before.

Chapter Nine

$\mathcal{D}$ust motes danced in the shaft of morning sunlight, the free-spirited swirl of the tiny gold sparkles at odds with her own conflicted mood. Perching a hip on the carved oak windowsill of the deserted picture gallery, Anna took a moment to try to sort out her thoughts.

The previous evening had been a subdued occasion. Both the ladies and the gentlemen had appeared tired from their sojourns into the inclement weather, and after supper, no one had lingered long over tea or cards. Even the marquess had been unnaturally quiet. That he seemed too preoccupied with his own thoughts to torment her with his teasings stirred yet more questions to tangle around the conundrum.

What the Devil was he up to? Was his brooding the sign of a guilty conscience? Or something else altogether?

Try as she might, she couldn't make any sense of it.

"My own heroine is far more clever than I am," murmured Anna. "Emmalina can solve all manner of convoluted mysteries, while I find myself doing naught but spinning in mental circles."

As the day had dawned clear and bright, all the men had set off early for a day-long trek through the moors. Several carts would carry a noontime picnic to a spot near the loch, so they wouldn't be returning until dusk. As for the ladies, a scenic walk to the nearby abbey ruins had been arranged, with an outdoor nuncheon overlooking the seaside cliffs.

Anna had once again begged off from the excursion—Lady Dunbar must think her more fragile than the most delicate Meissen porcelain figurine. Nothing, of course, could be further from the truth.

I am hardier than a horse. But clearly my brain is weaker than that of a fly.

While the others were strolling along the gentle meadow footpaths, she had found her way to a remote part of the castle, where the ancient picture galleries looked as if they hadn't been visited in years. Walking within their stretches of solitude, watched by only the dour stares of long-departed Dunbar ancestors, afforded a chance to mull over the situation in some much needed privacy.

It wasn't easy to find any solitude at a house party. Even in her own rooms, there were frequent interruptions as her own maid and the castle tweenies went about their daily tasks.

"Alone at long last," said Anna, exhaling a sigh.

The whisper of air echoed softly off the age-dark paneling, only to give way to a louder sound.

"Not quite."

Anna whirled around from the window, dislodging a fresh cloud of dust from the faded velvet drapery. She couldn't yet spot him in the gloom, but her whole body was suddenly prickling with the awareness of his closeness. "I—I thought you were out stalking birds with the others."

Devlin stepped out of the shifting shadows. "I decided to do my hunting in here today."

"I—I am not a grouse."

"Nor a pigeon," he agreed. "If anything, you are a finely feathered predator, a sharp-eyed hawk or eagle who is no less lethal for all its lithe, lovely lines and aerial grace."

"I have no idea what you are talking about," said Anna, yet even to her own ears, the assertion rang hollow.

He came a step closer and held up his hand. "I'm talking about *this*."

In the hazy half light, it appeared that the only thing grasped between his fingers was thin air.

"Is this another of your taunting tricks?" she demanded. "I see nothing."

"It's a tiny fragment of fabric."

"Grasping at threads, Lord Davenport?"

His bark of laughter held no amusement. "You are exceedingly clever with words, Miss Sloane. So let's play a little game with language, beginning with the words 'why' and 'how.'"

Her heart began to thud against her ribcage. "Unlike you, sir, I have no passion for sport."

"Methinks the lady doth protest too much."

"I don't really care what you think. I—" Her throat seized as he took a stride toward her. A panther-like stride, all sleek muscle and bristling strength.

"Nonetheless, you would do well to listen to what I have to say." His eyes blazed, though whether in fury or some other inner fire was impossible to say. Whatever the spark, his usual air of bored detachment had, in that instant, gone up in smoke.

To her dismay, Anna could not keep from falling back a step. No hawk, however fierce, could stand up to such overwhelming power.

"Go on," she whispered.

In answer, Devlin dangled the thread closer to her face. "An unusual shade of blue, don't you think? Rather like a late afternoon sky which has been darkened by storm-clouds."

"You a have a very poetic soul, sir," she replied, trying desperately to deflect his interrogation. "I never would have guessed that."

"Don't try to distract me." They were now nose to nose. She could see the faint stubbling of dark whiskers on his jaw, the tension radiating from his pores. "What were you doing in my rooms?"

Anna thought about denying it. A thread was awfully slender evidence. But then, her own ire suddenly ignited. "Don't ring a Holier-Than-Thou peal over my head, sir. I saw you sneaking around the castle the other night, and then when the comtesse's ring went missing, I couldn't help but be suspicious."

"I had a feeling that was you skulking behind the suit of armor," growled Devlin. "What were *you* doing out wandering the corridors at that hour?"

"I—I couldn't sleep, so I was going down to the library to fetch a book when I heard noises." She drew in a ragged gulp of air. It wasn't precisely a lie, just a slight stretch of the truth. "It's well known you are desperate for money. So after putting two and two together, I decided to have a look around your quarters."

"And what would you have done if you had found the ring?"

"I..." Anna swallowed hard. "I...hadn't thought that far."

He swore under his breath. "Of all the buffle-headed, bird-witted actions. Had it not occurred to you that walking into the lair of a criminal might have been *bloody* dangerous?"

"I had ascertained that you were out," she replied tersely.

A tiny muscle of his jaw twitched. "And if I had returned?"

She lifted her chin, refusing to be cowed by his scowl. "I suppose I could have shot you with that fancy pistol. By the by, does it fire golden bullets?"

"That," he said softly, "is *not* funny, Miss Sloane."

"It wasn't meant to be," she answered. "Gold, silver, pearls, diamonds, special enameling—that's quite an expensive, not to speak of unusual, firearm you are crafting. What's it for?"

"It has nothing—*nothing*—to do with the subject we are discussing."

Sensing a note of defensiveness in his voice, she pressed on. "Forgive me if I don't take your word for it. Perhaps we should allow Lord and Lady Dunbar to decide what is and isn't important in the search for Lady De Blois's missing ring."

"That would not be a wise move, Miss Sloane."

"You are aware that it hasn't been found, aren't you?" she replied.

"Assuming it exists," countered Devlin through gritted teeth.

"I suppose that's true. But for the moment, I see no reason not to take the comtesse at her word. While you—you appear to be hiding a dark secret."

"A secret." Suddenly his big hands were framing her face. The heat of them nearly made her jump out of her skin. "Yes, I confess, I do have a secret. However, it is not what you think. I ask that you...trust me."

"You have given me precious little reason to trust you, Lord Davenport," whispered Anna.

"Your sister and Lord Wrexham might disagree. Had they not trusted my information, despite my terrible reputation, the kidnapping of Wrexham's son might not have had a very happy ending."

Anna bit her lip. It was true. The marquess had provided critical information—and for no gain of his own. "Trust cuts both ways, sir. If I am to hold my tongue for now, I should like to be told the reason why."

"God give me the plague, rather than an aggravating, outspoken hellion to contend with," he muttered.

"Be careful what you wish for," said Anna.

A ghost of a smile flitted over his lips. "You are a very stubborn young lady. There are good reasons I can't reveal certain secrets. Is there nothing I can say or do to convince you to accept that for now?"

"No," replied Anna, trying not to let the sinuous curl of his mouth cloud her judgment. "Nothing."

"No?" The question was more a shiver of breath than a sound as he leaned in to close the tiny gap between them.

"No." This time a shove punctuated her refusal.

Devlin fell back a step. "No?"

Anna scowled. "For someone who just suggested playing a language game, this repetition is getting very tiresome."

"Ah. I see that I shall have to change tactics." He rubbed at his chest. "Do you train at Gentleman Jackson's Boxing Saloon? For a delicate creature, you throw a very hard punch."

"My father believed that ladies should know how to survive on their own in the world, including how to protect themselves from predators."

He regarded her clenched fists, unsure whether to feel bemused or exasperated. "Did his survival skills also include picking locks?"

"As a matter of fact, yes. If a lady finds herself an unwilling captive, the ability to open manacles or a locked door is a very useful talent to have."

"Who would have guessed that beneath the outward appearance of a demure demoiselle lies the spirit of an intrepid adventuress?" he murmured.

"Who would have guessed that beneath the outward appearance of a debauched devil lies the spirit of an artist," she countered.

"So, we have something in common. Secrets, which we wish to keep to ourselves."

She shifted, and as a momentary flicker of light illuminated her face, it seemed that her expression softened just a bit.

A hopeful sign, he mused, for her cleverness had put him in a deucedly difficult position.

How much of the truth can I tell her?

On one hand, he was sure that she could keep a secret. On the other hand, however absurd the conjecture might seem, he couldn't completely ignore the fact that she was a possible suspect. Her interest in firearms, her furtive foray into the wing of the castle where the prince was lodging...

"Lord Davenport?" Another small shuffle, and now she was wreathed in shadow.

"I am thinking," he replied slowly.

"Of what lies or deceptions you can tell me?"

He let out a grudging laugh. Oh, yes, she was clever. But he'd met scores of clever women before and handled them easily enough. This was no different.

"Partly," he answered.

She smiled. "Well, that at least was an honest answer. So perhaps I shall venture another question. Are you or are you not a jewel thief?"

"Forgive the tedious repetition of the word—but no," he replied. "Purloining jewelry is not among my admittedly many faults."

"But in Lord Dunbar's library I saw you hide a book in your pocket," she challenged. "If you weren't stealing it, why conceal the fact?"

"Caught that, did you?" Devlin blew out his cheeks. "The answer isn't nearly as intriguing as you think. It was a book on the history of mechanical devices—"

"Automata," interrupted Anna.

"Precisely." No harm in admitting it. The minx had seen the evidence. "I have a special interest in the subject. But would prefer to keep it private."

"I saw it on your worktable," she said. "Does that mean the golden pistol is some sort of automata, and not a real weapon?"

He nodded. "You are far too clever in puzzling out things."

"I wondered about the little bird on the table." Her fists

finally unclenching, Anna lowered her hands and set them on her hips. "What's it for?"

"Never mind." Seeing her eyes narrow, he quickly added. "I am not in the habit of talking about my projects. Making these devices is a very painstaking process. I have an idea in mind, but until I am sure that I can make it work, I don't like to discuss the details."

"Fair enough," she conceded, an odd little expression flitting across her features. "I can understand that."

"Then may I take it that you will agree to stay silent about my work?"

This time it was she who made a move to close the gap between them. "About your automata, yes. But I still think you are hiding something, sir." Her tone was defiant. "There was a sheet of paper tucked into the book. It listed all the guests here, and there was a penciled 'X' next to several names."

Damnation.

"Miss Sloane, don't play with fire," he replied in a measured voice. "Clever as you are with your mind and your nimble little fingers, you may very well end up getting burned."

"That's not an answer," she retorted. "That's a provocation."

Up close, her face was even more alluring. The luminous intelligence in her eyes blazed with a bright fury, while her mouth challenged him to . . .

Feeling a little off-balance, Devlin fought to regain his edge.

"It's *you* who are provocative," he growled. "I vow, you could drive St. Peter to drown himself in Blue Ruin."

"Are we going to stand here all day and trade quips," she demanded.

"That depends on you," said Devlin. "Honor requires—"

"You claim to have no sense of honor."

"I must have left a few crumbs in the corners when I swept out my conscience," he drawled.

"You," she said, "are utterly impossible."

"Agreed," answered Devlin.

She took a step closer. "Utterly outrageous."

"True."

"Utterly infuriating."

"Absolutely."

Her hands came up...

Devlin braced himself for a punch.

...and set on his shoulders.

A jolt of heat speared through the layers of wool and linen.

"Is there nothing I can say or do to convince you to tell me what you are up to?" she asked in a soft murmur.

Devlin blinked, trying to control the sudden hot and cold surges thrumming through his body. His brain was barking orders, but his body wasn't listening.

Anna slid her hands up and down the slope of his shoulders, her slim fingers tangling in his hair as she drew her touch up to the knot of his cravat.

His throat went slightly dry.

"It will be our little secret," she whispered.

Bloody Hell. Where had she learned to play the sultry siren-seductress? This was a side of Miss Anna Sloane that she had never, ever displayed in London.

"N-no," he said, not budging an inch. Manly pride demanded that he stand firm.

"Not even if I do this?" Her lips touched his skin as she gave a little nibble to the tip of his chin.

Every particle of his flesh now felt afire. "I—I will consider the request."

"And what if I do this?"

Ye gods, perhaps Miss Anna Sloane wasn't quite the innocent virgin that she appeared to be.

The thought ignited another burst of sparks in his belly. His whole body was now vibrating with lust. *With longing.*

Angry at himself for the momentary weakness, Devlin snapped out a brusque warning. "You are now not only playing with fire, but thrusting yourself into the roaring flames."

"Mmmm." Her tongue flicked over his lower lip as she pressed her body up against him. "You do feel a trifle warm."

Satan save me.

All he had to do was press his palms to her slender shoulders and put some distance between them. *A simple move.* One he had done often enough, for his cardinal rule was to keep any woman from getting too close. And yet his fingers curled instead around her arms and slid down the soft sleeves of her gown to capture her wrists.

"Miss Sloane…" He hesitated, surprised at how unsteady his voice sounded. Then, reminding himself that he was a ruthless rake, Devlin sucked in a harsh breath. "Warm is rather an understatement. You are dancing dangerously close to the razor-thin line of No Return." Forcing himself to loosen his grip, he gave her a final warning. "Flee now, else I can't be responsible for what happens next."

A lady should be a little dangerous.

That she could arouse such a look of molten desire in a rake's eyes emboldened Anna to arch into a more intimate embrace. "I spend more time than you might think trying to imagine what it's like to be daring and dangerous."

"Your imagination," rasped Devlin, "is far too active."

Anna knew that she should pull back. Every shred of sanity was echoing the Devil's warning. *Flee now—fly away, as fast as you can.*

Otherwise there was no going back.

A part of her knew this was madness . . .

A part of me doesn't care.

Anna lifted her gaze to lock with his. "I'm not sure whether it's active enough." Summoning her courage, she rubbed herself back and forth against the ridge of his arousal.

The reaction was immediate. Devlin's body tensed, and his breathing turned a little ragged.

A tingling took hold of her palms. There was something elementally exciting about having the power to make a jaded blade like the marquess lose control.

"Ye gods," he whispered, his voice somewhere between a groan and a growl. Grasping her waist, he drew her into a shadowed alcove. His hands then slipped down to the fastenings of his trousers.

Anna felt the fumbling of fabric—soft wool, smooth cotton—and then Devlin seized her hand and suddenly there was a primal, pulsing heat against her palm. Velvet flesh, hard as steel.

I should scream, I should swoon. Instead, she curled her fingers around his maleness and squeezed ever so gently.

Devlin made a sound in the back of his throat.

She tightened her hold and drew a gasp.

Thinking back to her father's books on primitive cultures—and the lengthy late-night chats with her older sister about the mysteries of desire—Anna slowly moved her hand up and down the rigid length of him.

"Am I getting this right?"

"Exquisitely so." Devlin circled his hand over hers. "It's for you to set the rhythm, like so," he added, guiding her stroke. "And adding pressure here…" A sharp exhale. "And here will drive a man mad."

Slowly, slowly. Anna closed her eyes, intent on learning every nuance of his shape and his reaction to her caresses. Oh, Society would think her worse than wicked, worse than wanton for breaking every rule of proper behavior. But for now…

His hand fell away.

But for now, to the Devil with all rules. Acting on instinct, she quickened her strokes while watching Devlin's face. His jaw muscles tightened and a sheen of sweat began to bead his brow.

"I like the feel of you," she whispered. "Though no doubt I will be damned to perdition for saying so."

His hips rocked in rhythm with her touch. "Perdition," he said through gritted teeth, "suddenly seems a rather attractive place."

"I imagine it's very hot." Anna tentatively ran her touch around the crest of his cock. "On account of all the flames."

"Flames." With a raspy groan, Devlin jerked her hand away.

A lick of chill air chased his warmth from her fingertips. "W-was I doing something wrong?"

It took him a moment to steady his ragged breathing. "Alas, you were doing it all too right, sweeting."

"I—I never imagined that passion was quite so…powerful." She pressed her palms together as he turned away to refasten his trousers, surprised by the fierce pulse of heat coming from within her own body. "It's one thing to read about it in books and quite another to experience it in the flesh."

"You've not yet experienced the pleasures of passion?" he asked in a devil-dark voice.

Anna wasn't sure how to answer.

As Devlin turned and set his hands on her shoulders, the alcove seemed to come alive. The slanting patterns of sunlight began to dip and dance over the woodwork, and the air around them started to crackle with unseen sparks. Whirling, twirling, whirling—everything became a blur, and then suddenly Anna found her body braced against the back wall.

"Have you?" he demanded. Their bodies were locked together in an intimate embrace.

Words tangled together too tightly for speech. All she could do was shake her head.

"I did warn you that playing with fire is dangerous." His whisper teased against her face. "Now it's your turn."

Go. Now.

Anna's heart began to thud against her ribs. "I don't think—" she began.

"That's right," said Devlin. "Don't think. Just feel."

In the next instant, Anna was overwhelmed by a swirl of sensations. His hand was skating down the curve of her thigh...her skirts were skittering against her legs...a cool draft was curling around her ankles.

Up, up the fabric inched, as if impelled by some ancient Highland spell. Lace tickled over her skin, and his hand...

She gasped. *Oh, surely his hand wasn't going to touch her there.*

Her body froze, and Devlin went very still. "If you wish for me to stop, you have only to say so. I may be a rogue, but I am not a cad."

Yes or no?

Anna hitched in a slow, shuddering breath. Against all rules, against all reason, she felt safe in his arms. "Oh, please. D-don't stop. I want to know...I want to know..."

Know what?

Anna wasn't quite certain how to put it into words. Her body speaking a strange language all its own.

And yet, Devlin seemed to have no trouble understanding exactly what it was saying.

"Let the tension melt away, sweeting," he murmured.

As he traced a light kiss along the line of her jaw, Anna felt a delicious warmth radiate out through her limbs. Her legs turned a trifle unsteady, and if not for Devlin's hold on her waist, she might well have slumped to the floor.

"Mmmm." Letting her eyelids fall half-closed, she twined her arms around his neck. "Being ravished is really rather pleasant."

He let out a low, husky chuckle that made her insides give a lopsided lurch. "Do pay attention. I shall lose all credibility as a rake if the object of my evil intentions should fall asleep during the seduction."

"*Are* you seducing me?" Anna nuzzled the starched points of his shirtcollar. "By the by, you smell very nice." Inhaling deeply, she held the tantalizing scent in her lungs for as long as she could. "Like spiced smoke and tawny port." *And a myriad of other intriguing pleasures that are forbidden to a lady.*

"I am not quite sure who is seducing whom," answered Devlin a little raggedly. His hand feathered higher.

And suddenly the world slipped off its axis.

Clutching at his coat, she held on for dear life as he grazed the top of her stocking, and bare flesh met bare flesh.

And then he delved into her core.

"Oh. Oh." A fresh wave of dizziness overwhelmed her.

Devlin stilled her trembling lips with a kiss. His taste and his touch sent shiver after shiver thrumming through every fiber of her being.

I am possessed...

An unfamiliar heat, silky and liquid as sun-drizzled honey, welled up within her as he found a hidden pearl within her feminine folds.

Whatever wicked enchantment held her in thrall, Anna found herself wishing it would go on forever.

"Spread your legs, Anna," coaxed Devlin.

With a wordless gasp, she slid her kidskin shoes over the smooth parquet.

His lips were now pressed to the hollow of her throat. He murmured something—she knew not what. The wild pounding of her pulse drowned out all else as a new surge of heat spiraled through her belly, seeking release.

Tightening her hold on his shoulders, Anna arched against his hand. *Want, need. Want, need.* "I want...I need..."

"Hush, sweeting," he soothed. "I know what you need."

His stroke quickened and she thought she might burst into flames.

Devlin shifted slightly, muffling her soft cries in the folds of his coat. And then, just when the molten heat was too much to bear, her body convulsed in a sudden burst of firegold sparks.

When at last the shuddering sensations subsided, Anna slowly opened her eyes, unsure whether she was in Heaven...

Or Hell.

No wonder young ladies were warned to stay far, far away from Temptation. The taste of Sin was far too sweet.

"Mmmm." *Like cinnamon-spiced sugar, warm and melting on the tongue.*

The sound of a door opening and closing jolted her out of the languid reverie. "What was that?"

"A maid—and all too close by the sound of it." Devlin hurriedly smoothed her skirts back in place. "Can you make it back to your rooms on your own?" he asked. "Ungentlemanly though it is to leave you in the lurch, it would be best if we are not seen together in this isolated part of the castle. I'm sure neither of us wishes to spark a scandal."

Her body still felt a little boneless, but the word "scandal" shocked Anna back to her senses. She took a tentative step and her legs, though a trifle wobbly, kept her upright. "Yes, yes, you must go," she hissed. "And quickly!"

The shadows rippled and the alcove was empty.

Anna pressed her forehead to the dark wood, taking just an instant to steady her heartbeat before making haste for the connecting corridor.

Chapter Ten

Anna eased her bedchamber's latch shut and leaned back against the door, still feeling a little dazed by the lingering fire inside her. A glance at her reflection in the cheval glass showed that her face and her figure remained unchanged.

How could that be? she wondered, when she felt like a completely different person.

Aware that her heart was still thumping erratically, she slowly drew in several deep breaths and tried to calm its beat.

No wonder the poets waxed ecstatic when they composed odes about physical love. The sensations were wildly wonderful—though lightning might strike her down for daring to think such wicked thoughts.

"I don't regret it," she whispered defiantly. No matter that Polite Society would brand her a harlot if they knew what she had done.

And perhaps they would be right. The blame did not lie with Davenport, conceded Anna. She had thrown herself at him, thinking it oh-so-clever to use a show of sultry flirtation to tease him into revealing his secret.

Instead, the rascally rogue had taken her seductive strategy and turned it to his own advantage. She had all but surrendered her virtue. And had received precious little in return.

Save for a taste of terrible temptation.

Feeling a little foolish, Anna made a place for herself on the cushioned window seat and stared out at the mist-shrouded moors. A myriad of puzzling questions were swirling inside her head. While a myriad of whirling-dervish desires were spinning through the rest of her body.

Research. Anna grimaced at her reflection in the glass. At least the experience could be counted as research. After all, a writer must be willing to make great sacrifices in order to create a compelling story.

Though if she dared describe the scene in lurid detail, her pen might scorch the paper.

Expelling a sigh, she drew her knees to her chest. *Who am I, really?* Perhaps the question was sparking too many impetuous urges, too many rash explorations. Her father had reveled in journeying into the unknown—apparently she had inherited the same adventurous streak, instead of a proper dowry.

A prickling sensation suddenly danced down her arms and she chafed her palms against the pebbled flesh. In many ways, experimenting with sliding into a different skin was exciting. Exhilarating. And yet it was also terrifying.

Good and bad. Dark and light.

Nothing seemed to be making any sense—least of all

her conflicting feelings. Up until now, she had been confident in her ability to plot out her own life, as well as those of her storybook characters.

So why do I feel like a puppet on a set of perversely tangled strings?

The only answer was a light knock on the door.

Her maid entered without waiting for an answer, two freshly pressed evening gowns draped over one arm.

"*Alors*, mademoiselle." Josette eyed the dust and cobwebs clinging to the hem of Anna's gown with a pained grimace. "Have my wits gone wandering?" She blew out a mournful sigh. "I am quite sure I would never have laid out your morning gown in such a shameful state."

"No, no, once again, the fault is all mine," assured Anna. "I did some exploring in the oldest wing of the castle, and the galleries there are rarely entered."

"Did you discover anything interesting?"

Anna felt a hot flush rise to her cheeks. "N-not really," she mumbled. "Just a number of ancient ancestral portraits and some fragments of Roman sculptures. It was all rather ordinary."

"Only ordinary?" Josette smoothed a tiny wrinkle from one of the gowns and then carefully hung them in the armoire. "Yet the servants here say that Lord Dunbar has acquired a great many valuable collections."

"Oh, yes, he has. But perhaps His Lordship's predecessors did not possess his discerning eye."

The maid accepted the explanation with a shrug. "Or his plump purse. One can have exquisite taste, but without money it hardly matters."

Anna had lived enough years in genteel poverty to know Josette's observation was in many ways true. And yet there was something a little sad about hearing someone so young express such a cynical outlook on life.

"Not all things of beauty or value can be measured in terms of money," she said slowly.

Josette curled a faint smile. "We have an ancient proverb in French that says some people see a glass as half empty, while others see it as half full. I think that you are, at heart, an optimist, Mademoiselle Anna. While I have a more pragmatic view of the world."

"I, too, consider myself a realist," she protested. "I am not blinded by schoolgirl fantasies."

Josette remained tactfully silent. Her expression, however, was eloquent in its skepticism.

"I'm not so naïve as to think that life always ends in a happily ever after," added Anna.

"You could hardly be blamed if you did. From what I have heard, your older sister's marriage was a fairytale come true."

"Trust me, there were quite a few bumps along the road to happiness," she quipped, thinking of the helter-pelter carriage chase that took Olivia and Wrexham across half of England.

"What about you, mademoiselle?" asked Josette after straightening the brushes and pinbox on the dressing table. "Do you expect to be happy in your choice of a husband?"

"I... I haven't really given the question much thought," she answered after a moment of hesitation.

Her maid let out a low snort. "Every woman thinks of that."

"What I meant was, until recently, I had a duty to my family to make a good match. Happiness was not part of the equation."

"But now you may choose whom you please?"

Anna forced a light laugh. "Perhaps things are done differently in France, but here in England, it is the gentleman who chooses, not the lady."

"Ah, *oui*, it is still the same in France, no matter that Napoleon has changed many traditions. But you know what I meant."

Rather than answer, she made a show of rising and shaking out her skirts. "I had better change out of this dusty gown. The hour is later than I thought, and I ought to begin dressing for supper. Which color would you suggest for tonight—the smoky emerald or the seafoam blue?"

"Hmmm." Josette regarded her thoughtfully as she tapped a finger to her chin. "Your mood seems pensive, and perhaps a little dark. So I would advise you to wear the emerald."

"You did not wish to join in the slaughter of birds today, Lord Davenport?"

Devlin turned as the Vicomte de Verdemont, Lady de Blois's overfed brother-in-law, joined him at the head of the grand staircase. "I was feeling a trifle lazy, so I decided to spend my day doing nothing more strenuous than viewing some of the earl's magnificent art collections."

"Ah, yes. You are the one who so nobly offered your services as a guide to Marie-Helene." Sarcasm further slurred Verdemont's voice as they started down the stairs. He had already started drinking freely of their host's vintage French brandy, judging by a whiff of his breath. "I hope the demands of my sister-in-law were not too strenuous. She can be a bit demanding."

"I always endeavor to rise to the occasion when it

presents itself," answered Devlin with a deliberate grin. "However, la comtesse was still too distraught over the loss of her bauble to stir from her quarters." A wink. "Perhaps tomorrow."

Verdemont's nostrils flared in irritation.

"You do not sound overly fond of shooting," Devlin went on. "Are you not an avid hunter?"

"I can think of more civilized ways to pass the time."

Like trying to seduce your wife's sister? wondered Devlin. Aloud he responded, "So why accept the invitation? The rough-hewn moors of Scotland offer little in the way of civilized pleasures."

"I might ask the same of you, Lord Davenport."

"Oh, I'm a keen sportsman," he replied. "When the moment is right, I am ready to—"

"Excellent! Then I shall expect you to join us on the morrow," bellowed McClellan as he emerged from one of the side corridors. "We leave at first light, so as to have a full day tramping the moors."

"There may be more guests dropping dead than game birds," observed Devlin dryly.

An evil glint momentarily lightened McClellan's granite-gray eyes. "Nay, nay. I'm a very good shot."

"As I said, more guests than birds might expire on the morrow."

The baron didn't crack a smile. "I shall be counting on your presence, too, Verdemont."

"I had planned on taking the day to finish some correspondence—" began the vicomte.

"Letters can wait." McClellan dismissed the excuse with a curt wave. "I need you to make up our line of fire. Several of the older gentlemen have already begged off, and Lady Dunbar would hate to disappoint the prince and his friends by not having enough shooters."

"If you insist," said the vicomte ungraciously.

"Then it's settled. We'll meet in the Gun Room at five."

Devlin heaved a martyred sigh. "As you see, there is a reason the Scots have a reputation for being a dour, grim-minded race," he said to Verdemont. "Rising before dawn just to shed blood is unnatural."

"Have you never fought a duel, Davenport?" demanded McClellan.

"Good heavens, no!" he drawled. "I have no honor to defend, so why would I bother?"

The exchange of barbs was brought to an end by the appearance of their hostess, who was escorting a half dozen of the ladies to the drawing room.

"Oh, dear, is my cousin offending everyone?" the countess inquired lightly.

Verdemont shrugged in wordless answer and walked away to join his wife by the hearth.

"Oh, please don't worry, milady," piped up Caro, who had come down from her rooms ahead of the rest of her family. "We have all learned to ignore his ill-tempered remarks."

Lady Dunbar laughed, but Devlin noted that McClellan did not appear at all amused.

"If you live by the proverbial sword, you must expect to die by the proverbial sword," he murmured, as he strolled past the baron to offer his arm to Anna's sister. "The young lady appears to have an even sharper tongue than you."

Alec responded with a phrase in Gaelic that needed no translation.

Suppressing a grin, Devlin turned his attention to Caro.

"I see that your sister is not with you. I trust she is not feeling ill?"

"No, no, she is simply taking a little longer than usual in dressing for supper," Caro assured him. "Which is rather odd."

"Indeed? I was under the impression that most young ladies spend an inordinate amount of time on their toilette."

"Not Anna," replied her sister. "Fashion bores her. She's much more interested in . . . um, other things."

What things?

His curiosity piqued, he quickly asked, "Such as?"

A guilty flush flooded her face. "B-books."

"That's nothing to be ashamed of," said Devlin.

"I'm not supposed to mention it," mumbled Caro. "Mama says gentlemen do not like ladies who are too clever."

"Your mother's pronouncements on what men like or don't like should not be taken as gospel," he said softly.

Caro expelled a harried sigh. "To be honest, even if she were right, it wouldn't matter. Neither Anna nor I would ever feel compelled to give up our interests just to please a man."

"Why should you?" murmured Devlin.

A look of surprise flickered in her eyes, only to be chased away by a flash of mirth. "Your ideas on the subject ought not be taken as gospel either, sir. It's well known you go out of your way to break every rule of propriety."

"True. That's because, like you and your sister, I don't feel compelled to behave according to the strictures of a gaggle of narrow-minded prigs."

Caro looked uncertain of how to reply.

"And it appears that neither does Lord McClellan," he added, as they passed through the entrance of the drawing room. The baron stalked in several moments after them and went to stand by himself in the archway of one of the side alcoves. "Though I daresay he'd bristle at the notion of having anything in common with me."

"You, at least, are entertaining," said Caro frankly. "While he is an odious, obnoxious oaf."

"You forgot 'opinionated.' It, too, begins with an 'O.'"

Her chin took on a slightly defiant tilt. It was, noted Devlin with an inward smile, an unconscious imitation of her older sister's look when she was annoyed.

"You may go ahead and mock me, sir," said Caro. "But I enjoy the rhythms and sounds of language."

"I wasn't mocking you, Miss Caro, I was merely bantering." He plucked two glasses of champagne from the tray of a passing footman and handed one to her. "Your sister mentioned you had an interest in poetry."

Caro choked on a swallow of the wine. "Sh-sh-she did?"

"In the library," he reminded her. "When the two of you were looking for some books of Robert Burns's verses, as well as the sonnets of Shakespeare."

"Oh, er, yes." A laugh, which for some reason sounded a little forced. "That's right."

Oddly enough, her blush was back. Though why the mention of verses and sonnets should be making her jumpy as a cat crossing a hot griddle was puzzling.

"There's nothing overly shocking about a young lady having an interest in poetry," he pointed out. "So there must be some other reason your face is now the same shade of crimson as Lady de Blois's gown."

"The wine," she stammered. "It must be the champagne. I am a little unused to strong spirits."

He refrained from smiling. Barely. "Would you prefer ratafia punch?"

"No, no, I shall just...sip it more slowly."

"Now that we've established your interest in poetry, I can't help but be curious as to what sort of books your sister prefers," he said, once she had taken a tiny swallow without further ill-effects. "She doesn't strike me as a truly serious, scholarly bluestocking. I can't quite picture her working on translating Homer from the original Greek or studying Newton's laws of motion."

"True, she's not overly interested in ancient classics or arcane science. Her tastes run to more modern works."

"Such as?"

Caro gave a vague wave. "Oh, you know, all the popular novels—the works of Mrs. Radcliffe and Charlotte Smith...that sort of thing."

"Novels." Devlin nodded. "Yes, what young lady doesn't enjoy an entertaining tale?"

And yet, something didn't feel quite right about the reply, though he couldn't say why. Perhaps it was because Miss Anna Sloane was not at all like the silly, simpering misses who paraded through the drawing rooms of Mayfair. For the most part, they were colorless pasteboard cut-outs, each one indistinguishable from the others.

Whereas Anna was unique. *Interesting. Intriguing. Unpredictable...*

Unlike Caro, he did not feel compelled to choose his adjectives for alliteration.

"Indeed, sir," responded Caro brightly. "We ladies do tend to be passionate about writing. That is to say," she hastily added, "the written word, and how authors can, if they are talented, transport us to a different world for a certain interlude."

"Because for ladies the real world is so very limited compared with the world of the imagination?"

She now looked utterly flustered. "I...I..." Caro heaved a sigh of relief. "Oh, look, I see that Anna has finally come down."

Devlin turned.

And his heart leaped into his throat.

Thump, thump.

In that single, pulsing moment, he couldn't speak. He couldn't breathe. He couldn't think.

The dark colored silk of her gown seemed to ripple over her body like a puff of exotic smoke. Several gold-sparked tendrils capered free of her upswept tresses, as if a lover had caught her in a quick caress. They danced down the arch of her neck, curling and kissing up against the bare skin.

That fabric and a few finespun wisps of hair could be so exquisitely erotic was a revelation.

His gaze then slid from her throat and his lungs had no choice but to suck in a much-needed gulp of air. That hitch of movement seemed to kick his brain back into working order.

How in the name of Lucifer had her mother allowed her to appear with such a plunging décolletage?

The answer was of course obvious. Lady Trumbull was determined to hook an impressive title and fortune for her second daughter. And the baroness wasn't above using Anna's considerable charms as bait.

All the gentlemen in the room had turned to stare as she

passed through the portal, and now they were whispering among themselves. That was to say, Devlin saw their lips moving, and yet the only sound he heard was the thrum of his own blood rushing through his veins.

Anna, seemingly oblivious to the effect she was having on half the guests, made her way around the display of flowers and came to stand by her sister.

As they exchanged a quick greeting, Devlin quaffed a swallow of champagne to lubricate his throat. "Perhaps you ought to consider hiring a new lady's maid," he said when they were finished. "She seems to be a trifle careless."

Anna turned and fixed him with a challenging stare. "You don't like the way I look?"

Actually I would rather remove every stitch of clothing from your body.

"She forgot a few hairpins." His gaze slid back to her breasts. "And a lace fichu to keep men from letting their eyes rove to places where they should not stray."

"Some men," she said slowly, "rove past all boundaries of propriety." With that, Anna turned to Caro. "What do you think of Josette's creative efforts with brush and comb?"

Her sister studied the casual creation. "Well, as Lord Davenport hinted, you do look a little rumpled. But strangely enough I think it suits you."

Rumpled. Caro's choice of word was all too fitting. Anna looked like she had just risen from bed. There was a heavy-lidded languor to her eyes—a touch of kohl, perhaps, wielded by a hand skilled in seduction.

"As Josette says," mused Caro. "A lady with nary a hair out of place is awfully bland."

This French maid was highly dangerous, decided Devlin. Highly dangerous to a man's peace of mind. But even more dangerous was Anna's sudden transformation from her usual self to a sultry Siren. He considered himself a savvy judge of woman, but she had him off balance.

"Um, do you think she could do something different with my coiffure tomorrow night?" continued Caro. She had lowered her voice, but not quite enough.

McClellan's rough-cut voice rumbled in a low laugh as he moved out from the shadow of the curio cabinet. "Aye, I daresay one of those towering designs from the previous century would look very fetching. You know, the ones that feature things like real fruit and stuffed songbirds woven into an elaborate nest."

"Ah, it appears that you do possess a sense of humor after all, McClellan," said Devlin lightly.

The baron's mouth curled up ever so slightly at the corners. "It wasn't meant to be funny."

"No," said Caro tightly. "It was meant to be beastly." Setting her wine glass on the display pedestal, she turned on her heel. "If you will excuse me, I had better go see what's keeping Mama."

"Is your sister always so excitable, Miss Sloane?" asked McClellan, after watching Caro storm off. "This afternoon I overheard her reciting poetry in one of the side parlors. Not bad poetry, though I didn't recognize the author. However, her emotions do tend to become enflamed."

"Only when provoked."

"Quite deliberately provoked," murmured Devlin.

"That," said Anna, turning her frown on him, "is rather like the pot calling the kettle black, sir."

"On the contrary. When I choose to wield my tongue

like a rapier, I do so only against opponents who know how to defend themselves," he replied.

McClellan's eyes darkened to a shade of gunmetal gray. "Just what, precisely, are you accusing me of, Lord Davenport?"

"Bad manners," answered Devlin. "I don't know you well enough to say for sure whether you are a cowardly cur."

"I should call you out for that insult," snarled McClellan through his clenched teeth.

"It would be a waste of breath. As I told you, I consider duels to be a nonsensical waste of energy as well as sleep."

"There are other ways of settling a matter of honor," growled McClellan. But before he could elaborate, Lady Dunbar approached with Count Rupert and Colonel Polianov in tow.

"Alec, might I draw you away from your present company to answer a few shooting questions these gentlemen have?"

"It would be my pleasure," he muttered. Inclining a curt bow to Anna, he moved off to join his cousin.

"Well, well," remarked Devlin, as the Russian envoy began to argue loudly with McClellan over what type of gunpowder performed best in the damp conditions of the Scottish moors. "What a jovial group of guests have been assembled here. It will be a miracle if the only blood shed this month is that of the game birds."

Chapter Eleven

"You appear to have made an enemy of the baron," said Anna.

Devlin shrugged. "I assure you, he is not the first."

"I don't doubt that." Despite McClellan's boorish behavior, a part of her was grateful to him for the distraction. The exchange of heated words had kept her from feeling unspeakably awkward in her first meeting with the marquess since...

"But I find it curious that you went out of your way to defend Caro," Anna went on. Or perhaps she had only imagined the spark of real anger in his eyes. At the moment, her usually solid judgment was subject to question. "You keep insisting that you have no sense of gentlemanly honor."

"Don't mistake my needling for nobility," shot back Devlin. "McClellan takes himself too seriously. I merely felt his pride needed a prick or two."

"You are not concerned that he possesses a volatile temper and a dislike of English aristocrats?" asked Anna.

"Not particularly."

"And yet," she replied, "it seems to me that he has a great deal of anger seething inside him."

"Oh, yes, he is angry." A sardonic twitch pulled at his mouth. "Mostly at himself because he is attracted to your sister and doesn't wish to be."

Anna wanted to dismiss the statement as absurd, but a momentary reflection on the baron's behavior around her sister compelled her to admit that the marquess raised an interesting point. "You think he's deliberately seeking to make her dislike him, so that there's no chance of an acquaintance developing?"

"Something like that," said Devlin, looking rather smug.

"You have a devious mind, Lord Davenport."

"Well, apparently we think alike."

For someone who took pains to appear a frivolous wastrel, he had a very clever wit.

To go along with his very clever imagination. And his very clever hands.

At the thought of his skilled fingers, and how adept they were at manipulating the most delicate of mechanisms, Anna felt her flesh begin to prickle with heat.

Don't, she warned herself. *Don't blush.* Don't betray how much his maddeningly masculine presence affected her rebellious body. Forcing her thoughts back to the baron, Anna suddenly recalled the list she had found in his work room.

"Speaking of devious, McClellan was one of the names you had marked with an 'X' on the paper hidden in your book. Why the interest in him?"

"Miss Sloane, as I've said before, you really ought to cease poking your nose in places it doesn't belong."

The condescending comment made her forget any lingering feelings of embarrassment. "Oh? And just how do you propose to stop me?" she challenged. "Here, in the drawing room, you can't resort to the same sort of distraction you used earlier today."

Devlin leaned in, a fraction closer than was proper in polite company. "You call what went on between us a *distraction*?"

"What would *you* call it?" demanded Anna, then immediately decided she had made a tactical mistake. "No, no, don't answer that," she muttered.

A devilish glint hung for an instant on the dark curl of his lashes...

The small valley between her breasts suddenly began to bead with sweat. Really, it was most unfair of the Almighty. No man ought to be blessed with such sensuous eyes.

And then he smiled.

Had he noticed her involuntary reaction? The dratted man seemed to have a sixth sense for Sin.

"Miss Sloane, there are a number of words I could use to describe our encounter. But no matter how softly I whisper"—his breath was now tickling her cheek—"none of them ought to be uttered in public."

She edged back a step, hoping he couldn't hear the quickening *thump-thump* of her heart.

"Miss Sloane, Lord Davenport, might I join you?" Prince Gunther paused politely by the display of roses. "Or am I interrupting a private conversation?"

"Not at all," responded Anna.

"Excellent." He came to stand by Devlin, who had assumed a bored slouch. "I wanted to tell you that I found a lovely fourteenth-century illuminated Book of Hours in the manuscript section of the library. The colors and gold leaf detailings are exquisite, and I thought you might like to see it tomorrow when I return from the moors."

"If I were you, I wouldn't plan any leisure activities," drawled Devlin. "Our Scottish Huntmaster has made it known—with fiendish delight, I might add—that he intends on driving us into the ground. To begin with, he demands that we assemble in the Gun Room at the God-benighted hour of five in the morning."

"Oh, I am quite used to early hours and vigorous exercise during a hunting excursion," replied the prince. "It's quite bracing."

"You are clearly a better fellow than I am." Devlin gave an exaggerated shudder. "I had better go find another drink to fortify myself for the coming ordeal."

Anna deliberately avoided meeting his gaze. "Retiring at an early hour after supper might be a better option, Lord Davenport."

"Sleep? What a tiresome thought," replied Devlin. "Especially when a house party presents so many more enjoyable activities to engage in." With that he sketched a bow and sauntered off.

"An interesting fellow," observed Prince Gunther.

Anna expelled an exasperated sigh. "That is a very charitable description."

He looked at her thoughtfully. "I had assumed the two of you were good friends, given how often Lord Davenport seeks out your company."

"Not exactly." She wasn't quite sure how explain their relationship. "As you have noticed, the marquess finds it diverting to needle people. That I react to his barbs seems to amuse him, so perhaps that's the reason."

The prince raised a brow. "That sounds rather ungentle-manly."

"Yes," agreed Anna. "So it does."

"Have you finally tired of young, innocent girls?"

Devlin looked up from the amber-dark depth of his whisky.

"They are so naïve, *non*?" went on Lady de Blois. "I confess, it surprised me that you paid them any attention." With a graceful little flourish—a gesture that had likely been perfected in front of a looking glass, he thought cynically—she tapped her fan lightly against his shoulder. "Until I heard that the elder one has recently been gifted with a very generous dowry."

He smiled, though his hand tightened around his glass. "Yes, money is very seductive."

A low, trilling laugh rippled through the air. "Yes, in-deed." Sidling closer, she toyed with the fringe of her shawl, shifting its folds just enough to expose a better view of her gown's low-cut bodice. "But so are other things."

"Like baubles?" he suggested.

Another laugh. "*Oui*. I like things of beauty, like pre-cious gems, gleaming gold." A pause. "And handsome men."

It was a blatant invitation to strike up a more heated flir-tation, which fitted perfectly with his duties for Thorncroft. And yet, he found himself ignoring the opportunity.

"Has your missing emerald been found?" he asked.

Her mouth pursed to a pout. "Not yet. The servant quar-ters have been thoroughly checked. However, Lord Dunbar is reluctant to offend his other guests by ordering a search of their rooms. He has, however, offered to reimburse me for its loss at the end of the house party if it hasn't been found."

"Most likely it has simply rolled into some hidden nook or cranny and will turn up before then."

"Perhaps." A Gallic sniff expressed quite the opposite sentiment. "Though I think it far more probable that it's tucked in someone's reticule or pocket." Lady de Blois flicked a gloved finger over the folds of his cravat. "Maybe I should demand to run my hands over your coat and waistcoat, Lord Davenport."

"Alas, you would be greatly disappointed, Lady de Blois."

"Oh, I think not." Her lashes fluttered. "And do call me Marie-Helene. After all, country house parties are notorious for their informality."

Notorious. Her understanding of the English language was either mediocre or superb.

"I am called—"

"*Le Diable*," she said. "The Devil. But surely your parents gave you a more proper Christian name."

"Devlin," he supplied. "Though I've been told they considered Lucifer, as I put my mother through hell in birthing me."

"Ah, so you were trouble from the start."

"So it would seem." As he spoke, the supper bell rang, signaling it was time to move into the dining salon.

"Since we are seated at opposite ends of the table, it seems we must continue this fascinating conversation at a later time," said Lady de Blois. "Midnight is a charming hour, don't you think?"

"An interlude of black velvet skies and diamond-bright stars, cloaked in the mystery of moonlight."

"La, you are a poet as well as a rogue," she intoned.

"Merely parroting the words of one," replied Devlin.

She regarded him with a faintly quizzical look before saying, "I am quartered on the third floor of the west wing. My door is the first one on your left as you enter the corridor. I shall not linger over tea with the ladies while you gentlemen enjoy your postprandial port and cigars. So don't dally too long."

The assignation should have stirred some enthusiasm in his thoughts—not to speak of his privy parts. However, the prospect of dallying with the lady no longer seemed quite so attractive.

Perhaps the combination of Scottish malt and French champagne was setting off an adverse chemical reaction.

Mayhap I should switch to Spanish brandy or German wine.

"*A bientôt*, Devlin," she said in a throaty whisper.

"Yes, until later," he murmured.

"Drat it." Freeing the tangled pin from her topknot, Anna tossed it on the dressing table. Several more *pings* followed.

"Was your evening's ensemble not a success?"

Anna whirled around as her maid emerged from the dressing alcove. "You really need not wait up for me in the evenings, Josette. I am quite capable of undressing myself."

"Forgive me if I am disturbing you. I was just putting away some freshly laundered nightrails. Things have been slow in the scullery because of all the extra work."

"I did not mean to sound snappish," apologized Anna. "I seem to be a little out of sorts tonight."

"Your gown..."

"Earned effusive compliments from most of the men present," she said, turning back to the looking glass to unknot the ribbon in her hair.

Josette carefully plumped the pillows on the bed. "But not from the dark-haired one they call the Devil?"

A harried exhale momentarily fogged her reflection. "W-what makes you say that?"

"Very little goes on upstairs that isn't discussed downstairs, mademoiselle," replied her maid.

"But of course. What a buffle-headed question." Anna loosened the last of the pins. "My wits don't seem to be working very well of late."

Josette maintained a tactful silence as she retrieved the ribbon from the carpet and twined it into a neat coil.

Biting her lip, Anna watched the slowly undulating flame of her candle as she started to brush out her hair, hoping its soft sway might help soothe her unsettled emotions. With a pang of longing, she realized how much she missed the company of her older sister. Olivia's steady good sense and sage wisdom could always be counted on to help untangle any problem.

Despite the flicker of firegold light, Anna felt her spirits sink deeper into darkness. It was dreadfully hard having no one to confide in. Caro was not yet experienced enough to give advice about men, and as for her mother...

Mama and I are as different as chalk and cheese.

A sniff slipped out of its own accord, causing the candleflame to waver.

"Is there a reason you are feeling...I think you English call it blue-deviled?" asked Josette softly.

"Oh, please." Anna forced a smile. "I would rather not hear the word 'devil' anymore tonight."

"Ah." Her maid perched a hip on the edge of the dressing table and tucked her skirts around her legs. "Men."

"Men," she echoed. If anyone had experience in the vagaries of life, and all its hard-edged realities, it was Josette. Drawing a deep breath, she ventured to add, "They can be awfully confusing."

"*Oui*," agreed her maid. "At times, one is tempted to strangle them—or rather him."

"Oh, I can't tell you how comforting it is to hear that," quipped Anna. "I thought perhaps it was just me."

"Trust me, if there is one sentiment all women share, it is that." Josette folded her hands in her lap. "If there is anything you wish to talk about, I am happy to listen." A pause. "Be assured that I don't gossip, mademoiselle."

Anna hesitated, but somehow felt that her maid could be taken at her word. "I ought to be able to ignore him. And yet, the Devil—that is, Lord Davenport—has the infuriating ability to make me lose my temper. And I *never* lose my temper." She frowned. "It's very puzzling."

"You wish for me to offer an answer?"

"Very much so."

"It's because you are very attracted to the man. Perhaps you are even a tiny bit in love with him."

"But that makes no sense," said Anna.

Josette's low laugh caused the pale curl of candle smoke to dissolve in the darkness. "That is the first thing you must understand about love, mademoiselle—it makes no sense. It comes from the heart, not the brain, and the heart can be very stupid about these things."

"I see there is much I have to learn on the subject." Anna was acutely aware of the *thump, thump* inside her chest. "I wish there were a book on the subject that, you know, spelled out the rules."

"There are a great many that claim to know the secrets. But I daresay they wouldn't do you much good. Love is not like a recipe for pigeon pie. There is no list of ingredients that can be mixed together to create a perfect result. It is different for every individual. You simply have to trust your instincts." Josette's mouth tweaked up at the corners. "Trust your passions."

"But passion can lead a lady into trouble," mused Anna.

"Yes, yes, I know. You English are cautious. Perhaps too cautious. We French believe that—"

"A lady should be a little dangerous," she finished.

"*Oui*. Risk makes you feel more alive."

"I—I think I know what you mean," said Anna, as the memory of the afternoon made her skin begin to prickle with heat. "It must be the same for men. Lord Davenport seems engaged in some strange—" Catching herself, she decided that her speculations were not something that ought to be mentioned. "Oh, never mind. I am quite likely wrong."

Josette rose. "I think perhaps you have enough to occupy your thoughts for now, so I shall bid you good night. Shall I lay out your nightrail before I go?"

"No, thank you," replied Anna. "I wish to make a few notes in my journal before I retire."

"Then I shall see you in the morning. *Bonne nuit*, mademoiselle."

The evening could hardly be termed "good," she thought wryly, as the latch closed with a soft *snick*. Upsetting wasn't quite right either, though the sight of Lady de Blois flirting shamelessly with Devlin had made her stomach feel rather bilious.

Josette thought her confused emotions had something to do with love?

Love? Oh, surely not. Granted, her body seemed to respond to the marquess with enthusiasm, while her mind was ordering quite the opposite reaction. And granted, Josette had spoken with the cool assurance of a woman who knew what she was talking about.

Still, it seemed illogical.

But as logic wasn't proving helpful in solving any of her conundrums, Anna decided to add some of her maid's observations on love to the notes for her current manuscript—the ideas offered some interesting ways to add some spark to her main characters. Emmalina and Alessandro were getting a little too predictable.

After scribbling a few quick pages, she sat back and closed her notebook. The hour was late, but her nerves were still too on edge for sleep. Instead, she rose and unlocked the bottom drawer of an old tea chest that was serving as a decorative plant stand. Hidden beneath a portfolio of blank writing paper lay the finished pages of the latest Sir Sharpe Quill adventure.

Gathering up the last few chapters, Anna curled up in the armchair by the hearth and read through the scenes. Things were shaping up rather nicely, she mused. The pacing felt right and the setting's description was wonderfully exotic, thanks to a book of engravings on the Ottoman coast that she had found in an antiquarian bookstore just before leaving London.

There was just one small, bothersome detail. Emmalina needed to fire off several shots with one of the new military-issue rifles, and while Anna knew that the cartridges and firing mechanisms differed from those of a standard musket, she wasn't quite sure of the exact details. She could, of course, omit any mention of them. But she liked to get things right.

Perhaps there was an illustrated book on modern weaponry in the earl's library. Shuffling the manuscript pages back in order, Anna went to relock them in her hiding place. She would check on the book first thing in the morning, while the men were out hunting. But as the key turned, the metallic click suddenly reminded her that the prince had mentioned bringing one of the latest model German hunting rifles with him, in case the opportunity arose to stalk the hills for the famous Highland stags.

The weapon would likely be stored in the Gun Room, and with the gentlemen having to rise so early, the place was certain to be deserted at this late hour.

It was worth a look, Anna decided. Taking up a pencil and her pocket sketchbook, she changed into a pair of soft-soled slippers and tiptoed out into the corridor.

Devlin hurried down the stairs, anxious to escape the cloying cloud of perfume that seemed to be shadowing his steps. He had managed to extract himself from Lady de Blois's clutches before having to take a tumble in her bed. But it had required some dexterous moves on his part. She hadn't been pleased by the excuse that the prince and his friends needed him to make up the right numbers for a late-night card game. He had promised to make amends.

Thank God I have no gentlemanly scruples about breaking my word.

England's needs must, after all, come before those of a randy widow.

Or was a lust for sexual dalliances the only reason she had come north?

That was only one of the many questions needed to be considered as he reviewed what progress he had made in his investigation.

Given the circumstances, Devlin decided he hadn't done too badly. Through casual conversation and careful observation during the evening gatherings, he had ruled out well over half the guests as possible suspects. The group of family and friends who had accompanied the young London heiress were conventional, conservative aristocrats who would likely expire from shock at the idea that they might be involved in any murderous plot. As for the local gentry, none of them possessed the imagination or boldness to attempt an assassination.

The German party who had accompanied the prince to Scotland presented more of a challenge to assess. But in the end, he had decided that they were likely just what they seemed—a pleasant, good-natured group of friends who seemed genuinely fond of their royal companion.

That left the French contingent, the ill-tempered Russian colonel, Lord McClellan...

And the Sloane family.

The baroness was a very unlikely villain. Again, a lack of imagination.

The two sisters were a different story, though. Caro, with her charming exuberance, did not seem to possess the necessary deviousness to carry off a crime. Anna, on the other hand, had both the cleverness and the self-control to be...dangerous.

Shaking off his suspicions, Devlin told himself that the French party were the far more likely suspects. He was aware of the fact that on a number of occasions, an exiled French aristocrat living in England had turned out to be a secret agent of Napoleon. Some did it out of idealism, some did it out of greed. He had a feeling that both Lady de Blois and her brother-in-law were not as plump in the pocket as they wished to appear. To begin with, he had taken a careful look at the comtesse's emerald necklace during one of the earlier amorous moments.

The jewels were paste.

And lurking beneath the trilling laughs and sensual smiles was a steely coldness that seemed at odds with her efforts to appear a seductive Siren.

That they might be working in tandem—one to create a diversion, one to create havoc—was a thought that couldn't be dismissed.

Still mulling over the comtesse and her behavior, Devlin turned down one of the side corridors, intent on taking a shortcut to his quarters in the men's wing. The passage led down a short flight of stairs and past the side portico. Just around the next corner was the Gun Room, where all too soon, the hunting party would be assembling in the wee hours of the morning.

No rest for the wicked, he thought wryly as he rounded the turn.

Up ahead, a faint pool of candlelight spilled into the corridor from a half-open door.

Strange. It seemed a trifle early for a ghillie to be up and checking the fowling guns or loading the cartridge bags. On instinct, Devlin ducked into the recessed doorway of a storage closet and cocked an ear to listen.

Nothing. No cocking of hammers, no shifting of canisters, no thumping of canvas. The silence made the situation even more suspicious. He waited, watching the erratic flicker of the light moving within the room.

Finally, after several long minutes, a figure emerged and drew the door shut.

First pistols, and now muskets and rifles?

Despite her protests to the contrary, Anna Sloane must have a *very* vivid imagination.

That, or something far more nefarious than a play was being scripted inside that clever little head.

Chapter Twelve

The following morning dawned gray and unsettled, with ominous clouds in the distance threatening rain.

The mood was somber as well, as the group started to climb into the hills. Or perhaps, observed Devlin, everyone was simply suffering the effects of too little sleep and too much brandy.

A dull ache was pulsing against the back of his skull, though not from a surfeit of spirits. Much as he wished to believe Anna incapable of being involved in any serious wrongdoing, her activities were becoming too alarming to ignore. Her explanations simply didn't ring true.

And yet, Devlin couldn't quite bring himself to accept that she was the agent in charge. She must be working with someone.

But whom?

Surely it had to be someone she knew from London. Colonel Polianov? His rudeness might only be an act, for the Russian government was meddling in German politics and had good reason to wish ill to befall Prince Gunther.

Or maybe the young heiress's father and Anna were having a clandestine affair, and the man had drawn her into an international intrigue.

Ye gods, he thought in some disgust, his conjectures were growing dangerously demented. There had to be a more reasonable answer.

"This way," called McClellan, interrupting Devlin's brooding. "Watch your step. The stones are slippery."

Ducking low to avoid snagging his hat on a branch of thorny gorse, Devlin made his way up the narrow path. He had deliberately chosen to bring up the rear, as it afforded a chance to keep an eye on all the rest of the hunters. But given the patches of fog and swirls of mist obscuring the moors, there wasn't much to see. The men ahead were naught but ghostly silhouettes.

"The grouse will likely have far more sense than we do," he grumbled, "and won't seek to stir from their nests."

"Ja, it is gloomy," came a disembodied voice from just ahead. Count Rupert rose from his crouch after making a final adjustment to the buckle of his hunting boot. "But I think I see a peek of sun to the east."

"Wishful thinking," said Devlin.

The winds had suddenly shifted just after daybreak, blowing a new squall in from the sea. However, the prince had been anxious not to miss another day on the grouse moors, so Lord Dunbar had prevailed upon his wife's cousin to carry on according to plan. A few of the gentlemen—the sensible ones, thought Devlin glumly—had demurred. But loath though he was to forgo the comforts of a roaring fire and glass of whisky on a rainy day, he had felt compelled to come along. After all, Thorncroft *was* paying him well.

"You don't like hunting, Lord Davenport?" asked the count.

"Not when it's colder and wetter than a witch's tit."

The other man looked puzzled for a moment, and then began to chuckle. "Ha, ha, ha. You English have a very peculiar sense of humor."

"Would you two stop cackling over bawdy jokes and pay attention?" called McClellan testily. "This is excellent terrain for the hunt, and if we spread out in a line parallel to the trail, the beaters and dogs can try to flush some birds before it's time to return to the castle."

Though several sarcastic quips came to mind, Devlin took his assigned place without comment. The prince, he noted, was positioned at one end of the line, next to Vicomte de Verdemont.

A signal from the head ghillie indicated that the hunt was about to start.

"We'll shoot in order, from left to right, as the birds take flight," called McClellan. "The prince will go first."

Cocking his fowling gun, Devlin set his stance and readied himself to take aim when his turn came.

The beaters began to thrash the bushes with their sticks, and in a matter of moments the whir of wings sounded as a startled grouse rose up from the heather.

BANG!

The bird kept on flying—it was Prince Gunther who fell to the ground like a sack of stones.

Dropping his weapon, Devlin sprinted to where the prince lay writhing in pain. McClellan was already kneeling beside him, wrapping a handkerchief around the injured man's bleeding hand.

"The gun misfired and the cartridge exploded inside the

barrel, shattering the stock," he explained. "The fellow is lucky. The wound isn't too serious." His glance went to the twisted metal and needle-sharp slivers of wood. "It could easily have been a good deal worse."

"It's just a scratch," said the prince gamely, though his face was pale as a puff of gunsmoke. "If you will help me up…"

His three friends were already there, lifting him to his feet. A sling was fashioned, and with his good arm draped over Count Rupert's shoulder, Prince Gunther was led to the path for the trek down to where the horses were waiting.

McClellan sent one of the beaters ahead to fetch a carriage from the castle, then began gathering the extra cartridge bag and the prince's rucksack as the other hunters began to file off after the Germans.

Crouching down, Devlin made a closer examination of the wrecked fowling gun. "Birdshot does not normally have enough gunpowder to cause such an explosion." As he spoke, he slanted a sidelong look at the baron, carefully watching to see what reaction his deliberately chosen words might provoke.

McClellan looked up slowly. It might have been naught but the shifting mist, but for a moment, it seemed that a spasm of emotion tightened his features. "I thought your expertise was in gambling and drinking, not ballistics."

"In my innocent youth, I did a fair amount of shooting on my family's estate." Devlin tapped a finger to the bent trigger. "Enough to know that the cartridge had the wrong charge of powder."

"Are you implying my cousin's gunkeepers are incompetent?" asked McClellan sharply.

"I am merely making an observation based on my experience."

A shrug. "In my experience, accidents like this one are not uncommon in hunting. My guess is that the cartridge simply jammed."

"Perhaps." But as a seasoned gamester, Devlin was not willing to wager any money on it.

"Have you heard?" said Caro, as Anna and their mother came into the drawing room. "Prince Gunther has been injured in a shooting accident."

"Oh, dear, I hope it isn't serious," exclaimed the baroness. She angled a concerned look at Anna. "What a pity it would be if he had to withdraw from the party, just when he is showing a marked interest in you, my dear."

"He is simply enjoying sharing his interest in books with me, Mama," she replied. "You ought not read anything more meaningful into it."

"That," announced Lady Trumbull with a note of triumph, "is exactly what Olivia said about Wrexham. And see where turning those pages led."

Anna knew the futility of arguing with their mother. Instead, she turned to her sister. "Have you any idea what happened?"

"Apparently his fowling gun misfired and the barrel exploded," explained Caro. "I heard Lord McClellan tell Lady Dunbar that he could have been killed."

"Oh, what a scandal that would have been for poor Miriam," murmured the baroness.

Anna thought she detected a tiny tinge of regret. But perhaps it was only because her nerves were a little on edge from lack of sleep.

"It would have had far more serious repercussions for our government," she pointed out. "With the all squabbling between our allies, the political situation in Eastern Europe is like a powder keg waiting to explode. The prince's death could be just the spark to ignite terrible trouble in the region."

"My dear, you really mustn't voice your thoughts about politics," chided their mother. "Men do not like ladies to have an opinion on such matters."

"Indeed. We prefer them to been seen and not heard." There was no danger of McClellan's overloud voice going unnoticed. "Especially when they are a lovely ornament to the room, like one of the pretty little Staffordshire figurines that my cousin collects."

"You think a lady should be as brainless as a lump of baked clay?" challenged Caro.

Lady Trumbull made a low warning sound in her throat.

"I think, milord, that you are deliberately trying to goad us into reacting to your words," interjected Anna. "However, we are much too intelligent to dignify such a silly statement with any arguments."

Caro had opened her mouth as if to say more, but then quickly curled a scornful sneer that spoke even more eloquently than words.

You Are An Idiot.

Only a complete bumblewit would have failed to comprehend the message. And the baron, although sadly remiss in his manners, was not lacking in brains. His jaw tightened and a tiny muscle up near his ear began to twitch. "You—" he began, only to be interrupted as another voice joined the conversation.

"Have cleverly silenced any further disparagements of

the female intellect," said Devlin. "Kudos, Miss Sloane," he added after inclining an exaggerated bow. "A man had better sharpen his steel if he wishes to cross swords with you."

"We weren't engaging in mortal combat, Lord Davenport," replied Anna lightly. What, she wondered, had kindled such a strangely martial fire in his eyes? "Merely a bit of friendly banter."

"It seemed to me," muttered Caro, "that Lord McClellan was deadly serious."

The baron threw her a daggered look.

"Girls, girls." Their mother huffed out an exasperated sigh. "Let us move on to more *ladylike* subjects."

"Like how to roast a man's liver with turnips and onions?" suggested Devlin.

Anna bit back a snort of laughter. She couldn't help responding to his scathingly wicked sense of humor, even though it appeared that his cleverness concealed a far darker side of his character.

Perhaps Polite Society was right to have labeled him the Devil. Lucifer was capable of great charm, but at heart he had chosen Evil over Good.

Looking up, she found him regarding her with a strangely intense look. It seemed to be both accusing and questioning.

As if that made any sense.

Lady Trumbull broke the momentary silence. "Really, sir, you ought not confuse young ladies with such shockingly inappropriate comments. It's gentlemen like you who give them the wrong idea of what is, and is not, the correct way to behave with propriety."

"Oh, have no fear, Lady Trumbull. I am not nearly as

pernicious an influence on your daughters as you seem to think. They are far too strong in their own views to be colored by mine."

"Ha, ha, ha." McClellan's flash of teeth was clearly not meant to be a smile. "That is what I call being damned with faint praise."

"You, sir, are no better," hissed the baroness. "Swearing in the presence of ladies is…is…"

"Unconscionably rude?" suggested Caro.

"We must be more forgiving of the poor fellow," murmured Devlin. "He likely has few conversational companions save for Highland sheep."

"And they, sir, are far better company than you Sassenach peacocks," retorted McClellan.

"Peacocks preen and take pride in their gaudy plumage. While I, alas, am considered a very dull bird in terms of dress. I don't find fashion terribly interesting compared to other things." Devlin looked down his well-shaped nose. "Nor, it would appear, do you."

Both men, observed Anna, appeared to be walking on a razor's edge tonight, and Devlin seemed intent on being even more provoking than usual. She wondered why. He usually knew just how far he could go without losing his balance.

"Whatever feathers you flaunt, they don't disguise the fact that you are an insolent arse," growled McClellan.

"On the contrary," piped up Caro. "Lord Davenport is amusing, not mean-spirited."

Lady Trumbull hitched in a horrified breath at hearing her youngest daughter give a tongue lashing to a titled lord…even though the barony was only a Scottish one.

Oh, bloody hell.

On several occasions in the past, her mother had fainted for dramatic effect. But in this case, decided Anna, a swoon might not be feigned. She had better intervene in the next moment, before the situation sunk into farce. With her guest of honor lying half dead upstairs, poor Lady Dunbar had suffered enough shocks for one day.

"Caro, kindly escort Mama to the punch table and find her a glass of sherry. A cough seems to be lodged in her throat." Removing her sister from the fray might keep the gentlemen from going for each other's jugular.

But before Caro could react, McClellan unclenched his jaw just enough to respond to her comment.

Anna prepared herself for the worst. *Smelling salts—I had better signal a footman to bring smelling salts. And a cudgel to bash both men on the head.*

She was, however, pleasantly surprised by the measured tone of his voice.

"You think it mean-spirited that I resent English lords and their oppressive treatment of my country?" he asked.

Caro appeared taken aback by the reasonableness of the question. "I...no, actually I think you have any number of legitimate grievances, sir. But you would do your cause better service to express them more thoughtfully, rather than indulge in childish pique."

The baron regarded her with an inscrutable stare. "In poetry, perhaps?" Strangely enough it was said more in humor than in anger.

"The Scots have a rich and distinguished heritage of expressing themselves in verse," replied her sister. "But if rhyming couplets are not to your taste, prose, or simply rational discourse, would be equally effective."

Devlin opened his mouth to speak, but on catching Anna's quelling look, he shut it again.

"Sherry," said their mother faintly as she fanned her face. "I do feel in need of a reviving sip."

"Caro..." murmured Anna, before the temporary truce could be broken.

Her sister dutifully offered an arm to their mother.

After watching them move off, McClellan excused himself with a brusque nod. "I had better go upstairs and see if my cousin requires some liquid fortitude." For a brief instant his steely eyes seemed to wink with a less martial glint. "Though I daresay she might prefer something stronger than sherry."

"It seems you have helped avert a second explosion of the day," said Devlin, once they were alone.

"No thanks to you." Anna let out her breath, suddenly aware of the tension coiled inside her. "You seemed intent on seeing blood spilled."

He shifted slightly, setting off a soft rustle of wool, and silent rippling of muscle as his body hardened along with his gaze. "Oddly enough, I find myself wondering whether to think the same thought about you."

Had he been drinking heavily? His words weren't slurred, and yet they weren't making any sense.

"I have no idea what you mean, sir."

"Don't you?"

Her head was beginning to ache, despite having had no more than a sip of champagne. "No. None whatsoever."

A flicker of uncertainty was quickly hidden beneath his dark lashes. "Your words say one thing and your actions quite another."

Had he spotted her foray to the Gun Room? Anna

fought back a guilty grimace, reminding herself that his own behavior was rather questionable.

"That may be," she replied coolly. "But I don't answer to you for my words or my deeds."

"Oh, quite right," he said, lowering his voice to a chilling softness. "The question is, to whom do you answer?"

If he was trying to frighten her, he was doing a damnably good job of it. Though why was even more confusing than the menacing slant of his brows.

"At the moment, it is to my stomach," said Anna, with a laugh that belied the lump of ice in her throat. "Which is demanding some of those delectable lobster patties that the footman has just brought to the refreshment table. So if you will excuse me—"

"Not so fast." Devlin shifted again, trapping her between the marble pedestal and his unyielding-as-granite body. "I, too, am hungry, Miss Sloane...to know what it is you are hiding."

"Ye gods, were you standing near the prince when his fowling gun exploded? For it seems to me that the force of the blast must have addled your wits. Do you truly imagine there is some dark, depraved secret..." A horrible thought suddenly flashed through her mind. *Gun. Gun Room.* Good heavens, surely he couldn't think for a moment that she had some irrational grudge against the prince.

"Go on," he said slowly.

It was so absurd as to be laughable. And yet her mouth was too frozen to form a smile.

"You are mad," she managed to whisper.

The peal of a brass hand bell prevented Devlin from replying.

"Ladies and gentlemen, I have some lovely news to announce," said Lady Dunbar, after following her butler into the drawing room. "Prince Gunther is resting quite comfortably."

Glasses clinked as the guests joined Count Rupert in raising a toast to a quick recovery.

"Indeed, he wished to join us tonight," continued the countess. "However, the doctor insisted that he be prudent and remain abed until morning."

"A wise decision," said her husband, who was standing with the German contingent by the hearth.

"But what with the dismal hunting weather and the unfortunate accident, I think that the prince—and all of us—deserve a special celebration on the morrow to brighten our spirits," she continued. "So I have arranged for a visit to Craigielochen Castle, a splendidly romantic fifteenth-century ruin situated on the ocean cliffs just up the coast. Mary, Queen of Scots, is said to have visited there."

Lady Dunbar paused to smile. "And so shall we, though I daresay in far more comfortable style. There are wonderful grounds and gardens to explore, and the servants will set up a sumptuous midday picnic repast. However, you have no need to fear wind or rain. The old banquet hall is intact, and we shall dine there in case of inclement weather. The men may enjoy fishing for trout in the river, and the ladies will find all sorts of lovely vistas for sketching."

A murmur of polite approval made its way around the room.

"The carriages will be waiting to transport us there after an early breakfast," she added. "Our head gardener is predicting lovely weather, and as he is rarely wrong, we should have a very enjoyable day."

"Assuming there are no further accidents," said Devlin, just loudly enough for Anna to hear. "I would advise the prince not to walk too close to the cliff's edge."

"Just one last thing," said the countess. "To start off a festive mood early, we shall have some dancing instead of cards after supper—just an informal interlude of country reels and gavottes." A discreet wave signaled the footmen to pop open more champagne. "Though our local musicians do know how to play a waltz."

To Anna's relief, she and Devlin were joined by Colonel Polianov. At the present moment, even his austere features and sour expression were a welcome sight.

The Russian surprised her by essaying a smile. "Are you pleased by the prospect of an outing, Miss Sloane? I have been told that all English ladies have a great fondness for the outdoors."

"Yes, fresh air and some exercise will be very welcome. I am looking forward to a leisurely stroll through the gardens," answered Anna, though her mind was already planning how to evade the outing without drawing undue notice to her absence.

"Perhaps I may be permitted to escort you," said the colonel.

For an instant, Anna thought that she must have misheard him. However, Devlin's sarcastic laugh dispelled any doubts.

"There are no wild wolves or bears here in Scotland, Polianov. And if there were, Miss Sloane would likely be quite capable of defending herself." He paused. "If a pistol or rifle weren't within reach, I daresay she would slay the beast with her bare hands."

Polianov's cheeks turned a mottled red as he looked to

her. "Forgive me," he said stiffly, "but I fail to understand the very peculiar sense of humor you English have. Have I made some error in etiquette?"

"Lord Davenport's sense of humor is entirely his own," she assured him. "Please pay him no heed. You have been quite correct in your deportment." Unlike some other men.

Looking somewhat mollified, the colonel smoothed at the sleeve of his gold braided tunic. "Then might I also request the pleasure of a dance—"

"My, my, it appears you have been polishing your manners along with your medals, Colonel." Devlin's sneer had turned even more offensive. "I hadn't realized that you had taken such a sudden interest in the young lady. Dancing, long walks through the roses, private meanderings behind the bushes—just think of all the interesting opportunities."

The colonel began to sputter. "What are you suggesting, sir?"

"Simply that you'll have a great deal of time for private conversation."

"That's hardly a crime," snapped Anna, then immediately rued her choice of words when she saw the look that came to his eyes.

Polianov chose to ignore Devlin's last provocation. "Until later, Miss Sloane," he said, bowing as he stepped back several paces and turned to rejoin the group of men by the far hearth.

His departure gave Anna an opening for escape. Slipping past the pedestal, she nearly collided with Lady de Blois, who had been standing half hidden by the bouquet of flowers conversing with her brother-in-law.

"*Pardon*," she muttered in French, brushing by the pair without slowing her step. She was in no mood for lingering near the widow, whose air of self-important superiority was beginning to grate on her nerves.

Spotting Caro and their mother in conversation with the other party from London, Anna quickly circled around the punch table and found a spot next to her sister.

Whatever addled twist of mind had provoked such wild fantasies in Devlin's head, she hoped he would soon come to his senses. Sarcasm was one thing, madness was quite another.

A delusional man could be dangerous.

Devlin exhaled a silent oath as he watched the first figures of a country gavotte form on the dance floor.

Damn. Damn. Damn. He had done his infuriating best to provoke a slip of the tongue. But neither Anna nor Polianov had given anything away. The Russian's sudden interest in her might be a signal that the conspirators were rattled by the failed attempt on the prince's life and needed to quickly make alternate plans.

Or it might simply mean that Polianov, like himself, had overheard several of the London ladies earlier in the evening speculating on how large a dowry the formerly poor-as-a-churchmouse Anna was likely to get from her wealthy new brother-in-law.

As for Anna, she masked her emotions better than most hardened gamesters. He had watched her closely during the past Season and had admired how coolly and calmly she had dealt with the bevy of suitors seeking her hand. All had been treated with charming smiles and gentle grace. It had made him curious as to what feelings lay beneath the flawless skin.

He had always sensed that she had intriguing depths at

odds with the outward show of sweetness. But given how hard she was to read, Miss Anna Sloane could make a fortune in the gambling hells—that is, assuming she still desperately needed money to support her family.

Which she didn't.

The soft *slap, slap* of the capering feet seemed to set the same insistent question to dancing round and round inside his head.

So why would she involve herself in such a nefarious plot?

Devlin considered himself very adept at piecing together the parts of a complicated puzzle. But this one had him flummoxed.

The lively music ended, and the laughing couples began to drift off for refreshments and to re-form into new pairs for the next set.

The violins ran through the first few notes to test their tuning.

A waltz, as promised.

Pretending that he didn't see the Come-Hither look from Lady de Blois, Devlin moved quickly along the stone colonnade to where Anna and her sister were standing with Count Rupert and Lord Saxe-Colza.

"Miss Sloane, I believe you are promised to me for this dance."

"Have I misunderstood—" began Count Rupert.

Anna's "No" was overridden by Devlin's "Yes."

"I did request the honor of your hand as soon as Lady Dunbar announced there would be a waltz," he added. "I should be wounded beyond measure if you tell me that you've already forgotten."

Count Rupert conceded with good grace. "It seems that

Lord Davenport's claim takes precedence over mine. I shall wait until the next one, for I'm sure our hostess will have the musicians play another."

A smile remained on Anna's lips but it came nowhere near her eyes. "The next one is most definitely yours, sir. And if any other gentleman claims a prior promise, he is telling an untruth."

"Now, who among us would do something so dishonorable?" murmured Devlin.

Anna didn't deign to reply.

"We had better take our place on the dance floor." As he placed a hand on the small of her back, he felt an unexpected pulse of electricity jolt through his palm. He would have dismissed it as anger heating her blood, but he felt her body react with equal surprise.

Neither of them said a word as he guided her to the least crowded corner of the polished parquet. For him, it was because speech was momentarily impossible—the jolt had sizzled up his arm and somehow tied his tongue in a terrible knot. He couldn't talk, he could only feel—the graceful sway of her hips beneath his hand, the soft swish of her silken skirts against his trousers. Tonight she was wearing a dusky lavender-colored gown trimmed with accents of a darker shade of plum. A perfectly ripe plum.

No wonder most of the men were eyeing her hungrily.

But all consciousness of anyone other than Anna disappeared in a blur as Devlin turned and they came close together in the intimate embrace of the waltz. Hands touching, heat thrumming—awareness spiked through him as the first notes of the music filled the air, and all at once his skin began to prickle and a tiny trickle of sweat started to tease down his spine.

Cursing himself for a fool, he somehow managed to move through the first intricate steps of the dance without tripping over his feet. His only consolation was that she, too, seemed affected by the same strange force.

A swirling turn seemed to dispel some of its power. Devlin recalled that he had brought her out here to prod her, to pressure her into giving him some answers about her recent activities. But he found himself caught up in the rhythm of the dance and the way their bodies moved in perfect harmony.

In a moment—I will confront her in a moment.

Anna spun through the moves with an effortless grace, feeling light as a fluff of eiderdown in his arms.

"I assume you did not ask me out here simply for the pleasure of dancing," she finally said, after they had whirled through another few turns. Her voice sounded a little fluttery, like the whisper-fine frothing of lace peeking out from beneath the hem of her gown.

"Correct," he replied.

"Well?"

"I—I seem to have forgotten the reason." Her scent filled his nostrils, making it hard to concentrate. "Let me think for a moment."

"You had better hurry," she said. "The dance is half over."

"Is it?" Time seemed to hang suspended. The other couples were naught but a whirling blur of jeweltone colors blending with flashes of black and white.

She looked away, to a spot somewhere in the distance over his right shoulder, her mouth pursing in a pensive frown. It gave him a brief moment to study her face and while he could see a quiet strength and stubborn resolution subtly shaping the fine-boned features, there was not a hint of guile or deception.

Around and around they turned, matching each other step for step.

But he would not be the first man ever to be taken in by a lady and her air of assumed innocence.

"Lord Davenport."

Another slow spin.

"Lord Davenport, the music has ended."

"So it has." Devlin reluctantly released her. "We shall talk another time."

Anna looked at him as if his wits had gone wandering. To somewhere beyond the moon.

"I hope that come morning, sir, you'll have realized that you are mistaken in thinking me...something which I am not."

Chapter Thirteen

Anna was already up and sitting on the window seat when her maid came in with a freshly brushed carriage cape for the morning's outing.

"Did you not sleep well, Mademoiselle Anna?" asked Josette. "Once again, you have dark circles under your eyes."

"Fitful dreams," she admitted.

"Shall I fetch you a tisane from the kitchens?"

"No, no, I am fine. Just a little restless, is all."

"Never fear, I know a little trick for disguising the shadows," said Josette. "A touch of rose lotion, a dab of rice powder, and *voilà*."

"How very fortunate that you possess so many different skills," murmured Anna, trying to sound appreciative though the state of her complexion was the least of her concerns.

The armoire door opened and closed. "The oppressive weather and the injury to the prince seem to have dampened everyone's spirits. I can't say that English house parties appear to be very enjoyable."

"We are in Scotland, where everything has a little sharper edge to it," quipped Anna. Eyeing the streaks of blue peeking through the scudding clouds, she added, "Lady Dunbar will be happy to see that the sun appears to be shining on her outing."

"Will all the guests be going?" asked Josette, as she selected a slate blue walking dress and fluffed out the skirts.

"Yes," answered Anna, deciding not to mention her own plans to abscond from the group picnic. A part of her regretted missing the outing. The historic castle and its scenic setting would likely afford some interesting inspiration for Emmalina's new adventures, but in her current unsettled state of mind, she preferred to escape for the day in her writing.

Especially as it ensured that Count Alessandro and the villainous Prince Malatesta would be the only men she would encounter.

"How nice." Josette held the gown at arm's length and cast a critical eye on how the sunlight played over the soft merino wool. "I think I would rather you wear the jade-colored gown. This shade of blue is not quite right for a seaside setting."

"I trust your judgment," said Anna, thinking that a burlap sack would serve just as well for curling up in a corner of her room with pen and paper.

"*Bon.*" A small shake set off a flutter of the smoky green fabric. "Come, you had better begin dressing, so as not to be late for breakfast."

Anna dutifully donned her clothing and allowed her maid to begin arranging her hair in a simple chignon.

"I daresay you will be spending some time with that handsome Lord Davenport." Josette seemed in a talkative mood this morning. "Perhaps an interlude alone? Downstairs, they say that the ancient castle has many lovely paths through the gardens and vistas looking out over the sea."

"Not if I can help it," replied Anna.

Josette paused in threading the hairpins into place. "*Non?*"

"Lord Davenport has...well, there seems to be a misunderstanding between us. For the time being, I would rather avoid him."

"With men, there is always some sort of misunderstanding. It is part of the challenge."

Anna thought about that for a moment. "You are far more daring than I am. You seem to embrace the idea of living dangerously, while I...I fear that I am less adventurous."

"Oh, I think perhaps you underestimate yourself." Josette artfully loosened a curl and stood back to survey her handiwork.

For an instant Anna wondered whether the maid had found some of her discarded manuscript notes. She was usually very careful about burning the scraps, but of late she had been making some mistakes.

"Perhaps." Anna sighed. "To be honest, I'm not sure I know myself very well these days."

The maid placed the brush and box of pins back in place.

"But never mind—I seem to be in a strange mood this morning." After submitting to the dabs of lotion and powder, she rose and took up her shawl. "You, too, ought to have a holiday. Please feel free to walk into town and explore the shops. I won't be needing any assistance until suppertime."

"Thank you, mademoiselle," said Josette.

Anna murmured a vague reply as she left the room. Her mind was already preoccupied with how to avoid the picnic without making a fuss. With any luck, few people would even notice her absence.

To her relief, Caro was already seated at the breakfast table.

"I need your assistance," murmured Anna as she slid into her chair. "I wish to avoid the trip to the castle, but would prefer to do it without raising a fuss."

Her sister's face brightened at the prospect of being involved in a little intrigue. "In other words, you wish it to be a secret."

Anna nodded. "Any ideas?"

Caro chewed thoughtfully on a piece of her buttered toast. "Ah, what about this?" she suggested after a quick swallow. "You sneak back to your quarters after we have finished with our meal. When the carriages arrive, I'll wait until the very last moment and then quietly inform Lady Dunbar that you've fallen ill with a stomach indisposition and don't wish to cast a pall over the picnic by announcing the fact. The countess will no doubt be grateful that her kitchens aren't called into question and will be equally discreet."

"Excellent," replied Anna. "As I've said before, you ought to consider writing novels as well as poetry."

Her sister grinned. "I'd rather be asked to assist with a more exciting plot, but I suppose this will have to do."

"I hope the only one experiencing any excitement will be Emmalina," said Anna. "My plans are to enjoy a very quiet workday with pen and paper."

"Perhaps," mused Caro, "the craggy cliffs and ocean

vistas will inspire a poem..." Her words trailed off as McClellan entered the room "...rather than the impulse to push a certain person into the churning waves below."

"Do try to control your emotions." Anna felt a little hypocritical offering such advice and quickly changed the subject. "Um, speaking of inspiration, would you mind making a few sketches of the castle and how it is situated on the cliffs. It sounds like it would make a perfect place for Malatesta to imprison Emmalina."

"Very well. But I favor the brooding ruins we spotted above the loch. You know, the one that looked like it had deep, dark dungeons cut into the ancient rock and subterranean passageways leading down to the water's edge."

"It sounds as if Craigielochen Castle might have its fair share of dungeons and secret tunnels. The North Sea allows clandestine ship travel between our Sceptered Isle and the Continent."

"A good point."

Anna allowed a small smile. "I've had to spend some time plotting how Emmalina came to be in Scotland."

Caro poured herself a fresh cup of tea. "Novels take a good deal more thought than poems. Unless, of course, one is writing an epic like Lord Byron's *Childe Harold's Pilgrimage*," she mused, slowly stirring in a generous dollop of cream. "But I shall need a great deal more experience in Life before I can ever attempt something as worldly as that."

"Cynical" was a better word for the poem. "I would hope that you never become as jaded as Lord Byron," murmured Anna. "At heart, he isn't a very happy soul."

"But one must suffer for Art," said Caro.

"Within moderation," replied Anna. She made herself

swallow several bites of a scone, even though she wasn't feeling at all hungry. "Great suffering does not guarantee great art."

"If it did, this current manuscript would be your best book by far," said her sister. "Ha, ha, ha."

"That's *not* amusing." Anna slanted a look out the bank of leaded windows. "Speaking of my book, I see the carriages coming up the drive." After a tiny pause, she added, "Please wait until the last moment before informing Lady Dunbar." She wasn't quite sure why she was being so secretive. Devlin's oblique suggestion that the prince's injury had been a deliberate act of sabotage must have put her nerves on edge. "And try not to let anyone overhear you."

"Oh, wait. One last thing—what if Lord Davenport inquires after you?" asked Caro.

"Just tell him I am feeling unwell. It won't be a lie." Suddenly recalling Polianov's attentions the previous evening, she added, "If the colonel asks after me, you may tell him the same thing."

"Leave it to me," assured her sister. "I am getting to be quite good at helping to manage these affairs of intrigue."

"Perhaps too good," said Anna. She hesitated, again thinking of Devlin's strangely menacing statements. "I don't mean to sound alarming, but please promise me that you will not go off alone with Polianov during the picnic. It's just a feeling, but I don't quite trust him."

"You think he might be a dastardly villain up to no good?" Caro's eyes slowly widened. "How exciting."

"Don't let your imagination fly away with you," she counseled. "The only dastardly plots going on are the ones that will take shape in my head. That is, assuming I get some peace and quiet for writing."

Seeing the guests at the other end of the table rise and head off toward the entrance hall, Anna pushed back her plate. "Come, we had best be going. I shall duck into one of the side corridors and then take refuge in the library. I've brought my notebook and will work there for a few hours while the servants finish their morning tasks upstairs. There are several reference books I wish to consult on what sort of plantings are typically found in a Scottish garden."

"It's a pity that you will miss seeing the castle," murmured Caro, as they left the breakfast room. "For however accurate books are, there is no substitute for the actual ambiance of a place to stir inspiration."

"Art demands sacrifice," quipped Anna. "With any luck, the Muse will offer enough inspiration on her own to keep me busy for the day."

From his vantage point high in the tower, Devlin watched the line of carriages set off down the drive. So far, his plan was rolling along quite smoothly. With the castle empty of all but the servants for the day, he had the perfect opportunity to pursue his suspicions.

Starting with the mysterious Miss Anna Sloane.

"Two can play at manipulations," he muttered, flexing his fingers. Picking locks was a skill that he, too, possessed. "What is good for the goose is good for the gander—let us see how the lady likes having a stranger pry into her most private secrets."

He waited for a quarter hour longer, then returned to the stairwell and made his way down to the corridor where Anna was quartered. *Patience, patience.* The precision required to make his automata had taught him to be very patient. From the shelter of a linen closet, he waited and watched, making sure that her lady's maid was not still at work.

After a lengthy interlude, satisfied that he would not be interrupted, Devlin slipped from his hiding place and with a deft twist of his metal probe, released her door's lock and entered her rooms.

The sitting room was decorated in heathered hues of stripes and floral chintzes. He made a cursory search of the cabinets and desk, though he sensed that her secrets would be hidden in a more private spot. As he drew a deep breath, the tantalizing hint of her fragrance seemed to wrap around him like a sinuous serpent and draw him toward the bed-chamber.

As he entered, Devlin tried to keep his eyes averted from the carved tester bed, where the faint rumpling of the coverlet stirred an unwilling reaction somewhere far beneath his brain.

Focus, he reminded himself. Thorncroft was not paying him to think with his privy parts.

Forcing his attention back to the task at hand, he approached the massive armoire and began a careful search through the clothing and bandboxes within its cavernous depths.

"Damnation."

With all the fancy frills and accessories needed for dressing in style, ladies had far more places in which to hide any incriminating evidence.

After finally finishing with checking inside the toes of her evening slippers—did a lady *really* require a dozen different pairs to appear *au courant*?—he shut the doors and moved on to the ornate oak bureau.

Nothing. Though the delicate lace of the folded under-garments caused another clench of distraction.

Turning around, he slowly surveyed the rest of the room. The escritoire seemed to be in frequent use. Papers were piled atop a small sketchbook, and several pens were poking up from the holder by the inkwell. As for the old mahogany tea chest, the thick, curling tendrils of the potted ivy nearly obscured the set of drawers. Likely they hadn't been opened since the last century...

A flicker of sunlight momentarily illuminated the dark wood before giving way to a scudding cloud. Devlin crossed the carpet and crouched down for a closer look. Sure enough, the inside of the keyhole showed a telltale glint of bright brass. The lock had been worked recently. More than a few times, judging by how much of the tarnish had been rubbed off.

"Let's see what you are hiding, shall we?" he murmured, once again drawing the steel probe from the sheath inside his boot.

The lock answered with a friendly little *snick.*

Devlin slid the drawer open, revealing a small portfolio bound in burgundy-colored Moroccan leather. Seizing it with both hands, he snapped open the cover and eagerly thumbed through the sheaf of papers.

All of which were blank.

Bloody Hell. Blowing out a disgusted sigh, he was about to drop it back in the drawer when he spotted a dog-eared corner of paper sticking up from beneath a pasteboard box of pencils and pen nibs.

He cautiously lifted it up and saw yet another pile of paper. The top sheet was covered with writing in a neat, feminine hand.

His hesitation lasted for only an instant. He would skim through the first few pages, and if it were a personal diary of girlish hopes and feelings, he would put the rest back unread. His unmerciful teasing to the contrary, he did have some scruples about violating a lady's privacy.

Taking up the pile—ye gods, it felt more like a novel than a diary—Devlin carried it over to the diamond-paned window. The script was rather small. To make out the letters, he angled the first page into the light and then began to read.

After reaching the bottom, he made himself go over it again before turning to the next page.

Perhaps he needed spectacles, for the words weren't making any sense. Unless...

No. Impossible.

Devlin made himself finish a few more pages, then took a random look at various sections throughout the manuscript, just to be sure he wasn't mistaken.

"Bloody Hell."

This time he said it aloud. Of all the things he had imagined that Anna was hiding, this was certainly not one of them.

And yet, the truth was undeniable. Even if the names "Emmalina" and "Count Alessandro" hadn't been familiar, the prose style was immediately recognizable.

He wondered what the *ton* would say if they ever learned that one of the most popular gentlemen in all of London was not a "he" but a "she."

On second thought, it was too gruesome to contemplate. Gossip was a blood sport in Town. The tabbies would tear her limb from literary limb.

Frowning, Devlin considered what he ought to do about

his discovery. But as he contemplated the conundrum, his gaze couldn't stop from straying back to the writing on the page...

Good Lord, where had she learned about a man doing *that* in the throes of amorous arousal? He quickly turned the page.

Or *that*?

His brows shot up. This would no doubt be Sir Sharpe Quill's best-selling novel yet. Assuming the printed pages didn't ignite in spontaneous combustion before they reached the bookshops.

And yet, despite all the heated passion, there were several little things that Anna did not seem to get quite right.

Which for some reason was rather pleasing.

Devlin was about to continue—in spite of its small flaws, the scene was becoming irresistibly interesting—when he heard the outer door open and shut.

Damnation. The chambermaids had no reason to be entering the rooms at this hour. Moving silently across the carpet, he peeked through the half-open connecting portal.

Improvise! He had a moment—maybe two—to decide on a strategy.

Chapter Fourteen

Stepping back to the center of the room, Devlin shot a quick look around and then squared his shoulders as he made up his mind to take the bull by the horns. Flight was not an option. And besides, the coming confrontation should prove extremely...

Explosive?

Anna shouldered open the door, her attention focused on the open notebook in her hands. "Drat," she muttered, not looking up. "What a pity there are no wolves left in Scotland. Their howls would have added a nicely menacing touch to the midnight scene on the moors..."

She would have bumped into him if he hadn't made a sudden noise.

"Grrrr."

Her feet stilled, her head snapped up.

"Why not simply add a pack of predators?" said Devlin. "After all, you are writing fiction, not fact." He gave a little wave of the manuscript. "Readers will allow you a little leeway with the truth if it adds to the story."

Anna's mouth went through a series of tiny contortions, ending in a perfect "O" of outrage.

Seeing as she had not yet mustered the powers of speech, Devlin pressed his advantage. "Speaking of stories, what an interesting plot twist we have here. Who would have guessed that the angelically prim and proper Miss Anna Sloane is really the wildly adventurous—and aggressively erotic—Sir Sharpe Quill?"

She had the grace to blush. Or perhaps it was fury that was bringing the beguiling shade of pink to her cheeks.

"Not I," he went on. "Even though I am considered to have a *very* evil mind."

A shiver of silence hung between them, as Anna slowly drew in a measured breath. "You are not only evil," she rasped. "You are wicked."

"Talk about wicked." He waved the pages again, setting off a crackling of paper. "Tsk, tsk."

Teasing her was irresistible. It was delightfully delicious to watch the play of emotions animate her lovely face. Normally, she kept her feelings hidden beneath a mask of polite good cheer, but at the moment, her features were far more expressive.

If those alluring green eyes were daggers, he would be flayed alive.

"You have had your fun, sir. Now hand back my pages," snapped Anna. "At once."

He pulled them back out of her reach.

"Do *not* trifle with me, Lord Davenport," she warned.

"Or what, Miss Sloane? You'll shoot me with one of Manton's pretty little pocket pistols?"

Sparks flashed on the tips of her golden lashes. "I have

a deadline to meet. So yes, I'm prepared to cut out your liver with my book knife if need be."

"I believe you would," he murmured.

She held out her hand.

"And what would be my fate if I were to make your little secret known to the public?"

"Oh, fie, sir. You wouldn't dare!"

The challenge stirred some Inner Demon. He felt a devilish smile form on his lips. "*Moi?* The Devil Davenport." He lowered his voice to a taunting whisper. "Surely you know by now that I have no scruples. About anything."

Anna's eyes flared wide in alarm and then steeled to a razored stare. "Give. Me. Back. My. Manuscript."

The demand awoke several more imps of Satan, who promptly joined the Demon in chorusing yet another provocation.

"But I haven't finished this chapter." He glanced down at the page and began reading aloud.

> *At the sound of footsteps on the marble tiles, Emmalina whirled around, clutching her towel tighter to her dripping wet body. Steam rose in vaporous clouds from the sunken bath, and yet she had no trouble identifying that all too familiar smile through the swirling mist.*
>
> *"You ought not be here," she said, belatedly aware that the cloth ended several inches above her navel.*

"Stop it," muttered Anna.

His smile stretched wider as he picked up where he had left off:

With a husky laugh, Alessandro put his hand on her quivering breast...

"Hmm, not bad. But don't you think it might be even more provocative if it read 'quivering mound of peach-colored flesh' instead?"

Anna uttered a very unladylike oath. "Why does every creature in Creation think he—or she—is a writer?"

Instead of responding to the remark, Devlin resumed reading aloud:

"Of course I shouldn't be here," he replied. "But when have you known me to obey anyone's rules, save for my own..."

"Hmm, sounds very much like me. Dare I hope that I've served to inspire your artistic imagination?"

"You flatter yourself, sir," said Anna tartly. "Ah, but wait, now that you mention it..."

Devlin wasn't sure he liked the new gleam that suddenly came to life in her eyes.

"Perhaps I shall have Emmalina discover that Alessandro has a secret passion—that of fashioning intricate *automata*." She tapped at her chin, letting the words sink in. "I wonder, what should I say he does with them? Sell them to the Sultan for a fortune in precious gems?"

All at once, the game of teasing was no longer proving quite so amusing. "Miss Sloane—"

"No, wait! I have it!" she exclaimed. "Alessandro will design an ingenious winged eagle, complete with real feathers, and just when the dastardly Prince Malatesta and his cohorts have Emmalina and Alessandro trapped at the top of a remote castle tower, he will push all sorts of intricate levers and buttons—and lo and behold, it will whir to life and fly them to safety."

"Let's return to the current story, shall we?" growled Devlin.

For the first time since she had entered the room, Anna smiled. Or perhaps it was better described as a smirk. "Oh, but we authors are always anxious to capture future plot twists and work out the details before they slip away. Trust me, ideas can be slippery as eels."

"I would rather see this one wriggle out of your fingers."

"The manuscript, Lord Davenport." Once again, she held out her hand. "I'm willing to negotiate. You keep my secret safe and I shall do the same with yours." A regretful sigh. "Though I really do like the eagle idea."

"Are you blackmailing me, Miss Sloane?" Ye god, writers were more ruthless than he had imagined.

"Call it a meeting of creative minds."

Watching the heated rise and fall of her bosom was enough to make a man's brain go blank. If that weren't enough, several honey-gold curls had come loose and were caressing the shapely curve of one shell pink ear.

If only a meeting of bodies would follow the cerebral connection.

Pulling a pained grimace, he handed over the pages.

"Thank you." Anna quickly returned the manuscript to its original hiding place and relocked the drawer with a small brass key pulled from a concealed pocket in her cuff.

"Clever," he commented.

"My maid is a very talented designer. She tells me that in France, it's called a *poche de billet-doux*."

"A pocket for love notes," he murmured.

"Yes, well, ladies must learn all sorts of little sub-terfuges." Anna smoothed the lace back in place. "That is, if they wish to have the same freedom as men to be a little adventurous."

"You have certainly created an inspiring example for those of your sex in Emmalina. However, speaking of sex, your characterization of Count Alessandro leaves a little to be desired."

Her expression turned a little wary. "In what way?"

"For one thing, a real rake wouldn't put his hand *here*." Devlin traced a fingertip along the ridge of her collarbone. "He would put it *here*."

She squeaked and backed up a few steps, then edged around the corner of the armoire.

Devlin followed, all primal male instincts now fully aroused. "You see, we men are, at heart, primitive crea-tures. The trappings of civilized manners often yield to the basic hunter-gatherer behavior of our ancient ancestors."

"M-my father was an expert on primitive cultures," said Anna. "I've read all about your primal urges."

"Reading is all very well, Miss Sloane. But if you wish to capture the real essence of animal attraction between a man and a woman in your novels, you ought to experience it in the flesh."

"I don't need to actually load and fire a cannon to com-prehend what it must feel like, Lord Davenport," she coun-tered. "I can do research and read first-hand accounts—"

Her voice cut off as he hooked a finger in the "V" of her gown's neckline. "Trust me, certain details get lost in the translation." Probing a little deeper beneath the fabric, Devlin drew a caress along the top edge of her corset.

She let out a little gasp.

"You see, certain sensations are not easy to describe in words." Delving past the lacy trim, his teasing finger dipped into the narrow gap between her breasts. "They require a skilled writer who understands the nuances of language."

Her skin began to quiver as the beat of her heart turned into a pulsing *thud, thud, thud.*

That she responded to his touch sent a surge of savage satisfaction through his body.

Oh yes, I am evil and wicked.

"Now pay attention," he whispered. "If a man were truly bold, he might even attempt…"

Anna pulled away and made another skittish retreat. She was now backed up against the far wall.

"You seem to have run out of room to maneuver." Devlin grinned as he closed the gap between them. "Now, I wonder—what would Emmalina do?"

Anna swallowed hard, mesmerized for a moment by the fire-bright gleam of his amber eyes. This must be how a helpless fawn felt when coming face to face with a prowling panther in the dead of night, she thought.

But I am not a helpless fawn.

"If you recall from *The Orphan's Revenge*, Emmalina knows some *very* underhanded and effective ways for dealing with aggressive men."

"Ouch," murmured Devlin. And yet, like an arrogant beast, supremely sure of his superior strength, he came a little closer. "You wouldn't dare."

She shifted her knee. "That's exactly the wrong thing to say to an intrepid female who has been forced by Cruel Fate to learn how to defend her honor."

Devlin began to laugh.

Anna tried to scowl, but instead her lips twitched upward. "Really, sir, this is absurd."

He seemed to be staring at the tiny pulsepoint beneath her jaw. She felt her blood begin to thrum and her heart kick up to an even faster beat.

"Is it?" he asked, lowering his mouth to within a hair's breadth of her throat.

Thump, thump. Her flesh began to tingle as heat spread from the pulsing point and spiraled downward.

"By the by, you have a very lovely neck. Its arch is as graceful as that of a regal swan."

Her breath seemed to stick in her lungs for just an instant. "D-do you always attempt to seduce your women by comparing them to birds?"

"That depends." Devlin touched the tip of his tongue to the throbbing spot and let out a soft chuckle on feeling her shiver.

"O-on w-what?"

"On the woman, of course." He licked again. And again.

"You shouldn't be doing this." Anna drew in a shuddering breath. "*I* shouldn't be doing this."

"Consider it research." He raised his head, and she was instantly aware of the loss of his warmth. "As I said, it's important to apply the same meticulous attention to detail that you show toward inanimate objects—like pistols—to your hero and heroine."

"Are you really criticizing my love scenes?"

"Merely saying they could be even better."

Anna tried to spear him with a daggered look, but feared that amusement was dulling its edge. "Really, sir. No novelist likes to hear that her prose leaves something to be desired."

"Your prose is delightful. I am simply trying to expand your knowledge of the subtle details of lovemaking."

"I suppose I must defer to your greater experience in the matter." Anna slanted a glance at the door. "However, what you suggest is too...dangerous."

"I distinctly remember you saying that a lady ought to be a little dangerous." Devlin leaned in again, this time to feather a kiss down to the base of her throat. "Besides, Emmalina is more than a little dangerous."

"I'm not Emmalina." Her hands, however, seemed to disagree. They crept up the front of his coat and set on the slope of his shoulders. "Well, not really."

"You don't sound very certain. I think, perhaps, we ought to engage in a spot of character development. Isn't that what authors do?"

"But—"

Devlin pulled away and in the space of several heartbeats he rebolted the door and returned to her side. "I doubt that any of the castle servants are as proficient as we are in lock picking," he murmured as he gathered her into a more intimate embrace. "Now, what page were we on?"

"I—I don't know. I seem to have lost my place." Anna swallowed hard. "I think I must start a new chapter."

"Ah, an excellent suggestion."

Do I dare?

The Inner Saint was warning that nothing but trouble could come from unleashing untamed passions. While the Inner Sinner was urging that caution—along with all the cursedly confining rules of Society—be cast to the wind.

"I'm not Emmalina," she whispered again, hoping that voicing the reminder aloud would help her resolve just who she really was.

Devlin pressed a kiss to her brow. "The Creative Muse might have an argument about that."

"I—I can't think straight when you do that," protested Anna.

"Sometimes it's best not to think, but to simply trust your feelings."

"But primal passions can be so very dangerous."

She felt his mouth quirk against her skin. "Ah, that word again." A note of humor shaded his voice, along with a softer undertone she couldn't quite define. "You must decide for yourself how much risk you are willing to take."

For a ruthless rake, he was acting with surprising gentleness. As if, in spite of all his predatory wiles, he was just as uncertain as she was about what scene ought to be written on the page.

Passion—their actions would be inscribed in indelible ink. There would be no chance for revisions, no crumpling of the paper and starting from scratch.

"Lord Davenport..."

"Devlin," he murmured. "Given the fact that we know each other's intimate secrets, formality seems a little silly."

"Devlin." His name, like his kisses, felt nice on her lips. Anna slipped her hands beneath the lapels of his coat and let her fingers explore the muscled contours of his shoulders. "For an indolent idler, you are surprisingly strong."

"I have my weaknesses. They are what most of Society sees."

"Why is it that you hide your talents under a haze of brandy and reckless behavior?"

"You, of all people, ought to know the myriad reasons for that, Anna," he answered.

"Yes, but I've always thought that for a man, it's different." She liked the way he felt. The hard chiseling of his shape was softened by a pulsing warmth. Drat the thin linen of his shirt—she itched to feel his skin against hers. "You are allowed to pursue your passions in every form."

"Only lowly peasants work with their hands," said Devlin in reply. "That I wish to refill the family coffers through the sweat of my own labors would be even more shocking to the *ton* than your plying the pen of a published author."

They locked eyes.

"You sell your artistic creations," she guessed. "And then use the money to restore your family estate?"

"A Herculean task, but yes. That is the idea." A sigh. "There, you know yet another sordid secret about me," he added.

"It appears that your horns and cloven hooves are just a clever disguise," she said, watching the amber depths of his gaze turn a little more molten.

"Don't deceive yourself," said Devlin a little roughly. "I am no angel."

Anna felt a sudden flutter inside her. Something akin to a winged creature breaking free from its cage. Her hands came out of his coat and entangled in his long hair.

"I—I don't think that I am either."

He held himself very still. "Are you sure?"

She hovered for an instant between Heaven and Hell.

And then took the plunge. "Yes. Very sure."

Devlin needed no further urging. With a low groan, he kissed her, a hard, demanding embrace that made her body feel boneless.

Slumping back against the wall, she twined her fingers

in his silky strands and opened her mouth fully, reveling in his textures, his taste. His heat.

A honeyed warmth seemed to melt through her limbs. No wonder she had more than once heard a fleeting phrase whispered in the ballrooms of Mayfair.

Sweeter than Sin.

"Sin." The sound stirred deep in her throat.

Devlin framed her face between his palms and moved his lips to the corner of her mouth. "Some would say so, sweeting," he murmured. "But in truth, Sin is not so easy to define. It can have a multitude of meanings."

"A philosopher? Again you surprise me," replied Anna, running the back of her knuckles along line of his jaw. "You had better be careful or your reputation as a dissolute wastrel will be ruined."

"Ruined." His husky laugh tickled against her flesh. "Ah, now that's another word open to interpretation. But as someone skilled in the nuances of language, you know that."

"I—I would rather not talk about l-language," stammered Anna. Speech was becoming increasingly difficult as he tilted up her chin and trailed a flutter of gossamer kisses down her neck.

"I agree." His tongue dipped into the hollow of her throat. "No words, just sensations."

A shiver skittered down her spine.

Devlin must have sensed her reaction. He laughed again, his breath a little like a puff of smoke, redolent with a hint of flames and fire.

Impelled by a need she didn't try to name, Anna caught the tails of his cravat. A tug and the knot came undone. Another pull sent the length of linen floating down to the floor.

Devlin responded by untying the tapes of her gown. She felt the fabric slip from her shoulders. A lick of cool air tickled down her arms as he slid off her sleeves, allowing the garment to bunch around her waist.

His fingers slipped around to her back, and she felt them graze the lacing of her corset. "You ladies really do make things difficult for us ruthless savages. Luckily, I'm used to working with my hands."

The delicate knot yielded to his deft touch. A series of tiny tugs loosened the silken strings. Anna sucked in a breath as the lace and whalebone stays pulled away from her skin.

"That's better," murmured Devlin. "You're beautiful," he added, gazing at her bared breasts. "Just like the Botticelli painting of Venus."

"N-no fluted clamshell," she stammered as a blush painted her flesh pink. She knew she ought to feel embarrassed, but the look in his eyes stirred a very different sentiment.

"Even better," he rasped, shifting his stance. "It would only crack under my weight."

His words trailed off as his mouth closed over her right nipple.

Anna nearly fainted—not from shock but from pleasure. The wet warmth sent a shiver spiraling through her body. Releasing a moan, she twined her fingers in his hair, reveling in the texture of the dark strands.

Devlin teased his tongue round and round—the tip of flesh felt on fire. Just when she was sure she couldn't bear it a moment longer, he released her.

Only to shift his caress.

He was right—there were no words for this.

She must have cried out, for Devlin lifted his head and suddenly his lips were on hers. "Hush, sweeting," he whispered, his voice a little ragged.

Anna clung to his shoulders, feeling weak in the knees. Her whole body was feeling strange, as if all her bones were melting to mush. "But I need..."

"I know what you need." He began hiking her skirts up. "And damn me for a scoundrel, but I need it too."

The ridge of his arousal was pressing hard against her belly. Easing a hand down and between their rumpled clothing, she found the fastening of his trousers.

The swooshing of fabric echoed the little gasps and groans now swirling through the air.

"Devlin." Muffling her cry against his coat, Anna slid her palm along the steeled velvet length of his cock.

In answer, he found the slit in her drawers and delved his fingers deep into her feminine folds.

Was it possible to expire from ecstasy?

The question hung hazily in her head for a brief moment. And then, as the head of his cock nudged between her thighs, all rational thought dissolved in a sigh.

"Spread your legs, Anna," urged Devlin.

Flesh against flesh—the intimacy was almost too much to bear. She arched up, wanting more.

More.

His tip teased over her slickened skin. With a groan, Devlin took hold of her hips.

"Yes, yes," she gasped, hardly recognizing the smoke-dark sound that slipped from her throat.

Closing her eyes, Anna leaned back and surrendered herself to the moment.

Chapter Fifteen

Thump, thump, THUD.

Anna slowly realized that the ever-loudening sounds were not her own hammering heartbeat but rather the efforts of someone trying to open the door.

The Devil take me.

Devlin froze, their bodies on the brink of joining.

Shooting up straight, she shook off the haze of passion and tried to move for the sitting room. But with Devlin's arms around her and her drooping skirts now tangling her feet, she would have fallen had not he managed to keep his hold.

"Damn," he swore, sounding just as fuzzed as she felt.

The latch rattled again.

"Oh, Lord," she whispered aloud, then in a louder voice called, "Just a moment! I'm coming."

Frantically feeling around the bunched folds of her gown, Anna found her sleeves and tried to thrust her arms inside them.

"Stop wiggling for a moment. I need to lace up your

corset." Devlin expertly threaded the strings through the tiny hooks, though she felt his hands were a little shaky. "Halfway done," he muttered, turning his efforts to fastening his trousers. "But it will do."

Anna yanked her bodice into place, madly searching her befuddled brain for some way to stave off scandal. "Oh, Lord," she repeated, casting a beseeching look to the heavens.

Her gaze stopped at the window...

Devlin followed her eyes. Leaving his shirttails flapping, he scooped up his coat, rushed to the sill and flung the casement open. "There's a wide enough ledge. I should be able to make my way around to your sister's room." One booted leg swung up through the opening. "Let us hope she's left the latch undone. I would rather not have to kick through the glass."

"On second thought—" she began, suddenly picturing what a dreadfully long drop it was to the ground.

Devlin cut her off. "There's no time to argue."

Given their disheveled state, he was right. "Please be careful."

"Don't worry. I've no desire to end up splattered like a pigeon egg on the stone terrace."

"Wait!" she hissed. "W-we need to talk. Meet me by the garden fountain in a half hour."

He hesitated, then gave a curt nod.

"You..." But he was already gone.

"Mademoiselle?" came Josette's muffled call.

"Yes, yes!" called Anna. Pushing a twist of loosened hair behind her ear, she hurried to the door and threw back the bolt. Thank God there was a good excuse for her disheveled appearance.

"Mademoiselle!" Josette quickly mastered her show of surprise. "I thought you were with the picnic party. Is—is something amiss?"

"I was feeling unwell at breakfast, and so I begged off from the excursion," answered Anna in a rush. "I came up to lie down and did not wish to be disturbed by the housemaids, so I decided to lock the door." Pressing her palms to her temples, she added, "And then I fell asleep and was plagued by horrible nightmares."

Her maid's expression remained impassive, save for a tiny twitch. Along with mastering the art of designing beautiful clothes, the French had perfected the subtle gesture of arching a skeptical brow.

Following Josette's gaze, Anna quickly tugged at a pesky little lump in her bodice, belatedly realizing that her half-unlaced corset was sitting askew. "Is it me, or is it awfully chilly in here?" she asked, snatching up the shawl she had earlier dropped on the sideboard and wrapping it tightly around her shoulders.

"Yes, there does seem to be a draft..." Her maid moved around the tea table and angled a look into the bedroom. "*Alors!* Look, the window is wide open."

Anna's gaze was instead riveted to a spot on the carpet, where Devlin's cravat lay in a tangled coil. "A gust must have blown the latch loose," she called, taking two rapid strides and kicking the offending garment under the sofa.

"Hmmph. We must ask the housemaids to be more careful," called Josette, as she leaned out to grab the heavy brass frame and swing it back into place.

Had Josette spotted the telltale twist of linen? Impossible to know, but her maid had awfully sharp eyes, especially when it came to matters of fashion.

Reminded of her own sartorial faux pas, Anna drew the shawl even tighter across her chest. "Thank you. That's much better."

"Shall I fetch a pot of chamomile tea from the kitchens?" asked her maid. "Its calming effect may help you to enjoy a restful sleep."

"Actually, I am feeling wide awake now," replied Anna. "Indeed, seeing as the weather is so nice, I think a walk outdoors may be just the tonic I need."

Another twitch of the raven-dark brow. "Would you prefer to change into another gown? That one appears a trifle wrinkled from your nap."

"Oh, no need to bother. I shall just smooth out the skirts."

"I can do that."

"No, no. I promised you the afternoon off. I'm perfectly capable of seeing to myself," she insisted. "We shall have to change for supper soon enough."

"As you wish." Josette put away the pile of freshly pressed handkerchiefs she had brought with her and quietly withdrew from the room.

Expelling a harried sigh, Anna fumbled her clothing into some semblance of order. The corset would have to remain undone, but her fretful tossing could explain the loosened lacing. After fishing out Devlin's cravat from under the sofa and hiding it beneath her shawl, she headed off to the side staircase leading down to the gardens.

Anna was early, noted Devlin, as he made his way past the privet hedge. So much for his hope that her resolve might wilt once she had a moment to reconsider how dangerous a path she was treading.

Yes, dangerous. Despite his making light of the word, he was concerned about drawing her any deeper into the shadowy netherworld of intrigue and deceit. Yes, she might have a spine of steel. But…

Unlike me, her heart is unblackened by sordid realities.

"I thought perhaps you might not come." Anna rose from her perch on the fountain's marble pool as he approached.

"I considered absenting myself, except I decided there wasn't a snowball's chance in hell that you wouldn't come track me down," he replied.

"A wise decision."

Sunlight played over her face and he felt a painful twist in his gut. She was sweetness and light, while he was dark as the Devil.

"No, it's a fool's decision," he murmured, offering her his arm. "Would you care to walk within the walled rose garden? The stones offer a shelter from the breeze, along with a modicum of privacy."

"Very well." Anna set her slim hand on his sleeve.

Devlin made himself look away, willing himself not to think about how her graceful fingers had felt entwined in his hair. It was, however, damnably hard as the heat of her gloved palm began to penetrate the layers of kidskin and wool.

Clearing his throat, he tried to distract his evil thoughts. "By the by, I am curious. You and your younger sister both pen literary works, and Miss Caro has informed me that one of the Oxford poetry journals has recently published one of her sonnets. Does your elder sister write as well?"

"Yes," answered Anna. But she did not elaborate.

"Is she, too, published?"

"Yes."

"What sort of writing?" he pressed.

Anna hesitated. "I am not at liberty to say."

Devlin considered the reply for a long moment. "Does Wrexham know?"

The question provoked a peal of laughter. "That is a story in itself, but yes, of course he knows."

"And the earl approves?"

Amusement gave way to a frown. "Whether he does or doesn't is beside the point. It wouldn't change Olivia's passion for what she does."

"And yet he could, by all husbandly rights, forbid her to publish."

Her expression turned martial. "Ha! I should like to see him try."

Devlin quirked a grin. "Actually, so would I." The earl was a highly decorated war hero who had vanquished countless French dragoons in hand-to-hand combat. But facing off against one of the Sloane sisters would be the ultimate test of a man's will and nerve. He wasn't quite sure on whom he would place his money.

"Be that as it may, there won't be any fight over her activities," said Anna. "Wrexham is quite proud of what she does."

Another novelist? Devlin tried to think of what other authors were wildly popular with the reading public. No name, other than Sir Sharpe Quill, came to mind.

"Scholarly books, perhaps?" he guessed. "Like your late father, is she an expert on some esoteric subject like rare beetles or butterflies?"

"No, Olivia is not overly fond of bugs," she replied dryly. "But enough of Olivia and her secrets—I assure you

I won't let the cat out of the bag. We have more important things to discuss."

"Such as?" asked Devlin, even though he was fairly certain he didn't want to know the answer.

"You are an experienced gamester," she went on.

He maintained a wary silence. A cardinal rule in gambling was to hide any show of emotion.

"So I suggest we lay our cards on the table, so to speak."

When he didn't react, Anna let out a small huff of impatience. "Must we continue to play games, sir? You are clearly up to something havey-cavey with your secret lists and midnight forays."

"So you wish to know yet more of my secrets?" he asked.

"It seems only fair. You know mine."

His voice turned a touch harder. "*All* of them?"

"Well, yes. Isn't the fact that I write racy novels enough?" Her brow pinched in consternation. "Ye gods, what other horrible deeds do you imagine I am doing?"

Unless his skill at judging people had gone wafting off with the North Sea squalls, she was telling the truth. The question was, should he respond with the same candor? Baring his private business arrangement with Thorncroft and the Home Office was not nearly as comfortable as baring his body.

"You have to admit that your skulking around the castle in the dead of night does raise some unsettling questions," he replied. "Like why you would have cause to visit the Gun Room at midnight?"

"Research," she said tersely. "I needed a closer look at the mechanisms of a rifle for the next scene in my book, and for obvious reasons didn't wish to answer questions as to why."

"Ah." Ducking under the low archway, Devlin led her into the enclosed rose garden.

"As for my other forays, I was following you," continued Anna. "Which leads me to the fact that you, sir, still have a great deal of explaining to do."

As in a game of high-stakes cards, a quick decision was called for. "I suppose I do owe you an explanation. But first I must have your solemn promise that you'll not tell a soul what I am about to reveal. Not even your sister."

She took a moment to think it over. "That's a reasonable request, assuming I have the same promise from you about keeping mum about my secret."

He nodded.

"Excellent. Then we have an agreement." Her lips curled up at the corners. "Do you wish for us to prick a finger on one of the thorns and sign a pact in blood?"

"Such drama would make an excellent scene for Emmalina and Count Alessandro," responded Devlin. "But no. I am content to take you at your word."

"Thank you." She set a hand on her hip, a gesture far more eloquent than words in conveying her impatience to hear what he had to say.

"You are correct in thinking I am here not merely to shoot Lord Dunbar's birds or drink his excellent wines. I have been asked by someone in the government—"

"Who?" demanded Anna.

"Never mind," he said brusquely. "There's no reason you need to know his identity."

She scowled but didn't argue, which he took as a signal to go on.

"I have been asked to keep an eye on Prince Gunther. As you know, he is not only a relation of the King, but also the sovereign of a small state in a region that is key to our alliance against Napoleon. The political situation there is rather tense at the moment, so if any accident were to befall him, it could have grave consequences for our country. That is to say, if we can't protect the King's own relative, how can we be counted on to be a reliable ally."

"I see."

Devlin was sure that she did. Anna was far too clever not to grasp the ramifications.

"So you are saying that the prince is in danger of being *murdered* by one of our fellow guests?"

"Not exactly. The man I work for says the information is unclear. There may be no threat at all. In which case I have wasted the effort of coming north." He shrugged. "But as I am well paid for my time, I have little reason to complain."

"You and the Home Office," she mused.

"I didn't say I worked for the Home Office."

"Oh come now. Who else would be handling a threat to the King's relative here on British soil?"

Damn. She was sharper than any other lady of his acquaintance. He would have to remember to be very careful with his words.

"I take it you have worked with the government before."

"They hire me occasionally for certain missions where my skills may come in handy," he replied.

"I did wonder how you obtained the precision instruments you lent to Wrexham when he was about to set off in pursuit of the villains." Anna pursed her lips in thought. "Good Lord—you made them, didn't you?"

"The man who employs me will once in a while have need of certain complex implements that are not easy to construct. He happens to know of my mechanical skills."

Her eyes widened slightly. "The automaton you are making in your room—what purpose does it play for this mission?"

Devlin allowed a tiny smile. "None whatsoever. It's purely personal. A wealthy collector has commissioned it, and if I can make it work, I will be paid a very large sum. Given the remote location and the filthy weather here at Dunbar Castle, it seemed likely that I would have time to kill, especially if the suspected plot proved nonexistent. So, like you, I brought along my work in progress to keep boredom at bay."

"And here we have been running back and forth spying on each other, like actors in a stage farce," said Anna with a rueful sigh.

"It has had its comedic moments." The breeze had kicked up, and the sting of salty air from the nearby sea was prickling against his cheeks. "Come, let us walk for a bit." Another archway led into another secluded space where the walls hung heavy with a profusion of tiny pink climbing roses.

She didn't miss the edge in his voice. As soon as they had passed through the opening, she said, "But I'm assuming the drama isn't over."

Once again the gears in her head were whirring with military precision.

"Correct," he admitted. "Yours is not the only room I've examined for telltale evidence. As of yet, I haven't found anything to indicate there is a plot to harm the prince. The hunting incident could have been just what it appears—an unfortunate accident."

"However, you aren't convinced the threat is a farri-diddle."

"No."

"Good Lord. Having seen me sneak into the Gun Room, it is no wonder you thought the worst." Anna grimaced. "Though I am curious—for whom did you think I was working? I live an awfully staid life in London and have precious little opportunity for involving myself in nefarious intrigue." She cleared her throat with a cough—or maybe she was simply disguising a laugh. "That is, except for those I create in my head."

"That was certainly something I had to consider."

This time, there was no mistaking her mirth. "Mayfair ballrooms are hardly a hotbed of treasonous plots and international deceptions. The only betrayals going on are those between husbands, wives, and lovers."

"You might be shocked at what people will do for money or power," said Devlin softly. "Or the simple thrill of doing something dangerous."

Anna's face paled. "And seeing as I was willing to sell myself to a rich husband in order to take care of my family, why wouldn't I sell myself for any task if the price were right."

Seeing her haunted expression, he quickly replied. "I didn't really consider you a likely suspect. However, I had to be sure."

"Are you now?" she challenged. "Perhaps I'm clever enough to conceal my true motives behind the ruse of penning a book."

Devlin shook his head. "That won't fadge—the writing is too good."

Her mouth slowly stretched into a grin. "You know exactly how to disarm an author."

"I shall remember that when you've got your book knife pointed at my liver."

"I'm not your enemy," replied Anna. "But I imagine you have some ideas on who is—or might be."

"There are several who stand out as possible suspects," admitted Devlin.

"Who?" she asked eagerly, turning so quickly that her shawl snagged in the thorny vines.

"Anna," he murmured, reaching out to untangle the finespun wool.

"That," she snapped, "is exactly the tone of voice men use when they are about to say 'don't worry your pretty little head about such things.'"

"It is an exceedingly pretty little head," he drawled. "And there really is no need to worry it with such things."

"That's not amusing." A yank freed the shawl. "I would like to help."

"I don't see how you can," he replied coolly.

"To begin with, if any one of your suspects is a lady— and I would wager that's a good possibility—I have a far better chance of entering her room for a clandestine look around. My presence in that part of the castle will draw no undue attention, while you will have a much harder time of gaining access."

She had a good point. He was not anxious to initiate another amorous encounter with Lady de Blois. Sacrifices for King and country were all very well, but the idea of taking her to bed had lost its allure.

Still, what she was suggesting was too . . .

"And as for the men," went on Anna. She paused to flash a brilliant smile. "I can employ certain wiles to charm information out of them that you cannot."

His jaw tightened. "Absolutely not."

"Why?"

"Because. It. Is. Dangerous."

She uttered an oath that he had not ever heard outside the slums of Southwark. "Oh, and you are not facing peril if there is an assassin among us?"

"It's different," he muttered.

Her gaze sharpened to a steely stare. "If you are implying that I am helpless because of my sex, I just might fetch my book knife after all."

Bloody Hell. How was it that Anna Sloane always found a way to put him on the defensive? He was usually adept at dealing with women and the diabolically complex way their brains worked. She, however, had gears and levers he had never encountered before.

Reminding himself that he was good at figuring out new mechanisms, he tried another approach. "Anna, this is not one of Emmalina's exciting little adventures. It's all very well to go dashing around courting danger on paper, but it's quite another thing when the stakes are real."

When she didn't answer right away, Devlin began to congratulate himself. Conundrums were easy to solve if one simply exercised some patience and fortitude—

"Adventures on paper." She stopped abruptly and perched a hip on one of the stone urns dotting the path's verge. "Come to think of it, a prince in danger would add a very exciting element to my book. Emmalina has just arrived at a remote Scottish castle, and…"

"You swore an oath to tell no one!" exclaimed Devlin, adding a few words that ought never be uttered in front of a lady.

The breeze had tugged a few locks of hair free from

her bonnet. Gleaming gold in the sunlight, they waved like tiny naval flags signaling the start of a battle.

Sure enough, the rumble of the big guns rolling out immediately followed.

"I swore to tell no one about this specific mission," pointed out Anna. "Using it to inspire fiction was not part of the agreement."

"The devil it wasn't!" he snapped.

She lifted a brow.

"You are an imp of Satan in disguise," he growled.

"Then we are well matched, aren't we?" she countered.

Devlin sucked in his cheeks, trying to control the fierce twisting in his gut. It wasn't just anger but fear. Fear for her safety...

Fear for his own detachment going up in smoke.

"I'm not a feather-headed widget," she added. "I won't do anything to imperil your mission."

"And what of yourself, Anna?"

She looked away. "Lord Davenport—Devlin—I have become quite skilled at playing a role. You have seen for yourself that London Society sees me as a demure, dutiful young lady, a perfect patterncard of propriety, when at heart, that isn't the real me at all. I am tougher than I might seem, and more of a pragmatist than you might think, because my family circumstances demanded I be so."

It was true, conceded Devlin. She had unselfishly accepted a heavy responsibility, and had proved herself strong and steady with its weight on her shoulders.

Anna seemed to sense his wavering, for she quickly added, "And because people see me as naught but a sweet, biddable girl, you would be amazed at how comfortable they feel in confiding things to me."

Devlin watched a scudding of shadows pass over her profile. "I'm frightened for your safety," he finally confessed.

Her lips curled ever so slightly upward. "First of all, I can't imagine you afraid of anything."

Ha! I'm terrified of your wonderfully clever mind. I'm terrified of your intriguingly impish smile. I'm terrified of your sweetly sensual body. I'm terrified at how the walls around my heart seem to be crumbling into dust.

"And secondly," she explained, "I am willing to set some parameters. I'm not a fool, and so I won't do anything foolish."

"Our definitions of 'foolish' may be at odds," he pointed out.

She pondered that for a drawn-out moment. "Fair enough. Then how about we settle on a compromise. Let us agree to work together to discover if there is a plot to harm Prince Gunther. However, if and when you feel it's getting too dangerous for me to be involved, I will stop."

"You will obey my order?"

"Yes."

His eyes narrowed in suspicion. "What verbal loopholes am I missing here?"

She laughed. "None that I can think of at the moment."

"Anna, I—"

"That was a jest. You have my promise. A word from you and I shall back off."

"Truly?"

"Truly."

Clasping his hands behind his back, Devlin took a silent turn around the urn. Did he dare make a deal with the Devil? She was right—her assistance would be invaluable.

And no doubt Thorncroft would expect him to accept it without batting an eye. No sacrifice was too great for King and country. Including her life as well as his own.

"Damnation," he muttered, uncertain, undecided. "If I say yes, I shall likely regret it."

Anna crossed her ankles and smoothed at her wind-ruffled skirts.

"Damn, damn, damn."

"Swearing and walking in circles is not the best way to come to a reasonable decision," she murmured.

"I'm not feeling very reasonable," retorted Devlin.

Because I'm devil-damned if I can describe the unreasonable emotions twisting my innards into a knot at this moment.

She eyed him as if he were a slightly slow-witted schoolboy struggling to add up a simple sum.

Her look provoked a fresh scowl. "You promise there will be no mechanical eagle or plot to murder a prince in your new book?"

"You drive a very hard bargain, sir. It is a great artistic sacrifice that you demand, but yes, you have my promise."

"Oh, bloody hell," he conceded, after pacing through another turn. "Very well. We have a deal. But I warn you, if you try to wiggle out of your promise I shall find the deepest, darkest dungeon in Christendom and lock you there until Doomsday."

"Fair enough." A smile bloomed on her lips. "Now enough of sparring with each other. Tell me whom you consider to be the most likely suspects."

Chapter Sixteen

You were missed at the picnic," said Caro, turning around from her dressing table as Anna entered her bedchamber. "I have much to tell you—"

"*Alors*, please sit still, Mademoiselle Carolina, while I fasten the last hairpins in place," chided Josette. "The supper bell rang several minutes ago and I should not like for you to be late in joining the other guests."

"Yes, do hurry. We ought not be rude," said Anna, impatient to join the party in the drawing room. Her sister's late return from the outing had precluded a private chat before the evening's activities began. And while she was curious to hear about the day, it would have to wait. "We can talk about it when we retire for the night."

"One of the carriages became stuck in a rut on the way back, and the one I was in stopped to help," explained Caro. "So a number of the others will be making a late entrance to the drawing room." Looking unhappy at having to hold her tongue, she added, "You ought to know before we go down that Colonel Polianov seemed upset that you had not come. He kept dogging my steps all afternoon, asking all sorts of impertinent questions about you."

"Indeed?" Anna's attention snapped to full alert. Devlin had seen her nocturnal wanderings, so it was possible that Polianov had too. "How very odd. What sort of questions?"

"Oh, ones concerning your likes and dislikes, your habits. That sort of thing. I found it exceedingly odd too, especially as he's been rather rude up until now." Caro's reflection in the looking glass sharpened to a speculative stare. "You must have had a reason for warning me to not to go off alone with him."

"I was simply worried that he seemed an aggressive sort of man," she answered, hoping to put an end to the subject. Given any encouragement, her sister's vivid imagination could prove an impediment to the investigation. It would take some adroit handling to keep her off the scent. "His behavior was unsettling, but I think I was merely overreacting. Russians are simply . . . very Russian."

"Lord McClellan's behavior was even more unsettling. He kept staring and scowling . . . and trying to overhear what Polianov and I were talking about," muttered Caro.

Yet another of Devlin's prime suspects. The conversation was veering onto treacherous ground.

Before she could react, her sister asked, "You've had more worldly experience with men than we have, Josette. What's your impression of the colonel and the baron?"

"I do not see much of the gentlemen guests," replied the maid. "But downstairs there is always gossip. The colonel's valet says he is a cold fish, and the house servants say Lord McClellan can be very moody."

"It's clear he dislikes the English," murmured Anna. Servants often knew a great deal of intimate information about the people they served. Perhaps she could learn some useful information. "Do they give any reason why?"

"They say he has some very radical views on politics and equality for all men."

"That must earn favor with the servants," she mused.

Josette shrugged. "Most people do not like change, mademoiselle."

A very keen observation. With her sharp eye and lively intelligence, the maid could be a very helpful ally, if handled with the utmost discretion, decided Anna.

Which would make it impossible for Devlin to deny the wisdom of sharing his secret and allowing her to be a partner in the hunt.

"I can't help but be curious," she said. "Is any other reason mentioned for Lord McClellan's feelings for the English? It almost seems that there is a personal grudge of some sort."

"Not that I have heard," answered Josette. She finished threading a ribbon through Caro's topknot and set the brush down. "Would you like me to ask?"

Yes or no?

Taking a moment to think, Anna bent down to retrieve a cast-off stocking from the carpet. Creating compelling stories was something she was very good at. This simply required a slightly different twist.

"Actually, I would," she said softly. "I can't help but notice Lord McClellan's interest in my sister—"

Caro made a rude noise.

"And a lady can't be too careful about knowing what a man is really like," she finished. "Our mother thinks only of a title, so I feel that I must be the one to consider the man behind the trappings of privilege."

"It is very wise to look at a man's character as well as his purse, mademoiselle. The world can be a harsh place for those of our sex, So yes, it is important for a lady to keep her eyes open so that she may look out for herself."

Once again Anna was grateful that her maid was so sensible and pragmatic, rather than a flighty featherhead.

The reflection in the looking glass showed Caro appeared thoughtful as she mulled over Josette's words. Which was all well and good, mused Anna. Such advice helped temper her sister's natural exuberance.

"Speaking of Mama," said Caro, slowly twisting around in her chair. "She said that the carriage ride gave her a beastly headache and she means to spend the evening in bed."

How fortuitous. Not having to contend with their mother's ham-handed matchmaking would be one less distraction from her newfound sleuthing duties. "What a relief," she replied with a wry smile. "I can pass the evening without fear of finding myself engaged to the prince before bedtime."

"According to his valet, the prince is not likely to ask for the hand of an English lady," murmured Josette. She took a moment to shift the box of hairpins. "Nor, for that matter, the hand of *any* lady."

It took several ticks of the mantel clock for the maid's meaning to sink in. "The prince does not...favor females?"

"Apparently he much prefers to spend his time with the other members of his club, a very small and exclusive group of gentlemen who are interested in rare books and fine art."

"You appear to be intimately acquainted with the details of his private life," mused Anna.

Josette gave another lift of her shoulders. "As I said, servants do like to gossip. Especially when trying to impress one another."

Ha—yet another reason Devlin had to admit that having a lady as an ally was useful.

The *tick, tick* seemed to grow louder in the flutter of silence. "*Voilà*, your toilette is finished, Mademoiselle Caro," said the maid, stepping back and casting a critical eye over both her charges. "The two of you look very well. Now you had best hurry to join the others."

"Thank you," murmured Anna, as Caro slid off her seat and fluffed her skirts. "We are very fortunate to have a person of your skills, Josette."

Devlin surveyed the room over the rim of his drink, trying to quell his impatience. He was *never* impatient, and most certainly not when a lady was concerned.

But this was no ordinary lady, he reminded himself.

A fact that he wasn't quite sure was very good or very bad.

His brain, however, had little time to parse the question. As Anna floated through the doorway in a rippling of shimmering sea-green silk, it went utterly blank, and all rational thoughts sunk into...

Some depth of demented crosscurrents he had never experienced before.

Breathe. Basic instincts seemed to be the only messages emanating from his head. His lungs slowly obeyed, and the rush of fresh oxygen seemed to dispel the sensation of drowning, drowning, drowning.

Turning away, Devlin gulped down a swallow of wine to steady his shaking hand.

"Where were you today?" growled McClellan, bringing him back onto firmer ground.

"I was feeling lazy," he replied. "We indolent idlers are not used to the rigors of tramping your moors. Satan must have been Scottish to have formed such hellishly steep climbs and bone-chilling mists to torture us soft Sassanach creatures."

McClellan's mouth twitched, showing the man wasn't completely devoid of a sense of humor. "Aye. How perceptive of you to have noticed that his cloven hooves are those of a shaggy Highland steer."

"Actually it was more of a lucky guess," drawled Devlin, the exchange stirring his senses back to some semblance of normal. "Next time I am in his presence, I shall be sure to take a closer look."

"A closer look? And here I had assumed the two of you were already intimately acquainted."

McClellan was drinking a dark red-gold whisky rather than champagne, and his eyes were already a little over-bright. "It's never wise to make assumptions when the Devil is involved," said Devlin. "All too often you will find that his red-hot pitchfork ends up jabbing you in the arse."

"Is that supposed to make me fearful, Davenport?"

He widened his eyes in mock surprise. "Good Heavens, no—it's supposed to make you laugh." He lifted his glass to his lips, this time to take a smaller sip. "What reason would I have to make you fearful?"

"A good question," answered the baron.

"What is a good question?" asked Caro, as she and her sister approached.

"Lord McClellan and I were just discussing theology," replied Devlin.

· At that, the baron did let out a snort of laughter. "Good and Evil is such an interesting topic, but let us not bore you ladies with such talk."

"Oh, Lord Davenport is never boring," replied Caro, in a voice that left little doubt as to what she was leaving unsaid.

Devlin remained silent, noting the glitter in the baron's eyes was now more like a dancing of fullblown flames. Heeding his own advice, he decided not to make any assumptions on why the fellow seemed in a volatile mood.

"I'm sure that Lord McClellan can converse intelligently on a number of topics," interjected Anna. "Like the poetry of Goethe. I happened to note that the assistant secretary had set several volumes aside in his name when I visited the library this morning."

Caro's expression went through an odd little series of contortions. "You read Goethe's poetry?"

A flush rose to McClellan's cheeks. "Unlike much verse, his work at least strives to capture the full range of human emotion."

Rather than respond with a caustic comment, the younger Sloane sister swallowed hard and asked, "Have you a favorite, sir?"

Anna quickly hooked Devlin's arm. "Let us leave these two to debate poetry. If you will kindly escort me to the refreshment table, I have a question to ask you concerning card games."

"Card games?" repeated Devlin, once they were out of earshot.

"I had to make up something that wouldn't stir Caro's suspicions," she replied. "It won't be easy to keep her from guessing something havey-cavey is afoot."

"You claimed to be good at intrigue."

"And so I am." Drawing him to a secluded spot by the bank of windows, she quickly explained what she had learned from her lady's maid.

"Interesting," he conceded, "though at the moment I don't see what relevance it has to my mission. If the prince is in danger, it's because of politics, not personal peccadilloes."

"I'm not sure it does have any relevance," answered Anna. "Save for the fact that Josette is privy to a great deal of gossip, and I've come up with a plausible reason for asking her details about the private lives of our two most likely male suspects."

"One of whom is now, thanks to your encouragement, conversing with your sister."

Anna waved off the comment. "Even if Lord McClellan is our villain—which by the by I think unlikely—he has absolutely no reason to suspect that Caro knows anything about his secrets." Her gaze lingered for a moment on the gardens outside the glass. Moonlight mizzled the orderly rows of ornamental bushes with a silvery light, softening the spiky edges of the sturdy hollies and yews. "If I were truly pragmatic, I might even point out that allowing her to befriend McClellan would also make him less likely to be suspicious of me."

Damnation. She was frighteningly familiar with thinking out how a villain's mind might work.

"Be that as it may," she went on, "my maid may prove helpful."

Devlin nodded slowly, unable to think of any reason for objecting. It was an excellent idea, but he didn't like it a whit. "As long as you are—"

"Careful. Yes, I know." She slanted a look around. "We've spent enough time together. You ought to go flirt with Lady de Blois, as we planned. She's been watching us and looks miffed, which will work in your favor."

A glance showed Anna was right. In the past, the provocative pout, the revealing gown, the flick of a fan would have stirred the desire for a casual dalliance. Now it did quite the opposite.

There must be something in the Scottish air. A Gaelic curse perhaps, meant to rob all Sassenach males of their manhood.

"Davenport?"

"Throwing me to the wolves?" he murmured.

Her flash of teeth had a faintly predatory gleam. "There are no wolves in Scotland, remember?"

"Perhaps not the four-footed kind."

"You don't sound overly pleased with giving chase. I thought you said all rakes were hunters," said Anna.

A clever quip seemed to elude his grasp. Instead, he quaffed the last of his wine and set the empty glass aside.

"You will need to keep her occupied for at least a half hour, after I retire from the card table. It will be too chilly for a stroll outdoors, but perhaps a walk to the conservatory to a look at the specimen plantings—"

"Thank you," he interrupted, "But as you so politely pointed out, we rakes have experience in pursuing our quarry. I don't need you to plot it out for me."

"My apologies," she said, sounding a little flustered. "I—I was merely making a suggestion."

Her face turned a very sweet shade of pink. It took all of his mental discipline—not overly steady except with his *automata*—to keep from leaning in and pressing his lips to the ridge of her cheekbone, where the color was at its most intense.

"You are adorable when you are angry," he murmured.

Her lashes dropped, not quite quickly enough to hide a flutter of...

Of what?

"I—I'm not angry," she answered.

"Shall I make another guess?"

"I would rather you didn't." Her eyes once again darted away to the windowpanes. Rain had begun to tap against the glass.

Devlin was suddenly aware that the thud of his heart was turning a little erratic. "Dare I hope it's jealousy?" he said, just loud enough for her to hear. The teasing note belied how much he wished to know what she was thinking.

The pink hue paled and then deepened to scarlet. "I..." she began.

"My interest in the widow is purely professional," he murmured.

"But she's very worldly," replied Anna, watching the mist curls through the plantings.

"And very manipulative."

"She's very beautiful."

"In a tawdry sort of way." Devlin shifted, forcing her to meet his gaze. "Trust me, her charms hold no seductive powers over me."

Her throat tightened as she swallowed. "A half hour, sir. I need a half hour to have a look around her room."

"You shall have it," he assured. "But remember your promise—if there's any danger of being seen, you must retreat. If there is a conspiracy afoot here, none of the varlets must suspect that you know of it."

"I understand." Anna stepped back. "You really ought to go. We wouldn't want Lady de Blois to think your interest in me is anything more than casual."

The minutes seemed to be mired in molasses. Anna stole yet another glance at the case clock, willing the gentlemen to finish their port and cigars and rejoin the ladies.

Caro caught her eye and drifted over to take a seat next to her on the settee by the curio cabinet. "Is there a reason you are so concerned with the clock?" she asked between sips of her tea. "A tryst with one of your many admirers, perhaps? I hope it's the prince. He is far more pleasant than the colonel."

"You heard Josette. The prince is...well, he is not likely to make Mama's wishes come true," replied Anna.

"That may be. But the colonel's interest is undeniable."

She was about to assure her sister that she had no interest in Polianov, but quickly thought better of it. He was one of Devlin's prime suspects, and so she fully intended to encourage his attentions.

"We ought not be too harsh on him. Granted he hasn't made a favorable first impression, but that may be due to his feeling uncomfortable expressing himself in English. Beneath the outward stiffness, he may be quite interesting and amusing."

Caro arched a skeptical brow. "Perhaps you've put too much sugar in your tea."

"As Mama would say, don't be cynical."

"Then I shall be blunt instead," retorted her sister. "I think the man is a pompous bore."

Repressing a chuckle, Anna glanced around at the clock

again. And found Lady de Blois watching her with a cat-in-the-creampot smile.

The sound of a satisfied purr was almost audible.

She looked away quickly, feeling her insides curdle at the thought of the widow sinking her claws into Devlin.

I have no right to feel possessive.

And yet she did.

Her palms began to tingle as Anna recalled the shape of his shoulders, the feel of his muscles. The idea of another lady exploring his body was...

She heard herself let out a sharp hiss.

Startled, Caro nearly dropped her spoon. "Are you feeling ill?"

"My tea has too much lemon rather than too much sugar." Anna set her cup down. "I wonder what is keeping the gentlemen tonight?"

"Lord Andover once confided to me that most of the time they linger over port and cigars is spent telling bawdy jokes," offered Caro. The corners of her mouth crept upward. "Perhaps Polianov is telling a rather lengthy one. In Russian."

Anna was too tense to let out a laugh. She rose and feigned an interest in the curio cabinet's display of Renaissance medallions while she tried to compose her emotions.

If her heroine Emmalina was too wise to fall in love with a rakish rogue, then surely that should mean that her own brain could function just as well as an ink and paper one.

Shouldn't it?

The question was still plaguing her thoughts when at last the gentlemen made their entrance into the drawing room, trailing a faint fugue of spirits and spiced smoke.

Devlin went to sit with Lady de Blois. It was all according to the strategy they had devised beforehand, but still Anna felt a twinge pinch in her chest at seeing the widow sidle closer and lay a hand on his thigh.

Her brooding was interrupted by the colonel, who greeted her in Russian.

Maybe her offhand remark had some truth to it. He smiled broadly when she replied in kind.

"You speak my language very well, Miss Sloane."

"Not nearly as well as you speak English, sir," she said. "But it is gallant of you to say so."

His chest puffed out a bit. "I have had a great deal more practice than you have."

In what? The sinister whispers of intrigue and murder?

Anna forced a smile. "I should like to visit your country some day. The city of St. Petersburg must be very beautiful. I have heard it is called the Venice of the North."

His eyes lit with a gleam—one sparked by hard-edged speculation, not any softer sentiment. "I am very delighted to hear of your interest. It is indeed a beautiful city, with magnificent buildings and all manner of sumptuous balls and entertainments." The colonel came a little closer and she could smell the sweetness of the wine on his breath. "I think you would feel right at home."

The man's sudden overt interest in her was a little alarming. During the course of the past Season she had experienced a broad range of flirtations, from frivolous to serious, and something felt false about the colonel's attentions.

The realization stirred a pebbling of gooseflesh along her bare arms. Once again she couldn't help thinking that if Devlin had spotted her nocturnal ramblings around the castle, Polianov might have as well.

"That may be," replied Anna lightly. "But alluring though it sounds, I don't expect to visit anytime soon."

"Perhaps it will happen sooner than you think."

Mystified by his words, she chose to ignore them. "Perhaps."

He shifted his booted feet, and the touch of his trousers against her skirts sent another little shiver down her limbs. "Allow me to fetch you some tea, sir," she added quickly.

That Devlin's brow seemed to raise a fraction as she passed him helped steady her fluttery nerves. She would *not* prove unequal to the challenge.

Polianov followed on her heels. "Like all Russians, I prefer my tea very sweet," he said.

Such information wasn't overly useful for the investigation. She would need to delve deeper. "Given Napoleon's march to the east, your position here in England must be *very* important, Colonel Polianov," she ventured after handing him his cup. "It must be very difficult to form a united alliance with the German states."

He shrugged. "*Da*. But that is all left to the diplomats, Miss Sloane. Let us talk about more pleasurable things, like your favorite leisure activities. English ladies seem to paint or play the pianoforte."

Anna clenched her teeth in frustration. She had expected him to snap like a hungry trout at her baited hook. But before she could cast out another lure, they were joined at the tea table by the Vicomte de Verdemont.

Another prime suspect. Perhaps she would have better luck with him.

"I cannot help but remark on how that unusual shade of blue-green tonight highlights your natural beauty, Miss

Sloane," murmured the fleshy Frenchman, contriving to catch her hand and raise it to his lips.

Anna made no move to pull it away. "La, what lady doesn't appreciate hearing a compliment?"

Polianov bristled at being cast in the shade. "Miss Sloane's beauty goes without saying," he snapped.

"Actually, I think it can't be said often enough," replied Verdemont a bit smugly. "We wouldn't want the fairer sex to think that we take them for granted."

"We were just talking about Napoleon's march to the east," said Anna, deliberately keeping her eyes on the vicomte. "You must be offering a prayer to the Heavens that the Allied forces will be able to defeat him."

Did his gaze darken for instant? Whatever the reaction, it was gone in the blink of an eye.

"More than one, mademoiselle," he replied, his voice betraying no hesitation. "Tyrants must be destroyed at all costs."

Polianov gave a gruff sound in his throat. "Let us not sully the lady's lovely ears with such talk of war."

Anna surrendered any hope of squeezing any useful information out of the pair at the present moment. The vicomte's reaction, however tenuous a clue, was at least something to offer to Devlin. And as soon as the group finished with the refreshments and moved on to the card tables, she could withdraw for the evening and head upstairs for her real mission.

"You are right, colonel. War and intrigue are such an ugly business." Taking up a platter of ginger biscuits, she offered it to Verdemont. "Tell me, does Lord Dunbar's gardener think the weather looks favorable for a hunt tomorrow?"

Chapter Seventeen

Careful, careful. The flickering flames of the wall sconces seemed like silent tongues, repeating the same warning that was whispering inside her head.

Anna checked up and down the dimly lit corridor before flattening herself against the dark wainscoting and inching forward. She had changed into breeches and a loose-fitting shirt—thanks to her insistence on meticulous research, she always had such clothing at hand in order to write accurately on what moves Emmalina could make when dressed as a male. No question that moving swiftly and stealthily was far easier when unencumbered by yards of silk and petticoats.

Pressing an ear to Lady de Blois's door, Anna listened intently for any sign of life within the chambers.

Nothing.

A second look around, a quick juggling, and she was safely inside.

So far, so good.

But there was precious little time to waste in self-congratulation.

After relocking the door, Anna turned in a slow circle, reviewing her options as she surveyed the sitting room. A half hour wouldn't allow for a search of the entire quarters. And so she would have to rely on female intuition as to where the most likely hiding place for intimate secrets would be.

A lady like the comtesse, she decided, would want to keep them close to her...bosom.

Without further hesitation, Anna rushed into the bedchamber and looked around for the jewel case. It wasn't hard to spot. A large brass-cornered domed box covered in emerald green leather sat on the dressing table between a half dozen ornate crystal scent bottles and a pair of silverback hair brushes.

A pair of locks were fitted into the heavy lid, and as a bead of moonlight flitted over the shiny metal, they seemed to wink in challenge.

"Perhaps it takes a lady to catch a lady," she murmured, flexing her sliver of steel. The small mechanisms proved surprisingly difficult, but with a few extra probes they finally yielded.

She didn't dare strike a flint to the brace of candles. Even the faintest curl of smoke left lingering in the air could give away the visit.

And so could a careless search of the box's contents. Despite her eagerness, Anna made herself study the arrangement of the brooches, pendants, and earrings before lifting the velvet-lined tray out and setting it aside. Several necklaces lay in the deeper compartment, but the fact that they lay twined in a careless tangle should work in her favor. Holding her breath, Anna ever so gently slid her fingers beneath the twists of gold and eased them up and onto the smooth tabletop.

The bare black velvet stared at her in silent reproach.

"Don't look at me like that. I doubt you are as innocent as you seem," she whispered in reply. A quick sidelong glance at the outside of the case had shown that the interior appeared to end far higher than it should.

Anna gingerly worked a fingernail between the fabric-covered pasteboard bottom and the wood and felt for any looseness.

Sure enough, the pasteboard shifted. A few gentle tugs and it came out smoothly, revealing a hidden compartment. In it was a packet of letters.

Anna quickly checked the clock on the mantel. *Twenty minutes left.* That should allow more than enough time to read through them.

Such optimism quickly dimmed. Unfolding the first one, she saw it was written in French.

Merde.

Luckily, there were only four missives and she was fairly fluent in the language. Still, she would have to work fast.

They were all penned in the same bold script—a man's hand, decided Anna, taking a quick peek at the signature on the first one she unfolded. It didn't confirm her guess—it was simply a large "V"—but she was sure she was right. Just as she was sure that "V" would turn out to be Verdemont. There was, after all, an old saying that lightning never struck the same place twice.

Her surmise on the letter writer's identity was soon confirmed as she read over the contents. It was indeed

Verdemont, and his words left no doubt that he and the comtesse were engaged in a passionate affair. Anna felt a momentary twinge of guilt for prying into the other lady's personal secrets, but then quelled her misgivings and moved on to the next letter.

Anyone willing to deceive her own sister in such an ugly way might very well be capable of even worse acts of betrayal.

The second and third letters were less overt in their meaning. The mood was more agitated, the innuendos more puzzling. Anna found herself struggling a little with the language.

Eight minutes left.

Did she dare read the last one? It took only a split second to judge it worth the risk.

This one had a slightly ominous tone... assuming her imagination wasn't running away with her. She needed to reread it several times, for there was a phrase that seemed to make no sense at all, even though she knew the meanings of the French words. *A code, perhaps?* Frowning, she committed it to memory, thinking that Devlin might have some ideas.

Four minutes.

Praying that Devlin's charm was holding strong, Anna hastily refolded the letters and placed them back in the secret compartment. After replacing the false bottom, she carefully lifted the necklaces...

Only to freeze at the sound of footsteps in the hallway.

"Don't panic," she whispered aloud as the gold began to chatter in her trembling hands. Willing herself to remain calm, Anna arranged the jewelry into the right configuration, then slipped the top tray into its slot.

Shutting the lid, she managed to work the locks into place and then slid the case into its original place.

A key rattled the front latch, the metallic scrape sounding loud as cannon fire.

Thirty seconds. Maybe less.

Anna spun around to the window. If Devlin could manage the ledge, so could she. Her feet were smaller, and dancing with any number of clumsy men had taught her agility and balance. She cracked open the tall leaded glass frame and slipped out—ye gods, it was cold—taking care to pull it firmly shut behind. A piercing gust of damp air cut through her thin stockings and suddenly the ledge felt narrow as a razor's blade.

She quickly edged out of view, just as a flash of candlelight illuminated the panes. Flattening her back against the rough stone, she drew in a gulp of air and held it in her lungs.

A grumbled mutter, the thump of a water jug, the scuff of shoes on the carpet coming close to the casement...

Anna bit her lip and offered up a prayer to the Celtic wind gods that the window wouldn't fly open.

All at once, the light disappeared as the heavy damask draperies were yanked closed. The steps receded and all she could hear was the keening of the wind through the turreted tower and the rustling of leaves below. Anna glanced down—and then wished she hadn't. The drop looked far greater than it had from inside the room.

Several deep breaths helped to steady her quaking knees. There was no going back. Which meant she had no choice but to swallow her fear and make herself start to move.

* * *

Devlin tossed down his cheroot and ground out the glow-ing coal beneath his boot. Still no signal, though it felt as if a century had passed since his parting with Lady de Blois. Anna should be back in her room by now, a single candle blazing bright in her bedchamber window to say that all was well.

"Damnation." He glanced up again. "Damn, damn, damn."

A fresh gust blew across the terrace, further tangling his wind-snarled hair. Too impatient to remain in the niche by the corner wall, he turned up his collar and began to pace along the stone railing.

Only a bloody fool—or an idiot besotted by a beguiling beauty—would have agreed to such a dangerous plan. Her oh-so-clever mind made it hard to remember that Anna had no experience in flesh-and-blood intrigue. It was all very well to pen swashbuckling feats of daring. Ink and paper did not bleed, imaginary heroines did not die from real-life bullets or blades.

A growl welled up in his throat.

Bracing his palms on the stone, Devlin stared out at the mist-shrouded moors and slowly counted to ten. He was allowing his mind to exaggerate the risks. In all likelihood, there was nothing more nefarious going on at Dunbar cas-tle than some illicit trysts.

Turning, he shot another glance up at the looming wall. *Then where was the bloody candle?*

Clenching his teeth, he resumed his pacing. Ten more minutes—he would give her ten more minutes. If no light had appeared by then, he would take matters into his own hands.

Where they should have been in the first place.

Pebbles crunched beneath his boots as he descended the terrace stairs and began walking along the graveled path in search of a better angle of view to Anna's bedchamber. Shadows swirled through the bushes, and a sudden gust ruffled the knife-edged holly leaves, hiding the west wing for a fleeting interlude.

Ducking low, Devlin shouldered his way through the prickly hedge and once again lifted his gaze.

A flame—faint but unmistakable—finally glimmered behind the glass.

Relief pulsed through him, followed by a spurt of anger. He stood for a long moment, staring at the light while he fought to bring his emotions under control.

When at last the pounding of his heart had subsided back to its normal beat, Devlin returned to the path and headed back for the terrace.

She had better have a good explanation for tying his insides into knots. But much as he wished to hear it now, it would have to wait until morning.

Falling, falling, falling . . .

Stifling a cry, Anna sat bolt upright in bed. It took several rat-a-tat thumps of her racing heart for the dizzy, disoriented feeling to subside. A dream—it was just a bad dream, she realized. Her toes were snug beneath an eiderdown coverlet, not sliding off a sliver of slippery stone.

She blew out a sigh and slumped back against the pillows, reveling in the welcoming softness and warmth. Still, she couldn't help feeling a shiver tiptoe down her spine. The inch-by-inch traverse along the ledge had been a nightmare ordeal, with every tiny step seeming to take an eternity.

A gust slapped against the windowpanes, provoking a rueful smile. Swashbuckling exploits seemed much easier to perform on paper.

Her throat dry as dust from her fitful sleep, Anna threw off the covers and padded over to the washstand to fetch a glass of water. Too restless to return to bed, she curled up on the window seat and gazed out at the silvery moonlight playing over the dark silhouettes of the shrubbery.

From this perspective, she mused, the scene had a cozy feel to it. The clouds were clearing, and with the wind dying down to a gentle breeze, a peaceful stillness was settling over the grounds...

A movement within the leafy shadows of the boxwood hedge suddenly caught her eye. Anna wiped the mist from the glass and leaned in for a closer look.

One...two—no, three—figures materialized from the gloom and hurriedly crossed an open swath of lawn to take shelter beneath a large oak tree not far from her window.

Anna quickly shifted on the seat to keep them in view.

One of the men she recognized. The untamed shock of reddish-gold hair made Lord McClellan hard to miss. The others were too well-swathed in broadbrimmed hats and dark scarves to make out their features. Their gestures, however, were clear enough in the dappled light— they seemed to be arguing with the baron, and quite heatedly.

Lying low on the cushions, she reached for the latch and cracked open the casement.

No luck. The voices were too low to carry through the whispery night sounds.

Pressing closer to the panes, Anna kept her eyes on McClellan, who was becoming more and more animated.

A clandestine meeting in the dead of night could have no explanation, save for one.

The baron was up to no good.

Her pulse began to pound. Was she watching the conspiracy against Prince Gunther in action?

The answer came quickly enough—McClellan's two companions each reached within the folds of his overcoat and reluctantly handed over a weapon.

Two muskets—no, two rifles! She recognized the distinctive silhouette of the short barrel as McClellan slung them over his shoulder.

With a curt wave, the baron dismissed the men, who slunk away into the darkness. He watched them go, his profile stony and expressionless, mirroring the distant granite outcroppings dotting the moors.

A very hard man, thought Anna, feeling her insides clench. And his fiery passions made him a very dangerous one to cross.

As if sensing her presence, McClellan suddenly turned to stare up at the castle.

She ducked beneath the casement, telling herself that his hawkish gaze couldn't possibly penetrate brass and stone. But much as she wished to slither down to the carpet, she waited for several moments and then ventured another peek. Devlin would want to know every detail, and she did not want to disappoint him.

The baron had already started walking—she could just make out the gleam of his fair hair and swirl of his coat around his boots as he took the stairs to the side entrance two at a time.

Her own feet twitched, and she darted a glance at the doorway. Devlin ought to be informed as soon as possible...

But reason quickly prevailed. Venturing out into the deserted hallways of the castle with an armed assassin on the prowl was not the wisest of ideas.

Perhaps my earlier adventure has tempered my taste for outrageous risks.

Deciding that discretion was the better part of valor, Anna crept back to the sanctuary of her bed. The downy softness felt blissfully good against her tired limbs, and she stifled a yawn as she burrowed deeper into the covers.

Unmasking the baron's perfidy could wait until morning.

"Still abed, mademoiselle?" Josette paused by the armoire, a pile of freshly laundered nightrails in her arms. "Shall I come back later?"

"No, no, it's quite all right." Anna pried an eye open and winced as a blade of sunlight cut across her face. "Oh, dear, is it fearfully late?"

"Not by the standards of your fellow guests. Most of the ladies don't rise until well after noon."

"I am not used to lazing in bed," she mumbled sleepily. But on flexing her aching shoulders, she was sorely tempted to remain cocooned within the covers for a while longer.

"An eventful evening?" inquired the maid.

The question quickly cleared the muzziness from her head.

Ye gods—the evening!

Anna sat up quickly and pushed a loosened hank of hair off her cheek. "N-no, not really."

Josette leaned down and fished a bedraggled stocking—an unmistakably male stocking—from beneath the bed. "Hmmm."

Drat! In her haste to strip off her male garments and hide them in one of the bandboxes, she had been a little careless.

After examining the item a fraction longer, Josette merely folded it neatly and placed it on the bureau without comment.

"I can explain," murmured Anna. "But I'd rather not."

"If you wish to sneak out for an assignation with that handsome dark-haired devil, that is entirely your own affair, mademoiselle," replied the maid. "As you know, I believe a woman ought to have the freedom to make her own choices, even if they are ones that may lead her into trouble."

"I wasn't having an assignation with the Devil," said Anna, then quickly amended her words. "Well, not exactly." Better to let Josette think her adventures were simply amorous. "I know that doesn't make sense—"

"Love rarely does," quipped Josette.

"But I'm not in love."

"*Bon*. That is good." The maid turned and began straightening up the brushes and boxes on the dressing table. "Men will only make you miserable if you give them your heart."

Anna smiled but felt a strange sort of pinch in her chest. *Was that true?* Her own mother's shrill unhappiness was in part due to the detachment of her father. He lived in his own world—a quite wonderful world, but the fact that his wife was uncomfortable in it did not deter him from living quite cheerfully on his own.

It must have been disappointing for Mama to realize that the tribal customs of Crete meant more to him than her needs and desires. Neither had been willing to compromise...

"Shall I fetch hot water for your morning toilette?"

Josette's quiet question roused Anna from her reveries. "No, no—that's not necessary." Rising, she hurried to the washstand and splashed some cold water on her face. "I'm anxious to go down to breakfast."

"I shall shake out your cerulean blue walking dress. The day is bright, but a bit chilly, so merino wool seems a good choice, just in case you wish to go for a stroll in the gardens."

Devlin signaled the footman for another pot of coffee— and promptly scalded his tongue on the first swallow. Sputtering a low oath, he slapped the cup down and shot an impatient glance at the breakfast room entrance.

"More toast, milord?"

Devlin waved off the question. He had already consumed enough food to feed a regiment of hungry Hussars while waiting for Anna to appear. For someone who normally rose at an ungodly early hour, she was proving perversely slow this morning.

At the sound of steps, he looked around again, but it was only McClellan.

Devlin didn't relish the company. The room had been his alone for the last half hour, allowing him to swear at will.

The baron went straight to the chafing dishes and helped himself to several slices of gammon and a ladleful of thick Scottish porridge. Taking a seat across the table, he proceeded to attack his breakfast without a word of greeting.

Noting the other man's haggard looks, Devlin couldn't refrain from venting his frustration with a little well-placed needling.

"Enjoyed a few drams too many of whisky with the moor banshees last night, McClellan?"

The baron didn't look up from his oats.

"I'm assuming your company naught but wild Gaelic spirits, for the ladies here don't seem to care for your manners. Or lack of them."

McClellan slowly set down his spoon. "Careful, laddie. Or in another moment you may be digging your teeth out of your gullet."

"I wouldn't wager on that." Though he normally considered fisticuffs an egregiously silly waste of energy, he was itching to hit something. The harder, the better.

McClellan's aquiline nose would do very nicely.

Speaking of which, that particular portion of the baron's anatomy had turned an angry shade of red. He, too, looked spoiling for a fight.

"You have a very high opinion of your wit, Davenport. Perhaps that illusion ought to be thumped down a notch or two."

"By you?" drawled Devlin. "That should be amusing."

McClellan's sun-bronzed face turned a shade darker. "I would pound you to a pulp here, but I might break some of my cousin's precious porcelain." His chair scraped back across the oaken floor. "Shall we take a stroll in the gardens?"

Devlin cracked his knuckles—a deliberately infuriating sound. "Oh, very well. If you insist. But only if you promise not to puke on my boots when I break your beak."

The comment provoked a sharp growl from the baron. Shooting up from his seat, he looked on the verge of lunging across the table—

"Oh, please don't rise on my account, Lord McClellan."

Intent on the confrontation, Devlin hadn't heard Anna enter the room.

"It's not necessary to stand on ceremony this early in the day," she went on brightly. "My, my, what a lovely day. Do you gentlemen plan to venture into the hills for more birds?"

The baron unclenched his fists. "Actually, I was thinking of organizing a hunt for vermin—foxes, stoats, and other pests who plague the estate."

Devlin met her gaze as she sat down next to him. Beneath the surface smile, her eyes looked troubled.

"In fact, Davenport and I were just about to take a stroll in the gardens to attend to the details," went on McClellan. "If you would excuse us—"

"It would be most impolite to abandon Miss Sloane," interrupted Devlin. "You go on. I shall join you anon."

The other man's jaw tightened, but after a tiny hesitation, he simply nodded with ill grace and stalked away.

Chapter Eighteen

$\mathcal{Y}$ou," uttered Devlin, "have a great deal of explaining to do."

"Please don't waste your breath ringing a peal over my head," replied Anna. "I do indeed have much to tell you." She glanced at the footman stationed at the far end of the serving sideboard. "But we ought to find a more private spot."

"You should eat something first." His tone softened considerably. "You're looking pale."

"Never mind that." The sight of McClellan in a temper had her stomach too jumpy to contemplate food. "I'm not hungry."

Ignoring the assertion, he rose and chose a generous selection from the breakfast offerings. "A pot of fresh coffee for the lady," he called as he set the plate down in front of her. "And please make sure it's dark and hot."

The heavenly aromas of fresh-baked pastries and shirred eggs reminded Anna that she hadn't eaten since supper, and even then, she had been too on edge to do more than pick at her meal.

"I shudder to think what you consume when you're feeling peckish," he murmured.

"Wretch," she said around a forkful of creamed mushrooms. The warmth was delicious and helped to melt the tension gripping her insides. "It seems that I was hungrier than I thought."

"That's better. The color is returning to your face."

Anna took a grateful gulp of the steaming coffee. "Thank you. This is divine. But we need—"

Devlin signaled her to silence. "When you are finished," he commanded.

Bemused in spite of her worries, Anna chewed thoughtfully on a piece of sultana-studded muffin. He was watching her with a rather peculiar expression— half exasperation and half something she couldn't quite define. "Tender" was the first word that came to mind, which was of course ridiculous. The Devil Davenport didn't have a tender bone or sinew in his body.

Cut him and he would bleed sarcasm.

Wouldn't he? She slanted another look at him through her lashes, suddenly feeling a flutter in her stomach that had nothing to do with hunger. Dare she think he might have softer sentiments hidden beneath his caustic quips? That would, of course, be asking for trouble...

No, it would be asking for heartbreak.

Anna looked down at the crumbs on her plate. Not that she had any intention of serving up her heart on a platter.

Brushing aside such conflicted musing, she popped the last morsel into her mouth. "There, I'm done. Now let us find somewhere quiet."

"The gardens," he suggested.

And risk encountering the murderous McClellan? "No, no, the library. At this hour it will be deserted."

"I would argue if I thought it would do any good." Devlin sighed. "Walls are more likely to have ears than the open air. But I agree that we should be safe enough."

Anna led the way to a recessed alcove hidden away in the back of the Geology section of the Natural Sciences Room. "I discovered this while searching for a secluded spot to write," she explained. "We won't be disturbed."

Rather than sit in one of the comfortable reading chairs, Devlin perched a hip on the edge of the work table and leaned forward. The pose accentuated his long legs—he had *very* long legs—and broad shoulders. The muscles seemed to twitch beneath the sleek black wool of his coat, bringing to mind the uncomfortable image of a stalking panther ready to pounce.

"You," he repeated, "have a great deal of explaining to do."

Tender? Her wits must still be addled by the dizzying height of the narrow ledge.

"Why in the name of Hades did it take you so long to light the signal?" he went on testily. "I gave you more than the allotted time. You should have been well away before Lady de Blois returned to her chamber."

"The signal isn't important. Nor, for that matter, is Lady de Blois, though I did discover some very interesting evidence tucked away in the false bottom of her jewel case."

Devlin frowned. "What are you saying?"

"That I've discovered the real villain behind the plot to harm Prince Gunther," she whispered.

"Who?"

A triumphant smile. "Lord McClellan!"

To her disappointment, his expression didn't alter on being told the momentous news.

"Explain," he said softly.

Anna quickly recounted what she had witnessed from her window.

Still no reaction, other than a curt "*Hmmph*."

She shifted her chair, feeling a little wounded at his failure to appear impressed by her sleuthing prowess. Given the scrapes and bruises on her aching body, a bit of praise would have been nice. "You seem uninterested in my discovery," she murmured. "I thought it was rather important."

"It's not uninteresting, just unexpected," he replied. "I find it hard to believe that McClellan would be involved in an assassination plot."

"But he's hot-tempered and passionate in his dislike of England," she pointed out. "And makes no secret of his wish for Scotland to be independent of our government's rule."

"True. But as you say, he's not a man who hides his feelings," countered Devlin. "Playing at high stakes games, I've come to be a good judge of character, and despite his thunder and lightning, the baron strikes me as a fellow who has his own set of moral principles. If he wished to harm Prince Gunther, he would be more likely to march up to him and challenge him to a duel with those fearsome-looking ancient claymores that hang in the Weapon Room."

An astute assessment. However, a key question remained unanswered. "So how do you explain the rifles?" she asked.

Devlin shrugged. "Haven't a clue. There's only one way to find out."

"Which is?"

He deflected the query with one of his own. "You haven't told me about what you discovered in Lady de Blois's jewel case."

"Letters," answered Anna. "Signed only with a 'V,' but there seems precious little doubt that they are from Verdemont."

"Well, go on," he prodded when she didn't volunteer any more.

"In truth, I'm not sure that there is much point. The contents made it clear they are having a torrid affair—and I can't help but think that if they are willing to deceive the comtesse's sister in such an ugly way, they might very well be capable of even worse acts of betrayal." Anna expelled a sigh. "However, aside from a line that made no sense at all, there wasn't anything other than personal matters expressed."

"I don't suppose you remember that odd line." He didn't sound sanguine.

"I'm not a feather-brained henwit," she responded tartly. "Of course I remember it." Lifting her chin, she rattled the phrase.

"*Hmmph.*"

Anna was getting very tired of hearing that muted snort. "*Hmmph* what?"

"*Hmmph* I am thinking." He darted a glance around the alcove. "Is there paper and pencil anywhere nearby?"

She reached beneath the lip of the tabletop and opened a slim storage drawer. "*Voilà.* And before you ask, my French is excellent, so I'm quite certain my translation is accurate."

"I'm not questioning your skill," he replied absently,

quickly writing down what she had told him. "It helps to see the words in black and white."

Craning her neck, Anna studied the paper for several long moments.

Have no fears—at the sign of the Witch, the double-faced eagle's feathers will turn to dust.

"They still don't make any sense. Unless, of course, they are a code."

His lips twitched. "How did you come to have such a frightfully devious mind?"

"Through a great deal of practice."

The grin became more pronounced. "No wonder your poor mother is hellbent to marry you off."

"Most ladies would take offense at that, Daven—"

"Devlin," he corrected. "But not you, Anna. You know me well enough to understand it wasn't a criticism."

"*Hmmph,*" she replied.

He laughed, and though it was barely more than a rumble of air, the sound sent a tiny thrill spiraling down to her very core.

A laugh shouldn't make me want to press my hand to his chest and feel the rise and fall of his breathing.

Thump, thump. In the silence of the alcove, Anna could suddenly hear the quickening beat of her heart.

The sound grew louder, and she realized it was Devlin drumming his pencil on the tabletop.

"Blast," he muttered. "I've an idea about what one part of message might mean. But as for the other...it may take some time to figure out." *Thump, thump.* "Assuming, of course, that it's not simply some private lover's code."

Which was, Anna realized, the most likely explanation.

She had been too flushed with her own cleverness to consider the obvious.

"So I haven't really accomplished anything." Anna tried
to mimic his nonchalant shrug but she feared her voice
gave away her dismay. That she had risked life and limb
for a mere billet-doux sent her spirits plummeting. "Save
to force you to fritter away time in discerning their secret
endearments."

A frown formed between his brows. "You've accomplished a great deal. Just knowing for sure that Verdemont
and Lady de Blois are lovers is very important. Missions
like this one rarely have such swashbuckling drama as you
portray in your novels. The villains are usually foiled by
painstakingly piecing together bits of evidence, rather than
catching them red-handed."

"You seem to know a lot about all this. Does the government hire you often?"

His expression turned shuttered. "Let us concentrate on
this particular assignment." Devlin nudged the paper toward her. "You've a creative mind. Any ideas on what this
could mean?"

She started to answer, but the stealthy footfalls of someone moving through the rows of bookcases nearby made
her pause.

Devlin was instantly alert to the intruder. His body
tensed and he cocked an ear to listen.

More steps, followed by the sound of books being
pulled from the shelves. The ruffle of turning pages.

A low oath.

Anna cast a questioning look at Devlin.

He nodded.

McClellan.

Her eyes widened as Devlin drew the Manton pocket pistol from inside his coat.

"But—" she began in a soft whisper.

He pressed a finger to lips. A tiny gesture, yet Anna immediately fell silent. Any lingering hint of the indolent rake was gone—in an instant he had taken command of the moment.

Rising, Devlin slipped to the side of the alcove's narrow entrance. His eyes steeled to a gunmetal gray glitter.

She found herself holding her breath.

A book snapped shut, nearly causing her to jump out of her skin. The air suddenly stirred, setting off a dance of dust motes through the trickle of sunlight coming in through the lone window.

McClellan stalked into the alcove, muttering darkly under his breath. It took him a moment to look up from his book and see that he wasn't alone.

"Miss Sloane." He didn't sound happy about the encounter.

Anna tried to speak, but her throat was dry as parchment. All that came out was a croak.

"Forgive me," growled the baron. "I'll find somewhere else to read."

"Actually, I'd prefer that you didn't."

McClellan whipped around to find Devlin blocking the entrance.

"Now that you are here, why don't we have a cozy little chat?"

The baron calmly eyed the weapon pointed at his chest. "About what? How high and mighty English lords are too lily-livered to settle their quarrels like men?"

"No, we can talk about that subject at another time.

Right now, I've a more pressing topic to discuss." Devlin gave a flick of the cocked pistol at the chair opposite hers. "Have a seat."

After tossing the books on the table, McClellan did as he was ordered.

Anna watched him fold his arms across his chest. Her own hands would have been shaking had they not been clasped tightly in her lap, but the baron appeared as unflappable as a sliver of Scottish granite.

But then, a hardened assassin would need to possess a heart of stone.

Devlin approached, and bared his teeth in a semblance of a smile. The baron responded with a contemptuous sneer.

Two lordly wolves, circling, circling, seeking a soft spot to attack.

"Are you going to stand there all day waggling your weapon?" demanded McClellan, after the silence had stretched tighter than a bowstring. "Or shall we dispense with the theatrics and get to the point of this confrontation?"

"You wish to cut to the chase, as it were?" Devlin remained standing. "Very well. Why don't we begin by having you tell us where you've hidden the rifles you received last night. Shall we find them secreted in your rooms? No, no, on second thought you'd not risk having the murder weapons spotted there. You'll have found a spot where no one is likely to stumble upon them. The castle affords so many hidey-holes."

McClellan tipped back in his chair. "Murder weapons?" He sounded genuinely bemused. "The only one present at this house party I'd contemplate shooting is you. However, if I were to desire your demise, I'd do it face to face, not with a faraway shot from a rifle."

"But I saw you skulking through the gardens late last night with your two cohorts," blurted out Anna. "The three of you had an argument, and in the end, you made them hand over the rifles." She lifted her chin. "There can be no explanation, sir, save for an evil one."

The baron snorted in disgust. "Spying can lead a lass into all sorts of trouble."

"I wasn't spying," she retorted. "I was simply sitting in my bedchamber looking out the window."

He lifted a red-gold brow. "At that hour?"

"I—I couldn't sleep."

"It's not Miss Sloane's behavior that is under question," snapped Devlin, deciding it was time to intervene. "It's yours."

"And just whom am I supposed to be intent on killing?" asked McClellan.

The baron ought to join the great John Kemble on the stage, for his acting skills were just as finely honed.

"You wish to play a childish game of hide and seek?" countered Devlin. "Frankly I'm in no mood for running in circles. Your target is Prince Gunther—and don't bother denying it. I know all about the plot. The only missing piece of the puzzle was the assassin's identity."

To his surprise, McClellan started laughing. "You think that *I* am planning to kill the prince?" he wheezed between guffaws. "By the bones of St. Andrew, you ought to take up novel writing."

Anna bit her lip.

"Why the devil would I want Prince Gunther dead?" added the baron.

Devlin felt a twinge of uncertainty. Anna's information on the weapons had seemed to confirm McClellan's guilt. But the man's reactions had him a little off balance. "Because it would create havoc for England," he answered slowly.

"I wish I had thought of that," retorted McClellan. "But I didn't."

"Then explain the rifles," demanded Anna.

The baron was no longer smiling. "It has nothing to do with you or any of the guests here."

"Forgive me for being skeptical..." Devlin now felt himself back on firmer ground. "But I find it rather hard to take you at your word."

McClellan cracked his knuckles. "Then I suppose you will have to go ahead and shoot me."

"Lord McClellan, be assured that none of us want to see blood shed," interceded Anna. "If you would offer an explanation—"

"Why bother?" The baron's chair came back to the floor with a *thunk*. "That spawn from English Hell has already indicated he won't believe anything I say."

"Then I shall speak up in your place!"

"Caro!" Anna shot out of her seat as her sister stepped out from the shadows of the corridor.

McClellan let out a heated oath in Gaelic.

Not that he could understand a word, but it certainly sounded like an oath to Devlin.

Caro fixed the baron with a defiant scowl. "I don't know why I bother defending you, you odious man, but my sense of honor demands that I tell the truth."

Devlin restrained the urge to take his head in his hands. This was fast descending from drama into farce. "Which is?" he asked, hoping Anna wasn't making notes of the scene for her next book.

"Lord McClellan met with two of his Scottish revolutionary friends late last night in one of the side parlors. They wished for him to help them raise arms and gunpowder for an ambush of a visiting English military commander." She darted a sidelong look at the baron, who was staring out the window. "He refused, saying violence was not the way to achieve their goals. When the meeting was over and they took their leave, he followed and saw them stealing weapons from the Gun Room. After trailing the pair into the gardens, he confronted them and demanded that they give the rifles back to him."

"How do you know all this?" he asked.

Caro blew out her breath. "Because I had been listening at the door, and then crept after them and heard all that was said outside."

"Ye gods," exclaimed Anna. "That was foolish beyond belief! What if they had, in fact, been bloodthirsty murderers?"

Caro lips twitched. "I should have run like a banshee, I suppose. Or figured out some suitably impressive heroics, just like a storybook heroine."

McClellan made a rude sound. "Ladies ought not be allowed to read. It addles their wits."

"On at least one thing we are in agreement," murmured Devlin.

Anna spared a moment to spear him with a glare before turning back to her sister. "That's *not* amusing."

"Neither is the fact that you have been keeping secrets from me." Caro's eyes sparked with indignation. "Talk about dangerous doings! You have been involved in smoking out a dastardly assassin and didn't think I could be trusted with the information."

"I...um..." Anna's voice faltered.

Caro didn't wait for her to go on. Her ire was now focused on him.

"And you, Lord Davenport, I wouldn't have thought *you* to be such a spineless mawworm as to conspire with my sister behind my back." Setting her hands on her hips, she ended with an oath that made Devlin's ears turn red.

McClellan was laughing again, though the sound was hardly louder than a zephyr. "You may be a Sassenach lady, but you've got the temper of a Highland warrior."

She whirled on him. "As for you, you big lummox—your brain must be thicker than porridge. Only a bloody sapskull would keep mum about the real reason for the rifles."

The baron's mouth thinned to a razored line. "And why—"

Caro cut him off. "Because if my sister and Lord Davenport are busy dealing you, that means the real culprit is free to carry out the nefarious deed."

Devlin decided to sit. Dealing with not one but two of the Sloane sisters was a little overwhelming.

"An excellent point," murmured Anna.

"Thank you." Her sister responded with a mock curtsey. "Now that we've eliminated Lord McClellan from your list, who is the most likely suspect?"

Anna looked to Devlin.

As did McClellan.

Devlin lifted his gaze to the ceiling, wishing some words of wisdom might be found in the spidery cobwebs clinging to the carved rosettes.

"Ah, well." He sighed. "The more the merrier."

Chapter Nineteen

$\mathcal{A}$ council of war." Caro quickly took a seat and propped her elbows on the table. "How exciting."

"Please try to keep a rein on your exuberance," murmured Anna. "This isn't a scene out of a Lord Byron poem."

"Or a novel," added Devlin.

How he was feeling about this unexpected turn of events was impossible to tell, she decided. His face was a cipher.

McClellan, like her sister, was far easier to read. At the moment his stormy expression was darker than a North Sea squall. "What in the name of Satan is going on here?" he demanded. "Murder? Mayhem?" Scowling at Devlin, he added, "And am I really supposed to believe that *you* are involved with the Sassenach government?"

"It's true," responded Anna.

"Ha! No wonder Napoleon is riding roughshod over England and her allies."

"Sarcasm is not helpful, Lord McClellan," snapped Caro. "If you wish to be part of our efforts to prevent a vile assassination, you must have a more positive attitude. Otherwise, I suggest you leave."

Anna fully expected the baron to stalk off in a huff. Instead he slouched back in his chair, lips pursed, and appeared to be giving her sister's challenge serious thought.

Interesting, she mused, before forcing her attention back to the threat facing the prince. The tangle of personal feelings was far too confusing to try to sort out when a murderer was lurking close by.

"It's not your fight," observed Devlin. "I don't expect you to give a rooster's tailfeather for whether the assassination of an obscure German prince causes trouble for England."

The room went very still, the only sound the faint scrabbling of a mouse behind the age-dark paneling.

McClellan finally broke his brooding silence. "Bloody hell. You're right—as far as I am concerned, your Mad King and rakehell Regent can go the Devil, along with your oppressive Parliament and laws. But Prince Gunther is a decent fellow, and assassination is a cowardly act. So I'll do what I can to help."

"Thank you," said Devlin.

Oddly enough, thought Anna, he sounded sincere.

The baron seemed to note the same nuance. Giving a grimace, he muttered, "Ye gods, just don't expect me to exchange comradely kisses." There was, however, no edge to his words.

Caro eyed both men but refrained from adding her own comment.

"Excellent," said Anna quickly. "Now that we've agreed to join forces, I'm sure that Dev—that is, Lord Davenport— will share what we've discovered so far."

Devlin fingered the paper on which he had written the puzzling phrase. A brusque flick moved it to the center of the table. "The prime suspects are Lord Verdemont and Lady de Blois. We managed to find some private correspondence hidden in the lady's rooms—never mind how—and have reason to suspect these phrases might be some sort of code, for they make no sense on their own."

"Of course, their meaning may only be of a personal nature," added Anna. "But it certainly does raise suspicions."

"As Miss Sloane so sagely pointed out to me, if they don't bat an eye at the fundamental betrayal of their own sister and wife, then they are likely capable of any evil."

"Like murder?" murmured Caro. "But why?"

"Money, for one thing," muttered McClellan. "Its power can corrupt most any conscience."

"That's awfully cynical, sir," replied her sister. "I would rather starve than betray my principles of right and wrong."

The baron regarded her for a long moment. "Yes, I rather believe you would." A shrug shifted his gaze. "But be that as it may, it is the French couple that concerns us. And it seems to me that in addition to money, there's also another powerful force to consider."

"Passion," said Devlin, before the baron could go on. "Verdemont has presented himself as an ardent French Royalist, a nobleman who lost his lands and wealth to Napoleon. But there are some of the Old Guard exiles living in England who secretly believe fervently in the revolutionary ideas, and they serve as spies for the current French government."

"Precisely." McClellan tapped his fingertips together. "Passion can be a dangerous thing."

Danger. Like a sinuous serpent, the word seemed intent on slithering over her skin and capturing her in its coils. Repressing a small shiver, Anna shook off the sensation.

A frown seemed to flit over Devlin's face. *Had he sensed her reaction?* If so, he let it pass unremarked.

"Any thoughts on what this blasted phrase might mean?" he asked the others.

Caro's face was a mask of concentration, while McClellan leaned back and clasped his hands behind his head. "Have no fears—at the sign of the Witch, the double-faced eagle's feathers will turn to dust," he recited. "I assume you tried a simple Caesar shift on the letters?"

"What's that?" asked Caro.

"A way of encrypting a message," answered Anna. "It involves shifting the letters of the alphabet—but that usually results in gibberish. And besides, the message was originally written in French, so that rules out the possibility."

"True," said McClellan, and then quickly added, "By the by, how do you know so much about codes?"

"I read a great deal," she replied blandly.

Devlin swallowed a snort before voicing his own observation. "It seems fairly clear to me that it's referring to the next attempt on the prince's life. The coat of arms of Schwarzburg-Rudolstadt contains a double-headed eagle."

"Drat, how could I have missed such an obvious clue?" murmured Anna.

He flashed her a private grin that made her insides give a lopsided lurch. "I have a bit more experience in clandestine missions than you do." His lips, however, quickly thinned to a grim line. "But I confess, I haven't a clue as to what the first part of the message means."

"I wonder, are they expecting another conspirator?" mused Caro.

"That's a very good point," said Devlin. "McClellan, can you make inquiries about whether any stranger has been spotted in the area?"

"Aye," answered the baron.

"Perhaps it's Polianov," said Anna. "His government has reason to covet Prince Gunther's land, and he's been acting very suspiciously of late. For one thing, he's developed a sudden interest in me, which is a little alarming. I fear he may have seen me moving around the castle at night."

"Forget Polianov," replied Devlin. "I searched his quarters quite thoroughly the other night and found a letter he had just written to one of his comrades in London. I regret to say that his interest in you is purely monetary. Lady Dunbar mentioned to him that you are an heiress, and apparently he's decided you are the answer to his prayers for a life of indolence, now that his family coffers are nearly bled dry."

"I see."

"Don't look so stricken," he murmured softly. "You've plenty of genuine admirers."

Flustered, she turned slightly, hiding her face in shadow. To her relief, Caro provided a distraction, by clearing her throat. "I have been thinking..."

Devlin signaled for her to go on.

"We also ought to consider whether 'witch' has some other meaning. After all, Shakespeare made Scotland rather famous for witches. Perhaps it's a metaphor."

Anna wasn't quite sure what McClellan's low grunt signified, but she herself was exceedingly impressed with her sister's thinking. "I think that's a splendid idea. Shall we fetch a copy of *Macbeth*? It may be that one of the scenes with the witches will provide the key."

Devlin nodded thoughtfully.

"Or," said McClellan suddenly, "it may not be a metaphor but rather an actual physical place or landmark."

"Yes, yes, that makes sense." Caro's voice thrummed with rising excitement. "And since you suggested it, I assume you have an idea of what that place might be."

"Aye. There is a set of wind-carved stones on the moors that resemble three figures leaning together in close conversation. The locals call the knoll 'the Witch Coven.' And in discussing the best hunting beats in this area with the prince and his party, I've made mention several times that I intend to lead our party to that spot tomorrow. The ghillies have scouted the hills there and report the grouse are quite plentiful."

"Would Verdemont know this?" asked Devlin.

McClellan looked faintly amused. "All of the hunting party does. Had you bothered to listen to my lectures during our breaks for food and drinks while shooting, you would, too. But no, you found wandering off to inspect the rocks and lichens infinitely more interesting."

"Tramping the hills is not my favorite activity. It's far too exhausting," drawled Devlin. "I was actually stealing a nap while you prosed on about the ideal habitats for the local flora and fauna."

"Let us not stray from the point, gentlemen," chided Anna. "It now seems inarguable that Verdemont and Lady de Blois are the villains—"

"I trust you will concede that confiding your secret to me and Lord McClellan was a wise move," interrupted Caro. "Despite your misgivings—all of your misgivings—

I'll have you know that I can be trusted to act with sense and caution."

McClellan opened his mouth to speak and then appeared to think better of it.

Wise man, mused Anna, understanding all too well her sister's feelings. It was not easy being the youngest, especially with two strong-willed older siblings. All too often, Caro had been told she was not yet mature enough to be treated as an equal. And while her emotions still got the better of her at times…

"I'll concede that, and more," murmured Anna. "If at times I seem unwilling to tell you certain things, it's because I am trying to protect you. Mama's concerns are quite limited, so I suppose that I have felt that I must play mother hen." She sighed. "I apologize if that is condescending."

Caro's cheeks flushed with color.

"But that does not mean I will stop."

Her sister smiled. "Fair enough. However—"

"Ladies, forgive me for interrupting this touching scene," growled McClellan. "But we have a murder to prevent."

"Have you no particle of romance in your soul?" murmured Devlin.

"That," jeered the baron, "is rather like the pot calling the kettle black."

"No one would ever accuse either of us of being knights in shining armor," he replied. "Nevertheless, we do need to crack off a bit of the coal dust and attempt to do a good deed."

"Though you haven't mentioned it, I assume you have some other government contact nearby," said Anna. "The

Home Office cannot have expected you to deal with an assassin—or assassins—without reinforcements."

"Correct," responded Devlin.

"Then cannot you have them swoop in and arrest the villains and be done with the threat?"

"I'm afraid it's not quite that simple. First of all, while we have strong evidence as to who the culprits are, it's not absolute proof."

"But—" began Caro.

"And I would rather not make a mistake," went on Devlin.

That silenced her sister.

"Secondly, the government would prefer to handle this very discreetly. The best scenario would be if I could contrive to, shall we say, confine the villains in some secure location, so the government operative could remove them with no one being the wiser as to the real reason. An excuse can be made that an emergency required their immediate departure for England."

"Which would be the truth," mused Anna.

"I see your point," said McClellan. "So what is your plan?"

Rather than answer, Devlin rose and went to look out the window. Anna could almost hear the tiny gears and levers whirring inside his head. Though in truth, she added to herself, the marquess's mental workings were infinitely more complex and complicated than his clever automata. She wished that she had an inkling of what he was thinking...

He turned, his mouth pursing in a wry grimace. "Haven't a clue yet. For the moment, I ask that the rest of you do nothing. I need to ponder the options. And I do that best alone."

McClellan rose and cast a sharp glance at Caro, who reluctantly followed his lead. "Then we shall leave you to your work."

"Anna," began her sister.

"I shall be along in a moment, just as soon as I have had a private word with Davenport."

Devlin waited until the retreating steps faded away into silence. "There's really nothing more to say, Anna. I need to mull over these new facts before I can decide on a next move."

"Truly?"

"You don't trust me?"

A laugh, low and soft, and yet it seemed to tease its way beneath his shirt and prickle against his bare skin. "Don't try to distract me, Devlin. I've learned your little tricks for changing the subject."

Distraction. He wrenched his gaze away from her upturned lips and retreated a step. "In this case, I am telling the truth."

Anna narrowed the distance between them. The gleam in her eye was pure Emmalina. "You wouldn't dream of coming up with a new strategy and putting it into action without telling me?"

Another step. *Damnation.* His back was now up against the wall.

"Would I do that?" A weak reply, he knew. But his brain seemed unable to come up with a more inventive quip.

"I think"—reaching out, she twined her fingers in the folds of his cravat—"that you are capable of anything."

A strange sort of sensation squeezed at his throat.

"Including devious deception." She leaned in close.

Her scent—that beguiling mix of sweetness and spice—was affecting his balance. How else to explain why the floor seemed to be canting at an odd angle?

"Where in the name of Lucifer have you learned such wiles?" he muttered.

"Oh, here…" Her palm pressed against his chest. "And there."

"Hell's teeth." His voice was muffled by the nuzzling of her lips.

Oh, I am a weak-willed, evil fellow. Abandoning all pretense of restraint, Devlin gave in to his inner demons and kissed her back.

Evil. Evil.

"We have come this far together," whispered Anna.

Not far enough, said his lust-hazed brain.

"We are comrades-in-arms, so to speak. So don't you dare try to sneak off and capture the miscreants on your own."

"Because you need to come up with a swashbuckling scene for your next chapter?" he asked.

"Because…" A flash of sunlight crossed her face, obscuring the rippling of shadows beneath her gold-tipped lashes. "Just because."

"I would expect a more articulate reason from a famous author." Hearing her sharp intake of breath, Devlin quickly added, "I am teasing, sweeting. I've not yet devised a plan, and when I do, I shall inform you."

"As a famous author, I am familiar enough with the nuances of language to know that 'inform' does not mean 'invite,' as in, 'I shall invite you to come along,' does it now?"

"Anna, we have an agreement," he reminded her. "If I deem it too dangerous, you promised that you would stand aside."

Her chin jutted up...and then slowly sunk. "Drat. Having a strict notion of right and wrong is a cursed inconvenience."

Smiling, he couldn't refrain from kissing the tip of her nose. "I wouldn't know."

"At least let me help you come up with some ideas of how to trap the traitors. You have to admit that I have certain creativity when it comes to dashing adventure."

Brave, bold, beautiful—a whole bookful of adjectives could not begin to capture her spirit. Anna was unlike any lady he had met before. *Unique beyond words.* All at once, Devlin felt a surge of emotion swell up in his chest. The force was so great he thought his ribs might crack.

Fear, lust, anger, aggression—all these he recognized. This was something utterly unknown.

Oh, surely it couldn't be love.

Clearing his throat, he managed a light reply. "Just as long as you don't expect me to swoop in on a mechanical eagle and carry them off to the Tower of London."

"Hmmm."

A shuffling in the neighboring room of books warned that with the morning hours waning, the castle was beginning to bustle with activity.

"Look, we cannot linger here any longer without attracting attention," he pointed out. "I've agreed to accompany Lord Dunbar on an afternoon ride to the sea cliffs, so I won't be free to strategize until the evening hours. I suggest that we meet in the deserted wing of the castle after everyone has retired. Unless, of course, you would rather not risk any more creeping through the corridors at midnight."

"Where?" she demanded.

"You remember the Portrait Gallery?"

A flush of color painted her cheeks. "Yes," she answered curtly. "But it's not quite as isolated as one might wish."

"I know another more private spot. But I had best lead you there, as it's hard to find."

"Very well. But if you deceive me—"

"Yes, yes, I know. My liver will be handed to the cook for use in her special pâté."

"You are wiggling worse than a Breton eel, this evening, mademoiselle," murmured Josette. "Is something amiss?"

"No." Anna tried to stop squirming in her seat, but her body didn't seem to be listening to her brain. "That is..." She groped for an explanation. "...I am unhappy that Mama keeps trying to push me together with Prince Gunther. Clearly the poor man isn't interested. It is embarrassing to both of us."

"I would imagine that the prince is no stranger to fending off matchmaking mamas," replied the maid. Her deft fingers snagged an errant curl and twisted it into place. "Perhaps your unhappiness has to do with another gentleman downstairs, eh? One that your Mama does not want to encourage?"

Anna felt herself blush. "*That* particular gentleman needs no encouragement to do whatever he pleases."

"A man with backbone. That is good, *non*?

No. The spineless fops of the *ton* were certainly easier to deal with emotionally than the marquess. Somehow he had taken her steely self-control and rearranged all the little gears and levers.

As if I were one of his mechanical creations, she thought wryly.

Josette let out a throaty little laugh when she didn't answer. "Men are impossible creatures." A hairpin slid into place and a clever little tug created an artful tumble of golden curls. "The key is not to take them to heart."

Illusions. Her maid had a knack for hiding any flaw.

"But...how do you manage that?" asked Anna. "I fear that the heart does not always listen to reason."

"You'll learn." Josette curled a midnight blue ribbon around her finger. "There is no easy answer to your question. We all will have different solutions. But keep in mind one thing—just as the heart doesn't listen to the head, the head can ignore the helter-pelter thumpings of the heart."

Can it? Anna wasn't so sure.

"You have a stronger will than I do," she replied, making a rueful face in the looking glass. "I seem to have no..." Squaring her shoulders, Anna sat up a little straighter. "But never mind my silly musings. There must be something in the Scottish air that puts me in a strange mood. I shall shake it off."

"Wild heather and rough magic—the ancient Celtic spirits are strong in this land of sea and stone," agreed her maid.

"Yes, that must be it." Anna regarded her reflection, surprised that she looked so outwardly calm when her insides were churning like the wind-whipped ocean waters. A glimmer—it had lasted for only an instant—had set off this surging, spinning, swirling force within.

A glimmer—a fire-kissed glimmer in Devlin's eye. She drew in a quick breath. Which was likely just a quirk of her own imagination.

"*Voilà.* You are ready to go down, mademoiselle." Josette set her hands on her hips. "Have no fear. You are more than a match for *amour* and its arrows."

Chapter Twenty

Devlin shifted his weight from foot to foot as he waited, shrouded in darkness, just inside the entrance to the Portrait Gallery. There was nothing to be nervous about—the chances of anyone stumbling onto the late-night rendezvous with Anna were almost nil. And yet, he found himself feeling unaccountably edgy.

Perhaps because over the course of the last few days, a number of new elements had been added to the mission. He preferred to work alone and for a very good reason. His experience in building complex mechanical mechanisms had taught him that the more moving parts in the design, the greater the risk for something to go awry.

To give them credit, his three coconspirators had performed admirably all evening. He had been a bit concerned about the younger Sloane sister, but Caro had betrayed no hint of interest in the French suspects. She had argued with McClellan over the artistic talents of Sir Thomas Lawrence—whether the tiff was feigned or real he couldn't tell. But regardless, the diversion had amused the other guests and given him a chance to keep a close eye on Verdemont and Lady de Blois. Neither had made any attempt to slip away from the drawing room. He hadn't really expected them to. Whatever evil they were planning, it was almost certainly going to take place on the moors.

Leaning a shoulder to the fluted molding, Devlin cocked an ear for any sound of movement.

She was late.

Mouthing a silent oath, he felt anxiety begin to gnaw at his insides. Yet another reason to remain a solitary operative.

Light steps drew him from his brooding. He recognized Anna's tread. Damnation, a great many things about her were imprinted on his consciousness—*the softness of her skin, the sweetness of her mouth, the lilt of her laughter.*

"Devlin?"

He reached out and caught her arm. "Shhhh."

She gave a little start but didn't make a sound as he yanked her into the gloom.

"It's not safe to talk here," Devlin whispered. "Follow me." Keeping hold of her hand, he ducked into a narrow passageway that led to the oldest part of the castle.

"I've been this way before, the night I followed you into the depths of the old wing. You entered a room with a heavy door, but I dared not follow. What were you doing there?"

"You'll see soon enough." It was pitch black within the rough stone walls but he didn't wish to light a candle. "Watch your step," he warned. "There are several sharp twists and a set of stairs up ahead, so be careful not to trip on your skirts."

Her answer sounded suspiciously like a snort.

Come to think of it, there was something odd about the swishing of fabric around her legs. Or lack of it.

He stopped abruptly and ran a hand over her derriere. "What in the name of Hades are you wearing?" Not that he objected. The feel of her body unencumbered by yards of silk and lace was rather lovely.

"Breeches," answered Anna. "You have no idea how much easier it is to move quickly. It's most unfair of you men to keep them to yourselves."

Devlin let his palm linger on the curve of her bum. "I'm all in favor of creating a new fashion for ladies."

She shuffled her feet, sending a frisson of heat up his arm. *Ye gods, her lower legs must look divine in stockings.*

"Um, shouldn't we keep going?" she murmured.

"Right." This was no time for erotic fantasies. Shoving aside his impure thoughts, he hurried through the last stretch of darkness and came to an ancient, iron-banded door.

Easing it open, he struck a flint to the pair of oil lanterns hanging just inside the entrance.

"Good Lord," intoned Anna, as the flames flared to life, casting a weak illumination over the front part of the cavernous room.

He shut the door and shot the bolt into place. "Interesting, isn't it?"

She moved through the circle of light to inspect a near life-size carved wood tiger with a hapless human trapped between its giant paws.

"McClellan would take great pleasure in this piece," said Devlin dryly. "The beast is about to devour an Englishman." He joined her by the automaton and reached out to flick a small brass lever.

The tiger began to grunt and growl as the man flapped a hand and made a wailing noise.

"Oh!" Her eyes widened and then she let out a laugh. "Wherever did it come from?"

"India," he replied. "It's called Tipu's Tiger and was made around a quarter century ago for Tipu Sultan, the ruler of the kingdom of Mysore. He hated the East India Company and the control it wielded over the native dominions."

"So it would seem," murmured Anna.

"The East India Company army found it when they captured the sultan's summer palace during the first Mahratta War. The Governor General sent it to London, where it was put on public exhibit at East India House." Devlin ran a hand over the painted head. "I had heard it was sold to a private collector, but hadn't realized that Lord Dunbar was the purchaser until I arrived here."

She glanced around, noting a number of other elaborate creations half shrouded in the shadows. "What other creations are secreted here?"

"A good many fascinating things." He unhooked one of the lanterns from its wall bracket. "Come, let me show you a few of my favorites."

Bypassing a massive chiming clock in the form of a brass peacock, Devlin drew her deeper into the gallery. "Here is a marvelous English mechanical model from the last century," he explained, stopping in front of a silver swan set on a shimmering stretch of glass rods. "Its workings are impressively complex—just watch." He wound the clockwork key, and a music box started to play as the glass rods began to rotate, giving the illusion of moving water. Little silver fish appeared within the rods as the swan moved its neck and preened. A moment later it appeared to notice the fish and bent down to catch one in its beak.

"Amazing," exclaimed Anna.

He smiled, glad that she found the automata as fascinating as he did.

"My eagle wasn't such a mad idea," she mused. She traced a fingertip along the graceful arch of the bird's neck. "This is wonderful, but I daresay your singing pistol is even more fiendishly difficult to create on account of the miniature size."

"It has its own unique challenges," he murmured. "But then, all automata require a willingness to let one's imagination run wild."

On impulse—the Devil's own wicked impulse—he took her hand and pulled her into a small anteroom off the main gallery. Unlike the main room, it had two narrow windows, mere slots in the mortared stone, originally made for archers and now covered with paned glass. A dribble of moonlight added a silvery cast to the flickering gold of the candle.

"Lord Dunbar keeps a few items in here that aren't designed for public view." Devlin indicated a length of black velvet draped over a large object. "Suffice it to say, they are rather provocative, so you might not care to view them."

Her brows angled up. "Is that a challenge?"

He shrugged in answer.

Anna hesitated no more than an instant before venturing a peek under the cloth. A sound—a laugh? a squeak?—seemed to lodge in her throat. "Help me unveil it. I think it needs to be seen in all its glory."

Devlin folded back the heavy fabric and dropped it atop a pile of other draperies. Lifting the lantern, he let the light play over the exquisite detailing of carved ivory and precious metals. The automaton showed a couple on a coverlet of scarlet silk, entwined in the throes of passion. On toggling one of the lady's upraised legs, the man's hips began to rise and fall.

As she watched intently, he tried to gauge her reaction. However, her expression, that bland Mayfair ballroom mask of politeness that she could slip on in the blink of an eye, gave nothing away.

"It's Italian and was made by a Florentine master craftsman in the seventeenth century." The lady's head began to turn from side to side, setting her luxurious tangle of tresses to caressing the silk. "Her hair is made of real gold threads, and her eyes are Chinese jade," he added. "Legend has it that Casanova once owned this piece."

"I can well believe it, given his appetite for the opposite sex." She crouched down for a closer look. "Good heavens, the anatomical rendering appears remarkably accurate." The male lover rose and fell again. "Um, for the most part, that is."

"Oh? Is something not quite right?" Devlin knelt down beside her.

After observing another gyration, Anna answered, "Not that I have a great deal of expertise in judging such matters, but the male appendage seems ... a trifle exaggerated."

"Are you saying I have a shortcoming?" he drawled.

Was it just the shadows or was she blushing?

"I—I haven't enough experience to say one way or another." Her eyes remained on the mechanical couple. "I have a feeling that the classical Greek and Roman statues

I've viewed are not true to life. Nor, for that matter, are the sketches in my father's books on primitive cultures and their rituals."

Without all the layers of feminine frills between them, Devlin was intimately aware of the heat radiating from her body. It was making his skin prickle.

He found his gaze drawn to the pile of folded cloths beneath the windows and found the black velvet stirred a sudden rush of evil thoughts.

Evil, evil.

He had brought her here for reasons of strategy, not seduction.

Ah, but I've always been a weak-willed devil.

"Marble and paper are no substitute for empirical observation." He curled his arm around her waist. "Come. Seeing as your father taught you to appreciate the importance of serious scholarship, I suggest that we further your education."

"I'm not sure my father would approve of this sort of empirical observation." And yet, Anna let herself be lifted up and carried to the bed of draperies. The stone-chilled air made her acutely aware of Devlin's warmth beneath the rippling of corded muscle and hard...

She shifted in his arms, feeling a naughty thrill tickle between her thighs as his arousal rubbed against her.

"On the contrary, it sounds to me as if he encouraged all his daughters to be curious." He set her down. "And adventurous."

The nap of the cloth was softly sensuous against her palms. Anna imagined it would feel very nice against her bare bum. A most improper thought, she knew. But somehow wearing a man's clothing seemed to free her of more than mere physical constraints.

Why can't I be a little wicked? Ladies ought to be allowed the same freedom as men. On that her father had wholeheartedly agreed.

Drawing her knees to her chest, she answered, "Yes, he did encourage us to explore. But he also took care to explain that there were dangers and that we must understand and accept the consequences of our actions."

"It sounds as if he was a very wise man."

"Yes, in many ways, he was." A sigh. "And yet, he had his faults. His devotion to his passion for science was unfair to Mama. It seems to me that a good relationship involves compromise."

"We all have faults, Anna." Devlin captured the tip of her shirtpoint between his fingertips and began to toy with the fabric. "Some are far worse than others. Believe me, I should know."

There was a strangely vulnerable note in his voice that belied the sardonic words. She caught his wrist, the sudden movement causing the lantern flame to flicker wildly within the glass globe. "Why is it that you keep casting yourself in such a harsh light? I think you are far more noble than you care to admit."

"I assure you..." He freed his hand with a quick flick and touched the top fastening of her shirt. "I am not feeling remotely noble at this moment."

Was she willing to step beyond the boundaries of her world? Anna watched the starlight skitter over the rough stone below the window. This time, there would be no going back.

"Neither am I," she whispered.

Devlin hesitated, as if giving her a last chance to rescind her words.

"I'm not afraid," she added. In truth, she was, just a little. The unknown was frightening—but also exhilarating.

Sinner or saint? Perhaps the difference wasn't black and white but a shadow-kissed shade somewhere in between.

Reaching out through the hazy half-light, Anna feathered a fingertip along the line of his jaw. "I'm not afraid," she repeated, this time a little louder.

The physical touch seemed to dispel whatever misgivings held him in thrall. Expelling a sharp *whoosh* of air, Devlin seized her wrist and pressed a kiss to her palm.

The petal-soft caress of his lips sent a spear of heat through her core. A sound—it must have come from her, for the automaton had gone silent—echoed off the walls.

"Sweeting," he whispered. One by one, her shirt's fastening yielded to his hurried tugs.

The fabric slipped over her head, leaving her upper body clad in just a thin chemise. Anna wasn't sure whether she was hot or cold—despite the fire inside her, the dark-misted air raised a pebbling along her bare arms.

And then, the chemise was gone and his mouth closed over her breast.

Dear God. Dear God. His tongue teased round and round until her nipple felt like a burning ember about to burst into flame.

She cried out again and again as wave after wave of pleasure rippled from her scalp to her toes. Fisting her hands in his shirt, she pulled it up over his back.

Devlin broke off his embrace just long enough to yank it off. The white linen fluttered away through the shadows.

Like the ghost of my old self, was Anna's fleeting thought. In the next instant, however, she was no longer thinking of the past or the future.

Only the magic of the present moment.

His wicked, wanton, wonderful mouth possessed hers. He tasted good. More than good. A hint of brandy-sweet heat, a potent male essence that sent desire bubbling through her blood.

Of their own volition, her fingers found the fall of his trousers.

A throaty groan, and Anna felt his hips shudder. That her touch could affect his self-control emboldened her to push the layer of wool and the cotton drawers beneath it down to his knees.

Another sound, low and rough, as Devlin kicked off his shoes and his rumpled garments.

"How very lovely that breeches are so much easier to remove from a pair of shapely legs than all those cursed layers of fluff," he murmured, expertly stripping off the rest of her clothing.

She laughed against his mouth. "You've had a good deal of practice, so no wonder you're so skilled at it."

"I've far more interesting skills to display, sweeting."

Anna found herself rolled onto her back, her shoulders sinking into the napped fabric with a velvety sigh.

Outside, the weather seemed to have turned stormy. A peltering rain drummed madly against the window glass, and a faraway thunder rumbled through the distant moors.

Or maybe it was just her vivid imagination. If she were to finally write a seduction scene for Emmalina and Alessandro, it would be one with a wildly romantic setting such as this one.

Looking up, she saw his face hovering close, its lean lines hazed in the swirl of shadows and the tangled strands of his dark hair. Only his eyes caught the weak flicker of the lantern, and within their depths an amber fire suddenly flared to life.

"Anna." Devlin dipped his head and now the sparks were dancing along the sinuous curl of his mouth.

Oh, that mouth.

Mesmerized by its sensuous shape, she arched up to touch her tongue to his lower lip.

"You," he rasped, "have been transformed by some ancient Highland sorcery into a temptress too powerful to resist."

"It's no sorcerer's spell," answered Anna. "It's..."

It's some far more personal alchemy. But she dared not voice such a thought aloud.

"It's some other potent force, though I can't yet give it a name."

"Whatever it is," responded Devlin, "it's as intoxicating as Scottish whisky."

The sliver of space between them gave way to a deeply intimate kiss. Their tongues teased and twined, sending a sudden rush of liquid heat coursing down to her feminine core.

A gasp, a shudder. Devlin seemed to need no words to understand. He covered her body with his, lithe muscle molding to her heated flesh. Instinctively her legs parted, allowing his maleness to nudge up against her feminine folds.

Fire on fire. Igniting a burning need.

Looping her arms around his neck, Anna whispered—she knew not what—in his ear. A cacophony of feelings was echoing in her head, but only two words rose above the din.

Need. Want. Need. Want.

She had teased tantalizingly close to the flames before. This time, she wished for them to consume her.

With a low groan, Devlin hitched his hips and suddenly he was inside her.

Anna felt a sharp pinch, and then the tightness softened as her body adjusted to their joining.

He stilled. "Did I hurt you?"

In answer, Anna arched up. "No, it feels wonderful— more than wonderful." Slowly, sweetly, he resumed his earlier rhythm, and somehow her body knew just how to move in elemental harmony with his.

Two as one.

Devlin shifted, and she was acutely aware of myriad subtle sensations—liquid heat, thudding hearts, the exquisite friction of flesh against flesh. Everything seemed to be quickening. Her breathing was turning into ragged little gasps. With each rise and fall, Anna felt the pressure inside her growing, a cresting force searching for release.

She knew what was coming, and yet the entwining intimacy seemed almost too intensely exquisite to bear.

Clutching his shoulders, she cried out, giving voice to its need. His skin was damp, his muscles bunched taut beneath her fingertips, and she could feel the same thrumming pulsing through him.

Gilded in the golden lamplight, their bodies arced on the makeshift bed, the velvety whisper of the cloth echoing the swirling sounds of passion.

Anna felt his mouth, warm and wanting, possess hers,

and for a perfect moment they seemed to be melting and molding together, two hearts beating as one.

Thud, thud.

And then...and then...

The exquisite sensation was too much to bear. As Devlin's hips thrust against hers, she felt herself shatter into swirling shards of crystalline light.

Chapter Twenty-One

The stirring was soft as a dream at first, but quickly became more insistent, drawing him out of a honeyed sleep.

"I have been thinking," announced Anna.

"Mmmm?" Devlin opened one eye, just enough to make out the quicksilver play of moonlight and shadows dancing across the plaster ceiling. "No thinking, remember?" He was still savoring the delightful languor suffusing his limbs. "It's against the Rake's Rules of Midnight Lovemaking."

She shifted on the velvet.

"Page eight in the handbook," he added drowsily.

"Davenport—"

"Devlin," he corrected, adding a smile despite the fact that her reversion to his title stirred a small frisson of unease.

"Very well then, Devlin," said Anna.

Something in her voice brought him wide awake.

She rolled over to face him and propped herself up on one elbow. "It may be against the rules, but nonetheless,

something important has occurred to me and I should like
to discuss it with you."

He had an inkling of what it was. And while he had already made up his mind on what to do, he was hoping to
linger just a little while longer in the blissful haze of sweet
oblivion.

"May we talk about it later?" he asked.

"I would rather do it now."

Devlin had come to recognize that tone. It indicated that
the earth might tremble and monuments might crumble,
but her mind, once resolved on a course of action, would
let nothing stand in its way.

"You," he said, heaving a martyred sigh, "can be exceedingly stubborn."

"Like you, I concede that I have more than a few faults,"
said Anna sweetly. "Stubbornness is one of them."

The show of toughness belied the vision before his
eyes. With her unpinned hair tumbled over her lovely
shoulders and the rumpled fabric tucked loosely around
her slender body, she looked exceedingly vulnerable.

A teasing comment died on his lips. Instead, he hitched
himself up against the wall.

"Very well. But instead of beating around the bushes,
why don't we simply cut to the chase and avoid any awk-
wardness about the subject. I fully intend to marry you.
Though I hope you will spare me the spectacle of a fancy
wedding at St. George's of Hanover Square."

"Marry?" Shock slowly spread over her face. "Ye gods,
Devlin, you don't want to marry me."

"After this…" He gestured at the glimmers of their
moonlit nakedness peeking through the black velvet,
"honor demands it."

"Be damned with honor!" exclaimed Anna. She frowned. "Besides, you don't have any."

"That may be true, but I do have a shred of common decency left. And common decency demands that I marry you."

"Because I'm *ruined*?"

Damn.

Either way he answered the question would land him in a very deep and unpleasant hole.

Taking his silence as surrender, Anna quickly went on. "So, you may put the notion out of your head."

"Because I'm an unprincipled scoundrel?"

That took a little of the wind out of her sails. "I—I didn't say that."

"You implied it. The Devil Davenport has the morals of a snake, so of course he can put the notion—as you so charmingly call it—out of his head."

"I've hurt your feelings," she said, sounding surprised.

"How could you?" Devlin replied, assuming his most offensive drawl. He did not wish for her to see, that yes, she had cut him, more than he cared to admit. "I have none of those either."

Anna looked away. In the shifting shadows, it was impossible to read her expression. "Forgive me, I should have worded my reaction differently."

The iron fist in the velvet glove, rather than bare steel smacking him square in the gut?

"You took me by surprise," she added softly.

"My apologies," he said stiffly, "for upsetting you with such an outrageous proposal."

"Being surprised is not the same thing as being upset."

"Clearly I don't understand the nuances of language as you do," he growled. "I'm an idiot, remember?"

"Are you now going to sulk?" she inquired.

His temper, which had been hanging on by a thread, suddenly snapped. "Satan stick me with his pitchfork! I am *not* sulking!"

She lifted a brow.

"Men don't sulk."

"Apparently they do," replied Anna calmly. "I've seen a great many sulks, and you are definitely sulking."

Trying to maintain some stitch of dignity—his manly pride seemed to have been lost in the helter-pelter jumble of clothing on the floor—Devlin decided to prove her wrong. "Let us drop the subject, shall we? If not marriage, what was it you wanted to talk about?"

Anna smoothed the velvet down over her bare toes. "I really have hurt your feelings."

"Let us drop the subject, shall we?"

Hitching closer, a move that revealed an all-too-tantalizing peek at her breasts, Anna touched a hand to his cheek. "I'm sorry. I truly didn't mean to."

At her touch, his resolve to remain angry seemed to flit away like a midnight shadow. "You didn't hurt my feelings, you wounded my vanity." He forced a smile. "There is a great difference."

"Men!" she declared, sounding exasperated. "I swear, for all your fearsome huffing and puffing, you are even more delicate creatures than women."

"Are you now questioning my manhood?" Chuckling, Devlin pulled her into his arms. "I shall be happy to give another demonstration to prove that I am not a wilting flower."

Anna snuggled against his chest, her breath tickling sweetly against his skin. "I was speaking metaphorically."

"Use small words, please, so that my delicate brain can understand them."

She laughed softly, dispelling the worst of the darkness that had settled in the pit of his belly. "Did we just have our first quarrel?"

He gave a mock grimace. "Hardly. We have been spatting like cats and hounds ever since we met."

"I suppose we did go at it tooth and nail for the first few confrontations," she mused. "But then..."

Devlin waited for her to go on.

"But then, it became more of...a game is not at all the right word. Perhaps a better way to describe is a test of wits."

"And wills?" he suggested. "You are used to being adored. That I didn't fawn over you piqued your interest."

"You are used to being reviled. That I wasn't afraid of you was something you found intriguing." She pulled a face. "At least I knew you weren't paying attention to me because of my money. I had none to speak of."

He felt himself stiffen as her words stirred an unpleasant thought. Did she think his mention of marriage had anything to do with her newfound wealth? Wrexham was a very rich man, and it was said he had gifted both of the younger Sloanes with generous dowries. As to the amount, he hadn't a clue.

"Are you chilled?" she asked, flattening her palm and slowly circling it against his chest.

"Nothing—not cold nor heat nor tender sentiment—permeates my thick hide," he replied mockingly, afraid to betray how vulnerable he felt.

As for my heart, it feels like shards of ice are prickling like daggers against the sensitive flesh.

Silence seized the moment. Anna drew her knees up to her chin and sat lost in thought for a while before responding. "I am not sure why you are so terrified to admit to having a sense of honor."

"This is getting tedious," said Devlin through his clenched teeth. "I don't have one."

"And yet you engage in dangerous work for the government to defend our country from harm."

"That's because the government pays me very well."

Anna cocked her head. "Yes, you sound very convincing, and no doubt your assertions fool most people. However, you forget, I, too, have had a great deal of experience in hiding my true feelings from the world, so I recognize all the telltale signs of subterfuge."

That she could penetrate his defenses so easily was frightening. In an instant he was back to brooding.

"Oh, dear," she murmured. "It seems our second spat is following hard on the heels of the first."

"Stop that," he growled.

"You mean this?" Anna ran her fingertips lightly through the coarse curls peppering his chest. "But I like all your different textures and the way they feel against my skin."

"I—" Devlin expelled a harried sigh as she did it again. "Damnation, I am trying to stay angry with you."

In response Anna twined a curl around a fingertip.

An apt metaphor, he decided glumly, for how easily she could wrap him around her pinkie. "You are impossible."

The sweetness of her laugh nearly took his breath away. "Which only goes to show that we are truly kindred souls."

Then why won't you marry me?

Devlin held back from asking. He had already been rejected once. Twice in one night might crush even as callous a heart as his own.

Besides, he didn't blame her. What lady in her right mind would choose a rake with an unsteady temperament and a near-empty purse when she had her choice of far more attractive suitors?

"Cry pax, Devlin?" she added softly.

"*We* are not at war," he said quickly. Enough of personal battles that he had no chance of winning. "There are real enemies out there and we had better turn our thoughts to defeating their plan."

She sat up a little straighter. "I was wondering when you were going to stop being so secretive and tell me what you have in mind. How are you going to stop Verdemont, and what can I do to help?"

"I've come up with a strategy for the moors, but I need to work out the final details with McClellan first thing in the morning," replied Devlin. "As for your role, well, part of the reason I brought you here was because I wanted you to become familiar with the layout. As you might have noticed, there's a storeroom right outside this alcove with one of those massive ancient doors that weighs more than a Highland ox. More importantly, it's equipped with an iron padlock."

"Perhaps I should feel offended that seduction wasn't your primary plan?" she interrupted.

He waved off the suggestion. "Don't change the subject. You know I am easily distracted."

She lifted a brow.

"It would be exceedingly helpful if you could lure Lady de Blois here when we go off to the hunt. Make up some farriddiddle—tell her you've discovered a jewel collection that seems to have been forgotten, and need her help to discern what gems are the most valuable. Act excited—she'll understand greed as an elemental emotion."

"Yes, yes," interrupted Anna. "I understand the scenario. Leave the details to me. I shall come up with a compelling scene." She thought for a moment. "It should be easy enough to trick her into entering the storeroom...a special chest filled with Viking gold, perhaps. Or a horde of Elizabethan earrings. However, just in case she needs additional persuasion, I ought to have a weapon."

Devlin heaved an unhappy sigh. "I supposed you are right. I'll give you my pocket pistol tomorrow. But blast it all, Manton's handiwork cost me a fortune, so please see that it comes to no harm."

"Ye gods, you and your precious pistol." She made a face. "Don't worry. It will be safe with me."

As opposed to my heart, which I've discovered is surprisingly fragile.

"I shall expect you to replace it if it's lost or damaged."

Anna rolled her eyes. "When Caro was six, she had a favorite doll with a porcelain head and—"

"We had better not linger here any longer," interrupted Devlin, in no mood to suffer further indignities. He leaned over and felt around for his shirt. "Only Lucifer knows what demands the coming day will bring, so I suggest we return to our rooms and get a few hours of sleep."

Anna watched him fish his clothing up from the stone tiles. Something was wrong. She felt it too. "Wait," she murmured, as a stocking slapped against the velvet.

He found her breeches and dropped them in her lap. "Dawn is already creeping up to the horizon. So I suggest you hurry and dress. We both need to face the enemy with a clear head."

"Then it's best we clear the air between us," she answered. "You're upset. We should talk about why."

Anna saw his body stiffen for just an instant. "I'm tired," he shot back. "And have done quite enough talking for one night."

Could it be that she had wounded more than just pride with her refusal?

"That may be, but I've a few things to say, if you please."

Devlin stilled, but did not bring his gaze around to meet hers.

Drat, he seems determined to make this difficult.

"You spoke about marriage earlier," she began hesitantly.

"And you rejected the idea out of hand," he replied. "What more needs to be said?"

"You mentioned honor and duty."

You did not speak of love.

At that, he slowly turned to face her. "Did I leave something out?" His smile was sardonic, but it didn't reach his eyes. A different emotion seemed pooled beneath the fringe of his lashes.

"Yes." Her heart was thumping against her ribs. "You did."

He smoothed at the crumpled sleeve of his shirt. "What?"

"Oh, you big lummox," she muttered under her breath.

A spark of amusement lit the darkness for just an instant, the first sign of warmth in a while.

"Are you hinting a lady likes to be wooed?"

It was her turn to look away.

I don't want to be wooed, I want to be loved. But maybe

Devlin had been telling the truth when he had said that he didn't have a heart.

"Anna, your Mama wouldn't approve. Wrexham wouldn't approve. Polite Society wouldn't approve. Hell's teeth—I can't think of *anyone* who would approve."

"And since when are you so concerned with the opinion of others?" she demanded.

He opened his mouth and then shut it.

To her dismay, Anna felt tears sting against her lids. *Love.* Was it that hard a word to say?

Throwing off the velvet covering, she grabbed up her shirt and pulled it on. "You're right," she muttered. "We ought to be going."

Devlin didn't budge. In the fire-kissed light, his torso had a smooth, classical beauty, as if it were sculpted out of marble.

Hermes, the ancient Greek god of thieves.

No, no, that wasn't quite fair. He hadn't stolen her heart. She had given it freely. The fact that he didn't want it wasn't his fault.

Swallowing a sigh, Anna jammed one leg, then the other into her breeches. "Have you seen my stockings?"

"Now who is upset?"

"Oh, never mind. Here they are."

"Anna, there truly isn't time to continue this discussion right now," Devlin pointed out. "But be assured, we haven't finished with the subject."

"On the contrary, as you so eloquently put it, what more needs to be said?"

"This." He pulled her close and kissed her. Quite thoroughly. "I'm not as clever with words as you are. Give me some time to compose my thoughts. But first we have a pair of cunning criminals to catch."

Chapter Twenty-Two

$\mathcal{D}$espite a fitful few hours of tossing and turning, Anna rose early and was already at her dressing table unplaiting her hair when Josette came in for her morning duties. With her she brought a cup of steaming hot chocolate.

"I thought you might like some sustenance to start the morning, mademoiselle. You have seemed a little peaked of late."

"Thank you." Anna set it aside, her stomach too jumpy for food or drink. "How very thoughtful."

"Smudges." Her maid was not eyeing any of the clothing in the armoire. "You've even darker smudges under your eyes this morning."

"I…"

"*Amour*," intoned Josette with a knowing nod. "Oh, a bit of rice powder can hide the signs of love for now. But you ought to think of the future, and decide whether it's wise to trust your heart to a rogue."

Shifting uncomfortably in her chair, Anna found herself wishing that Josette was not quite so clever. "Are you sure that you are not a Gypsy in disguise? You seem to have an uncanny knack for seeing beneath a person's skin."

The maid turned abruptly, spilling a bit of the powder. "Pardon," she muttered. A quick swipe of her handkerchief dusted the tabletop clean. "I have no supernatural powers, nor do I possess the Evil Eye, mademoiselle. Moving from place to place has taught me to be observant, that is all."

Anna bit her lip. She seemed to be offending everyone around her. Josette's tumultuous childhood had slipped her mind. *The maid's loss of her well-to-do family, the up-heaval of her way of life…the poverty that had forced her into service…* Ye gods, the Gypsy remark had been a clumsy and careless reminder that she too, was a homeless vagabond.

"Please forgive me, Josette. It was meant as a jest, but my tongue seems to be tripping over itself lately."

"Perhaps I should learn fortune-telling," said Josette with a shrug that signaled no umbrage had been taken. "I hear that reading the cards is just as popular in England as it is in France. I could make some extra pin money."

"I daresay you would be very good at it. And think of the wonderful costumes you could design…" To Anna's relief, the rest of the dressing interlude passed in friendly chatter.

"Oh, excellent! I was hoping you were up and dressed." Caro entered the bedchamber just as Josette fixed the last few hairpins into the place. "I…I have something I wish to discuss with you."

"I shall take these shifts and chemises down to the laundry room," said Josette, quickly gathering up an armful of garments from the floor of the armoire and discreetly withdrawing.

As soon as the outer door closed, Caro perched herself on the edge of the dressing table. "Well? Did you meet with Davenport after we all had retired?"

"Yes."

"Oooo, how exciting. I wish that I could experience a midnight adventure."

Before her sister could demand any details of the encounter, Anna hurriedly confided the outline of Devlin's plan and her assignment to lure Lady de Blois to the remote automata gallery. "But first I need to meet Dev—Davenport in his room at ten, when it's least likely for anyone to be moving through the corridors. He is going to lend me his pocket pistol, just in case."

Caro leaned forward expectantly. "In case of what?" Her glance fell on the cup of chocolate. "By the by, are you going to drink that?"

"In case of trouble," she answered. "And no, I'm not," she added. "You are welcome to have it."

"Oh, do go on," said her sister after a long swallow. "Why, exactly does he want you to take her to that particular place?"

"Because it has a storage room with a very heavy door and a sturdy lock. My task is to confine her there until Devlin can arrange to have both of the miscreants taken away by his government contact," she explained. "I have an idea on how to trick her into entering it. However, if anything goes awry, I wish to have something more convincing than words to make the comtesse doing my bidding."

"How…" Caro paused to pat back a yawn. "How can I help?"

"Actually, I think it best to for me to deal with her

alone," replied Anna. "She may get wary if I say that you are accompanying us."

Her sister plainly didn't like being left out of the action, but she held back any complaints and merely nodded. "I suppose that makes sense. But surely there is *some* role I can play."

"Actually there is. Can you find McClellan and alert him that Davenport will be looking for him before the hunting party assembles to leave for the moors?" she asked. "You might also warn him that Davenport plans to make his move just before the hunt reaches the Witch Coven and may need help to spirit Verdemont away." She paused for a fraction. "It never hurts to have message passed on by you too, just as a precaution in case they miss each other beforehand."

Caro nodded, not before stifling a second yawn.

So, I am not the only one plagued by sleepless nights.

Anna couldn't help but wonder just how much her sister's feelings for the rough-mannered McClellan had changed since their initial clashes. But for the moment, she pretended not to see the tiny gesture.

"Never fear." For some reason, Caro chose to drop her voice to a conspiratorial whisper. "I'll handle it." Hurrying away from the table, she flung open the bedchamber door—

And nearly knocked Josette off her feet.

"I'm so sorry! I—I didn't hear you come in," stammered Caro.

"No harm done," said Josette as she hastily gathered the clothing she had dropped. "I did not wish to intrude on your sisterly confidences, so I was just going to leave these items on the sideboard." She held out the same shifts and chemises that she had gathered up earlier and explained, "The laundry room's main tub has sprung a leak, so they have put off the wash day until tomorrow. I thought it best to bring your things back here, so they wouldn't get lost."

"I'm very grateful that you manage things so well, Josette," replied Anna. "I am aware of how fortunate I am to have found you."

"I try to be efficient, mademoiselle," said her maid. She carefully folded the garments and placed them on the sideboard. "*Voilà*. I shall now leave you and Mademoiselle Caro to finish your tête-à-tête in private."

"Oh, I was just leaving," said Caro, casting a meaningful look at Anna. "I promised Mama that I would see if she left her embroidery box in the Morning Room."

"Yes, by all means, do. You know how cross she gets when she's misplaced something," she said.

With that, her sister lost no more time in quitting the room.

"Shall I take away the chocolate?" asked Josette, spotting the empty cup.

"Yes, thank you." Feeling a bit guilty from earlier, Anna quickly added, "It was delicious."

"*Bon*." Her maid did a last bit of tidying to the vials and boxes on the dressing table. "Shall you be needing me to change for nuncheon?"

"No, no. Your time is your own until the supper hour."

Josette turned to leave.

"Thank you again—for everything," said Anna, nervousness making her edgy. "I hope you know how much I have come to value not only your skills but also your sage advice. I am grateful."

The maid quirked a half-smile. "That is kind of you, mademoiselle. Though I fear the differences in our stations of life make it very hard to be true friends, I sense that we are, in many ways, kindred souls, *non*?"

"Would that I had your worldly confidence and experience," murmured Anna. Thinking of the coming challenges had her stomach all aflutter.

"Be careful what you wish for," responded Josette. With that, she bobbed a parting nod and quietly drew the door shut behind her.

Devlin paced back and forth before the sitting room hearth, mentally reviewing his plan for thwarting the vicomte's attempt to kill the prince while he waited for Anna to make her way to his chambers. Unlike the designs for his intricate automata, he had decided that it was best to keep things simple. As the hunt approached the Witch Coven, McClellan would add a little extra distance between each shooter, making sure to assign Verdemont the lead position. Devlin would be next in line, and when they wound their way into the rocky outcroppings at the foot of the knoll, he would creep in to close the gap. At the first sign of foul play, he would pounce and disarm the Frenchman with the help of two of the burly local ghillies that the baron would station in hiding.

The gunpowder in Verdemont's cartridges and powder case had been replaced with a harmless substitute, so his weapon would be useless. Even without that precaution, the man would have little chance against three opponents. And McClellan would keep watch on the top of the knoll, in case an accomplice was lurking.

Pursing his lips, Devlin tried to think of any flaw he was missing, but things seemed well in order. The prince should be safe and the conspirator caught in the act, allowing the government to eliminate a very cunning foreign agent from British soil.

The only cause for concern was Anna's role. He was starting to have second thoughts about having her lure Lady de Blois to the remote automata gallery. The comtesse might appear to be nothing more than a sexual temptress, but the fact that she was involved in a traitorous conspiracy meant she was scheming, cold-blooded, and likely dangerous as a viper if cornered. Anna was clever and intrepid, but if matched against someone who knew a number of sordid tricks—

He spun around at the soft click of the door latch releasing. "I was beginning to worry that you had been spotted."

"I had to wait for the maid to finish dusting the suit of armor outside the Weapon Room," answered Anna, after pausing to catch her breath. "I've sent Caro to alert McClellan that you wish to meet with him before assembling for the hunt."

"I've asked one of the ghillies to deliver the same message, but thank you."

"She wishes to feel involved in the action," said Anna. "I can't say I blame her. It is deucedly hard to accept being constantly told you are too young or too inexperienced to help."

Devlin cleared his throat. "Then I daresay you aren't going to like what I say next."

The glint of anticipation in her eyes was replaced by a more martial light.

"We made an agreement," he hastened to add. "You

promised to withdraw if I decide things have become too dangerous."

"Having proved myself capable of looking out for myself—need I remind you it was me who found the incriminating letters and then was quick-witted enough to escape without being seen—don't you think that I have earned the right to argue the point?"

"We don't have time," he muttered.

"If you're worried that I don't know how to handle a pistol, you're wrong. My father believed all his daughters should know how to defend themselves. Granted, I've not handled one of Manton's pocket pistols, but the principle is the same. And I'll have you know that I'm an excellent shot."

"Lady de Blois might have a pocket pistol as well, or a dagger hidden away in her skirts," he countered. "And no compunction about striking a mortal blow."

"You're worried that I'm not a match for her?" asked Anna in a measured voice.

"Yes." A breath broke free from his lungs. "No. I'm worried that you might be hurt." *And I couldn't bear it.*

Her expression softened. "You don't think I worry about you?"

"I'm just a big lummox, remember?"

"You are," she said, a tiny smile tugging at the corners of her mouth. "And I must be a feather-witted fool, for my heart seems intent on overlooking such an egregious fault."

Her heart? His insides gave an odd little lurch.

She eyed the mantel clock. "You're right in that we don't have a moment to dally in argument. Come, open your workroom, and let us fetch the pistol. At least let me show you that I know how to use it. If you're not satisfied with my prowess, I'll do as you ask and won't confront Lady de Blois."

Devlin knew he should not be swayed by that smile. "Very well. But I warn you that I won't change my mind, regardless. It's too dangerous."

"Fine." She said something under her breath that sounded suspiciously like "We'll see about that," before adding, "We really must hurry!"

Pulling the key from his pocket, he led the way into his bedchamber. "I will likely regret this," he muttered.

"No, you won't," answered Anna sweetly, as she took up a position at the head of his work table. "By the by, how is your feathery weapon coming?"

"It's finished. You may have a look if you wish. It's under the chamois cloth by the paint box."

He heard a soft gasp as she lifted the covering. It was, he reflected a little proudly, rather a magnificent piece of work. The gold and jeweled detailings gleamed in the windowless light, and the actual workings of the weapon were an exact replica of the real thing. All in all, it was the finest thing he had ever made, and that she admired his handiwork—

"Actually Miss Sloane, I regret to say that Lord Davenport is right. He *will* regret this."

Devlin whipped around to see Verdemont and Lady de Blois standing in the doorway. The vicomte had a pistol pointed at his heart. "And so will you, Miss Sloane."

"I don't know why the two of you chose to interfere with us," added Lady de Blois. She, too, was armed, which didn't surprise him. During their earlier interlude of flirtation, he had noticed that her eyes had a flat, reptilian coldness to them.

"But you will now pay for it dearly," went on the comtesse, a note of ugly anticipation in her voice as she flecked the point of her lethal-looking dagger back and forth through the air.

"How did you discover that we knew?" asked Anna.

"Never mind that," snarled Verdemont. "Come with me, Davenport. If you do as you're told, the girl won't get hurt." A nasty grin. "But I'd hurry if I were you. Marie-Helene sometimes likes to amuse herself with her blade if she grows bored with standing guard."

"Surely you can see that your plans have run amok," said Devlin, feeling a chill skate down his spine. "If you're wise, you'll flee while you can."

"Be quiet," ordered Lady de Blois. "We are far more clever than you and that silly little chit you've chosen to take up with."

A sound rumbled in Anna's throat, but he shot her a warning look that silenced any retort.

"You were a fool, Davenport," she added. "You should have been satisfied with having a pleasant little dalliance with me—and be assured, you would have been very well satisfied. But no, for some reason you felt compelled to poke your nose where it didn't belong."

"Aren't you curious as to why?"

A flicker of doubt shaded the comtesse's gaze.

"It doesn't matter," snapped Verdemont. "Now move— slowly and around the far end of the table—unless you want to see Marie-Helene get angry. She has a very violent temper."

Damnation. He was too far away to make a lunge at the vicomte. There seemed no choice but to obey and hope to escape once the two of them were alone.

As for Anna...

A desperate idea suddenly came to mind. It was risky, but he had no illusion that their captors had any intention of releasing them.

"Just behave like an automaton, Anna," he said, hoping she would understand the cryptic message. "You heard what the vicomte said—everything will be fine if we obey orders."

Anna watched Devlin follow the vicomte's directions and edge slowly toward the door. He turned for one last look but she had only a chance to flutter her lashes once before the vicomte jammed the pistol barrel in his ribs and made him move on.

Think! If ever there was a time to be as bold and resourceful as her pen-and-ink heroine, it was now.

"Ha!" Lady de Blois let out an evil laugh as soon as the outer door closed. "Men are such trusting creatures, but you and I know better, don't we, Miss Sloane?"

Anna answered with a girlish whimper.

The comtesse curled a look of contempt. "What a spoiled, lily-livered little chit you are. It's a pity, really. It's far more interesting to best a worthy opponent. But you..." She ran the blade of her dagger lightly over her thumb. "I've known lambs with more fight than you have."

"Lord Davenport is right. Your plans have been foiled." It was worth a try, decided Anna, to try to rattle her captor's composure. "Lord McClellan knows everything."

"We're aware of that," snapped the comtesse. "But you see, the key to being truly clever is knowing how to improvise." Her mouth now formed a mocking smile. "As we speak, Pierre is taking Davenport to the prince's chambers.

Two shots and *voilà*! What a scandal—an English peer murders a relative of the English King, but not before being mortally wounded himself. Pierre will say he heard the fight, but arrived too late to help poor Gunther, only to hear the dastardly Davenport's confession of being an agent for the French."

It was a diabolically clever plan. Given Devlin's awful reputation and the rumors of how badly he needed money, the story would be believed by most people.

"What about m-me?"

"Alas, you were also a victim of the deranged marquess," answered Lady de Blois. He had seduced you, but had grown weary of your tearful demands that he marry you. When you came here this morning and threatened to make a scene, he had to silence you."

Anna didn't need to muster much acting ability to appear frightened. But the fear bubbling up inside her was for Devlin. There wasn't much time, and the seconds were slipping away with each step.

Feigning a swoon, she moaned and let her knees buckle.

The comtesse laughed as Anna caught herself on the table and slumped forward, arms outstretched as if begging for mercy.

Steady, steady. Her fingers slid over the waxed wood, feeling for the chamois. A touch of soft leather, then blessedly hard metal.

"It is pitiful how you weak English roses wilt," taunted the comtesse. But her mirth pinched in mid-breath to a strangled snarl as she found herself looking down the shiny barrel of a bejeweled pocket pistol.

"Drop the dagger," ordered Anna coolly as she snapped upright.

Lady de Blois stared in disbelief, then spat out a string of obscenities.

"Drop it *now*." She cocked the hammer, praying it wouldn't trigger the music mechanism. "I won't ask again."

After an excruciating pause, the blade clattered to the floor.

"Now kick it away."

"Devil-bitch," uttered Lady de Blois, her face red with rage. But after a tiny hesitation, a swipe of her foot sent the razored steel skittering into the shadows.

Darting a glance at the doorway, Anna started to edge around the table. "Now kindly move back a step," she said.

The comtesse did as she was told.

One, two ... a half dozen strides and she would be free.

A rush of elation began to tingle through her limbs, and yet a tiny voice in her head reminded her of Devlin's warning that Lady de Blois was dangerous as a viper.

She wrenched her eyes back just in time to see the comtesse whip out a small stiletto from her skirts and lunge.

Twisting away, she flung herself sideways and threw up an arm to block the vicious stab aimed at her heart. The blade sliced through her sleeve, and cut a gash through her flesh.

The pistol fell to the table.

Lady de Blois snatched it up and with a bark of triumph, took dead aim and pulled the trigger.

A tiny bird exploded from the barrel and began to spin and flap its tiny feathered wings.

Anna swallowed the half-crazed urge to laugh. As the comtesse stared in mute shock, the trilling notes of a high-pitched birdsong began to flutter through the air.

Oh, Devlin was a genius—a maddeningly clever, winsome, infuriating genius.

And one who would soon be meeting his Maker if she didn't quickly gather her wits and rush to his rescue.

She dashed for the door and slammed it shut just as Lady de Blois made a grab for her skirts. The key was still in the lock, and a quick turn shot the bolt into place.

Fists hammered against the paneled oak, punctuated by a howl.

No matter that the sounds were nearly as sweet to her ears as the twitter of the pistol, she wasted no time in savoring her victory. Spinning around, Anna flew for the darkened corridor.

Chapter Twenty-Three

$\mathcal{D}$amn. Devlin cursed his stupidity. He had made the cardinal mistake of underestimating an enemy. And now Anna was going to pay for his mistake.

His blood curdled at the idea of her alone and at the mercy of the comtesse.

"I wonder that you can bear to take a viper to bed," he said aloud. "But then, I suppose that two poisonous snakes twine together quite nicely."

"Shut your mouth," snarled Verdemont, drawing back the snout of the pistol and jamming it hard against his ribs.

That gave Devlin an idea—a rather far-fetched one, but he was running out of time.

"Or what?" he retorted. "You'll sink your ugly fangs into my neck?"

This time, he anticipated the blow and jerked sideways just as the steel touched his side. The barrel skidded awkwardly and for an instant its aim wavered. A lashing kick staggered Verdemont just enough to break free of his grasp.

Grunting in pain, the vicomte smashed the butt of the weapon into Devlin's temple.

Pain shot through his head but he managed to dodge a second blow and counter with a punch to the other man's gut. Both of them fell to the floor in a welter of flailing arms and legs.

Though still a little dazed, Devlin managed to roll free.

Verdemont still had a grip on the pistol and was levering to his knees. Spotting the ancient suit of armor just ahead, Devlin slithered on his belly and grabbed hold of the gauntlet. A shove toppled the hulking mass of steel and sent it careening across the floor.

He heard a thud but was already scrambling through the doorway of the Weapon Room. Grabbing a claymore—the traditional two-handed Scottish longsword—from the wall display, he ducked behind one of the stone columns and waited.

Verdemont limped in, pistol at the ready. "You miserable whoreson. I should have put a bullet in your brain to begin with." Eyes narrowing to a slitted stare, he surveyed the room. "That will soon be rectified."

"Give it up," called Devlin. "Surrender now, and release Miss Sloane. In return, you have my word that I'll let you and your comrade-in-crime have an hour's headstart before I alert the authorities."   •

Several French epithets, each one more filthy than the last, expressed the vicomte's reaction to the offer.

"You've had fair warning." As he spoke, Devlin was assessing the situation. It was, he decided, less than ideal. The sword's prodigious length was of no advantage against a bullet, and it was heavier than Hades, making it difficult to wield with any speed. Just hefting the point several inches off the stone tiles sent a spasm of protest through his shoulder muscles.

Wincing, he glanced across the room. A crossbow would have been a far smarter choice—

"Devlin—watch out!" The warning shout had an all-too-familiar ring. "Verdemont is angling for a shot!"

Damnation. His momentary lapse in attention had allowed the vicomte to seize the advantage. Moving with surprising agility, Verdemont had darted past the display of stag-handled *sgian-dubh* and now had a clean sightline. Already his arm was raised...

Out of the corner of his eye, Devlin saw a blur of motion, accompanied by the whoosh of flapping skirts.

"DON'T!" he cried.

Too late. Anna slammed into the Frenchman with enough force to send them both sprawling.

Devlin sprinted for his fallen foe, somehow summoning the strength to brandish the claymore. As Verdemont tried to raise his groggy-eyed head, Devlin thrust a boot atop the vicomte's throat and forced him down. "I suggest you lie very still," he growled, placing the massive point on the Frenchman's quivering windpipe. "My arms are getting tired and the slightest jiggle..." A bead of blood welled up. "Oops."

Verdemont swallowed a gurgled groan and closed his eyes.

It was only then that Devlin dared look around.

Anna sat up slowly. Her hair was hanging in disarray around her shoulders, her nose was streaked with dust, and her face had a slightly lopsided look due to a nasty scrape on the left side of her chin.

She had never looked so utterly adorable.

"Are you utterly mad?" he said softly. "What in the unholy name of Lucifer possessed you to attack an armed assassin with naught but your bare hands?"

"I was," answered Anna, "possessed by the notion that I didn't care to see your brains spattered all over the display of quoits." She grimaced as she flexed her fingers. "Ye gods, why are you men always so anxious to engage in fisticuffs? It hurts like the devil to land a punch on someone's skull."

"You're supposed to aim for the chin," he murmured.

"Ah." She rubbed her knuckles. "I shall keep that in mind for next time."

Next time, he decided, was a battle to fight at some future moment. For now, he simply stared at her smile and felt his insides turn upside down.

"How did you get away?"

"A little bird helped me." Before she could say more, a gasp sounded from the doorway.

"Mademoiselle?"

Devlin recognized the petite figure of Anna's maid silhouetted in the soft light.

"W-what is happening here?" Another gasp. "*Sacre Coeur!* There is blood on your sleeve!"

A low oath slipped from his lips. For an instant, he was tempted to slit Verdemont's throat.

"Don't be alarmed, Josette, it's just a scratch," answered Anna. "There has been some trouble, but Lord Davenport has everything in hand. However, you could do us both a great favor if you would go find Lord Dunbar and ask him to come join us here. Please do it discreetly—oh, and mention that he ought to bring three of his largest footmen."

"Yes, of course," replied Josette. "But…but first let me help you up."

"Oh, you need not…"

Devlin wasn't unhappy to see the maid was already at Anna's side, smoothing a gentle hand through her tangled curls. "Merci," he muttered, quelling his murderous impulse for the moment. Still, he couldn't resist shifting his grip on the hilt, just enough to draw a squeak from the vicomte. "Miss Sloane is very fortunate to have such a loyal servant."

Like a spark from flint striking steel, Josette's smile flashed bright and then disappeared. "Actually, sir, I serve no one but myself."

Perhaps the earlier blow had indeed scrambled his wits, for he seemed to be hallucinating. A pistol had materialized from the maid's somber-hued skirts and its barrel was now pressed to Anna's temple.

"Put down the sword, Lord Davenport." The voice was all too real. "Enough of these cat-and-mouse games. Get up, Pierre. We must be off."

"Shoot her, Josie," moaned Verdemont. "Shoot them both."

"Impetuous, as always, *mon oncle*. That is why you must leave the decisions to me." She heaved a sigh. "Please do as I say, Lord Davenport. I'm willing to be reasonable, but only if you don't make me waste time in arguing."

Devlin lifted the claymore and let it fall to the floor.

"*Mon oncle?*" Anna's voice betrayed no fear, only curiosity. "The vicomte is your *uncle*?"

"*Oui*," replied Josette.

"I see." She fixed her maid with an appraising stare. "At

the time, I thought the fact that you chose to come work for our family, rather than a rich and influential one, was too good to be true. And now, I guess that I was right."

"You have a very sharp mind, Anna Sloane. Please believe me that I truly admire that," replied Josette. "Yes, it was no coincidence that I chose to come work for you. I needed an excuse to come to Dunbar Castle, and once we uncovered the fact that the countess was an old friend of your mother, a plan came to mind."

"Clever," conceded Anna. "And if I hadn't been looking to hire a maid?"

"Oh, I would have come up with some way to enter your household. I can be very creative." Her tone was light, but Devlin noted that the pistol's barrel didn't budge from Anna's head. "But alas, we have no time for a comfortable coze. Come, Pierre, on your feet. It's time to take our leave."

"But the prince," protested Verdemont as he gingerly got to his knees.

"I fear we must forget the prince. Miss Sloane and Lord Davenport have proved an unexpected obstacle to our attack, and we have lost this skirmish. A wise general knows when to withdraw in order to fight again another day." She retreated a step, pulling Anna with her. "We shall have other opportunities to hurt the British, *mon oncle*, but only if we go now."

"Wait," called Devlin. "You've no need to take Anna with you. I give you my word that we won't raise the alarm until you are well away."

"Your word as a gentleman?" Josette smiled. "You English have noble notions, but I prefer to trust in more practical guarantees. Like having a hostage."

"You forget that we have Lady de Blois," countered Devlin. "Forget nobility—I'm offering an exchange of prisoners."

Verdemont spat out a laugh. "Bah, keep her. As you pointed out, she's a viper. And of late, her fangs were growing a little too sharp."

"As you see, we have no need of bargaining, my lord." Josette started backing up toward the doorway. "And please, do not attempt to be a hero. Much as I like Miss Sloane, I will not hesitate to harm her if we are cornered."

The maid's cool calmness was far more chilling than wild-eyed anger. Devlin felt as if a vise was tightening around his chest.

"Don't try to be Emmalina," he said to Anna. A weak parting, but his brain wasn't functioning very well. "I'll...I'll make sure you come to no harm."

Anna's lips twitched in a rueful quirk. "Alessandro usually does figure out a way to save the day. I—"

A tug cut off her words. "Enough, mademoiselle. Bid your love good-bye. If both of you refrain from doing anything stupid, there's a good chance it won't be your last."

Love.

"Anna, I...I..." Devlin tried to swallow the lump in his throat.

"I love you too, so there's nothing to fear," she murmured. "Because we both know that love conquers all."

"A poetic sentiment," said Josette, as she led the way down a shallow set of stairs and turned into a narrow side corridor. "Did you learn that in one of the books you are so fond of reading?"

Anna answered the question with one of her own. "Where are we going? I thought you were eager to escape."

"While you had your nose buried in some horrid novel, I was spending my leisure time in more practical pursuits, like exploring the castle," replied her erstwhile maid. "This was dangerous territory in centuries past, so most ancient strongholds were built with a means for the inhabitants to leave if attacked by a more powerful enemy. The hill where we sit has several underground passages cut through it that lead out to a hidden egress. I took the precaution of stationing horses at one of them this morning, in case our improvised plan went awry."

"Josie," warned the vicomte.

"I'm revealing no great secret, Pierre. Miss Sloane is clever enough to figure it out for herself, once we enter the tunnel." Josette finally lowered the pistol just a fraction. "How did you and your Devil discover our plan?"

"I don't intend to reveal that."

"I could loosen your tongue quite quickly if I wished to, but it's not important."

"I don't have to ask how you knew about our activities," said Anna.

"You were careful in talking to your sister, but not careful enough," replied Josette. "I must say, you intrigue me, mademoiselle. Always reading, always scribbling in one of your little notebooks. Though I must say, I did sneak a peek at them, and they were filled with all sorts of odd observations that made little sense."

"Like you, I am observant," answered Anna.

"Unfortunately too observant." Josette turned down another passageway. The way was getting narrower, the air damper. She halted for a moment, then pushed Anna behind her. "From here on, we must go in single file."

Verdemont swore as he bumped his head on the rock ceiling. "Stop gabbling, *ma petite*, and quicken your steps. The sooner we are out of this cursed tunnel the better," he grumbled.

"What made you betray your heritage..." began Anna, then paused for a moment. "A silly question," she went on. "I suppose the story about your aristocratic family being executed during the Revolution is all fabricated, and you're simply radicals who've been planted here as spies."

"No, my background is all true," said Josette. "As for why..." Another turn, this one leading down. "I should think it would be obvious to a female with brains. The Old Order oppresses those of our sex—we are considered good for being nothing but brood mares or kitchen drudges. The New France allows clever women to use their abilities. My work is not a betrayal but an affirmation. I am helping to create a more perfect world."

"Through violence and assassination?" murmured Anna. "It does not bother you that so much innocent blood has been spilled?"

"The ends justify the means," snapped Josette.

She could see that argument was pointless. Zealots were rarely open to reason. The more important question was how to prevent them from escaping to commit more violence in the future.

True, Devlin had warned her not to attempt any heroics, but...

Josette's small lantern cast a flicker of light over the way ahead, showing another set of steps twisting down through a turn in the rough-hewn rock.

It was, she knew, a risky move to try. She would need perfect timing—and perfect luck. But the idea of making no attempt to prevent the pair from escaping and causing more bloodshed and mayhem for her country was not something she could live with.

Devlin was not the only one with a sense of justice and honor. She steadied her nervousness with a deep breath, glad she had told him that she loved him. Perhaps she had appeared a romantic fool, but his expression as she was pulled away had seemed to say otherwise.

Wrenching her thoughts back to the present, Anna began counting the steps to come. *One, two, three...* As her foot slid to the top edge of the stairs, she made her move.

Devlin grabbed a dagger from the wall display. He had heard Anna and her captors turn down one of the side passageways, which he knew led into the ancient part of the castle rather than any of the closer exits to the outdoors.

What the maid had in mind was a mystery. But despite her warning, he couldn't simply sit still and hope for the best. Tightening his grip on the dagger, he moved to the doorway and ventured a look up and down the main corridor. Still no sign that the household was aware that anything was amiss.

Praying his luck would hold, Devlin crept into the shadows and hurried to the turn up ahead. A quick glance showed the way was clear. Josette was setting a fast pace. Clearly she had a plan.

He was just about to set off when the sound of approaching steps made him quickly turn the corner and flatten himself against the dark wainscoting. With luck, whoever was coming would pass without noticing him.

"You are sure the rendezvous was for Davenport's quarters?" Though the question was uttered in a whisper, McClellan's voice was unmistakable.

"Yes," insisted Caro. She sounded a little woozy. "But I'm not sure how long I was asleep."

"I'm damnably glad to see you." Devlin stepped out from his hiding place. "How well do you know the castle?" he demanded of the baron.

"I spent countless hours of my childhood here. I'm familiar with every crack and cranny," he replied.

"Is there a way out from the ancient tower, other than windows?"

"Yes," said McClellan without hesitation. "There's a secret tunnel that branches off to several exits within the walled grounds. But—"

"How many?" interrupted Devlin. "Verdemont and his cohort have taken Anna as a hostage to ensure their escape."

Caro sucked in a sharp breath. "It's Josette, isn't it?"

"How did you guess?" he asked.

"The chocolate she brought to Anna's room—it was drugged. I drank it instead."

"I found Miss Caro slumped in a chair in the parlor and was able to rouse her. Otherwise I'd be waiting for you by the stables," explained the baron. "What happened?"

"Never mind that now. Again, how many exits are there?"

"Two—no, three," responded McClellan.

"Damn," swore Devlin. He had to make a decision, and quickly. Grabbing the baron's arm, he gave him a small shove. "Pick the two most likely and let us fly."

"I—I'm c-coming with you," cried Caro, though her knees nearly buckled as she tried to match their stride.

He turned. "I applaud your pluck, but you'll only slow us down."

"If you truly wish to help," interrupted McClellan, "hurry and find Lord Dunbar. Tell him to take some men to the stone cistern by the rose garden. Explain what's happened—"

"That's too dangerous," protested Devlin. "The maid must be taken by surprise. Or...or Anna may come to harm."

"Scotland is a rough land, Davenport, with many feuds that bubble up into violence." He signaled Caro to be off, adding, "Dunbar will know how to take them by surprise if they come out there."

"Let us pray so," muttered Devlin as he watched Anna's sister lift her skirts and hurry off as fast as her wobbly legs would allow.

"Prayers are all very well. But action speaks louder than words." The baron drew a pistol from inside his coat. "Follow me."

Chapter Twenty-Four

$\mathcal{T}$he vicomte was right on her heels, his impatience to be out of the cramped tunnel evident in his jumpy step. Steeling her nerve and her body, Anna stopped abruptly on the edge of the stair and let him slam into her. A twist of her hip knocked him further off balance, and a shove sent him pitching forward.

An oath echoed off the jagged stone, punctuated by the thud of colliding flesh and the clang of the brass lantern hitting the treads.

Then all went black.

Anna knew she would have only moment or two to seize the advantage. Bracing her hands against the walls to keep from falling, she rushed down the steps, scuffing over tangled limbs and skirts.

Had Josette lost hold of the pistol?

Dropping to her hands and knees, Anna began a frantic search of the ground below the shallow stairs. The lantern...bits of broken glass...a pool of wax still hot to the touch...

Thank God. Her fingers curled around the butt of the weapon.

Scrambling out of reach of her still-thrashing captors, Anna cocked the hammer, taking heart from the loud metallic click. "Don't move," she ordered. Unfortunately, her voice didn't sound quite as intimidating as the pistol's sound.

"Clever," came Josette's reply from out of the gloom. "But you have been reading too many novels. Miss Sloane. You have one bullet and there are two of us."

"I have a knife," lied Anna. "I shall shoot your uncle and take my chances with you, Josette."

A laugh, more amused than angry. "And you would use it?"

"My father was an eccentric explorer," she countered. "One of his quirks was that he taught his daughters how to defend themselves."

That drew a quiver of silence.

Anna tried to swallow, but her throat was dry as dust. *Could she pull the trigger?*

Verdemont swore, the guttural sound amplified by the darkness. "I shall cut out your—"

"Be quiet, Pierre, and leave this to me," ordered Josette. "Men. They are not as pragmatic as women." She paused, and Anna could almost hear her thinking. "Well, well, what are we to do? I could call your bluff and charge, hoping you won't have the nerve to shoot. But then, there is a good chance that my uncle or I will die, for despite the darkness, you are likely to hit one of us."

Anna felt her palm grow slippery with sweat. The pistol suddenly felt awfully heavy in her hand.

"Or Pierre and I could retreat and take the turn just a

short way back, which leads us out to another exit. That, of course, is assuming you won't shoot one of us down in cold blood."

More silence—or so it seemed. Anna's ears were thrumming with the pounding of her heart.

"I think," said Josette, "that in this case, I shall choose to err on prudence. You have won this skirmish, mademoiselle. Indeed, you have been as resourceful as the heroine in those novels you are so fond of reading."

The swoosh of silk, the scrape of boot leather as Josette ordered her uncle to start crawling back up the stairs.

"*Alors*, now you have a choice to make, Miss Sloane."

Not really, decided Anna. She lowered her weapon. Yes, she believed in stopping a murderous enemy. But not at the cost of becoming one herself. She waited until the sounds of retreat faded away, then got to her feet and limped off in the opposite direction.

Following McClellan's lead, Devlin vaulted over the low stone wall and skidded through a turn on the slippery grass. After they threaded their way through a small grove of apple trees, the baron signaled for a halt.

"We're almost there," he said in a low voice. "The two exits are not far apart. My guess is that they will have horses stationed by the one they plan to use."

Devlin nodded. That made sense. He did not think Josette had acted on a whim.

"So, we can either both wait at the most likely place, which doubles our chances of overpowering them before anything can go amiss. Or, to be sure we don't miss them, we can split up to cover the two spots." McClellan fixed him with a questioning look. "The choice is yours."

The pistol in his coat pocket—he had managed to grab a weapon from the Gun Room as they had raced out the side door—seemed to double in weight. "Let's go to the nearest exit," he replied. "I'll make up my mind there."

Turning away without a further word, the baron crouched low and led the way over a wooded rise. Below was a stretch of wild meadowland, with a half dozen sheep grazing among the long fescue.

"There." He pointed to an outcropping of rocks jutting up from the grass. "The tunnel opens up there." His hand shifted slightly. "And look." Tethered among the copse of oak just below them were three saddled horses.

God help me if I am wrong. Devlin made up his mind. "This seems the right choice. But I feel we can't leave a spot uncovered. Dunbar has the cistern, and so you should move on to the third place."

McClellan's eyes betrayed a hint of hesitation, but he made no protest. "If they come my way, I shall keep your lassie safe," was all he said before slipping off.

My lassie . . . nay, my Love.

"I should have said it aloud," whispered Devlin, as he circled around the sheep and approached the opening in the rocks from the rear.

In answer the breeze ruffled softly through the grasses.

Slowly, silently, he edged his way close to the gap and cocked an ear to listen.

Nothing.

A sound in the trees caused him whirl around, pistol at the ready. But it was only a large hawk perched on a branch. With a harsh cry, it finished stretching its wings and began preening its feathers.

Devlin inched closer, this time, ducking his head into

the darkness. The dampness of the air sent a shiver through him.

Was it his own limbs quaking, or was there a faint rustling from within?

He tried to hold himself very still.

"Damn."

The accent didn't sound French.

"Damn, *damn* these cursed skirts. Mud makes them weigh more than a cannonball."

No, definitely not French. Casting caution to the wind, Devlin slithered inside the tunnel.

A tiny trickle of light penetrated the gloom. He could just make out a smaller black opening between two slabs of charcoal-gray stone.

The scuffling was growing louder, and in the next instant a head emerged from the opening.

"Anna." It came out no louder than a breath of air.

She wriggled free of the stones and looked up.

Their eyes met.

"I love you," he blurted out.

Her dirt-streaked face went through a series of odd contortions before wreathing a smile. "No, no, first you're supposed to say, 'However did you manage to escape from the dastardly villains?' so I can tell you how clever I was."

"Clearly I've no idea how to be a proper hero." He reached out and clasped her hand. "I love you," he repeated. "Now, however did you manage to escape from the dastardly villains?"

Anna pulled herself closer. "Kiss me first."

"Gladly. But wouldn't you rather we first get outside into the fresh air and sunlight?"

"Mmmm, no. This is more romantic," answered Anna.

"Though manacles and chains would add even more atmosphere."

He curled his fingers around her wrists. "You have a wonderfully vivid imagination, but let's confine dark dungeons and dangerous villains to your novels, shall we? I've had quite enough bloodcurdling excitement for one day." His lips found hers. "Well, almost."

Anna wasn't sure how long their kiss lasted. *A moment? An hour? An afternoon?* Freeing a hand, she traced the line of his jaw and entangled her touch in the silky strands of his wind-tangled hair, wishing it would go on for an eternity.

His mouth was doing the most exquisitely erotic things to her earlobe. The aching bumps and scrapes on the rest of her body seemed to have melted away into a puddle of pleasure...

A shout suddenly pierced the sweet reverie.

"Hell." Devlin lifted his lips, sounding just as dazed as she felt.

"Davenport! Davenport!" The bellowing was coming from just outside the hidden entrance. "Where the devil are you? The cistern—Dunbar has spotted them fleeing from the cistern. We must hurry!"

"Come, we had better let him know you are safe," murmured Devlin.

"Yes, of course."

With a bit of scooting and squirming, they managed to emerge into the daylight.

"Anna is here!" he called.

McClellan hurried out from the trees, leading the three horses. "By the bones of St. Andrew, you are a sight for sore eyes, Miss Sloane."

"Sore is rather an apt word," said Anna, wincing as she flexed her bruised knee. "Scotland has rather a lot of rocks."

"That," said the baron, "is why we Scots are known for our flinty reserve."

She smiled. The man was beginning to soften around the edges. A good sign, but if he wished to spend any more time around her sister, he had better be prepared for a hammer and chisel to pound away at that flint.

"Be that as it may, shall we join Dunbar and his men in the pursuit of the villains?" asked McClellan, offering her the reins to one of the mounts.

Devlin looked at her, but she shook her head. "I have a feeling they won't catch Josette. She'll have taken precautions to ensure her escape."

"A cunning little chit, isn't she?" remarked McClellan.

Anna blew out a sigh. "It's a pity. She was right to say England offers women with ability little opportunity to exercise their talent. They must either work in secret or turn to crime. It's no wonder that Bonaparte and his radical social ideas appeal to her."

McClellan grunted. "Bonaparte's promised freedoms are mostly illusions."

"Speaking of Josette, how did you manage to free yourself from her clutches?" asked Devlin.

"It's really not all that exciting." Anna quickly recounted what had happened.

"Ye gods, you're hurt," he muttered, touching her sleeve. "On second thought, I shall ride like a bat out of hell after that woman."

"Oh." She had forgotten about the cut. "It's hardly a scratch, and it wasn't Josette who wielded the blade. It was Lady de Blois."

"By the by, if the comtesse did not flee with her other two cohorts, where is she?" asked McClellan.

"Locked in Davenport's dressing room," she answered, glancing at Devlin. "I do hope she hasn't vented her ire on your personal possessions."

"Never mind that. I'm taking you back to the manor this instant so you can have that wound treated," said Devlin, in a tone that brooked no argument. "And once there, I will try to refrain from murdering her with my bare hands."

"Not on horseback," said Anna. She had several bruises on her posterior from bumping along in the tunnel. "I would rather walk."

"And I," he said, lifting her into his arms, "would rather carry you."

His shoulder felt reassuringly warm and solid.

She decided not to protest.

The rest of the afternoon passed in a bit of a blur. The manor was in an uproar over the events, but Devlin quickly quieted speculation by passing word that the French trio were jewel thieves, who had escaped after Anna had spotted them trying to steal a pair of Lady Dunbar's diamond necklaces. The countess and her husband went along with the story when the truth of the assassination plot was confided to them. As for Lady de Blois, she was taken away by Devlin's local government contact with no one being the wiser.

At the news of Anna's injury, her mother had taken to her bed in a fit of vapors, demanding a dose of laudanum to calm her nerves. Which was, decided Anna, just as well, for Caro's barrage of questions while she had her wound bandaged by the housekeeper was tiring enough. Indeed, all she wanted to do was sleep for the next several days. However, Prince Gunther insisted on having a gala celebration to laud her for her bravery, and it seemed best to accept the accolades. There was no need for him to know how close he had come to death.

"And to think I missed all the excitement," groused Caro after lifting her glass of champagne in toast. "That dratted cup of chocolate put me to sleep for *hours*."

"You would not have liked it," said Anna. A childhood mishap in the caves near one of her father's work sites had left her sister deathly afraid of dark, cramped spaces. "The tunnel was black as Hades, and I was forced to crawl for much of the way out."

Caro's face paled, and she took a quick swallow of wine.

"Besides, you played a key role in the adventure. You found McClellan—"

"Actually, *he* found *me*." Caro grimaced. "And I'm sure he'll never let me hear the end of it. No doubt he thinks me a ninnyhammer."

"I doubt that," began Anna, but before she could say more, the baron approached, carrying a freshly uncorked bottle of bubbly.

"Another salute to the intrepid heroine," he murmured.

Caro allowed him to refill her glass, but Anna shook her head. Suddenly the glittering candles, the crowded room, the loud voices felt too overwhelming. And despite his earlier declaration of love, Devlin was nowhere to be seen.

Love. She wished she could slide her palm inside his shirt and feel the beat of his heart against her skin.

"Thank you but no. If you'll excuse me, I think I shall

retire from the party," she murmured. "I'm feeling rather fatigued."

McClellan nodded in understanding. "In that case, I shall drink for both of us." His eyes were a trifle over-bright, and given how often sparks had flown between him and her sister...

Tonight, Anna decided, Caro would have to control the fire by herself.

"I shall see you in the morning." Slipping out to the corridor through the side salon, she hurried up the stairs, anxious to gain the solitude of her quarters. The door was almost within reach when all at once the flitting shadows came to life as one dark silhouette stepping away from the wainscoting.

"It's about time you tired of the festivities." Devlin pulled her into the side corridor. "I have a more private celebration in mind to acknowledge the victory of Good over Evil."

"We shouldn't," said Anna, seeing where his steps were headed.

"Oh, surely you are intrepid enough for one more adventure before the night is over." His candle's flame caught the roguish curl of his grin.

"You are a bad influence on me. Before I met you, I was a paragon of propriety. I only wrote about outrageous exploits, I didn't dream of actually doing them."

"Very bad," agreed Devlin. "Wicked, in fact." Opening the door to the Automata Gallery, he led her into the moon-dappled alcove. "I shall reform—perhaps—but first, we have an unfinished matter to resolve."

"I thought we had resolved things rather nicely last time we were here," said Anna, as he lay her down on the black velvet draperies and stretched out beside her. Snuggling into the crook of his arm, she set her chin on his chest. The faint sweetness of malt whisky and tobacco scented his skin, along with an earthy male essence that tickled her nostrils.

The Devil's own scent. And suddenly her whole body was pulsing with a hellfire heat.

"Quite nicely," he agreed. "However, something was missing."

Flesh on flesh. Fire sparking fire. Two hearts beating as one. A shiver of longing coursed through her. "It was?"

"Allow me to demonstrate." Gently, ever so gently, he eased off her gown. Her chemise was next, the whisper of fabric against her skin nearly as soft as the kisses he trailed over her injured arm.

She sucked in a breath, watching him strip off his shirt. In the pale pearlescent light, his chiseled torso glowed like burnished bronze.

Swiftly, silently, the rest of their clothes fell away. Moving in unspoken harmony, their bodies came together.

Anna held him close, reveling in the wondrous textures of hard muscle, coarse curls, and sculpted shoulders. With her tongue she traced the curve of his collarbone, tasting salt and a smoky spice too ethereal for words.

No fancy words, no well-turned phrases, she told herself. All rational thought surrendered to the magic of the moment.

Devlin let out a raspy sigh as he slowly eased himself inside her. She arched up to meet his thrust, match his rhythm. Her hands skimmed over the contours of his back, feeling his skin turn slick with heat.

Faster, faster. Devlin's hips rose and fell—she could

sense the tension taking hold of him. Need was cresting inside her, seeking release.

A cry, the ragged sound taking form as his name, as she came undone in his arms.

An instant later his body shuddered in climax.

Waves of pleasure washed through her, the first rush slowly ebbing to a soft ripple. He pressed a kiss to her brow, her cheek, the corner of her mouth. And they lay very still.

She must have drifted into sleep, for the next time she opened her eyes, the candle had burned down to a guttering stub.

"So, have I convinced you?" asked Devlin.

"That something is missing?" responded Anna. "I can't imagine what could make it any more perfect for us."

He reached to brush his fingers through her hair. "Marry me, Anna." He was smiling, but a hint of uncertainty flickered in his eyes. "A storybook hero would likely spout an eloquent speech, but all I can say is I love you. I may not be worthy of you, but I am trying to be a better man than I am."

Love. Her heart gave a lurch. That was more than enough.

"And I can't bear the idea of not having you in my life. Please say yes."

"Yes—on one condition," replied Anna. "Promise me that I can use the idea of the winged eagle automaton in my next book."

He rolled his eyes. "You drive a hard bargain, but very well. I look forward to writing a number of adventures with you."

"Oh, I'm *so* happy."

He chuckled. "About the plot device or me?"

"Both," said Anna, and then allowed a mischievous smile to curl on her lips. "But it's you, my dear scamp of Satan, who truly makes my heart soar."

"Well, it's taken you a devil of a long time to say so."

"Then I'll make up for it..." Her lips touched his and lingered there for a long, long moment. "By saying it again."

Acknowledgments

Creating a story is, at heart, a solitary endeavor. But creating a book is a real group effort, and I am incredibly lucky to have a fabulous team to work with.

Special thanks go to my wonderful agent, Gail Fortune, who is not only a great brainstorming partner but also a great friend.

And hugs to my amazing editor Lauren Plude, whose passion and perfect feel for romance have helped make me a better writer. We have such fun together working on my books!

Kudos also go to the terrific production and publicity people at Grand Central! Jessica Bromberg, Kallie Shimek, Sylvia Cannizzaro, and Diane Luger and the Art Department—you guys are the best!

Aspiring young poet Caro Sloane yearns for
a romantic adventure. And when she runs
into an achingly handsome Scottish baron,
she discovers he may just be the bit
of danger she's looking for...

Please see the next page
for a preview of

Passionately Yours.

Chapter One

$\mathcal{A}$ slip sent stones skittering down the slope of the narrow country road.

"Watch your step," cautioned Carolina Sloane, as the rough-edged echo faded into the shadows. "The way turns steeper here, and the ground is very uneven."

She paused to glance up at the ominous gray clouds and then looked back at her companion, who was struggling to keep pace with her. "We can rest for a few minutes if you like, but we ought not linger longer than that."

Thunder rumbled off in the distance.

"The light seems to be dying awfully fast," she added.

"No, no, I—I shall manage," answered Isobel Urquehart in between gasps for breath. "I'm so sorry to be lagging—"

"Oh, please, don't apologize," said Caro quickly. "It's my fault—I should have paid more attention to the time." She squinted into the gloom up ahead, hoping to see some flicker of light from the outskirts of town. But if anything the shadows seemed to deepen and darken as the road wended its way into a copse of trees.

A gust of wind, its bite already sharp with the chill of evening, suddenly rustled through the overhanging branches, stirring a prickling of unease at the back of her neck.

"We haven't much farther to go." Repressing an oath, Caro forced herself to sound more cheerful than she felt. "It can't be more than a mile or so until we reach town."

"Yes, yes, it must be close, given how long we've been walking." Isobel hitched her shawl a little tighter around her shoulders. Her cheeks looked unnaturally pale in the fading flickers of sunlight but she managed a smile. "And if night falls before we get there, we shall just pretend we are having a marvelous adventure."

Caro was relieved that her companion had such pluck and a sense of humor, for she hadn't realized that Isobel's health was so fragile.

That was because the two young ladies had only just met the previous afternoon. On discovering a shared interest in antiquities—as well as literature—they had made spur-of-the-moment plans for a walk out to see one of the Roman ruins that dotted the countryside around the spa town of Bath.

The day had dawned warm and sunny, so they had set out after nuncheon, thinking to be gone no more than several hours. But the setting had proved wildly romantic, and the two of them had lost track of the time as they chatted about books and history over a picnic of pastries among the weathered limestone columns.

But now, with dusk cloaking them in a swirl of shadows and stormclouds threatening rain, the decision did not seem so wise.

Impetuous. Caro gave an inward wince, knowing she did have a tendency to go off half-cocked—

"Why, just listen to the wind keening through the trees," went on Isobel, interrupting Caro's brooding. "If you use your imagination, you can almost picture yourself in the wild mountains of Sicily, evading a band of cutthroat brigands on your way to a midnight rendezvous with a swashbuckling count at the ancient ruins of Taormina."

Caro picked her way over a patch of loose stones. "Yes, I can see what you mean." A pause, and then she laughed. "So, you've read *Escape from the Barbary Pirates* as well as *The Prince's Evil Intentions*?"

"I confess, I've read *all* of Sir Sharpe Quill's novels." Isobel gave a shy grin. "Although I daresay I shouldn't admit it, I find them scathingly funny. Not to speak of intriguingly interesting when, um, Count Alessandro starts removing Emmalina's clothing."

"Oh, your secret is safe with me," replied Caro.

"You've read them, too?" asked Isobel.

"Every word," she assured her new friend.

And in truth, the statement was no exaggeration. That was because the reclusive author, considered by the *ton* to be the most intriguing gentleman in all of London, was not actually a *he*, but a she—more specifically Caro's older sister Anna.

But that was a secret she was not at liberty to share.

And at the moment, there were far more pressing concerns than clever *noms de plume* or dangerous pen-and-paper plots. Perhaps it was merely the rising whoosh and crackle of the leaves overhead, but it seemed that Isobel's breathing was becoming more labored.

Damn, damn, damn.

Caro bit her lip, wishing she dared quicken the pace. The prickling sensation at the back of her neck had turned sharper, like daggerpoints digging into her flesh. It was foolish, she knew, to let talk of ruthless villains and exotic dangers spook her. This dark stretch of road was a quiet country lane in England, and the black silhouettes were placid oak and beech trees, not gnarled claws of doom stretching out to grab...

"And then, of course, the scene where Emmalina slithers down a cliff"—behind her, Isobel had begun to recount the plot of the latest Sir Sharpe Quill novel—"and pounces on the pirate leader who is about to skewer Count Alessandro is very exciting."

"Indeed," murmured Caro, trying not to be distracted by the jumpy black shadows flitting in and out of the surrounding trees.

"Of course, it's not very realistic to expect that a young lady would know how to fight tooth and nail against a muscled villain..."

Ha! thought Caro wryly. Her late father, a noted explorer specializing in exotic tribal cultures, had taken his three young daughters on several expeditions to primitive places. Being a very practical man as well as a serious scholar, he had made sure that they knew how to defend themselves with some *very* unladylike tricks.

"But of course, fiction allows—"

A loud *snap* startled Isobel into silence.

Caro whirled around, trying to spot any movement within the glade, but the softly swaying tendrils of mist seemed to mock her fears.

"W-what was that?" whispered Isobel.

"It's probably just a fox setting off on a hunt," answered Caro quickly, her gaze still probing among the muddled trees.

Her friend let out a nervous laugh. "Then it is a good thing we are not mice."

Or helpless little pigeons—the perfect prey for any hungry predator stalking through the shadows.

Shaking off such disturbing thoughts, she freed the ribbons of her bonnet from the folds of her shawl. "We had best keep moving."

Isobel sucked in a lungful of air. "Yes, of course."

They walked on in silence, which seemed to amplify the night sounds. *The screech of an owl, the crack of a twig, the rustle of—*

Another snap, this one even louder.

The echo reverberated through the woods like a gunshot.

Hurry, hurry.

As the road narrowed and turned sharply past a thicket of brambles, Caro slapped aside a twist of thorns, and in her haste to put the grove behind them, nearly slid into a puddle of brackish water. Before she could call out a warning, Isobel stumbled on the wet ground too, and lost her footing.

"Oooh!"

Caro caught her just as she was about to take a nasty tumble. "Steady now," she murmured, keeping hold of her friend's trembling hand.

"Sorry to be such a ninnyhammer."

"Nonsense. You are a far more intrepid adventurer than any storybook heroine."

"J-just as long as I don't step on any c-cobras." Though

she appeared on the verge of tears, Isobel managed an exhausted smile.

"Oh, there aren't any snakes in this part of Somerset." That might be stretching the truth a bit, but as reptiles did not come out in the chill of night, it didn't matter.

"Let's rest for a moment."

They slowed to a halt. And yet, Isobel's breathing only seemed to grow more ragged.

If only a cart would come by, thought Caro. But given the hour, that hope was unrealistic. There was no option save to forge ahead on their own.

Tightening her grip, she started forward again, hoping that the next bend would bring them free of the trees. There was something oppressive about the heaviness of the air and the canopy of leafy branches that nearly blocked out the twilight sky.

Rain—only a soaking shower could make matters worse.

She angled a look up at the scudding clouds, just as a sudden movement in the bushes caught her eye.

A scream caught in her throat as branches snapped and a man dressed all in black burst out from between two ancient oaks.

Seizing Isobel from behind, he tried to drag her back into the tangle of leaves.

But Caro reacted in the same instant and held on to her friend's hand for dear life. "Let go of her, you fiend!" she cried, then raised her voice to an even higher pitch. "Help! Help!"

Isobel struggled to fend him off. She was putting up a game fight, though in size and weight she was no match for her assailant.

He gave another wrenching yank, then swore a vicious oath as Isobel's flailing elbow caught him flush on the windpipe.

"Help, help—let me go!" She, too, had started screaming at the top of her lungs.

"Bloody Hell, shut your gobs," he snarled, clapping a beefy hand over Isobel's mouth. "And you, you hell-bitch..."

The epithet was directed at Caro.

"Back off or I'll break every last bone in your body." The brute—for brute he was, with muscled arms and legs thick as tree trunks—punctuated the threat with a lashing kick aimed at Caro's knees.

She caught his boot and jerked upward with all her might.

Yanked off balance, the man fell heavily to the ground, his skull hitting the hard-packed earth with a thud.

The force of his fall took Isobel down, too. But she managed to roll free and scramble to her feet.

"Run!" urged Caro. "Run!"

However slight the chances were of outracing him, flight was their only option. Trying to outfight him was madness. Still, she snatched up a rock as she turned to follow her friend.

All too quickly, the man was up and after them, cursing with rage. His heavy footfalls were coming closer and closer...

Caro whirled and flung her missile at his forehead. *Thank God for the games of hunting skill she had played with the tribal children in Crete.* Hours of practice had honed her aim to a lethal accuracy.

Whomp.

The rock smashed into his right eye, drawing a pained howl. Half-stunned, half-blinded, he staggered on, fists flailing wildly.

As she dipped and dodged the blows, Caro decided that the only hope in escape lay in trying one last, desperate measure. Ducking low, she darted straight at him and brought her knee up hard between his legs.

Very hard.

The brute dropped like a sack of stones, his curses turning to a mewling whimper.

"Run!" she called again, seeing that Isobel had stopped and was staring in open-mouthed shock. The trick had bought them more time, but when he recovered, he would be out for her blood.

"How—" began her friend.

"Never mind that now," she said, shoving Isobel into action. "We must fly like the wind."

But they hadn't gone more than several strides when two more figures appeared from the shadows up ahead.

"Bull!" shouted the one in the lead. "Wot's wrong? Why ain't ye grabbed 'em?"

A pack of abductors?

The thought sent a spike of fear through her.

Things looked rather hopeless, but Caro wasn't yet willing to go down meekly.

Think! Think!

A quick glance around showed one last chance. Grabbing Isobel's arm, she pushed her off the road and toward the woods. The tangle of brush and trees might slow down their pursuers.

"Try to lose yourself in the darkness," she hissed. "I'll see if I can distract them for another few moments."

"But—"

"GO!"

To her relief, Isobel had the good sense not to waste precious seconds in further argument.

Scooping up a handful of rocks, Caro peltered the new assailants with a quick barrage, then turned to seek safety in the shadows.

With luck…

But luck chose that moment to desert her. Her shoe caught in a rut and she tripped, entangled in her skirts.

Cursing the constraints of female dress, she twisted free of the fabric, scrambled to her feet, and was moving again within the space of several rapidfire heartbeats.

Quick, but not quick enough.

The first trees were only a stride away when the one of the men snagged her trailing sash and whirled her around.

"Poxy slut," he snapped.

Caro blocked the first slap and countered with a punch that bloodied his lip. The second blow caught her on the side of the head with a force that set her ears to ringing. She tried to pull away but he yanked her back, and then his fist drove the air from her lungs.

The ground began to spin and blur.

Dizzy with pain, Caro felt herself slipping into a daze. Squeezing her eyes shut, she fought down a rising nausea. But things seemed to be spinning out of control. The voices around her were suddenly sounding strangely agitated and the ringing was turning into an odd pounding.

Like the beat of galloping hooves?

Wishful thinking, she mused as she slumped to her knees. And yet, her captor seemed to have released her…

Forcing her lids open, she saw a jumble of dark shapes.

A horse. A rider flinging himself from the saddle. Flying fists. Her assailant knocked arse over teakettle.

"Shoot the devil, Bull!" he croaked.

As her gaze slowly refocused, Caro saw their first attacker rise and run off, still clutching his groin, into trees on the opposite side of the road.

"Your lily-livered friend doesn't seem inclined to come to your rescue," came a deep baritone shout. "That leaves two of you—whose neck shall I break first?"

Her wits must be so addled that she was hallucinating. How else to explain why the voice sounded oddly familiar?

The man who had hit her scuttled like a crab across the road. "Billy!" he cried in a high-pitched squeal.

The only answer was a scrabbling in the bushes that quickly faded to silence.

"Vermin," muttered her rescuer, as he watched the man join his cohorts in beating a hasty retreat. Turning, he then gently lifted her to her feet. "Are you hurt, Miss?"

"I…"

I never swoon, she wanted to reply, if only her tongue would obey her brain. *Only peagoose heroines in horrid novels swoon.*

However, on catching sight of the chiseled lips, the too-long nose, and the shock of red-gold hair now looming just inches above her face, Caro promptly did just that.

Fall in Love with Forever Romance

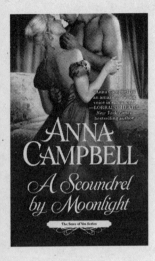

A SCOUNDREL BY MOONLIGHT
by Anna Campbell

Justice. That's all Nell Trim wants—for the countless young women the Marquess of Leath has ruined with his wildly seductive ways. But can she can resist the scoundrel's temptations herself? Check out this fourth sensual historical romance in the Sons of Sin Regency series from bestselling author Anna Campbell!

SINFULLY YOURS
by Cara Elliott

Secret passions are wont to lead a lady into trouble... The second rebellious Sloane sister gets her chance at true love in the next Hellions of High Street Regency romance from bestselling author Cara Elliott.

Fall in Love with Forever Romance

A GOOD ROGUE
IS HARD TO FIND
by Kelly Bowen

The rogue's life has been good to William Somerhall, until he moves in with his mother and her paid companion, Miss Jenna Hughes. To keep the eccentric dowager duchess from ruin, he'll have to keep his friends close—and the tempting Miss Hughes closer still. Fans of Sarah MacLean and Tessa Dare will fall in love with the newest book in Kelly Bowen's Lords of Worth series!

WILD HEAT
by Lucy Monroe

The days may be cold, but the nights are red-hot in *USA Today* bestselling author Lucy Monroe's new Northern Fire contemporary romance series. Kitty Grant decides that the best way to heal her broken heart is to come back home. But she gets a shock when she sees how sexy her childhood friend Tack has become. Before she knows it, they're reigniting sparks that could set the whole state of Alaska on fire.

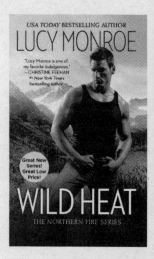

Fall in Love with Forever Romance

SUGAR ON TOP
by Marina Adair

It's about to get even sweeter in Sugar! When scandal forces Glory Mann to co-chair the Miss Sugar Peach Pageant with sexy single dad Cal MacGraw, sparks fly. Fans of Carly Phillips, Rachel Gibson, and Jill Shalvis will love the latest in the Sugar, Georgia series!

A MATCH MADE
ON MAIN STREET
by Olivia Miles

When Anna Madison's high-end restaurant is damaged by a fire, there's only one place she can cook: her sexy ex's diner kitchen. But can they both handle the heat? The second book of the Briar Creek series is "sure to warm any reader's heart" (*RT Book Reviews* on *Mistletoe on Main Street*).

Fall in Love with Forever Romance

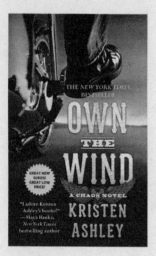

OWN THE WIND
by Kristen Ashley

Only $5.00 for a limited time! Tabitha Allen is everything Shy Cage has ever wanted, but everything he thinks he can't have. When Tabby indicates she wants more—*much* more—than friendship, he feels like the luckiest man alive. But even lucky men can crash and burn...The first book in the Chaos series from *New York Times* bestselling author Kristen Ashley!

FIRE INSIDE
by Kristen Ashley

Only $5.00 for a limited time! When Lanie Heron propositions Hop Kincaid, all she wants is one wild night with the hot-as-hell biker. She gets more than she bargained for, and it's up to Hop to convince Lanie that he's the best thing that's ever happened to her...Fans of Lori Foster and Julie Ann Walker will love this book!

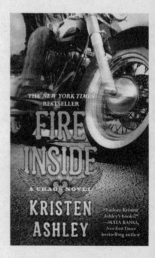